MEDIA DARLING

Praise for Fiona Riley

Room Service

"The sexual tension between Olivia and Savannah is combustible and I was hoping with every flirtious moment they would jump each other… [A] sexy summer read."—*Les Rêveur*

"*Room Service* is a slow-burn romance written from the point of view of both main characters. Ms. Riley excels at building their chemistry that slowly grows to sizzling hot."—*Lez Review Books*

"*Room Service* by Fiona Riley is a steamy workplace romance that is all kinds of fabulous…Fiona Riley is so good at writing characters who are extremely likeable, even as they have issues to work through. I was happy see that the leading ladies in *Room Service* are no exception! They're both fun, sweet, funny, and smart, which is a brilliant combo. They also have chemistry that sizzles almost from the get-go, making it especially fun to watch them grow in ways that are good for them as individuals and as a couple."—*The Lesbian Review*

Strike a Match

"Riley balances romance, wit, and story complexity in this contemporary charmer…Readers of all stripes will enjoy this lyrically phrased, deftly plotted work about opposites attracting."—*Publishers Weekly*

"While I recommend all of the books in the Perfect Match series, I especially recommend *Strike a Match*, and definitely in audio if you're at all inclined towards listening to books. Fans of the other two installments will be happy to see their leads again, but you don't have to have read them to pick this one up. It's sweet, hot, and funny, making it a great way to spend a day when you just want to hide away from the world and immerse yourself in a lovely story."—*Smart Bitches, Trashy Books*

"*Strike a Match* is Fiona Riley's best book yet. Whether you're a fan of the other books in the series or you've never read anything by her before, I recommend checking this one out. It's the perfect remedy to a bad day and a great way to relax on a weekend!"—*The Lesbian Review*

"I love this series and Sasha is by far my favourite character yet. I absolutely loved the gritty firefighter details. The romance between Abby and Sasha is perfectly paced and full of wonderful grand gestures, magical dates, and tender, intimate moments."—*Wicked Reads*

"Fiona Riley does a nice job of creating thorny internal and external conflicts for each heroine…I was rooting for Abby and Sasha, not only to be together, but also that both of them would grow and change enough to find a true HEA. The supporting cast of family members, friends, and colleagues is charming and well-portrayed. I'm looking forward to more from Fiona Riley."—*TBQ's Book Palace*

Unlikely Match

"The leads have great chemistry and the author's writing style is very engaging."—*Melina Bickard, Librarian, Waterloo Library (UK)*

"Two strong women that make their way towards each other with a tiny little nudge from some friends, what's not to like?"—*The Reading Penguin's Reviews*

"*Unlikely Match* is super easy to read with its great pacing, character work, and dialogue that's fun and engaging…Whether you've read *Miss Match* or not, *Unlikely Match* is worth picking up. It was the perfect romance to balance out a tough week at work and I'm looking forward to seeing what Fiona Riley has in store for us next." —*The Lesbian Review*

Miss Match

"In this sweet, sensual debut, Riley brings together likable characters, setting them against a colorful supporting cast and exploring their relationship through charming interactions and red-hot erotic scenes… Rich in characterization and emotional appeal, this one is sure to please."—*Publishers Weekly*

"*Miss Match* by Fiona Riley is an adorable romance with a lot of amazing chemistry, steamy sex scenes, and fun dialogue. I can't believe it's the author's first book, even though she assured me on Twitter that it is."—*The Lesbian Review*

"This was a beautiful love story, chock full of love and emotion, and I felt I had a big grin on my face the whole time I was reading it. I adored both main characters as they were strong, independent women with good hearts and were just waiting for the right person to come along and make them whole. I felt I smiled for days after reading this wonderful book."—*Inked Rainbow Reads*

By the Author

Miss Match

Unlikely Match

Strike a Match

Room Service

Media Darling

Visit us at www.boldstrokesbooks.com

MEDIA DARLING

by
Fiona Riley

2018

ISBN 13: 978-1-63555-278-2

This Trade Paperback Original Is Published By
Bold Strokes Books, Inc.
P.O. Box 249
Valley Falls, NY 12185

First Edition: November 2018

Credits
Editor: Ruth Sternglantz
Production Design: Stacia Seaman
Cover Design by Tammy Seidick

Acknowledgments

The best part about being an author is learning new things and experiencing life from a different angle, a different perspective. And in this case, if you're into that kind of thing, it was also an excuse to binge on *TMZ*, *E News*, *Huffington Post*, and other celebrity "news" sites. *Media Darling* gave me the chance to see the complexities and dimensions of celebrity today, and it was an eye-opening experience. Writing this also helped to remind me that the internet is forever, which is a valuable thing to remember these days. Careful out there, friends!

I want to thank Tonieh Kaikor Ellis for his help with the behind-the-scenes knowledge of the film industry. I really hope I did you proud. I can't thank you enough for the late-night phone calls and endless patience you showed me when I asked you about the minutiae of your work. I think you are so, so cool. Have I told you that recently? Thank you for being in my life.

To Ruth Sternglantz, thank you for the title inspiration! You are gracious in your comments regarding the editing process and are always willing to discuss a concern, even ad nauseam on my part. You're a wise word wizard and I am grateful for you. Thank you.

To my BSB family—you're the best! Thank you for always being just a tweet, text, FB comment, phone call, or FaceTime away. Without all of your support, I'm not sure I would ever meet a deadline or maintain my sanity. Special thanks to Kris Bryant for always talking me off the ledge. You're a unicorn, never change.

And to the readers—Thank you for taking this journey with me. Your reviews and feedback are everything. Thank you for taking the time to check in with me and tell me your thoughts. I truly appreciate it. XO!

For Jenn.

Thank you for brainstorming with me
when I write myself into a corner.
You're the best writing partner a girl could ask for.
And I sort of love you forever, too. So there's that.

CHAPTER ONE

Hayley Carpenter adjusted the lanyard around her neck for the fifth time in the last twenty minutes. She hated these things. She hated wearing a name badge and she hated the large, obnoxious lettering identifying the *Hollywood Sun* as her place of employment. She knew it was a matter of safety and was required for backstage access, but it still felt like a target on her chest. There was a part of her that cringed at the bold PRESS letters under her name. Her dreams of becoming a screenwriter wilted a little more every time she got the inevitable side-eye associated with this tag. Deep down she knew that her beloved grandmother would roll over in her grave if she found out that Hayley was working some throwaway entertainment piece for one of the largest gossip sites in the country. She was better than this and she knew it.

"Ms. Carpenter? From the *Hollywood Sun*? Are you here?" a short, balding man in a headset called out into the press room.

"I'm here." Hayley stepped forward and walked toward the door as he motioned her and a few other reporters toward the side entrance.

He blinked at her and made a note on the tablet in his hand before addressing her and the people around her. "Okay, you stand here, you over there, and you are the corner. Don't touch anyone. You can call their name to get their attention, but otherwise remain behind the barrier at all times."

"Yeah, yeah, Dennis. This isn't our first rodeo," a blond woman drawled out next to her.

Dennis turned toward her voice and narrowed his eyes. "Even if that is true, Ms. Teslan, I would like to remind you all of last week's debacle at the Daytime Awards. Stay behind the barrier."

Someone next to Ms. Teslan growled. "Jesus. One nut ball jumps a guardrail with a fake press pass and suddenly we're all in time-out."

"You're new." The woman looked at Hayley expectantly. "Where's Sharon?"

"Sharon couldn't make it. I'm just covering for her." She didn't bother mentioning that she was filling in for senior gossip writer Sharon Ferguson because she was in hot water with Sharon over an article she had written recently. Work was hard enough as it was right now. She didn't need to make any more waves. She extended her hand. "Hayley Carpenter."

"Anna Mae Teslan. *LA Life*. Nice to meet you."

"She doesn't care who you are, sugar tits." The owner of a gruff voice from before emerged over Anna Mae's shoulder. He scoffed, "She's the one that wrote that op-ed piece on celebrity fragility in the current media market."

Hayley glanced down at his name badge and swallowed hard. He was James Drake from the *Hollywood Daily Mail*. His work was *infamous*. He was known for causing drama with other reporters and going out of his way to ambush celebrities with his intense scrutiny and questioning. Drake had made a career of ruining other people's.

"Drake, try and use your professional language." Anna Mae blinked and gave Hayley a once-over. "So you're the one rattling the cage over there. I was wondering what had Sharon all wound up."

"Someone gunning for her job, obviously." Drake rolled his eyes and adjusted his glasses.

"I'm not gunning for anyone's job," Hayley replied coolly. Drake was nothing more than a bully. And she didn't deal kindly with bullies.

Anna Mae placed a hand on her shoulder. "Ignore him. He's as irritable as they come."

"Right. Listen to the Southern Belle and you are bound to get bowled over." Drake added with a smirk, "She's only sweet until you steal an interview from her, then the claws come out."

"You're one to talk. I don't think I would count getting slapped with a restraining order *stealing an interview*, Drake," Anna Mae quipped, her red nails glittering with her air quotes.

A gentle tap on Hayley's shoulder distracted her from Drake's reply.

"I see you met Sharon's usual sparring partners." Scotty McDoyle's tall, fiery haired frame paired with the enormous video camera on his shoulder nearly blocked the bright California sun. He was so much taller than her that his *Hollywood Sun* press pass was at her eye level. She made note of the broad grin on his photo ID. It was just *so* Scotty of him.

"Hey, Scotty." She'd expected to only be doing some audio work behind the scenes and maybe snag an interview with someone at the event, but when she'd arrived today, she'd been informed that she would be on the red carpet and possibly on camera. She was trying not to think about that.

Scotty leaned close and nodded toward the other reporters. "Anna Mae's pretty cool, but she's got an edge to her. And Drake, well, you've heard the rumors about Drake, I'm sure. Just FYI—they're all true. He's ruthless. He and Anna Mae get into it at every event and red carpet. Sharon butters them both up to keep the peace."

"I'm not particularly interested in getting in the middle, if that's what you mean." Hayley looked over at the bickering reporters in front of her and stepped back a bit more. "Please tell me this will be painless."

"No can do. This is going to be long and boring and frustrating as hell."

Hayley pouted. "I figured."

"Cheer up, buttercup. My friend is here tonight with the *Entertainment TV* crew. I'll tell him you're a little green to this and see if he can get us a quick interview for your fluff piece."

Hayley could tell Scotty was trying to be helpful, but she hated everything about this assignment. She had interviewed at the *Hollywood Sun* as a favor to a friend who'd taken a position as a temp agency job placement coordinator. She needed to set up a certain number of job interviews per week to meet her quota, and she'd called Hayley in desperation. What had started out as a favor had somehow ended up as a job at the *Sun* that she didn't particularly want to be doing in the research and receiving department.

That was five years ago. On the plus side, it was a paying position that left her lots of time to work on her personal writing projects and gave her endless resources for research and experience. But this was far from what she'd imagined herself doing when she was a naïve undergrad. This was not the glamorous screenwriting dream gig she'd hoped for when she moved to LA so many years ago.

Nonetheless, she was grateful for Scotty. He'd started at the paper a short time before her, and they had become fast friends. They both had dreams of doing something more, but money was money, and at the end of the day, it paid the bills. She didn't get to work with him much since he was on the entertainment department staff, so she was happy to be in his company today.

As the rest of the media zone around them began to fill in, there was a sudden surge of excitement. It was palpable. Hayley checked her watch. The first round of celebrities would be arriving soon. Her attention was drawn back toward Anna Mae and Drake when their exchange increased in volume.

"Just watch yourself, Blondie. I'm getting that sound bite from Emerson Sterling tonight. You can bet your fake tan on that." Drake adjusted his shoulder bag and blew Anna Mae a taunting kiss.

"Ha." She cocked her head to the side. "You think she'll walk the carpet tonight?" She let out a low whistle. "That's a bold call."

"She's presenting. She'd be foolish to miss the opportunity for the positive press after this morning's bombshell," Drake said.

Hayley had been half listening to them up to that point, but something about Drake's tone caught her attention. "What bombshell?"

They both looked at her like she had three heads.

"Amateur." Drake's wicked Cheshire cat grin gave her the chills.

"Oh, honey. You're gonna need to prepare a little better if you ever hope to take over Sharon's spot." Anna Mae fluttered her eyelashes but the friendliness from before was missing. So this was what Scotty had been talking about.

"I'm not interested in taking anyone's job—"

"That's your second mistake." Drake turned his back to her and cracked his neck.

Anna Mae shook her head and sighed. "Look. You seem nice and all, but I don't think this is your calling. It was nice meeting you, though."

And with that, she was dismissed. Not that she had been welcomed in the first place, but still. She was too flustered by the exchange to be angry. What had even just happened?

The hum around her from the arriving camera and sound crews for the other media outlets increased in volume as the number of bodies doubled and nearly tripled. People were moving around like a swarm of angry ants. Everywhere she looked, people were frantically running cords and doing sound checks. This was the biggest event she had ever been assigned to, and the hustle and bustle around her was making her head spin. She felt nauseous. "I can't do this."

She stepped back and bumped right into Scotty. She hadn't realized how close he was. How close everyone was. Great. Now she felt claustrophobic, too.

"Yes, you can. This is how you get out from behind the desk doing Sharon's bitch work. You wanna write the movie that gets nominated? You gotta get in there and get a little dirty. This is a tough town, but you can do this. Ask a couple of questions. What've you got to lose?" Scotty's expression was encouraging.

"My job?" This pep talk was falling flat.

"Unlikely. You need a little sidebar puff piece, right? Not even a full page. We can do that. *You* can do that. I'll help." He gave her a broad smile and adjusted the camera on his shoulder. His confidence in her was reassuring. She felt a teensy bit better.

"Hey. What bombshell were they talking about?" She motioned to the backs of Anna Mae and Drake. They stood up against the rail, just millimeters apart. They were both hurriedly talking to their respective camera crews.

"Hmm?" Scotty was looking through the lens of his camera and fiddling with buttons and knobs that looked expensive.

"Emerson Sterling. They said there was a bombshell today." Emerson *was* a bombshell. Hayley knew that clear as she knew her own name. Everyone knew who Emerson was. She was gorgeous. And talented. And had a complex Hollywood history that was only further complicated when she was cast in the most anticipated movie of the year opposite Rachel Blanche and Johnny Pietro. Which in and of itself wasn't complicated, but what happened next was: halfway through filming, Rachel left the project *due to scheduling issues*, quote-unquote, which Hayley had come to realize was code around here for Rachel was fired.

"Oh, yeah. You didn't hear?" Scotty pulled out his phone and loaded Twitter. He pointed to the trending topics, and there in bold read the headline, "Blanche Blames Bust-up on Set to Bedroom Fallout with Sterling."

Hayley grabbed his phone and scrolled through the feed in shock. "You're kidding me."

"Nope." Scotty took his phone back and pocketed it. "It's the biggest news story of the day. Probably the year. And so far, it's just a teaser. Rachel released a snippet of an interview—some transcript or something—with a promise to fill in the details later. This is big news."

Hayley wondered what bedroom fallout meant. Well, she assumed she knew what it meant—Rachel and Emerson had been in a relationship, that took place in a *bedroom*—but no. No. There was no way. Right?

She mulled this over a bit. Shit. This was huge. "When did that come out?"

Scotty shrugged. "A couple of hours ago, just over two, I'd guess."

"Literally right in time for the red carpet."

"Yup. With Emerson and Johnny both presenting tonight, it's—"

"Ballsy." And fucked up, Hayley thought, but she kept that to herself. Rachel Blanche was America's Sweetheart: blond, blue-eyed, and charming as hell. She was the kind of girl every guy wanted to be with and every girl wanted to be. She was the white picket fence, homecoming queen kind of beauty that you hoped would move in next door and fall madly in love with you. Hell, she'd been *People*'s Most Beautiful Person twice in the past six years. So when her role was recast, and filming had to be reshot with a new actress, Piper Sanderson, pretty much all of Hollywood and the planet had assumed it was because of actor feuding. And everyone wanted to blame it on a catfight. Emerson Sterling with her dark hair and sordid past was quickly labeled the problem in the court of public opinion even though the film studio had released a statement denying that assumption. There were rumors, but nothing was substantiated. Rachel had gone dark for a while. Clearly, that had ended.

"Okay. It's showtime. Buckle up." Scotty's height gave him an advantage over most of the camera people around them. He must have seen something no one else did. Before she could ask him what he meant, he was pushing her forward and using his large frame to box out Drake's and Anna Mae's crews from blocking Hayley's access to the railing. Next thing she knew, she was front and center and she had a bird's eye view of the warm-up wave of B-list celebrities starting to walk down the carpet in their direction.

"You got this." Scotty's encouragement was accompanied by a wink. But she didn't miss the glare Anna Mae was casting in her direction. Or the snarl on Drake's face.

CHAPTER TWO

Emerson Sterling looked at the shattered remnants of the champagne flute just outside the balcony door and frowned. Her anger management coach would not approve. Nor would her PR rep, her manager, or her fans. Well, that last part was yet to be determined. If she was out of the limelight for too long, people talked. But if she was in it for too long or too often, people talked. Basically, as long as people were talking, things were okay. Or they weren't. That seemed to be the rub as of late. Regardless, she was down a champagne flute and it was entirely her fault. Or Rachel Blanche's fault. Maybe she could blame it on the media?

The two male voices arguing outside her bedroom door had become impossible to ignore. She could hear her manager, David Stilton, clucking and stuttering some point at her personal assistant, Tremont. She smiled as Tremont Winter's soprano pierced the air in fiery retort. He was good to her, he always had been. Tremont had been with her through the good and the bad, and she trusted him implicitly. She'd be kidding herself if she didn't admit that Tremont had been her savior all these years. He made sure she was always on her A game, he helped her with her looks and her lines, and he kept her humble. Without him, she'd be lost. Literally. She had a terrible sense of direction. It was almost comical. And David, well, David managed her. Or *tried* to. He had a hand in setting up her auditions and helping coordinate her appearances and press work, but her relationship with him had been rocky for a while now. She couldn't quite make out what they were saying, but it sounded like David was mad and

Tremont was—Yup. He definitely just called David a heartless bitch. Good. Things must be going swimmingly.

She twirled the empty mini champagne bottle on the table in front of her and wondered if David was stopping Tremont from bringing an adult-sized beverage through the door. He was like that, so damn limiting. It's not like she had any vices anymore. She never drank, except for champagne, and she never did it before a public event. But this was different. This was war, and in times of war, anything goes.

She stood and strode toward the door. She was tired of waiting and even more tired of the angry hum of voices just outside of earshot.

"Boys," she barked and yanked open the door. David jumped back with a startled expression. Tremont, on the other hand, had his arms crossed across his chest, with his eyebrow raised in challenge. Tremont never spooked. It was one of his best qualities.

Emerson could see the gold foil of the top of the champagne bottle under Tremont's arm. She reached for it.

"Do you really think that's a good idea, Emerson?" David barely got the question out before Tremont started in on him again.

Emerson held her hand up and silenced them both. She nodded toward the bottle, and Tremont opened it with a satisfying pop and handed it to her. She brought it to her lips and sipped before looking at Tremont and motioning toward David.

"Did you tell him that the hotel only stocks mini-bottles of champagne? Mini-bottles. What if there was a champagne emergency and I needed a full-sized bottle immediately? What if I couldn't wait for them to bring one up? Someone should write a review of this place. The nerve." Tremont laughed and took a sip from the offered bottle. She didn't bother offering any to David. He was such a curmudgeon.

"Emerson. Please. No more destruction. We're doing the best we can to do damage control already," David whined. He was always whining.

"It was a glass, David. It...slipped."

"It didn't slip, and you know it." David huffed and looked flushed.

"You look a little sweaty, David. Why don't you sit down and have some water?" She took the bottle back from Tremont and turned, heading back into her room. She didn't wait for him to answer. It was an empty pleasantry. They all knew she didn't want him around. Not after this screwup.

"Emerson, I tried—"

She spun on her heel and pointed the bottle at him. "You tried? When did you try, David? When Rachel squeezed you like a pimple for information and you popped like an overly hormonal virgin on a first date?"

David looked scandalized. Emerson felt like someone had thrown gasoline on the simmering she was barely keeping contained.

"Was it her tits? Is that what convinced you to sell me out? Because I've seen them, David, and they're awfully nice, but they aren't worth the price of my soul. Maybe they're worth the price of yours, though. I'd never given that much thought. Maybe that's my fault. I had no idea I employed someone so *soulless*."

"How was I supposed to know she'd turn on you, Emerson? How?" David dug the hole deeper and Emerson saw red.

"It's your job to have my best interests in mind, David. Why do I have to be the one to tell you that this work requires a backbone? I had no idea you were so incredibly useless"—she growled—"but lesson learned."

"She warned you," David spat back at her. "She warned you when you cast her aside like some jilted lover—"

"Leave." She couldn't stand the sight of him. If David hadn't planted the seed, Rachel might never have figured it all out. But that fucking moron wasn't thinking with his head. Or maybe he was, just the wrong one. Rachel could be very convincing when she wanted something. He was just too stupid to realize he was being played.

"You knew this was coming. It was only a matter of time." David's flush had spread into his neck. His nostrils flared, and Emerson raged.

"Are you serious right now?" Her blood boiled as she stepped toward him. "Did you just fucking say that?"

Tremont stepped between them and held up his hands. "We'll be downstairs in a bit. You should go, David."

"Fifteen minutes. She has fifteen minutes to throw her tantrum. Make sure she gets in that car and smiles like she's supposed to. We all knew that article was coming—we've already prepared a statement." David avoided eye contact with her and spoke only to Tremont. That was probably a wise idea since the bottle felt heavy in her hands.

Tremont scoffed. "This is why you're single, David. Because you're heartless."

"And I hear you're also a *bitch*." Emerson couldn't help herself. Tremont snickered next to her.

"Fifteen minutes," David called over his shoulder as he slammed the door to her hotel suite.

She headed to the balcony and lowered herself onto the lounge chair facing the million-dollar view of the mountains off in the horizon. She sipped the bottle in her hands and willed them to stop trembling. This was everything she had feared would happen, except it was a thousand times worse than she had ever anticipated.

"He just doesn't get it, Em. He doesn't have the whole story, so he can't understand." Tremont sank into the seat beside her with a sigh. "Not that he should have said anything to Rachel, but still."

She nodded and handed him the bottle. No one had the whole story. Well, except for her and Tremont. He knew just about everything. That helped ease some of the isolation she was feeling. But even that wasn't entirely true. He knew most of what she was feeling, but not all of it. She didn't think anyone would really understand.

"I just…I never thought she'd actually do it." She took the bottle back from him and ran her thumb over the slightly curled edge of the label. "And I'm mad at myself for being so naïve about it."

Tremont didn't say anything for a long time. She'd almost forgotten he was there. "I don't think I've ever seen you more scared or more hurt than I did this morning when we got that call. I think it's best we just accept this for what it is: a betrayal. She betrayed you, and whatever you had with her—whatever friendship or professional courtesy you might have shared—it's gone. Rachel is seeking her revenge in the most public way possible, and you are the object in her crosshairs."

"That sounds a little dirty."

Tremont shrugged. "I heard that on *NCIS* last week. You know how I love me some DiNozzo."

"You can do better." She winked at him.

"So can you." Ouch.

"Just give me a few minutes, okay? Let me wallow in my self-pity and armor myself for what is going to be the worst night of my life." She hoped he didn't notice the pleading in her voice.

His face told her he did. "That's a little dramatic. I'm sure you'll have much worse nights."

She deadpanned, "You're too good to me."

"Someone has to look out for your overly emotional and hormonal ass. And you don't pay me enough to deal with David's bad breath on top of his usual condemnation. I want a raise." Tremont pretended to flip his nonexistent hair and left her on the balcony to collect her thoughts. She loved that man. She wasn't sure where she'd be without him.

She let his words wash over her and her chest felt heavy. Behind the rage and blind panic that came with the call from her PR agency letting her know about Rachel's big reveal, there was a level of disappointment and pain that had floored her. But as much as Tremont was right, so was David. Rachel had warned her this was coming. She just didn't want to believe it.

She placed the bottle down on the table next to her and sighed. She'd need her wits about her for tonight's red carpet. It was not a coincidence that Rachel's statement came out today of all days. Tonight's presenter gig with Johnny was part of the studio's marketing campaign to generate buzz on the upcoming movie's release. This was the first big push of what would be many exhausting weeks and months of interviews, press, attending events, and smiling for the camera. In just a few months, *The Willow Path Convergence* would be shown to critics and then to audiences across America. She sighed. This role was supposed to change her life. It was supposed to change her career. And it had. But it also brought Rachel into her life. And at the release, her name would be in the credits and Rachel's wouldn't. So, no, she shouldn't be surprised that Rachel's teaser tell-all came today. Or any day, for that matter. But that fact didn't make it hurt any less.

She stretched in the chair and thought about the whirlwind that had been the last year. Getting this role was the kind of stuff that dreams were made of. It was a chance for her to catapult her acting career into the kind of legacy status that she'd always hoped for. This was the chance of a lifetime. But it was a risk. And the studio was taking a risk on her. It was a dark and complex film, and the emotional depth required had been grueling, but it had taught her a lot about herself during the filming as well. And it had brought Hurricane Rachel with it. Everything had changed with this role. Everything.

She knew that tonight's presenter gig was an attempt to amplify her public persona. Even though the film was still in editing, it was already getting hyped as one of the best films of the year. She had thought this would be her chance to change her image. She'd hoped that the days of her Hollywood Bad Girl status were long gone. It looked as though this role was going to do just that, until Rachel was let go from the film under a cloud of suspicion. And now she was the villain to Rachel's one-sided sob story.

"It's time." Tremont held out her clutch and lipstick. "You need to reapply. Thank Gucci the makeup artist left this behind. That champagne bottle is wearing all your lipstick."

She glanced down and laughed. "So it is."

"Ready?"

They both knew she wasn't.

"No." She sighed. "Let's go."

"So remember, smile and let Chandra field all the questions. Don't go off script. We released the statement on the ride over here. All you have to do is say *no comment*. Got it?" David said. Emerson knew that wasn't really a question.

"Don't worry, David. I'll be on my best behavior." Emerson turned back toward the commotion outside the limo's window. "All the vultures are circling. Must be foulness afoot."

David dared to take her hand and gave it a squeeze. "It's going to be fine, Emerson."

She had to will herself not to snatch her hand away. "Let's not kid ourselves, David. It's going to be a veritable shit show. And I'm the main attraction."

"Good thing we packed an umbrella." Tremont held up his designer messenger bag and tapped it confidently. "Shit shield in tow."

Chandra Patel, her PR rep, knocked on the window and opened the door. "All right, Emerson. We're ready for you."

The cameras flashed, and Emerson's name rang out from every media outlet imaginable. Tremont stepped out and took her hand, guiding her and her designer gown onto the red carpet. He held his hand up to deflect some of the glaring lights as Chandra stepped forward and addressed the group.

"Ms. Sterling will pose for some pictures, but she is not giving any statements at this time. If you ask, she will move on without a shot." Chandra's announcement was met with disgruntled groans.

"Emerson, Emerson! Over here! To the left!"

Emerson raised her head as she stepped onto the marked *X* on the carpet in front of her and flashed that perfect Hollywood smile she'd paid a fortune for.

The lights were always more blinding than she expected. She'd been on plenty of red carpets and press junkets before, and yet every time, it felt a little overwhelming. There was no getting out of the center of attention at these things. That was the point, right? To be there and generate buzz, to make people want you. To make people want to be you. To make them want to see what you were up to. It was all part of the game. It was a part of the big, scary Hollywood machine: Show face. Smile. Look pretty. Sell the illusion. That's what this all was, just an illusion.

"Emerson! Here! Up here. Smile!"

She turned toward the voice and obliged. It was difficult for her to see any specific person during these walks. The lighting was complimentary but made it impossible for the actors to see any of the media's faces until the flashes faded. If it wasn't for Tremont following closely behind and guiding her over the occasional rogue cord or bump in the carpet, she'd face-plant. That would be almost as interesting as Rachel's attempt at a distraction. She considered it.

"I know that look. You're up to something," Tremont said when the flashing lights stopped. He stood by her side and offered her a bottle of water with a straw.

She turned her back to the media line and waited for her signal to move on to the next photo stop on the carpet. "Mm. Is that so?"

"Oh, yeah. Girl, I can practically smell your mischief." He took back the bottle and capped it. "What're you thinking?"

"Truthfully?"

"Always."

"I was wondering if I accidentally intentionally fell if that would get me off this carpet before our little smile-but-don't-talk charade fell apart."

"Don't you dare." Tremont's face was far too serious. She'd only been joking. Sort of.

"I can totally do it. I did all my own stunts in that car movie last year. They told me I looked like a seasoned stunt double." She took the compact he held out for her and touched up her lipstick.

"Oh, I have no doubt that you can gracefully fall. What I doubt is that it will do anything but amplify the attention on you. Plus, I know you aren't wearing any underwear under that dress, so with the way things are going for you, you'd probably end up showing everyone your hoo-ha."

"Hoo-ha? What are you, twelve?" She used her finger to blend the color across her bottom lip.

"Would you prefer I call it your lady bits? How about your pink—"

"You could call it a *vagina*. Because that's what it is."

Tremont grimaced and put his hand up. "That sounds so dirty. Ew. The whole thing is gross and wet and ew. I'm going to puke. I don't understand you people."

"You people? And what *people* would that be?" Emerson was so glad he was here with her. She felt safe.

Tremont looked left and right before he leaned in and whispered, "You *lesbians*."

"You and your labels." Emerson didn't bother trying to contain the deep, throaty laugh that bubbled up. She felt no need to align herself with a label or to follow anyone else's rules about who she could be attracted to. She'd had male and female partners in her life. She was drawn to the *person*, and it just so happened that most of those people were female. "You know, I could say a whole lot about your extracurricular activities, but I'm too much of a lady for that."

Tremont's skeptical look was so comical she laughed harder. "Girl, please. I can't get any man to go on more than one date with me because you are needy as fuck and require all my attention, all the time. No man wants to date someone who is at the beck and call of some prima donna."

There was a truth in that statement that sobered her momentary joyfulness. Tremont didn't date anyone seriously. He hadn't in a long time. But it wasn't that he couldn't find the right guy. It was his job that got in the way. And not in the way he teased her about now, she wasn't overly demanding—at least she didn't think she was, anyway. It was more than that. She was a target for attention and exploitation, and Rachel was making that clear with her statement today. Tremont had stopped dating when people started recognizing him as her best friend and personal assistant. Too many dates had shown more interest in her fame and celebrity than in him. And though he joked about it, she knew it bothered him. It bothered her, too. She'd found that her celebrity ruined people's lives, one way or another. And that was the same reason why she was single. She'd broken her vow to remain unattached when she got involved with Rachel. She thought that maybe it could work since they were both in the public eye. But clearly that had backfired in the most gloriously devastating way. Rachel was just like everyone else—the only exception being she had a bigger audience to air Emerson's dirty laundry to. No, this proved it—she could never trust anyone. Ever. Except for Tremont. And her sister. Shit. She had to call her sister.

"What? I was joking. Don't look so serious," Tremont replied.

"Did you call Deidre?" Emerson started to panic. How could she have forgotten to call her sister? "Tremont, I need to call her. I need to—"

He stepped close and reached out to take her elbow. His touch was gentle and his tone was soft as he said, "Em. It's okay. I called her. She knows. She said she'd be free tomorrow to talk. Don't worry."

She was still holding the mirrored compact, but her hand was frozen in midair. A part of her was afraid she might drop it. Tremont must have noticed because he reached out and took it from her, but not before she got a glimpse of the people standing in front of the next marked spot on the carpet.

"Fuck. James Drake is here."

Tremont looked over her shoulder and scowled. "I hate that asshole. Hold on."

He waved back toward Chandra and motioned for her to join them. She had been hovering off in the distance, looking down at her tablet and talking quickly into her headset as usual. She was always conducting some sort of complicated PR dance at these things. Emerson had asked about it once. She wanted to know why it looked so stressful. Chandra had laughed and told her that there were seating changes and set updates that happened up until the very moment of each event. Sometimes that meant Emerson had to be someplace entirely different than was previously planned. And depending on where that was, a little negotiating might be needed. She was grateful to be ignorant of most of it.

Chandra jogged over. Her expression was bleak. "You heard, huh?"

"Heard what?" Emerson didn't like it when Chandra looked worried.

"Yeah, what are you talking about?" Tremont was annoyed.

"Well, that depends"—she was stalling—"on why you waved me over."

Emerson and Tremont shared a look. Chandra's headset squawked, and she grabbed her ear. She spoke quietly into the mouthpiece and frowned.

"Spit it out, Chandra. You're freaking us out," Tremont said.

"Rachel's here. Five marks back," Chandra replied.

"She's here?" Emerson felt herself start to unravel.

Tremont shushed her. "Don't lose your shit now. Not in front of that Drake fool and his camera crew." He looked at Chandra and shook his head. "We're skipping the next mark. All the marks. No more carpet."

Chandra looked as stressed as Emerson felt. "Do you think that's wise?"

"I'm not doing it." Emerson was careful to keep a false smile on her face as she spoke. The last thing she needed was to give anyone any reason to think she was freaking out as badly as she was *freaking out*. "Get me out of here."

Chandra nodded and spoke into her headset. The person stationed at the next mark was calling out to them and waving them forward, but Emerson had no intention of stopping. Rachel was closing in on them, and she knew she couldn't face her without falling to pieces in the process.

"Emerson! Here! Look here!" She ignored the calls and looked for a way out. Chandra had to figure something out fast, or she was going to tear a hole in that award show banner backdrop and book it.

"Emerson!" A sharp, piercing whistle caught her off guard and she turned without thinking.

The sound came from a pretty auburn-haired woman who was hanging over the railing at the next mark. She didn't recognize her, but that wasn't anything unusual. She didn't know a lot of media at these things. But she did recognize the man standing directly next to the mystery woman, and he was staring right at her.

"Emerson, is it true that your sexual relationship with Rachel Blanche got her fired?" Drake's voice was deafening in the silence that followed the shrill whistle. The cameras flashed. Emerson was too stunned to answer.

"Go." Tremont grabbed her elbow and hurried her into an opening in the backdrop that Chandra held back for her.

She had no idea how things had gotten so out of hand so fast.

"It's okay, just breathe."

Tremont pushed the water bottle into her hand, but she couldn't drink it. All she could think about was what her expression had been when Drake got his question out. Had she reacted? She'd been so stunned by the whistle she didn't have a chance to stifle her emotions.

"Find out who that woman was." Her voice sounded far away.

"What woman?" Tremont continued to pull her along the back of the red carpet toward the amphitheater.

"The banshee whistler that works for Drake. Find out who she is and make sure we never cross paths again." She tugged her elbow from Tremont's grasp and increased her pace toward the building. She needed to get inside before anything else happened. She needed to get inside before everyone saw just how badly she was shaking.

CHAPTER THREE

A re we almost done?" Hayley looked over her notes and confirmed that all her interviews had loaded to the cloud at work. She was particular about rechecking that, after one assignment ended with her phone in a toilet and all the recordings flushed down the drain with it.

Scotty adjusted the strap on his camera bag and patted it. "Yup, all packed up and ready to go. I'll call over for the car. Meet you out back?"

Hayley nodded and pulled off her lanyard, shoving it into her pocket as she waited in the corner of the backstage press area. Most of the other reporters had filtered out, and it appeared that only staff came back toward this section, if the rolls of cable coiled and thrown about, discarded folding chairs, and empty coffee cups littering the floor were any indication. It was hardly the place for anyone of importance—that was one of the reasons she'd come back here. She wanted to be hidden from view for a chance to catch her breath.

She leaned against the corner as she took off one of her shoes and massaged her foot. She was not used to standing around in heels, and she was eager to get home and banish these back to her closet where they belonged. She was happy with the work she'd gotten done with Scotty today. They'd talked to a few celebrities and their PR people, and it hadn't been nearly as bad as she'd anticipated it being. She had plenty of fodder for her two-hundred-word border piece. Sharon would be pleased, and hopefully she could get back to her own work without any more controversy.

But she knew the real story was the one that nearly got away: Emerson Sterling. And the only reason it was *nearly* at all was because of Grandma Ginny's notorious dinner whistle. Had she not resorted to the secret, sonic boom signal that had been passed down to her and honed through a lifetime of summers in Maine trying to wrangle her cousins from the woods behind the family cabin, she never would have gotten Emerson to stop long enough for her to see that there was definitely something going on with the troubled starlet. She had looked more than shocked. She looked almost scared. And Hayley had instantly regretted her actions.

Her assumptions had been all but confirmed when Rachel showed up just moments after Emerson's Houdini impersonation. They'd missed each other by less than three minutes. It was almost as if Emerson had gotten some intel to flee.

In contrast to Emerson's team stating that she would not be giving any statements, Rachel had been more than candid and willing to talk to Drake and anyone that would listen. She managed to keep it mostly vague, but she encouraged everyone to wait for the rest of her statement and played to the affections of the camera. It was almost sickening after having seen Emerson's reaction immediately before. Rachel seemed to be flourishing in the attention and adoration.

Hayley couldn't shake the feeling that she had set something in motion with that whistle. She'd practically set Drake up for a home run with his question—she'd literally silenced the crowd for him to be heard. He'd thanked her for it afterward. The guilt she felt rivaled her dislike for him in that moment.

The sound of approaching voices jarred her out of her daze.

"Don't talk to me." An angry female hiss came from around the corner as the footsteps got louder. It was so fast and sharp Hayley couldn't recognize the voice's owner.

"Oh, please, don't kid yourself, Em. I'm just trying to get out of here in one piece." Rachel Blanche's voice, on the other hand, was unmistakable.

A male voice chimed in, "I'll believe *that* when you can prove to me more than ten percent of what is on your head isn't weave."

"Oh, joy. Tremont is here to add commentary." Rachel turned the corner and stepped into Hayley's sight line, where she turned and faced the male voice. "Call off your gay dog, Emerson, before I neuter him."

"Fuck off, Rachel." Emerson Sterling stepped forward with a threatening glare. "You've done enough damage for one day."

Rachel laughed and crossed her arms. "What's the matter, Em baby? You didn't like my headline? I thought it was rather creative."

"You mean that starved-for-attention ploy to steal some of my celebrity since you got canned? I've been warned to stay away from falling stars and burning bridges—and you, Rachel, are white hot," Emerson spit back.

Drake materialized next to Hayley and reached for his phone just as a furious looking Rachel lunged forward and grabbed Emerson by the arm, spinning her on the spot. The sound of Drake dropping his bag must have caught Rachel's attention, because in a single motion she leaned close to whisper something into Emerson's ear and flashed Drake a quick smile as he aimed to take the shot. Something in Hayley snapped. Before she realized what she was doing she'd reached out and smacked the phone out of his hand. The phone hit the ground with a thud and someone near the starlets called out for security.

Drake swore and shoved Hayley as he reached for his phone, almost knocking her to the floor in the process. She grabbed the back of one of the folding chairs nearby to steady herself and watched the rest of the action unfold in front of her. Rachel's distraction and pose for Drake had given Emerson's assistant enough time to step between the women. Rachel had lowered her voice but whatever she was saying was being heard loud and clear by Emerson, who looked somewhere between furious and mortified. Someone she assumed was from Rachel's team emerged and dragged Rachel off in the other direction. It had happened in a blink, and it was over just as fast as it had begun.

"What's your fucking problem?" Drake growled at Hayley and took a menacing step toward her.

"The show's over." Hayley squared her shoulders and narrowed her gaze. She'd made one mistake tonight already. She wasn't about to let him capitalize on her naïveté again. "Go home."

"Sharon was right about you. You're as underhanded as they come." He leaned back and gave her a once-over. "I underestimated you. That won't happen again. I'm going to make sure you pay for this."

"Hey, back up there, fella." Scotty's voice came from over Drake's shoulder as he pulled him away from Hayley.

Drake shrugged off Scotty's hand and stormed past Emerson's assistant just as security arrived. Emerson's expression was blank and unreadable. Hayley wondered what she was thinking.

"Let's go, Hayley." Scotty nudged her toward the exit.

Hayley nodded and glanced back once more, briefly making eye contact with Emerson. Though they were a distance apart in the backstage area, Hayley could still see the vividness of Emerson's eyes. They were a perfect storm of blue and green. Her eyes were one of her signature attributes and Hayley could now attest to them being more incredible in person. The magazines and paparazzi shots did them no justice at all. Hayley could have sworn there was something brewing behind those eyes just now.

As Scotty ushered her toward the back door and into the night, a nagging sensation settled in the pit of her stomach. Something told her that the events of tonight were far from over. And the uncertainty of that made her feel sick.

❖

"Hayley, my office, now." The voice of her boss, Jonathan Ula, boomed over the intercom on her desk phone.

"What now?" Hayley whined and shoved her chair back. She'd not had the best week. In fact, since that press event she covered for Sharon, her life had been miserable. The fluff piece she did was well received, but rumors swirled about a heated backstage confrontation between Hollywood's two most dynamic and explosive stars. And though it had been far from a catfight in Hayley's humble opinion, there was definitely something happening between Emerson and Rachel. It was undeniable. But what it was, she doubted she'd ever know.

One of those rumors was started by Drake and placed Hayley right in the thick of it. It turned out Drake had teased, *Someone close to the wounded star Rachel Blanche reported a heated quarrel with her speculated ex-lover Emerson Sterling backstage*. He went on to further accuse Emerson of having spies that infiltrated opposing media sources to keep the fight a secret. It didn't take long for his insinuations and carefully worded articles to lead to the conclusion that said spy worked for the *Hollywood Sun* and her name rhymed with *Bailey*. When Sharon got in the next day, she'd made it clear that not only was their debt not settled, but that Hayley was not to be trusted. A point she made known to all the other writers and staff at the *Sun*. God, she disliked that woman.

Hayley trudged to Jonathan's office, trying to ignore the side-eye half the staff was shooting her way. Sharon had forged a lot of loyalty over her years working in entertainment, and Hayley was feeling like the odd woman out, again.

She knocked and waited. She'd missed a deadline earlier in the week, and when she did submit the piece—late—it was disorganized at best. She'd been expecting to be disciplined, but that didn't make her any less nervous in this moment.

"Come in," Jonathan called from behind the frosted glass.

"You wanted to see me, Jonathan?"

"Close the door, have a seat," Jonathan grumbled in reply.

He walked around to the front of his desk and sat down. Even though he was barely in his fifties, his face looked tired and worn. Something that long nights, lots of coffee, and dozens of cigarettes between deadlines did little to improve upon. "Tell me about Emerson Sterling."

"What?"

"Listen, I heard the murmurs around the office. I know that Sharon and her little minions are irate. I also know that James Drake has made three blatant jabs at you in his daily column over the last week and speculation is flying that you have something going on with Ms. Sterling. I had seven calls today alone asking for your employment records to see if you are on her payroll. The higher-ups are considering actually investigating this to make sure we have not been compromised as a media source. So tell me, what's up?"

Hayley's jaw went slack. "I have no idea what you're talking about."

Jonathan rubbed his forehead and pinched the bridge of his nose. "Why don't I believe you, Hayley? I know this isn't what you want to do forever, but you make more waves than anyone else here, and you still seem to end up ahead. How is that?"

Hayley shrugged, expecting to be fired. "Wait, ahead of what?"

Jonathan reached behind him and picked up a piece of paper. "Emerson's PR rep just called, looking to set up a meeting with you tomorrow about a prospective project Emerson is at the helm of that needs media coverage. They refused any senior reporters and demanded that only you represent the *Sun*. No further details were given. None." He cleared his throat. "How does someone who has never covered a major entertainment event before end up with the most coveted interview in all of Hollywood?"

"I have no idea." Hayley was at a loss for words, which was unusual for her. Usually she had *lots* of words, and most of those words got her in all sorts of trouble. But right now, she was speechless.

"Are you working for Emerson Sterling?"

Hayley gaped. "What? No. I've never even spoken to the woman."

Hayley racked her brain but came up with nothing. If she'd ever spoken to Emerson, she would surely remember it. That woman was unforgettable. Hayley hadn't been able to stop thinking about the look Emerson had given her after she'd blocked Drake's attempt to film her. She'd felt like an energy had passed between them in that moment, which she realized sounded ridiculous. But still, she'd thought of it often over this past week all the same.

Jonathan seemed to mull over her response before he stood and extended the paper toward Hayley, pulling it back briefly before finally handing it over to her. "Hayley, if I find out that you are on her payroll and have been twisting the facts of this story to meet her needs, I will not protect you from the wolves. Do you understand?"

"Yes." Hayley nodded and looked down at the paper in her hand like it was combustible.

"I expect a full report following your meeting. They want you at the Parisian tomorrow at noon. Don't be late." He walked back to his chair and waved her out before she could say anything else.

Chapter Four

S o let me get this straight." Her colleague and her closest friend in LA, Alison Pope, stared at her from across the table, her martini suspended in air. "Tomorrow at noon, you're meeting with Emerson's *people* because she personally requested you?"

"It would appear that way, yes." Hayley finished her first martini in record time and reached for her water. She needed to slow down if she was going to have any time to review tomorrow before the meeting. Jonathan had handed off her other assignments for the rest of the week and had *advised* her to prepare. When Alison suggested they go to their favorite watering hole, Lilly's, after work, she'd hesitated before agreeing. Jonathan's words were fresh in her mind. Alison was having none of that, though, so she didn't put up much of a fight. Now, as they split two appetizers and people watched, Alison got right to it.

"You've got to be kidding me." Alison shook her head in disbelief. "All right, spill. Why is Hollywood's hottest bachelorette asking to see you?"

Hayley shrugged. She was getting tired of all the backhanded compliments she'd received about this today. Was it really that otherworldly for someone as attractive and famous as Emerson to have an interest in her? Yes. Yes, it was. But Emerson wasn't *interested* interested in her. She wanted to meet with her for some press work. Which was nearly unfathomable in and of itself. But she didn't need everyone else pointing that out as well. She was nervous enough as it was.

"I know what you're thinking, and yes, this is so fucking weird," Alison supplied over her glass.

Hayley laughed. Alison just got her. They'd both started at the *Sun* around the same time, and though they worked in different departments, they'd managed to get close over the years. Alison's sincerity and down-to-earth qualities were a breath of fresh air in a city known for its fakeness. "I have no idea how to prep for this. What do I even say?"

Alison paused and waved to the waiter, indicating she needed a refill, before pulling out her cell phone and typing something onto the screen.

"What are you doing?" Hayley was afraid to ask.

"Googling. Duh." Alison accepted the new drink the waiter dropped off and returned her attention to her screen.

"Of course." Hayley was being sarcastic, but she had fully intended to do that very same thing later during her prep. Alison was saving her a step. Sort of. Maybe she could get that second drink after all. Alison had no problem making that decision for herself, it seemed.

"Let's go over the facts: Emerson was a child actress and teen television star, typical SMActress, right? Singer. Model. Actress. The Hollywood triple threat. She won the damn talent lottery." Alison nodded as though this was common knowledge. It was, and it wasn't for Hayley. Her work required her to binge on celebrity gossip—that was true—but she shied away from it in her personal life if at all possible. She knew enough to be good at her job. But she couldn't name Beyoncé's kids without giving herself a serious brain cramp in the process.

"She's been on Hollywood's hotlist every year since she was eighteen. She signed her first multi-million-dollar movie contract at nineteen and made the formal move from television to the silver screen around that time. It says here that she is one of the highest-grossing movie actresses of her generation thanks in large part to her involvement in that car movie franchise crash-boom-rah thing that Rob raves about. He loves her." Alison snorted.

"You don't say." There was no love lost for Alison's boyfriend Rob from Hayley. They'd been dating a little over a year and Hayley tolerated him at best. He was a typical postcollege frat boy who didn't have a ton of direction in life and had taken a position in his daddy's company out of convenience and laziness. He made good money and spoiled Alison, but Hayley knew she could do better. He was a total dud. And to make matters worse, once he found out Hayley was into women, he regularly went out of his way to say the most ignorant and suggestive things. She hated it.

"Yup. She was nominated for an Oscar for that gritty drug movie she did in her early twenties…Oh—this is news to me—it says here that she won an Emmy for a song she performed as that little cartoon frog, Zelda Frog, on that kids' show, the *Adventure Frog* series. This says here that she's done the voice work for that character since the beginning. I hear the author is a real recluse, no one ever sees her… Rafaela Silver or something. Anyway, I heard they're making a feature film with that frog. My nieces love that series. Zelda is like the perfect feminist role model," Alison said.

"A feminist role model frog?" Hayley was not up to date on this aspect of Emerson's career.

"Yeah, she's like super-smart and creative. The stories have a moral and teach empathy and kindness and all that other shit. It's actually kinda awesome. You should watch it sometime. There's a lot of funny, hidden adult humor."

Hayley made a mental note to look into it.

Alison continued, "Looks like she was on the *Forbes* celebrity list once or twice and—oh, it says that she's being courted to portray a young Angelina Jolie in the upcoming biopic about her life entitled *Lip Service*." Alison's jaw hung open dramatically. "Can you imagine that? With her dark hair and pouty lips with those light eyes, I mean, she'd be perfect for that role."

"Agreed." Hayley thought back to the backstage exchange she'd witnessed. Emerson's long dark hair fell in choreographed waves across her shoulders. She'd looked striking on the red carpet, but seeing her in action backstage was what had stayed with Hayley. The way her bicep flexed in her attempt to pull her arm away from Rachel's grasp…the way her full lips parted when she snapped back at Rachel's insults to her assistant. She probably shouldn't have found her attractive in that moment, but she most certainly had. In fact, the fiery look Emerson gave Rachel had made Hayley shiver. But definitely not out of fear. No. That was the problem. She was attracted to Emerson because she had eyes, and Emerson was clearly perfect. And a big part of her was worried about falling to pieces in her presence tomorrow. "What if I'm a bumbling mess?"

"Like, more than usual?"

Hayley sighed. "Alison."

"Well, she's super hot. And you know how you get around hot women," Alison replied.

Hayley gave her a look.

"I'm just saying, you've got no game, that's all." Alison's expression was playful. "I'm kidding. Kidding. Seriously, don't pout. It's so sad looking."

That only made Hayley pout more.

"Why are you worried? We both know you're better than this job, Hay. You're way too smart to be writing puff entertainment pieces. Maybe this is your chance to strike out on your own. You know, finally get that script of yours out."

"Screenplay," Hayley corrected.

"Exactly. Even better." Alison smiled, and Hayley matched it. She knew Alison was teasing her. Hayley had been working on that screenplay for over two years now, and Alison had been one of her biggest cheerleaders throughout the process.

Alison continued, "All I'm saying is that this is an incredible and, let's be honest, an insanely unrealistic opportunity to fall into your lap."

"Rude." But she was totally right. All day Hayley had been feeling like someone had made a grave mistake, and that when she showed up at the hotel to meet Emerson and her team tomorrow, they would be shocked, fully expecting someone else to be there instead. Like this was all some silly misunderstanding. Because it had to be, right?

"It's true. You've got nothing to lose. Bat for the fences. Kick that touchdown. You know, do the thing, win the points." Alison gave her a mock cheer from her seat.

Hayley picked up a truffle fry and waved it at Alison before popping it into her mouth. "Your sports analogies are awful."

"And your choice to always wear that red and black plaid shirt when we go out after work for drinks is offensive. But I still hang out with you," Alison said as she took a fry from the shared plate and dusted off the grated parmesan cheese before eating it.

Hayley wrapped her arms across her chest defensively. "Hey. I love this shirt."

"I know. And so does everyone in this bar because you wear it all the time," Alison replied as she reached across the table to pat her shoulder. "It is soft, though, I'll give you that."

Hayley nodded because duh. Alison worked primarily in the fashion department at the *Sun*. She always managed to look flawless and perfectly put together. In that regard, she and Hayley were very different. Hayley was all about comfort and practicality. Alison, on the other hand, was willing to endure discomfort to look good. It was very LA of her. That was something that had always impressed Hayley. She lived here, she worked here, she occasionally dated here, but she never really felt like she fit in here. Alison's friendship helped that a little. "Look, we can't all be fashionistas. I get cold in the air-conditioning, okay? And it reminds me of home."

"And by *home* you mean Maine, right? Because it's putting out a serious Maine vibe." Alison's bubbly laugh was contagious.

"Precisely." Hayley finished her water and waved her hand at Alison's phone. "Well, don't stop now, we're waist deep in research here."

"Right. I digress. Back to the important stuff. Blah, blah, blah, she's been featured as Best Hollywood Beach Bod for four years in a row. Yada, yada, yada, she's gorgeous, on a million magazine covers. She donates a third of her salary to animal shelters and children's hospitals here and in Colorado. Oh, here's the good stuff—she's rumored to be bisexual, although nothing has ever been formally announced." Alison paused. "Wow. She's beautiful, she donates her money to orphaned pets and sick kids, and she's probably most likely definitely into women. She's, like, perfect. I think I'm nervous for you."

Hayley sighed and sank lower into her seat. "You are not helping, by the way."

"You make a fair point"—Alison nodded—"sorry."

Hayley signaled to the waiter for another drink. She was doomed no matter what. She might as well take advantage of the end of happy hour. "It's fine. Go on."

Encouraged, Alison continued, "Okay, that's what her *Wikipedia* says, but the gossip rags tell a different tale." She scrolled down some more.

Hayley knew a little bit of this next part. Emerson's successes had been shrouded in controversy. Multiple reports stated that she'd slept her way—with both male and female directors—into two of her three biggest-grossing movie roles. She was reported to have a violent and volatile temper that landed her in anger management in her mid to late teens and early twenties. Rumors abounded that she was a diva on television sets in her youth, and that she made unrealistic demands while working on movies even to this day.

"Remember that little bit like eleven years ago when she was accused of lighting fire to her ex-manager's car?" Alison stole a sip of Hayley's newly delivered martini before stripping another fry of its cheesy goodness. The horror.

"No charges were pressed, though," Hayley pointed out, even though she understood the societal assumed guilt was punishment enough. There were murmurings that Emerson was dropped from two projects following that media frenzy and that that was the primary reason why she started working as a voice-over actress on that kids' show, *Adventure Frog*. People around the *Sun* said she had to get out of the limelight for a little while to let things blow over.

"Are you sure you aren't working for her?" Alison asked.

That was probably the most ludicrous part of this whole shit show. How anyone could think that Hayley was employed by Emerson or her PR team was beyond her. Really. "Positive."

"All right, whatever you say." After a moment, Alison's expression got serious. "This is all well and good, but the fact of the matter is this— the most important part of this puzzle is the Rachel piece. Agreed?"

Hayley nodded. "Yeah, there's that."

The internet had practically broken down when Rachel left the movie they were costarring in. Initial speculation blamed Rachel's departure on fighting between her and Emerson over screen time, and Emerson was painted as the instigator by *insiders*—whoever that was. But Rachel's recent publicity teaser turned that theory on its head. She was blaming her dismissal on a steamy affair with Emerson that unraveled because of jealousy over fame, salary, and their male costar. And if you were to believe Rachel's media baiting, this was just the tip of the iceberg. It felt like any day now Rachel would spill a little more tea. But for the moment, she was surprisingly quiet. It was almost as if she was biding her time before the next big reveal, and the media outlets were positively salivating over it.

"Not to make this any worse for you…"

"That's literally the worst thing to say before saying something that is going to make it worse for me." Hayley frowned.

Alison ignored her. "The supposed sexual relationship bombshell is on every major—and minor—news outlet in the world. It's trending on Twitter, Facebook, Instagram. Everywhere. All sorts of secret pictures of them together on set are being leaked. None of them indecent—yet—but it feels inevitable. There is a ticker on the bottom of every show on *TMZ* with hourly updates of any new information and a loop of footage of their near run-in on the red carpet, and snippets of Rachel's wounded but vague interview with James Drake that night even made it to three different primetime television news shows. This is the most exciting—and scandalous—thing that has happened in a long time."

"I know. It's—"

"Sensational. And creating a hell of a buzz." Alison leaned back in her seat, seeming to contemplate this. "What do you think? You think there's any truth to it?"

Hayley considered this question. It wasn't like she'd been able to think of much else this past week with Drake dragging her in the gossip columns and Emerson's face on every single screen on every channel and website in varying stages of reaction. Some smiling, some tight lipped, all of them beautiful. But people were already taking sides and writing their own narrative. The most popular theory was that Rachel had most likely been seduced by Emerson and duped into a relationship that ended her tenure on the film. Everything Rachel had said or implied up to this point made it appear as though she had been coaxed and coerced into any perceived misdoings on her part, further making Emerson out as the villain. Hayley wasn't so sure. She'd seen the backstage exchange—Rachel had been the instigator. She'd seen the fear in Emerson's eyes on the carpet. And the hurt in them later that night. There was more to this story. She was sure of it.

"I don't know. I think there's some truth there. But I think there's a lot more we don't know, too. It can't be that simple. It can't be that black and white." Hayley placed her empty glass on the table and shook her head. She had told Alison a little about what she'd witnessed that night, but she kept some of her observations to herself. The ones that felt like an invasion of privacy for Emerson. Which, if she was being honest, was all of them. "Something happened between them. I'm sure of it."

"Well, if it's true, I think it's hot"—Alison added with a nod—"but more than that, I want to know what happened to turn two of

Hollywood's most powerful actresses against each other." Alison raised her water glass and nodded toward Hayley. "Lucky for us, you're on the case."

"Lucky indeed." Hayley groaned and signaled for the check. Tomorrow was going to be a big day.

CHAPTER FIVE

Your two o'clock fitting just got bumped up to twelve thirty," Tremont said, his voice missing its usual warmth.

Emerson sighed but nodded. Had her hands not been currently immersed in warm water, her cuticles soaking, she would have flipped off Tremont for his tone alone. He'd been giving her attitude since yesterday when she'd asked for Chandra to come in and speak with her privately.

"Tremont," she said.

"Emerson," he answered, with the same flat tone as before.

She exhaled and shifted in her chair as the technician began drying her hands and prepping them for polish. "I can't tell for sure, but I feel like you might be upset. You do such a wonderful job at hiding it. I think maybe you should be the Oscar-nominated one here."

He clucked and stood, tossing the magazine in his hands to the side as he leaned over her and said, "Nominated and lost. Don't forget that little tidbit for your memoir."

The technician looked up at Emerson fearfully, averting her eyes when Emerson glanced at her.

She pressed on. "Montie, I'm going to need you to get over this hissy fit sooner rather than later."

"Don't call me *Montie* like you give a damn about what I have to say. That's reserved for my mama and my sisters—people who appreciate my opinion."

"Your poor mother doesn't ever want your opinion, and your sisters think you're a diva. Let's slow the bullshit train before it flies off the tracks, shall we?"

Tremont pursed his lips and pulled out his phone. He scrolled through the screen and gave her his best impression of indifference, which was actually quite good. "You have to pick out an outfit for the gala on Saturday night. It's the same woman who is doing the fitting for the film's wardrobe department. Two for one, to accommodate your busy schedule."

Emerson looked over at her old friend and contemplated her next choice of words carefully. She needed his help for this to work, but she also needed to corral his broodiness. They couldn't both be on the brink of instability, not when she had so much at stake.

The technician finished applying the polish and top coat before setting up the hand dryer. Emerson nodded and told the woman to come back in a few minutes, promising to stay put so as to not smudge anything. Once their audience departed, she tried again.

"Tremont. I know you think this is a bad idea. But something has to be done," she said.

Tremont gave her a look. "I don't understand why you aren't letting David and Chandra worry about this. You know that this is a hot topic, Emerson. Why put yourself in the position to make a mistake that you can't correct?"

"Maybe because they did such a bang-up job the first time around, I'm a little leery of their help, ever consider that?" She bristled, irritated that she couldn't move her hands to help vent some of her frustration.

"You know there was nothing they could do, Em." His reply was soft as his usual warmth returned. He was trying to manage her, and that made her bristle even more.

"Everyone spends so much time telling me that there is nothing that can be done and doing nothing that it's a fucking miracle anything happens in this camp at all."

Tremont frowned. "We only want to help you, Emerson. We're not the bad guys."

"Then let me have my day in court, Tremont. Let me have a chance to actually dictate the pace of this sideshow for once," she replied.

"You and I both know that the speed is out of our hands," he said.

That wasn't entirely true, but Emerson didn't bother arguing the point. She had a plan to bring this to a full stop, but she needed his support.

"But the direction doesn't have to be. I'm tired of being a pawn in everyone's agenda," she replied.

Tremont let out a tired sigh as he sat next to her and stroked his hands through her hair. "I hope you know what you're getting into, Emerson. Because once you start this, there's no way to stop it."

She closed her eyes and let his words settle a bit before shooting him a sly smile. "Don't get soft on me now. I'm going to need you to make sure this doesn't blow up in my face."

Tremont stopped playing with her hair and ran a file over his nails. "Oh, please. If you go down, I'm out of a job. I have bills to pay, boyfriends to throw money at, an image to uphold…I can't have my Hollywood connection washing up and ruining the brand I've been working on for so long. Don't kid yourself."

"That's the sassy best friend I've been missing. Welcome back."

He pushed her wheatgrass smoothie toward her. "Shut up and drink your nasty green juice. You're gonna need all the energy you can get."

"Yes, ma'am." Emerson went to salute her friend, smudging her nails in the process. "Shit. Go get her for me, would you?"

"You. Are. Hopeless."

❖

"How's it going in Tinseltown?" Deidre's voice on the line was like a breath of fresh air.

"Oh, you know, gloriously sunny and fake as the day is long. As usual." Emerson glanced out the window of her rental home and surveyed the mountain view before her. The sky was blue and free of clouds, but the city just a short drive away was full of vultures.

"Mm-hmm. How are you holding up?"

Up to that moment, Emerson would have said she was doing okay. But hearing the sympathetic tone in her sister's voice brought all the emotions to the surface. Her lip trembled as she spoke. "Dee, I'm struggling. This is so hard."

"I know, Em. I know," Deidre said.

Deidre was quiet as Emerson's tears fell in steady streams. She loved that about her sister. She loved that her sister wasn't afraid to feel and let feelings exist. It was something that Deidre had always supported in her—to acknowledge and feel things. That was such a foreign concept in this town. In this world. But she never hid her true feelings from her sister. She never blunted her emotions. She couldn't. And she knew she was a better person for it. She owed that to her sister. She owed a lot to her sister.

She wiped her cheeks and took a steadying breath. "How are the kids?"

"They're good." They both knew what she was asking, but Deidre had the decency to pretend it was a normal question. "Alex is trying out for the lead in the school play—"

"What play?"

"*Macbeth*." Her sister laughed, and she felt lighter.

"Isn't that a little heavy for fourth-graders?" Emerson smiled at the thought of her nephew dressed in oversized robes reciting lines he didn't understand. He would be fantastic as Macbeth. That kid oozed charm and charisma.

"They're putting a modern-day spin on it. The students helped to rewrite the script a bit to make it more relevant to current day. Like— for instance—instead of witches, there are zombies."

"Obviously." That made perfect sense.

"It's your fault, you know," Deidre teased. "He wants to be just like his famous aunt. Plus, you send them to that bougie school where they encourage development in the *arts*…as if that's a thing."

Emerson laughed at the way her sister dramatically drew out the word. "It's a good school, Dee. You and Tom wouldn't have agreed to let them go there if you didn't think so, too."

"I know. Secretly I love that they have as much music and art classwork as math and science. But I'm still going to mock you for it because it's so very Hollywood of you," she said.

"Says the woman who lives in a town that has a school like that nearby." Deidre lived near enough to Aspen to capitalize on the posh private schools that had opened to accommodate the rich and famous families while they skied and shopped in the winter months. But over the years, Aspen had become more than just a winter getaway. More and more entrepreneurs and celebrities were taking year-round residence there to escape the hustle and bustle of Southern California. The two-hour flight was quick enough to be convenient, considering you could sit in two hours of traffic just trying to get in or out of LA these days. And although the unmatched natural beauty was what attracted Emerson to the area, the five-star restaurants and boutique shopping helped, too. Colorado offered Deidre and her family the privacy she and her husband desired while still giving Emerson quick access to them. It also afforded her the chance to make sure her niece and nephew had everything they could ever want or need. It was a win-win. Well, except for the small fact that Emerson seemed to have developed a fear of flying over the last few years, but she was working on that. Sort of.

"Touché. Feel free to fund their college educations as well." Deidre laughed.

"Already done." That was one of the first things Emerson had arranged once the kids were born—she'd made sure they would never want for anything, but she left what that meant up to her sister. She didn't want to interfere or eclipse her sister's parenting approach. That was something very important to them both, and it was why this relationship worked.

"Oh, and Rory requested a unicorn for her twelfth birthday. Maybe you could work on that, too," Deidre replied. She was the best.

Emerson paused. It was now or never. "Rory. How is she?"

Deidre was quiet for a moment. Emerson could hear a door closing softly on the near silent line. Her sister was going somewhere more private. That couldn't be good.

"She's okay." A pause. "She's worried about you."

Emerson felt a pit form in her stomach—no eleven-year-old girl should worry about her aunt. "How much does she know?"

"You're kidding, right? Em, you're on every channel. Everywhere. We can't even turn on the radio on the ride to school because every thirty minutes one station or another is giving their celebrity update and you're the main topic. Like, seriously. We even tried NPR and the classical station. You've peaked, sis. You are officially the center of everyone's universe," Deidre answered.

"You mean my alleged relationship and alleged subsequent breakup with Rachel are the center of everyone's universe. I highly doubt it's little old me." Emerson didn't bother trying to hide her bitterness about this whole mess.

"Well, yeah. That's true. Although—to be fair—without you none of this would even be an issue. So it *is* about you," Deidre said.

She frowned. "Thanks, Dee."

"Anytime."

Obviously, Deidre was going to make her work for this. Fine. That was fine. She deserved it. "What can I do?"

"To fix this mess?" Deidre sounded skeptical.

"No, I'm working on that. I meant to help with Rory." She meant that first part—she had a plan in place. She just had to implement it. The second thing, though…that was another story entirely.

"It's time, Em. I know we talked about it and I know we agreed on a decision, but things are different now. She's not a little girl anymore, Emerson. She's growing up so fast, too fast. And it's time," Deidre said.

"You say it like it's going to be so easy, Dee. Like telling Rory I'm her mother and not her aunt is just no big deal." She clapped her hand over her mouth. She hadn't meant to say that out loud. She almost never did.

Deidre responded with a harsh intake of breath. "Don't you think I wish it never came to this, Emerson?" she whispered. "Don't you think I've dreaded this conversation for nearly twelve years? Of course it's a big deal. It's the biggest deal. It's the only deal we ever made together that we've never faulted on. Because we couldn't. Because we are in this together. A family. We'll still be a family afterward, it'll just be… different." The sadness in her voice was palpable. Emerson felt every word.

Emerson was crying again, but this time it wasn't just because she was overwhelmed. It was because she was hurt. Because she felt lost. Because she'd failed her sister and her niece. This was all her fault. "I-I'm so sorry, Dee."

Deidre sighed. "You didn't do anything wrong, Em. You have the right to take a chance on love. Now, you picked a real flaming bitch in Rachel, but you still deserve the chance to be happy. Lesson learned, right? Next time I want to weigh in on the more serious dating prospects. Especially if one of those prospects threatens to tell the world that you have a secret daughter being raised by your sister. Or, you know, something like that."

Deidre's joke didn't make Emerson feel any better. There wouldn't be a next time. She'd lost her chance. This was the life she was meant to live—alone, renting a house to avoid the hordes of paparazzi and gawkers outside her primary residence that had descended on her like locusts after Rachel's red-carpet reveal. But Deidre was right. None of this would have happened if Emerson wasn't involved in the first place. She could never seem to get out of her own way. Her celebrity managed to fuck something up eventually. This was no different.

"How much time do we have?" Deidre's voice was soft. She sounded as heartbroken as Emerson felt.

"I think we're out of it." She'd realized that when the press release came out. Rachel had forced her hand. She knew it was only a matter of time before Rachel spilled the bigger story, the truth about Rory. Up to now she was just gathering sympathy for a relationship gone awry, but Emerson knew that she was only building her fictional backstory so that when she dropped the inevitable secret child bomb, she'd seem less like a heartless woman scorned and more like a betrayed and abandoned ex-lover. Emerson could already tell that the public was eating up Rachel's side of the story. She'd seen the fan pages—she was quickly becoming public enemy number one. Emerson sighed. "What does Tom think?"

"Mostly homicidal thoughts toward Rachel with occasional outbursts of tears. Luckily, I have the kids convinced it's *man*-opause. That should hold them until you get here." Deidre chuckled before getting serious and saying, "You are going to come here for this, right, Emerson?"

"Of course"—Emerson wouldn't dream of doing this over the phone—"this is a family emergency. We need to be together."

"Good." When Deidre sniffled, Emerson's soul quaked. She knew this was going to change everything for all of them. But she knew that Deidre and Tom were going to get the worst of it up front. Maybe, maybe over time she could repair things with Rory. And with Alex. But nothing would protect her sister and her family once the truth came out. They might as well kiss their privacy good-bye, which was what Emerson had been trying to prevent since the day Rory was born. Rory deserved a life outside of Emerson's shadow. She deserved a chance at normalcy. That would be impossible now. There wasn't enough *anything* in the world to make this right again. And that was what kept her up at night: the countdown to the fallout. It was inevitable, and it was happening right that very second.

CHAPTER SIX

Chandra Patel's face had been in a scowl for the entire time Hayley had been in her presence. While she'd formally introduced herself, she hadn't bothered disconnecting the call she was on. Hayley imagined her look of frustrated concentration was probably a common occurrence if the stress lines etched in her forehead were any indication. Chandra had handed Hayley some papers, mumbling something about giving them to legal, before she wandered out of the room.

Hayley shifted the file folder of documents into her messenger bag. She looked at the pack of gum tucked into the pocket and considered whether it would be rude to be chewing something when she finally met with Emerson. A quick survey of the waiting area she was in didn't help her decision; there was no trash can to use in the disposal process, and she would never swallow gum again after that near-choking incident in sixth grade scarred her for life.

After forty-five minutes of waiting beyond her scheduled meeting time, she began to wonder if she was going to meet with Emerson at all. Chandra had come in and out a dozen times in the last twenty minutes, always mumbling something into her headset, barely acknowledging Hayley's presence. About five minutes ago, the handsome and stylishly dressed black man who'd been with Emerson the other night had stepped out and looked at her before he sighed and left without a word.

Hayley checked her phone and started texting Alison when the door to her left opened, startling her.

"Emerson is ready for you." The man she assumed was Emerson's PA spoke briskly as he motioned for her to enter. Hayley tried not to stare, but his subtle eye makeup was freaking incredible. His eyeliner application was perfect, and his eye shadow blending was unbelievable. She wondered if it would be inappropriate to ask him for a few tips.

"I'm Tremont Winters, her assistant. I'll be with you at all times, so get used to the idea," he added curtly.

"Could you try to be a little more welcoming, Tremont?" Emerson's voice called out from behind the changing screen erected in the corner of the room. The sounds of hangers sliding along metal almost muted his clucked response.

Emerson emerged from behind the screen with a small smile on her face. Her tight black tank top was rolled up, exposing her firm abdomen, while a woman with her hair in a messy gray bun struggled to keep a tape measure loosely around her hips.

"Sorry for the delay. It turns out I have a dress fitting that is happening in my room at the moment." Emerson winced when a pin scratched across her skin as the seamstress adjusted her glasses and stumbled, jerking Emerson back by the tape measure.

Hayley laughed and then clamped her hand over her mouth when she noticed Tremont glaring at her. "Uh, it's okay."

Emerson cocked her head to the side and replied seriously. "No, it's not. But unfortunately this is not an uncommon occurrence. You should know that up front."

"Up front of what?" Hayley adjusted the strap of her bag and made every attempt to maintain eye contact with Emerson while her stage of undress continued to change—the tank top appeared to be up higher now.

Emerson raised her arms at the gentle nudging of the seamstress, clasping her hands behind her head and leaning back slightly. Hayley didn't miss how the loose pants along her hips slid down with the motion.

"I need you to write an article. There will be frustrating delays. I just wanted to warn you," Emerson replied. Her tone was sincere, her voice calm.

Oh, right. She had asked a question. "An article about what?"

The seamstress whispered something to Emerson. She nodded and pulled her tank top off completely while slowly stepping out of the pants that barely encased her hips. She returned her hands to their clasped position behind her head, standing only in matching black lace underwear as she playfully rolled her eyes at Hayley. "About me. The naked truth, so to speak."

Hayley knew she was blushing. Astronauts in space could see she was blushing. She might spontaneously combust. It was that serious. Emerson Sterling was just about naked in front of her, standing in an oddly suggestive position, asking her to write about her naked truth. Naked. Also, truth. Right, truth. She was there for the truth. *You can do this. Get it together, Hayley.*

She arched her eyebrow and asked, "Will all our meetings end with one of us scantily clad, or is this just how you welcome new people into your inner circle?"

Emerson laughed, putting one foot forward as the seamstress took measurements along her toned leg. "No one said I was welcoming you into my inner circle, Ms. Carpenter."

"Hayley."

Emerson nodded. "And the answer to your other question is—I guess we'll just wait and see."

❖

"Here's some coffee. She's waiting for you on the balcony," Tremont said as he handed her a cup and pointed toward the second-floor terrace of the home Emerson was renting near the movie studio. "I have to run an errand. Call me if you need anything."

Hayley followed behind him, making a mental note that although he was still rigid with their interactions, the iciness of the first day seemed to have thawed a little. This was her third meeting with Emerson in the past week. Once the legal department at the *Sun* had gone over all the paperwork and had her sign a bunch of things, she was given a loose schedule of dates and times. Today was the first day she would have more than an hour of Emerson's time, and it was time that according to the schedule would be exclusively their own. No fittings, no meetings, no phone calls. The lack of distractions made her a little nervous.

Emerson was reclining in a lounge chair when Hayley found her on the balcony. She was dressed casually, her ankles crossed in front of her. Her hair was pulled up today in a sloppy and yet annoyingly perfect twisted updo. She looked cute. Almost like any other attractive

LA person, save for the fact that Hayley knew behind the large dark sunglasses were those amazingly expressive eyes she'd been dreaming about all day and night since they'd crossed paths at that awards ceremony.

Emerson was reading over a thick bound sheaf of paper that Hayley noticed had intermittent highlighted passages. She didn't look up when Hayley sat down at the lounger next to her, only waving her fingers briefly to acknowledge her presence. After about ten minutes she put the bound papers down and surveyed Hayley.

"He likes you, you know," she said.

"Who does?"

"Tremont," Emerson replied simply.

"Why do you say that? I get the distinct impression he hates me." Hayley pulled out her tablet and began loading a blank document to take notes.

Emerson pushed her dark glasses up into her hair and smiled. "He's bringing you coffee."

"I've just been assuming that he's tampering with it in some way"—Hayley shrugged and typed in her password—"and I've only been polite in taking it from him. I haven't actually been drinking it."

Emerson sat up and swung her legs around so that she was facing Hayley. "Give me your cup."

Hayley leaned forward and hesitantly obliged the strange request.

Emerson brought the cup to her lips and sipped it. "Nope, no poison, bleach, or salt. But it's pretty heavy on the cream, is that how you like it?"

Hayley took back the cup and looked at the lipstick mark on the rim. "How do you know? And yes, I like a lot of cream in my coffee."

"There was a time when Tremont used to intentionally ruin my beverages as payback for what he called Bitch Breakdowns. I got pretty adept at identifying foreign substances in my drinks." She leaned back and reclined on the lounger again, her gaze out at the view in front of them.

Hayley's brow furrowed at the comment as she turned the mug and drank from the clean side, sighing happily at the robust flavor. She typed into the tablet for a moment and looked up again. "So, how do you take your coffee?"

"You have unrestricted access to ask me anything you choose, with no chaperone to limit or accost you, and that's your first question?" Emerson looked amused.

"It feels like a good place to start. We're having coffee together, aren't we?"

A slight smile settled on Emerson's full lips. Hayley tried not to stare. "I don't drink coffee. It makes me jumpy."

"What's in the mug then?" Hayley motioned to the cup by Emerson's side.

"Vodka."

Hayley's fingers stopped typing. "Seriously?"

"No." Emerson's eyes twinkled, and Hayley's heart skipped a beat. She liked playful Emerson.

Hayley shook her head and laughed, returning her fingers to the keyboard.

"What are you typing?" Emerson looked at her curiously as she sipped the unknown contents of her mug.

"Just little notes so that I remember what we talk about," she said. Emerson's camp had expressly requested that no audio or video would be used during the article writing process. Hayley could take as many notes as she'd like, but that was it.

"Can I see?" Emerson reached her hand out and waited.

"Uh"—Hayley glanced down at the blinking cursor in front of her and frowned—"I'm not sure that's how this is supposed to work."

Undeterred, Emerson extended her hand another inch in Hayley's direction.

"Okay, but only if you promise not to laugh," she said before relinquishing the tablet.

Emerson paused before looking at it. "I can't make that promise."

"Hey!"

Emerson replied with a smile, "You should learn to get confirmation on your conditions before you give up your power, Hayley."

Hayley leaned back into the chair. "Who told you that?"

"My grandmother," Emerson replied as she skimmed the tablet screen. She raised her eyebrow and pursed her lips. "Hayley, the only thing on the screen is a grocery list."

Hayley smiled. "If your grandmother is anything like mine, then she also told you not to show your hand to your opponent."

Emerson seemed to consider this. "Do you think of me as your opponent, Hayley?"

Hayley shrugged. "Not exactly. But I think you have a lot more to gain than I do in this relationship, so I'm being cautious."

"Ooh, we're in a relationship, are we? Do tell, what does that entail?" Emerson's lips curved up slightly and Hayley warmed a bit.

Hayley narrowed her eyes at the playful grin on Emerson's lips. "Emerson, this is only going to work if you are open and honest with me. I promise to be candid in my interpretation of our time together, but I can only work with what you give me."

Emerson watched her for a moment. She maintained eye contact while her fingers moved quickly along the keys of Hayley's tablet keyboard. "What's it like having a brother?"

"What?" Hayley watched Emerson's fingers continue their uninterrupted dance along her keys as those intense blue-green eyes trapped her again.

"A brother. What's it like?" Emerson repeated.

"It's…fine. I don't know, I've never known anything else. What's it like having a sister?" Hayley considered the information she knew about Emerson. She was the youngest of two. She and her older sister were raised by a single mother in California. They moved around quite a bit, but it appeared as though she'd spent her childhood in and around LA. Her sister was quite a few years older, but they looked very much alike. Save for the fact that her sister had dark brown eyes and Emerson's were that magical turquoise color. But both women were clearly blessed in the looks department, that was obvious.

"Lots of hair braiding and being a guinea pig for makeup disasters. I was never bored," Emerson said.

Hayley nodded. "Do you—"

"Tell me about your summer vacations in Maine," Emerson interrupted.

"My grandmother had a cottage on a lake. I spent my summers there…it was the best part of my childhood," Hayley answered without hesitation. That was true. Maine was a big part of who she was. She felt as if she'd found her peace and true self during those Maine summers. It was the most comfortable she'd ever felt in her own skin. "Wait, who told you about Maine?"

Emerson ignored her question. "Did you have cats or dogs growing up?"

"Two cats, a brother and sister," Hayley answered, unsure of why that mattered.

Emerson continued typing, her eyes never leaving Hayley's face. "What's your favorite color?"

"Purple. Aren't I supposed to be asking you questions?"

Again, she was ignored. "How old are you?"

"Twenty-eight." Hayley settled back into her chair and let the irony of the situation wash over her. This was the first time in any of her interactions with Emerson that she felt like she had Emerson's full attention. And somehow, she was the one in the hot seat.

"What's your sign?" Emerson's eye contact never waivered, which was both thrilling and intimidating. Hayley wasn't sure which feeling was stronger.

"Libra," she answered.

"Did you play softball in high school?"

"No." That was sort of true. Kinda. The question was complicated, but she got the impression from the speed with which Emerson was firing the questions at her that the answers she wanted should be short and succinct, not drawn out and boring.

"How old were you when you lost your virginity?" Emerson's expression remained unchanged, but the tone of her questioning appeared to have shifted.

"S-sixteen." Hayley stuttered through her answer, unsure of why she'd responded at all. This line of questioning had moved into a level of personal that she wasn't entirely comfortable with. Yet she couldn't look away from Emerson either. It was like she had her under some kind of spell.

Emerson raised an eyebrow as she asked, "When did you first realize you were interested in women?"

"I never said I was." Hayley was too shocked by the bluntness of the question to stop her automatic responses. The spell continued, it seemed.

"Why do you work for the *Hollywood Sun*?" Emerson's questioning pace increased.

"I'm a writer," Hayley replied.

"Is that what you think your Yale degree says about you? Or is that how you feel when you wake up in the morning?" Emerson blinked.

"Hey—" Hayley attempted to argue but was waved off again.

"What possessed you to pair that shirt with those pants today?"

Hayley snapped her mouth shut to stop from saying the angry comments that were mounting in her head.

Emerson's blank expression changed into something darker as she fired off more questions without giving Hayley the chance to respond. "Why did you stay back in kindergarten? How do you still have your license after three citations for speeding in the last eleven months? Why didn't you go to your senior prom? How long have you been exclusively dating women? Did you find it odd that I contacted you for this job considering you have no experience in this whatsoever? How many partners have you had? What makes you think you can hack it here in LA?"

"Emerson, I don't know what it is you want from me." Hayley crossed her arms and sat taller in her seat. She had no idea why their playful getting-to-know-you banter had suddenly changed, but the threatening glare Emerson was directing at her made her more angry than anxious. Hayley felt attacked and ambushed by the very specific and obviously researched questions being hurled at her in rapid-fire succession.

"I want you to answer me." Emerson's fingers halted on the keyboard. Her voice was low as she added, "Answer my questions or this ends here."

"You can't just demand me to answer shit that has nothing to do with this assignment," Hayley scoffed, her anger bubbling over as she began to stand.

"Sit down." Emerson's voice was cold, but it didn't compare to the iciness of her gaze. Hayley dropped back into her seat out of shock. What was wrong with this woman?

"Answer my questions, Hayley." Emerson was clearly not going to budge on this. She had to decide to play along and give Emerson what she wanted or to stand up and walk out of here—and likely, her job. It was one or the other.

She took a deep breath and dived in. "I broke my arm and missed two months of kindergarten, so they held me back. My brother is a cop back home, so he called in a few favors to get me out of the tickets—I have a need for speed. I was suspended for a fight with another girl and not allowed to go to the prom even though she started it, but that's another whole story entirely. I've been dating women since college. I have no idea why you want me here or what is going on in your head. I've had about eleven partners, maybe more? I never calculated a total, nor do I think that's any of your fucking business, but…whatever. And as for hacking it in LA—I'm here with you, aren't I?"

Emerson resumed typing feverishly for a moment before she pushed the tablet off her lap and picked up her mug. She blinked once slowly. "Honey and warm water."

Hayley was fuming. She felt like she had been shaken and dropped on her head by the sudden change in Emerson's demeanor. "What are you talking about?"

Emerson nodded to her cup. "In my mug. I don't drink coffee. But I start every morning with honey and warm water."

Hayley looked at Emerson like she had ten heads. "What the hell was that?"

Emerson let out a tired sigh and looked at Hayley again. The intensity from before was present, but the darkness had retreated. "You were wrong before. I have more to lose than I have to gain from working with you. You may be cautious and feel like I'm an opponent, but you have all the power in this relationship. You've seen my hand. You know more about me than I will ever know about you because I have no privacy and everything that happens in my life—even the mundane way I take my morning beverage—is something for someone to write about and benefit from. So you're wrong. I have more to lose than you do from this relationship. It's a gamble for me to even try to make this work with you—or anyone, for that matter. But I'm going to try."

She paused, her expression softening. "I just wanted you to know what it felt like to be under attack. For you to understand what it's like to have your words twisted and misinterpreted and your actions second-guessed. Because for this to work"—she gestured between the two of them—"I need you to understand what you think you know isn't all based in fact, and that's why I need someone who is willing to really hear me out."

Hayley's head was swimming. She closed her eyes and considered everything Emerson said. Her heart was still thumping quickly in her chest, but her adrenaline was starting to slow as she realized she wasn't in any real imminent danger. She paused for a second before opening her eyes and asking, "How did you know all that stuff about me?"

Emerson chuckled and reclined on the lounger again, her head turned to face Hayley. "I do my research on all projects I undertake. I like to be prepared for everything. I don't like surprises."

Hayley nodded, her heart rate slowing a bit more. "Why did you pick me to do this, Emerson?"

Emerson's expression became serious, but her voice was soft when she said, "Because you had the chance to exploit me when anyone else in your position would have, and you didn't."

Hayley thought back to that night and remembered her moral compass flashing red when Drake attempted to record the exchange between Emerson and Rachel. "It wouldn't have been right. I couldn't."

Emerson nodded and sat up. She picked up Hayley's tablet and handed it to her. "I'm going to trust you when you say that, Hayley, because my gut tells me you're being honest, and even though everyone else may think I'm crazy, at the end of the day I have to be able to trust my intuition."

Hayley took the tablet blindly and replied, "I'll do my best, Emerson. That's all I can promise you."

"That's all I ask." Emerson smiled and adjusted her sunglasses over her eyes as she stood and stretched. "You're a hell of a writer, Hayley."

She tossed the bound stack of paper onto the chair next to Hayley and pointed to it before walking back inside. "I made some notes on my favorite parts—read them over before our next meeting. Tremont will give you the schedule."

Hayley thumbed through the papers and noticed Emerson had assembled every article, story, blog entry, or essay that she had ever written. They were organized chronologically starting back from high school and ending with her tiny entertainment piece from the night she and Emerson first crossed paths. She noticed delicate slanting notes in the margins, and the highlighted portions she'd spied before.

Tremont clearing his throat drew her attention to his presence on the terrace. "Emerson has a meeting with her trainer now. I'll show you out."

Hayley just nodded, still unbelieving of what had transpired. She packed her bag and followed Tremont to the elevator, down through the lobby, to a car he had waiting for her.

"I'll email you the schedule for this upcoming week," he said.

"Thanks."

He gave her a kind look. "Hey, Hayley?"

"Yeah?" She wasn't used to him regarding her in such a...friendly manner. It unnerved her a bit.

He looked a little shy. "I never messed with your coffee."

Hayley's confusion deepened as she realized Tremont was probably nearby the whole time all along. "You never left, did you?"

"And leave you alone with Emerson? Not on your life." His usual confidence resurfaced. This Tremont was more like the one she was used to.

He helped her into the car and gave the driver orders to take Hayley wherever she wanted to go. "You could have been some secretly obsessed rabid fan. One can never be too careful these days."

"Something tells me Emerson is plenty capable of taking care of herself." After today's interview, Hayley didn't doubt that for a second.

"Everyone needs a little help from time to time"—Tremont gave her a small smile—"but you held your own just fine, Hayley."

Hayley didn't feel that way, but she appreciated the encouragement. "Thanks."

"See you next week."

As the car pulled away and eased into the traffic of the 101, Hayley couldn't help but smile at the compliment Tremont had given her. At least, she was considering it a compliment. And she had a feeling he didn't give those out very often.

Her thoughts drifted to her interaction with Emerson, and a wave of guilt washed over her. She'd ended up on the red carpet because Sharon was pissed that Hayley's article about celebrity fragility in the current media market had interested Jonathan enough that he'd bumped one of Sharon's pieces to feature Hayley's for the week. Hayley was proud of that article; she'd spent an inordinate amount of time studying trends and the overexposure of current day celebrities, but not once had she been able to put herself in their shoes. To be fair, she'd never been in the presence of someone with as much celebrity as Emerson, either. But she'd also neglected to take her own conclusions to heart.

Emerson had turned the tables on her in their exchange today, and Hayley had immediately gone on the defensive. She couldn't imagine what it was like to live your entire life with other people knowing and assuming things about you on a large and small scale. Her article had been well intended and well received. But clearly she had some serious reevaluation to do. Writing about the media and its impact on the existence of celebrity and experiencing it firsthand were two very different things. She wondered just how much exposure to celebrity she would have and just how long this work with Emerson would last. She found herself hoping it would be a very long time.

Chapter Seven

You were hard on her." Tremont sat down next to Emerson with a bottle of water and a fresh towel.

Emerson brushed the wet hair off her forehead and continued with her vertical crunches. "I thought you would be pleased I put her through the wringer."

"I didn't think you'd traumatize her," he added sarcastically as he checked his fauxhawk in the mirror across from them.

"She'll be fine." Emerson grunted as she pulled her ankles out of the brackets and signaled her trainer, Sebastian Diaz, to bring over the medicine ball. "And if she's not, then it wasn't meant to be."

"Catch the ball, twist, lift your legs, and toss it back. Ready?" Sebastian held the ten-pound ball and waited for Emerson to nod before he began.

Emerson caught the ball and exhaled. She could see the sheen of sweat on her chest in the mirror as she rocked to the side. Her abdominal muscles burned with exertion. "I hate you."

"You love me every time you make the top five of Best Bikini Bod and Hollywood's Most Enviable Abs lists. Go faster. Now, flip," Sebastian challenged and threw the medicine ball at her with more force, causing Emerson to huff out a sharp breath.

Tremont cheered. "Yeah, Sebastian. Give it to her, give it to her hard. She's been a bad, bad girl."

Emerson caught the weight and rolled, transitioning to fast push-ups with her palms on the ball and toes en pointe. She kept her body straight and her muscles engaged as she tried to stifle her laughter while Tremont whooped and catcalled.

"Time! Good work." Sebastian clapped and pulled her up into a standing position. She accepted his high five and splashed Tremont with the remaining contents of her water bottle.

"Just so you know, I've been number one on those lists. Every time. Not just top five. That's why I put up with your torture." She winked and patted Sebastian on the chest. "Now, if you'll excuse me, I have to go jump on a bike and burn off the warm water I had for breakfast."

Tremont waved her off without so much as a second thought, but she wasn't offended. She knew he had a total thing for Sebastian. She couldn't imagine who wouldn't. Sebastian was smart and sweet and ripped. Totally, insanely ripped. Which she happened to know was one of Tremont's weakness. She'd been doing a little investigative work on her own and felt confident that Tremont had caught Sebastian's eye as well. She'd kept that little tidbit to herself, though. She didn't want Tremont freaking out like he usually did when he found out a guy liked him. But she was rooting for them to figure it out soon. Not that she had any desire to have to hire a new trainer if things went south—for as much shit as she gave him, she'd be a fool to deny that Sebastian was a fitness guru. Almost nothing made her sweat and her heart race like her workouts with him did. God. She needed to get laid, and soon.

She slipped in her wireless earbuds and trotted over to the bike. She dialed up the resistance and logged on to the monitor attached to the handlebars before queuing up one of her favorite high-octane training sessions. This was a scenic session, but there was nothing leisurely about it. The screen depicted an interactive training experience set on rocky mountain roads with sharp pitches and steep inclines. The music in the background beat hard and fast, encouraging her to match the intensity as she pedaled. She glanced up on a familiar resting turn and saw Tremont flirting with Sebastian by the mat where she left them. Tremont was waving his arms in a dramatic birdlike fashion, and Sebastian was in near tears laughing. Whatever this mating ritual was, it appeared to be working.

The resistance of the bike doubled, and Emerson sucked in a breath to accommodate the increased challenge. She returned her attention to the screen and lifted off the seat, standing on the pedals as she forced them down in a practiced and automatic descent she'd honed during the last ten months of cycle training. She could feel her heart rate pick up and her mind wandered to her previous thoughts. She'd been wrong before. Sebastian wasn't the only one who got her heart racing. Hayley did, too.

She'd been trying to ignore that fact for the past few days, but she couldn't seem to let it go. There was something about Hayley. Something about the passion behind her eyes that drew Emerson in. They hadn't had the best first impression—more specifically, Emerson had thought she was working for that asshole Drake—but Hayley had proven herself to be more of an ally than an opponent in the short time they'd spent together. Emerson just had a feeling in her gut that this woman was different. And smart. God, Hayley was smart. And sarcastic. And funny. Her writing was what had initially captivated Emerson beyond the bravery she showed standing up to Drake. She loved the way Hayley used language to draw the reader into her work. Once Emerson's team had tracked down all of Hayley's public works, she had settled into a few entertaining nights of reading. And it took nights, plural. Because though she'd considered herself a fast reader from all her script work and memorization, Hayley's body of work was significant. And surprisingly varied.

She'd followed Hayley's work at the *Sun* and had been impressed by how easily she was sucked into the topics. Hayley had managed to make a write-up on plastic and glass bottle waste impacting the beaches along the Santa Monica Pier sound not only interesting but heart wrenching as well. Emerson had been so moved by her interview with famed marine biologist Dr. Massimo Andiamo that she'd fallen into a rabbit hole researching his marine work and totally got sidetracked. All of Hayley's work—from the serious to the more recent puff pieces in the entertainment section—had heart. All of it. There was something there—between the lines, hidden in the text—that made Emerson feel that if anyone could tell her story, it would be Hayley. And it didn't hurt that Hayley had the most beautiful green-flecked hazel eyes she had ever seen. Or that she was bold and fearless. And feisty. She liked the way Hayley had flared against her interrogation today. It was more than a turn-on that Hayley was no pushover. She'd have to be strong to take on this challenge. She'd have to meet Emerson halfway—maybe more—to make this work.

What troubled Emerson was that she wasn't sure what *this* actually was. She'd caught Hayley checking her out during the dress fitting—

that wasn't all that unusual for Emerson, people admired her often—but for whatever reason, it excited her in a way she wasn't expecting. She liked being noticed by Hayley. She felt like she was developing a bit of a crush. Which was not in the cards. No way. She had gotten in this mess by giving in to her libido. The last thing she needed was a distraction on her road to public redemption. She needed to keep this strictly professional. She needed Hayley's help, and there was no way falling into bed with her would be helpful. Except maybe it would take the edge off a bit. She'd been feeling awfully lonely in that department lately. Focus, Emerson.

The image in front of her changed from the dry, clay-covered mountain path to a lush downhill forest trail with tree roots and dirt pits obstructing her route. She was glad for the redirection from her wandering thoughts. She strained to the right to maintain her form and accommodate the tipping motion of the bike on the pivoting platform as the forest path before her dropped sharply into a bumpy and fast flowing creek at the forest's edge. The background music thumped in her ears, but she didn't hear any of the lyrics. All she could hear was the deafening sound of her heartbeat as the bike resistance continued to fluctuate from easy to hard with little if any rest. This was how she trained—hard and fast. She liked to challenge her muscles to accommodate the short rest intervals by forcing them to recover quickly and improve their efficiency. She had built the last few years of her career around some key changes to her fitness goals. This was one of them. Hard. Fast. Relentless. Just like her life as of late.

Rachel's simmer was heating up and it was making everyone sweat. Chandra had hired extra staff to keep a round-the-clock watch on any and all things about Emerson in the media. Emerson would have appreciated the diligence if it wasn't all being done to save her image. To save the movie studio's ass was more like it.

"They called again." David's voice was laced with anxiety—which Emerson had no trouble ignoring—but the incessant foot tapping was driving her insane.

"Unless you are trying out for the new Savion Glover biopic that's in the works, I'm going to need you to stop that." She pointed to his foot and tried to relax her jaw. She'd been gritting her teeth for the past fifteen minutes to stop herself from yelling at him about it.

David's foot paused, and he glared at her. "You ought to show a little more concern about this, Emerson. We're effectively being blackmailed—"

"We? When did *I* become a *we*?" Emerson still hadn't forgiven David for the slipup that put Rachel in the position to ruin her life and career—thank you very much. "Last time I checked, I was the one being tarred and feathered by the public. Evidently, I've been home-wrecking every person I've come in contact with over the last decade and have been seducing poor, naïve, innocent straight girls in mass numbers. But please, take some of that burden from me if you'd like."

David muttered under his breath and looked away. She knew he felt bad for what had happened. But it didn't change anything. She was still the target, and all this was going to land squarely on her shoulders, not his.

"I'm just saying, you seem awfully calm is all," David replied. He seemed more and more weaselly as the days progressed, she decided. She'd given serious consideration to severing their relationship. She'd had her lawyers looking into their contract since Rachel's press release. She couldn't stand the sight of him these days. It wasn't good for either of them.

"Well, I am an award-winning actress, David. Did you ever consider that?" She had to stop talking to him before she said something she shouldn't. Where was Tremont? She could use his filter right about now. The truth was, she wasn't calm. She was more than panicked. She just didn't need the added attention of anyone else noticing it. So she was doing her best zen impression and trying to seem unconcerned. Which had David fooled, but that wasn't any real prize, was it?

"Fear not, my loyal subjects. I come bearing sustenance." Like a fairy gay-mother, Tremont swept into the room and saved her from herself.

"I thought you'd never come." Emerson gave him a dramatic sigh and wrapped her arms around his waist.

"That's what she said." He snickered and kissed her on the cheek. His hands were full of treats and something green, which Emerson assumed was for her.

"You're a perv." She accepted the green shake and frowned as he handed David a bag of hot, delicious-smelling doughnuts.

"I learned from the best." Tremont pointed toward her pout. "Drink up. It's got kale, whey protein, some banana, and—because I love you—a little pineapple."

"Ooh, pineapple. You spoil me." Emerson had to strain to get the dense contents up the metal straw to her mouth. "Jesus. This is thick."

"And that's what *he* said." Tremont cracked himself up.

Emerson laughed along with him, happy to have the distraction. "Who whipped this up? It's got an interesting aftertaste. Like—"

"Toasted almond?" Tremont washed his hands and dried them with a paper towel before reaching into one of the bags he brought and procuring another smoothie. This one was a bit larger than hers and purple in color.

"Yeah, exactly. Why?" She stirred the drink and warmed it in her hands to thin the liquid a bit. The second sip was even tastier than the first. "This is good."

"It's got almond milk as the base with some pulverized baked almond mixed in for fiber." Tremont put another metal straw in the other cup and held it up to eye level, appearing to examine the contents.

"Who's drinking that one?" Emerson leaned back against the kitchen counter and savored the delightful flavor of the smoothie.

"Me. It's got purple carrots, beets, and blueberries." Tremont sipped it and smiled. "This is delicious."

"Since when do you drink protein shakes?" Emerson reached for his to try it and he pulled it away from her.

"Since when did you get so entitled that you thought what's mine was yours?" He used his significant height difference to hold it in the air, out of her reach.

"Please?" Emerson smiled as he rewarded her with a taste. "Oh, let's trade."

"No way. You need the vitamins and minerals in the green one. This is like a protein shake lite. I'm easing into the healthy food lifestyle." He took back his smoothie and patted her on the head.

This was not the usual, junk food loving Tremont she was used to. This Tremont was into fitness. This Tremont was an imposter. A thought occurred to her. "Why were you late today?"

"Late? What is this, a nine to five? Since when do I have to be here at a certain time? If you have to know, I went for a run." Tremont was deflecting. He was never late. They had a meeting in a half hour with the movie studio to go over damage control from the Rachel backlash, and any other time he would have been here an hour and a half early to help her get ready. To help calm her nerves if she had any. Which—today—she definitely did.

"You don't run." That was also true. She examined his appearance. He was dressed in his usual designer pants and was wearing a pair of his fabulous Italian leather shoes from his extensive collection. His shirt was freshly pressed and tucked in with his sleeves rolled up on his forearms and displaying the obnoxious diamond-encrusted Patek Phillipe watch that she'd given him as a birthday present last year. He'd been fawning over it for ages. He'd kept saying it was the exact accent piece he'd needed in his wardrobe. Something about it making his wrist so cold he could ice skate with it. Or maybe it was *ice* that was so cold it could stop traffic? She couldn't remember exactly, but she knew he wanted it, and she gave it to him because she could, and because she loved him and wanted him to be happy. He wore it on special occasions. Today's meeting wasn't a special occasion per se. Or was it?

She stared at Tremont. He'd changed his haircut. He often changed his appearance, but he'd clearly just had his edges lined up. And he had on his fake eyelashes, the short ones that almost looked real but were too fabulous to be natural. "You had a date."

Tremont looked up at her, his mouth opened in surprise. He regained his composure before he answered. "Is that a crime?"

She hopped up on the counter and swung her legs while sipping her drink. "No. Keeping it from me is, though." She pointed to his shirt. "You look good. Fit. Strong. Been working out?"

Tremont's eyes bulged, and she cheered, hopping off the counter.

"I knew it. Sebastian made these smoothies, didn't he? You had a date with Sebastian and that's why you're late for work."

Tremont scoffed. "I'm not late for work. The meeting isn't for another twenty-five minutes. And they're coming to you. So we don't have to worry about traffic or anything. I'm right on time." He pointed to her drink. "And I came bearing gifts."

"*Bribes* is more like it. You came with bribes of sugary delicious death for David and emulsified kale for me. Don't think I didn't notice the difference there." She glanced over at David in the other room. He was stuffing his face, stress-eating doughnuts while on the phone with his back to them.

"You should thank me for giving him a distraction. When I walked in, you looked like you were going to murder him." Tremont never missed her emotions, no matter how well she tried to conceal them. He was like Deidre that way. She pushed that thought aside. She didn't want to think about Deidre right now. She was scheduled to fly to Colorado next weekend, and just thinking about the flight made her nauseous enough, forget about the reason she was going there. She swore she could feel that old ulcer from her teens making its presence known again.

"It was close. He was nervously tapping his foot and pacing. I thought I'd have to restrain him with barbed wire. That was my only option."

"Clearly," Tremont replied. He gave her a serious look. "He's worried about you."

"He's worried about himself." She knew she was being childish, but she was feeling her own anxiety about the impending meeting and she didn't want his burden as well.

He cast a glance toward David, who seemed oblivious to them. Tremont stepped closer. "Do you want to talk about the plan?"

This time it was her turn to deflect. "Do you want to tell me about your date with Sebastian?"

Tremont gave her a look. "You are such a meddlesome little wench. Fine. It was a quick brunch. Except there was no food and only discussions of exercise and sweating. And smoothies. The man doesn't eat bacon. Only fiber and lean protein."

"It shows. He's practically godlike," Emerson said.

Tremont nodded in agreement. "I asked him if his middle name was Adonis. He said no, but he blushed a little. So I'm taking that as a win."

"So that's why you're drinking fortified carrot juice—because Sebastian recommended it." She gave him a smug smile and he rolled his eyes. "I think you two are cute together. I support it. Plus, you eat like a sugar addicted college kid. It'll be good for you to change your lifestyle in your advanced years."

"You did not just call me old." Tremont looked scandalized. "I'm still younger than you, Grandma."

"By two months," she pointed out.

"Still makes me younger." Tremont motioned between his body and hers with a sly smile. "You're just jealous of my genetics and my incredibly fast metabolism. You have to work to look that good. I was born this way."

Emerson clinked her straw with his. "To good genes."

Tremont laughed and took a pull from his metal straw. "I like these. They keep the drink colder than the plastic ones."

"Plus they're better for the environment." Emerson had stopped using straws after reading Hayley's piece about ocean pollution. She hadn't told Tremont that was the reason, but that's what instigated it. She felt good about the change. She wondered what Hayley was up to at this moment. She wondered that a lot when they were apart.

"They're here." David stood at the edge of the kitchen looking twitchy.

"I'll be in shortly." Emerson watched him walk away.

"Are you ready for this?" Tremont's face showed the concern she felt.

"No." The movie studio execs had reached out to David and her camp a few times in the last couple of days. They were getting nervous. They all seemed to be worried about her brand. Truthfully, she wasn't exactly sure what her brand was anymore. One minute she was a victim to Rachel's one-sided storytelling in which people commended her and her team for not responding to Rachel's baiting in the media. The rest of the time she was made out to be a salacious media whore who got Rachel fired with her magical vagina that somehow influenced all the people she had supposedly slept with to get the role in *Willow Path* to begin with. If you believed the dark-web polls, Emerson must have over a thousand discarded lovers in her wake. Male. Female. It appeared the trolls thought she was nondiscriminatory in that department. Which was the only truth to any of this. But that wasn't the point, was it? No. The point was the movie studio was having a conniption because *Willow Path* was supposed to be their *Titanic*. It was supposed to blow the competition out of the water and set the studio up for an awards season sweep next year. They'd agreed to have this meeting at Emerson's rental property to keep it as private as possible. The last thing anyone wanted was some studio intern or onstage extra seeing them all getting together—looking serious—and calling *TMZ*. The plan was to act as if nothing Rachel said had any merit. They couldn't well do that if it looked like they were circling the wagons. Which they were.

"Let's go before I lose my nerve." Emerson left the remainder of her drink at the side of the sink and walked toward the sun porch to join the meeting. As she passed the grand picture window in the kitchen overlooking the backyard, she cast one last glimpse at the quiet and peaceful outdoor patio with the mountain view. Oh, what she would give to be able to take back every moment she'd ever shared with Rachel Blanche.

CHAPTER EIGHT

Hayley went for a run after the driver took her home. She grabbed her phone and took off along a hiking trail near her house. As she keyed into her apartment building and stopped by the mailboxes, she ran into Greta, her elderly neighbor next door.

"Hi, Hayley." Greta smiled and gave her a kiss on the cheek. "How's the entertainment biz?"

Hayley took the grocery bags Greta had been struggling with and followed her up the three flights to the floor their apartments were on. "Oh, you know, thrilling."

"I bet." Greta missed her sarcasm. "You're so young and beautiful. Did you find a girlfriend yet?"

"No, Greta." Hayley helped her get the key in the lock, her gnarled and arthritic hands too clumsy to get the job done quickly. "I'm not dating anyone."

"You'll find someone, dear. No worries." Greta patted her cheek and forced her to take a piece of coconut pie with her as she retreated to her own apartment next door. She liked Greta. She reminded her of her grandmother.

By the time she got home from her run, she had three missed calls from Alison, one from the office, and an email from Tremont. She was mighty popular these days, it seemed.

She slumped into the kitchen chair and powered up her laptop as she let the events of this morning run through her mind. She'd been surprised by the passion she had seen in Emerson's eyes when she challenged her. The fire had been intense and commanding. Emerson was easily the most attractive woman Hayley had ever seen, in person or in media. The magazines and photo spreads did no justice to the radiance she had in natural light. Her dark hair and light eyes were so unique, it was captivating. Hayley could see the appeal—Emerson was physical perfection.

Hayley stared off into the distance for a moment before refocusing on the screen in front of her. She had a big job ahead. The *Sun* and Emerson's camp had decided to promote the project with a series of teaser pieces over the next few months to ensure that the release of the complete article would match up with the release of *Willow Path* at the start of summer. In that time, Hayley had to uncover Emerson's secrets and make sure that the story she told was a fair representation of the woman, her journey, and the *Hollywood Sun*. Oh, and somewhere in there she also had to prove she was a good enough writer to deserve the opportunity that had basically fallen in her lap. No pressure.

She loaded her email and opened the file Tremont sent her. It was packed. Red flags and highlighted segments blurred the screen as she tried to see where she fit into Emerson's schedule. She sighed as she attempted to decipher the abbreviations. After fifteen minutes of trying to decode this mess, she gave up and emailed him back asking for clarification. She listened to her voicemail and smiled as Alison's enthusiastic and well-intentioned prodding came through the speaker of her cell. And Jonathan was calling for an update—that could wait.

Hayley stretched in her chair and walked over to the fridge to pull out some water. When she settled back into her seat she noticed a file saved to the desktop that wasn't there before. Her curiosity piqued, she opened the file and sipped her water as she scrolled down the text. It was from earlier, it was Emerson's work. Hayley had forgotten Emerson was typing during her interrogation. She'd been too distracted by the panic and feelings of being attacked.

Hayley tilted her head and rested it on the back of the chair as she slid down, bringing one knee up to her chest. She relished the soft ache in her leg from the stretch. She ignored the phone that buzzed beside her on the table, focusing instead on the words in front of her.

The document started with Emerson's questions and Hayley's responses. After the first few questions, Hayley noticed new information tacked on.

What's your favorite color? Purple. ES: blue
How old are you? 28. ES: 27
What's your sign? Libra. ES: Cancer
Did you play softball in high school? No. ES: you're lying,
　　first base

Hayley chuckled at Emerson's note. That was true. She did sort of play softball in high school, but only for half a season, and she never played during a live game. She was never good enough to be anything more than a member of the practice squad. She wondered how Emerson knew that, but her thoughts halted when she noticed the next bit.

The deepest pools are not found in the ground. They are not in a hollow, they are not man-made, they are man-born. The deepest pools are found in the soul. They hide secrets in shadows and keep mysteries from being discovered. Those pools protect the fragileness of its owner's mortality, the weaknesses, the passions, the deepest, darkest parts of oneself. The soul of it. The heart of it. And when something breaks through the surface of those pools—when it is breached, and its security put into question—ripples spread throughout. Those ripples go on and on until they contact the walls encasing that pool. One small stone, one pebble, one tiny moment can disrupt the calm and the quiet and it can damage the safety of the environment. Because souls may be deep, but they are delicate. And once someone invades their boundaries, the damage done is irreversible. Every ripple causes a change.

You won't find the answers to your questions here. Everyone has something worth protecting. It's why most people don't make direct eye contact when they speak—they're fearful someone will see something they want to hide. But when you talk to me, you do. Almost unafraid. Maybe you should be. But as I said before, I am not your opponent. I am merely someone who wants to be heard and seen for my authentic truth. I want to be seen as a human being with a beating heart and a living soul who is more than a headline on a page. I didn't mean to offend you with my questions today. I just wanted you to see some of what it's like to be me these days. All the days. I'm sorry if I hurt your feelings. And I didn't mean what I said about your outfit. I think you look nice.

Hayley smiled at the last bit. Emerson had a way of continually surprising her. She wondered how she had managed to type that during all the accusing and intimidating. She closed the file and renamed it *ES Musings*, leaving it on the desktop to go back to later. Hayley reached into her messenger bag and pulled out the stack of her writings. This was a nifty collection—she had it all saved electronically but hadn't reread the old stuff in years. It would be fun—and probably super embarrassing—to revisit some of this. She sipped her water and laughed at the amusing notations Emerson sprinkled throughout. She liked that woman more and more every moment.

❖

A week had passed before Hayley had the chance to meet up with Emerson again. They shared what one might call a lunch, but it was really a thirty-minute car ride to the movie studio with Tremont hovering over them both in the back of a limo. Emerson had to do automatic dialogue recording voice-over work for some of the scenes reshot with Piper, and she seemed uncomfortable about it.

Emerson ate fruit and sipped water; Hayley skipped a meal in favor of taking notes instead. They talked a little about Emerson's life growing up, but she was mostly vague.

"You have a unique first name. Is there any significance to it?" Hayley started with the easy questions to warm Emerson up to the harder ones she had planned.

"My mother went through a transcendentalist phase where she exclusively read Ralph Waldo Emerson works for the last few months of pregnancy. I guess she didn't think Waldo was an appropriate name for a little girl." Emerson shrugged. Hayley much preferred Emerson to Waldo. Hayley much preferred Emerson, in general, to *most* things, but she was trying to avoid falling into that rabbit hole and to focus on the task at hand. The task of getting to know Emerson. Which, she was finding, was making her prefer Emerson more and more, over and over again. This was a vicious cycle.

"What did you want to be when you grew up?" Hayley watched Emerson as she quietly chewed her grapes and gazed out the window.

"This," Emerson replied simply, her attention directed to Hayley.

"An actress?"

"Of sorts, yes." She paused. "What about you?"

"Um, I've always wanted to write, I guess." Hayley chewed

her bottom lip and tried to decide whether she should be annoyed by Emerson's deflection or surprised by the way the redirected question felt heavy to her.

"That sounds confident"—Emerson had the ghost of a smile on her lips as she leaned back and crossed her legs—"so let's try that again. What did you want to be when you grew up, Hayley?"

"A writer," Hayley said with more conviction. She furrowed her brow. "You didn't really answer my question, Emerson."

Emerson smiled at this response. "Yes, I did. I had dreams of being in a life much like the one I am in now. You, on the other hand, seem unconvinced that you've accomplished your childhood dreams."

When Hayley didn't reply, Emerson leaned forward and pushed the remainder of her fruit into Hayley's hand. "You need to eat something, Hayley. It's lunch."

Hayley accepted the fruit and Emerson started again. "What kind of writer did you want to be?"

"I guess I always wanted to be a screenwriter," she replied, feeling a little shy at her admission. Emerson had a way of making her feel... things. Shy was one of them apparently.

"Oh?" Emerson's expression was genuine. Hayley knew she had her full attention now. That made her feel things as well.

Hayley picked out the honeydew melon and chewed it slowly. "Yes. But I don't think I knew what that was at the time. I wanted to make stories for people to see in real life. Not just on a page. Not just in a fantasy world of written text."

Emerson nodded. "To bring a story to life, make it real—I understand that."

"Is that what you wanted? Is that the life you envisioned for yourself?" Hayley tried again.

Emerson looked at her with that intense stare she'd seen before. After a beat, she replied, "I suppose, yes. I can remember wanting to be a princess in a tower, with loyal subjects and love and the safety of the guards in a castle. I remember wanting to ride horses in open fields and play with puppies on hot summer nights by a lake. I remember wanting to sing songs that people knew the words to and dance with strangers, laughing along with me. So I guess I always dreamed of something like this—a life of making a living by pretending to be something I'm not.

An actress is the perfect career for a dreamer who refuses to be tied to one dream. Don't you think?"

Hayley nodded and thought back to the *ES Musings* file on her desktop. Emerson had a way with words, just one more sign of perfection to add to the list. "Maybe you should write, Emerson. That was beautiful."

A soft laugh from Emerson's plump lips had Hayley swooning. Focus, Hayley, focus. "Thank you, but I think I'll leave that up to you."

Hayley felt like Emerson was loosening up a bit, so she decided to leap into the more important details she was searching for. "Tell me about *The Willow Path Convergence*. Why did you take that role?"

Emerson paused, seeming to collect her thoughts. "I think, in a lot of ways, this role picked me."

Hayley waited for her to elaborate.

Emerson shifted and straightened up a bit. "Willow Path is everyone and no one, right? I mean, you've read the synopsis by now, I'd assume."

Hayley nodded. She'd seen the trailers about a thousand times in preparation for working with Emerson. The movie was based on the record-setting *New York Times* best seller, and with its author, Kate Stanton, involved in the script development and lauded female director Paige Montgomery at the helm, it was promising to be a groundbreaking film for the women's empowerment movement.

"Yes. Rhea and her boyfriend Kevin are falling out of love. Rhea proposes a cross-country road trip to help reignite their relationship, and along the way they meet a drifter named Willow Path. She's a catalyst for all kinds of self-discovery and change." Hayley would have seen it regardless of her current situation. As a wannabe screenwriter, the dimly lit single-shot cinematography of it alone was appealing to her. It added to the rawness alluded to in all the press about the movie. And a storyline with a love triangle featuring two women, that had major studio backing? Consider her interest off the charts. "It sounds fascinating."

Emerson's smile was genuine. "Wait until you see how they modified the ending."

"I'd be lying if I didn't tell you I'm beyond excited. But enough fangirling—back to the question. Why did you audition for the role of

Willow and not Rhea? Especially when most people are assuming Rhea is the main character."

Emerson sighed. "I've been acting for almost my entire life. And I've seen the same scripts—year after year—arrive at my doorstep. The stories are the same. Hero needs busty brunette love interest to rescue to justify his violent problem-solving tactics. Or art heist with ensuing car chase necessary to redeem wronged con artist on quest for redemption. The one I see most, though—the one that makes my skin crawl—is the story about the college frat boy with the endless privilege who learns about life the hard way by having to get back the girl of his dreams after he inadvertently cheats on her, forgets an important event, is a thoughtless asshole, whatever. That's the character arc that crosses my table: beautiful girl needed to fulfill male sidekick or damsel role to make money for the movie studios. That's the gist of it. Look pretty, don't make too many waves. Get paid. It's as easy as that."

Hayley felt like deep down she knew that, but hearing it confirmed so matter-of-factly made her feel sick. And selfishly, a little hopeless in the screenwriting department. "Jesus. That's depressing."

Emerson nodded. "So depressing. But I can see the tide changing. I can see things shifting in a new direction. Little by little, projects with heart are making their way to the table. And the writers behind them are finally reflecting the greater populace. Women are writing women and the results are incredible."

She leaned forward, her passion palpable. "This movie is a gritty, three-actor led film where two-thirds of the leads are female. The female characters are strong and well developed and they have such complexity and depth that even hearing about something like this is thrilling. But having the chance to be in it? Having the chance to land a possibly life changing role like Willow? I'd never miss that chance. I could never forgive myself for not trying."

She took a breath. "So to answer your question, Hayley—Willow Path represents the fork in the road in all our lives. She's the person, place, or instance that turns everything we thought we knew on its head. I've played Rhea a thousand times before, but never once have I had the chance to bring Willow to life. And I'd do it again in a heartbeat."

"Wow." Hayley didn't know what to say. But she felt charged. Something Emerson said resonated with her. "You said the role of Willow was possibly life changing—do you mean for you?"

Emerson gave her a small smile. "I suppose I did. She was. Or she is. Maybe she will be. I don't know. But when I said it just then, I meant it more for the audience. Willow lives by her own rules. She's untethered and free with her love and her life. She doesn't beg forgiveness or ask permission. What an incredible representation for a young woman to see on the big screen: a fearless image of themselves faced with impossible challenges and conditions, not only surviving but thriving in the process." Her expression turned playful. "Plus, I love to see a woman embrace her sexuality and own it. Good on you, Willow."

That was the crack in the armor she'd been hoping for—Emerson was finally letting her in a little. Of course, now all she could think about was Emerson portraying the brooding bisexual drifter and the likely inevitable sex scene featuring Emerson making out with another woman that was sure to be in the film—which would probably be even more explicit than the book's version. Was it hot in here? It was definitely hot in here.

Before she had a chance to ask a follow-up question, the car pulled up to the curb, effectively ending their time together. As Emerson exited the car, she paused and caught Hayley's eye. "To be continued, I suppose."

Hayley sat in the car, unsure of what to do. Or feel. She didn't have long to consider either before Tremont poked his head back into the car.

Tremont said, "It's a mostly closed studio today. If you wanted to observe some of the goings-on, I think I could convince Emerson to agree to it."

This was unexpected. Hayley was usually given a lot of notice to things she would be included or excluded from. "I'd like that."

Tremont held the door open for her and walked slowly next to her. "She talks to you, like, really talks to you. I think it's good for her"—he paused—"and to be honest, she's not looking forward to this voice-over scene. We've pushed it back three times already. I think if you're there she'll soldier through it."

"Okay." Hayley frowned at this information. She'd not seen Emerson uncomfortable often, and Tremont never let on to it if she ever was. "What about this scene is so stressful for her?"

Tremont stopped dead in his tracks and turned to her. "It's the pinnacle sex scene between the female leads in the movie. The entire mood of the film changes with this exchange between the main characters—everything changes after this." He shrugged. "I can see why she's anxious about it."

Hayley swallowed. Now she was anxious about it, too. Anxious with a mix of something else. Excitement? Maybe. The writer in her was excited to see Emerson's process behind the scenes. But she had a feeling it was more than that. Her feelings regarding Emerson were complicated as of late. This would surely only complicate things more.

"Are you coming, Hayley?" Tremont asked impatiently as he held that back door open to the ADR studio.

Hayley thought his word choice was questionable, but she kept that to herself. The thought of watching Emerson climax or bring another woman to climax on screen in front of her made a pressure form between her hips. So the answer to his question was *not yet*, but she settled on, "Uh, yeah."

CHAPTER NINE

"One more time, Ms. Sterling." The disembodied voice of a recording engineer spoke into her headset encouraging her to repeat the last line.

She nodded and complied. This was probably her least favorite part of acting. She found it difficult to summon the correct emotions without the scene playing in front of her, but she hated seeing herself act, so she found this more frustrating than most.

"Great work. Let's take a quick break before we do the last three scenes," the voice in her headset replied.

Emerson pulled off the headset and placed it to the side. She could see Tremont on the phone on the other side of the glass. He'd asked if she minded Hayley observing. She did, and she didn't. She didn't mind because spending time with Hayley was easy. But she did mind because today's scenes were promising to be emotionally draining, and she didn't want to fail in front of her. That was a new thing, the fear of failure...in front of Hayley specifically. She was aware that Hayley had gotten under her skin a bit. She wasn't sure how she felt about that.

At the moment, Hayley was focused on what she was typing, and her eyes were directed downward. Emerson took the time to appreciate how attractive Hayley was. She was effortlessly beautiful. She furrowed her brow when she focused and chewed the end of her glasses as she worked on the content in front of her. Emerson found the glasses thing particularly adorable. She swept her hair behind her ear inefficiently, more as if a nervous habit than with any real purpose. Emerson had grown to love watching her work. She wondered what Hayley was writing, what she was thinking…she wondered that more than she'd like to admit.

One of the techs came into the booth after a brisk knock. He handed her a bottle of water and gave her the next scene to review. Emerson swallowed hard as she scanned the text. This was the sex scene she'd been dreading. It had fast become her least favorite scene to shoot. Once Rachel was fired, she had needed to reshoot it with Piper. It was sort of a pinnacle scene in the movie: Rhea and Willow engage in a brief tryst before being discovered by Kevin. This was one of the scenes that had drawn Emerson to the role initially. It was raw and unadulterated. The depiction was carnal and explicit, full of passion and heat. It was Rhea's first time with a woman—an eye-opening experience under the careful guidance of the much more experienced Willow. The chemistry in this scene was vital to the remainder of the movie. And she'd managed to ace the physical portrayal, but some of the audio was obscured. With all the movement and choreographed position changes that were necessary, it wasn't unusual to have to rerecord audio for sex scenes. But she wasn't sure she had this in her today. There was so much happening outside of her control these days, she felt a little lost.

"We're ready when you are," the engineer said over the loudspeaker in the room, and she reached for her headset.

The scene began in front of her as she adjusted the headset and followed the script markers. She started the voice-over narration but stopped abruptly midsentence.

"Everything okay?" the engineer asked.

"Change the film." Her tone was flat. She did her best to make sure her expression remained vacant as she stared at the screen.

"I'm sorry?" the voice crackled in her ear.

"You cued the wrong scene. Change the film." Rachel's face, not Piper's, was frozen on the screen in front of her, her mouth in a tight O as the audience saw the back of Emerson's head at Rachel's chest and Rachel's hands threaded into Emerson's hair.

"Oh, dear. I'm sorry. We'll fix it right away." The screen went black. Emerson closed her eyes to try to purge the image. That only made it worse.

"I'm taking a break. Find me when you fix the problem." Emerson was careful to keep the rage out of her voice. But she had rage. Definite rage.

Emerson pulled off the headset and used every ounce of her anger management training to keep from launching it at the glass separating her from the engineers and the sound editors. She turned and intentionally exited the booth through the door opposite Tremont and Hayley to avoid them. She needed a moment to herself, to collect herself. She hated how much Rachel's image affected her.

Emerson pushed through the exit door into the semiprivate back lot of the ADR studio. She sat heavily on the concrete stairs, her eyes scanning the lot for any possible unwanted spectators. It was unusually quiet back here and she was grateful.

She let her head drop and her shoulders sag. The weight of the last few weeks settled squarely across her upper back, a headache threatening to bloom over her left temple. Even though it had been years since she'd smoked, old habits stirred, and she found herself reaching for a cigarette to soothe her nerves. A bitter chuckle spilled from her lips as she slid her hands along the faux pockets of her pants. Tremont always told her to avoid unnecessary lines in her clothing. Pockets were unnecessary when you had someone around you to carry your belongings. If you even needed belongings. It wasn't like she needed to have her ID on her these days. She didn't drive because the paparazzi were relentless, and it was dangerous. She didn't purchase anything with her own card because there was always the risk of a fan or stalker getting her information. She had two locks on her cell phone and had her email encrypted automatically. She hadn't manned her own social media pages in over a year. Every *t* was crossed and every *i* was dotted by someone other than herself.

"What I would give for a stiff drink and a long, slow drag," she muttered to no one in particular.

"How long has it been since you smoked?" Hayley's voice over her shoulder startled her.

Emerson dropped her head and gently rolled her neck. "According to the tabloids or real life?"

Hayley sat next to her, leaving a little space between them. She leaned against the metal railing to her left. "Someone once told me that the information in the tabloids isn't correct and should not be trusted. So real life, I suppose."

"I used to smoke when I was younger, in my late teens and early twenties. But I did it for all the wrong reasons, not that there is ever a good reason to smoke." Emerson leaned back and rested her elbows on the step above her. She kept her eyes on the small delivery parking lot in front of them.

"And a drink?" Hayley asked.

"Champagne is the only thing I dabble in these days. At award ceremonies or events. But even that's rare"—Emerson turned and looked at Hayley—"because I don't like to be numb if I don't have to. You find a reason to numb a lot of things in this business. It's addicting, it's so commonplace. I prefer to stay off Page Six, if possible."

"You are more cautious than I expect most people realize," Hayley replied.

"I think to retain any sort of sanity in this fishbowl, you have to be," Emerson added wistfully.

Hayley nodded but didn't say anything in response. She held Emerson's gaze, something that Emerson noticed Hayley had always done. Not many people made direct eye contact with her for very long. She'd assumed it was because of her celebrity or their own insecurities. Eye contact was important to Emerson—it always had been. She looked for people's truths, their true intentions, in their eyes. Hayley never turned from her gaze. She didn't seem to hide anything. Ever. That was one of the things Emerson liked most about her—she felt like what you saw was what you got with Hayley. The reliability of it made her feel safe.

"You have beautiful eyes." Hayley's gaze remained unwavering when she spoke, and Emerson felt like she could bask in that feeling forever.

Emerson could tell by Hayley's expression that she was being genuine. She felt her heart flutter in her chest at Hayley's honesty. "You are very sweet."

Emerson closed her eyes and leaned her head back. She let the late-day sun wash over her skin. "Besides this piece we're doing together, what else have you been up to?"

"You mean for the *Sun*?" Hayley replied.

"No." Emerson shook her head but kept her eyes closed as she lounged onto her elbows. "I mean for you. What are you doing for you?"

"Ah. Actually, I've been doing a little work on a screenplay I started a while ago."

Emerson picked up her head and looked at her. "Why did you stop?"

Hayley looked shy again. She'd shown that shyness in the car earlier. That conversation felt like an eternity ago. It was funny how a mere flash of Rachel's face could ruin everything. Always.

"Um, life gets in the way of the creative process, I guess. That's what I tell myself anyway." Hayley reached out and absentmindedly ran her fingers along the tips of Emerson's hair. "I've been inspired a lot though, lately. The Muse has visited me."

Emerson watched Hayley distractedly play with her hair. She smiled at the innocence of the action and spoke softly so as to not disturb her. "What are you writing about?"

Hayley twirled the ends around her finger as she chewed her bottom lip. "It's fiction, sort of headed in the direction of a romance piece. But that wasn't my intention."

That was awfully vague. Emerson watched Hayley worry her bottom lip with her teeth for a moment. The desire to find out if Hayley's lips were as soft as they looked was suddenly all she could think about. Emerson tried to remember what they were talking about before she got lost in her lusty haze…shyness. Hayley seemed shy. Right. That. "Does it make you uncomfortable to talk about your writing?"

Hayley shook her head, pausing midshake when she seemed to realize what she was doing with her fingers. "Oh, sorry, nervous habit." She released Emerson's hair and looked up as she answered. "Not usually."

"But it does now?" she asked. There was that look again, that intense focus. They were sitting awfully close, weren't they?

Hayley blinked. "Evidently."

"Do I make you nervous?" Emerson found this information amusing. She liked the idea that she might make Hayley nervous. It made her feel like she wasn't the only one with some baggage involved.

"Today you do," Hayley said, looking unsure of herself.

Emerson raised her eyebrows. "Why today in particular?"

A few people walked through the parking lot and Hayley shifted, positioning herself closer. Her eyes traced the outline of Emerson's face, momentarily pausing at Emerson's lips before returning to Emerson's eyes. Emerson didn't miss that.

"You seemed tense and unsettled in there." Her voice was softer, almost as if she was trying to keep their discussion private. She hesitated before adding, "And I think I missed being around you. So I don't want to upset you during the short time I get to spend with you."

Emerson considered this, the admission warming her a little. The scene snafu back there did little to ease her discomfort, but the truth was she was more worried about her impending visit to Colorado. They'd pushed it off so Rory wouldn't have to miss spring break plans with her friends, but things were so unpredictable around here, she didn't trust that they had time on their side before the news hit the press. She was simultaneously eager and dreading the conversation. She wanted to tell Rory about being her biological mother herself before she read it on the internet. She decided to omit that bit in her response. "I've had a longish few weeks. The movie release is fast approaching, and I think I'm a little stressed."

Hayley nodded, staying close.

Emerson thought about what Hayley had said. There was something about Hayley that drew her in. She found a strength in her presence. And an attraction, too. She'd be a fool to deny that she found herself more and more attracted to Hayley each day. "I think I missed being around you, too." She wanted to clarify something. "You don't upset me when you're around, even though you're the media. You make me feel very relaxed, actually. Like I can be myself with you. And it—"

"Frightens you a little?" Hayley asked. Yes. Yes, it did.

"Maybe." Emerson regarded Hayley. She was close enough to touch. She remembered the way Hayley's eyes flicked down to her lips before, and she had a feeling that if she kissed Hayley, Hayley would kiss her back. The desire to test that theory was very strong. This was dangerous.

"A good frightened or a bad frightened?" Hayley seemed to read her mind and spoke directly to Emerson's lips, desire written across her face. This felt like too much. Too much to ignore. Too much work to pretend like she didn't feel the same way.

Emerson caved and reached out to caress her cheek. She grazed her thumb along the edge of Hayley's jaw and marveled at the softness of her skin. She teased the skin below Hayley's lip, causing her bottom lip to protrude a bit before she leaned back and put a little distance between them. "Good frightened."

Hayley looked like she was going to say something when the

sound of approaching footsteps on the other side of the heavy door behind them drew their attention.

A tech poked his head out the door. "Ms. Sterling? Are you ready to continue?"

She nodded, her mood markedly improved. "I'll be right in."

He gave her a hesitant look before he ducked back inside.

"He's afraid of you," Hayley observed.

Emerson stood and reached out her hand to pull Hayley up with her. "Are you?"

"No. Not in the least bit." Hayley took her hand and smiled as Emerson entwined their fingers before she tugged her up the stairs and toward the door.

"Maybe you should be." Emerson was surprised when the words left her lips, but Hayley didn't bat an eye. She had a feeling that maybe she was projecting. Maybe it was she who was afraid of Hayley.

"I doubt that." Hayley pulled back and held Emerson on the landing for a moment. "You're going to be great in there. I can feel it."

Emerson could feel it, too. Whatever *it* was, was powerful. There was something brewing between them, and she could feel the heat of it from across a room. She just wasn't sure what to do about it, but she had a few ideas. Standing this close to Hayley now made the feeling that much more blindingly hot. She couldn't ignore it if she tried, so she decided she wouldn't.

She leaned close, basking in the warmth radiating off Hayley's body as she brought her lips to Hayley's ear. "Time for me to make that sex scene sound believable."

Emerson stretched out on the bed and groaned as her muscles protested yesterday's very long day. Her internal clock willed her to wake up, but she resisted. Some days she had no idea what time zone she was even in, but she knew this time that she was in her bed, in her rented house. Safe. She looked over at the clock on her bedside table and smiled. She had time to enjoy the warmth of her bed and the quiet for a little bit longer.

She closed her eyes and exhaled slowly. This was her favorite time of day—the calm before the storm, the peace before the war—her favorite time because it was the only time she had entirely to herself. No schedule, no appointments, no questions to answer, nothing. She paused and thought of Hayley. Answering Hayley's questions never felt like work, though. Her questions never felt like an invasion of her privacy. If anything, she found herself feeling like she was learning things about herself that she had suppressed. Answering Hayley's questions felt a lot like rediscovering herself, like finding her way after being lost. Like a beacon on a dark path, Hayley felt like a light, like a way out. And she could use some guidance right now.

She sighed out loud and looked up at the ceiling before she checked her phone again—she was waiting for Tremont's message telling her that Hayley's most recent teaser installment had hit the web. They had been doing a little hype work and had generated quite the buzz. People were talking more about Emerson and *Willow Path* than about Rachel and the mud she was slinging. Still, she knew the public was fickle and that there was still a possibility this could all blow up in her face. But she trusted Hayley to portray the narrative in a fair way. And so far, she had done just that. Emerson had been more than pleased she'd taken the chance on Hayley.

When she didn't find any update from Tremont, she tossed the phone aside and sat up. The sheets and blankets fell to her waist and exposed her naked skin to the room air. She shivered and stood before walking into her bathroom and starting the hot water in the shower. Once the steam clouded the glass, she stepped in. She took a deep breath and reached for the soap to lather her body under the continuous stream running over her shoulders and down her back. She moved her hands over her hip bones, across her abdomen, and under her breasts as she collected suds under her fingertips and massaged them into her skin. Her head fell back into the hot stream as she glided lower. She slipped her hand between her thighs and stroked the sensitive skin with care.

Her mind wandered back to yesterday's voice-over break. Someone had snapped a picture of her and Hayley sitting closely on the back step. She had scanned the lot before sitting but hadn't seen anyone, so she'd been surprised when Tremont had texted her the screenshot from *TMZ*'s nightly show. She'd been angry that someone had invaded a private moment, but more upset that Hayley was possibly drawn into this circus. Her face had been hidden by her hair, but it was just a matter of time before another photo emerged with the two of them together. That would surely fuel whatever speculation might run amok. She felt protective of Hayley in that moment, but also grateful that she hadn't given in to her urge to kiss her. Not because she didn't want to kiss her—she did—but because she didn't want to jeopardize her trip to Colorado this weekend.

The last thing she needed was to give Rachel more fuel and push her over the edge. Up to now Rachel was just trying to fuck with her career. She hadn't released anything personal—yet. But she knew it was only a matter of time before Rachel broke out the big guns. She didn't want to think about that right now. She wanted to think about Hayley and the way she'd looked at her yesterday. There was an affection there and lust. Emerson had felt the same.

She exhaled through her mouth as the shampoo rinsed from her hair. Her fingers playfully scratched up and down her thighs and stirred all sorts of wonderful feelings between her hips. She loved the slippery warmth the shower granted her—it had been a while since she'd had sex. She was horny.

She turned under the rain showerhead and let her front rinse clean of the suds. She spread her legs and soothed the skin on her thighs. She teased a little as she closed her eyes again and let herself enjoy the moment. The look on Hayley's face while she did the voice-over yesterday was fresh in her mind as she gently rubbed her clit. Emerson had used that look to help her get into the frame of mind for that sex scene. The memory fueled the heat spreading in her lower abdomen as her hand worked between her legs. She whimpered as her insides began to contract from the stimulation of her fingers. This felt good. She needed this.

Her mind returned to Hayley's eyes on her lips as they spoke quietly just inches apart on the step and the darkness in those same eyes when Emerson gave the voice-over performance of her lifetime—partly for Hayley's benefit, partly for herself. Emerson had watched Hayley closely. She had this look of…hunger. It was more than lust. She'd seen lust in Hayley's eyes briefly at the dress fitting during their first meeting together. This look, the one from the voice-over, was different. It was affectionate and adoring, but also piercing and protective. And wanting. She had seen a glimpse of it when Hayley complimented her eyes. That had been what spurred her to nearly kiss Hayley and to caress her cheek. Oh, how she'd wanted to suck on her bottom lip and feel the flesh between her teeth.

That look in Hayley's eyes was what she thought of now as she brought herself to climax in the privacy of her shower while hidden in clouds of steam. Her quiet moans of pleasure were shushed by the sounds of rushing water and her mind flirted with the easy smile of Hayley sitting in the sun on that step behind the studio. She thought of how that look of affection turned to something more when Emerson had almost kissed her. She thought of the slight blush on Hayley's cheeks when she had intentionally teased her about recording sex noises and of the turned-on, flushed look on her face when Emerson's voice performance was complete. That was the thought Emerson let flutter behind her eyelids as she felt each diminishing tremor roll through her.

She let out a contented sigh as she finished her shower and turned off the water. She wondered if that solo performance was the best idea, considering she was supposed to see Hayley again in the near future.

"Probably not," Emerson said to no one in particular as she reached for the towel on the heated rack to her left. But she regretted nothing. If anything, she wanted to do that all again, this time with Hayley here in person.

Chapter Ten

It had been five days since Hayley had seen Emerson or been in her whirlwind. Something—Tremont didn't elaborate—took Emerson out of town and their plans to get together had fallen by the wayside. She'd been actively writing in the time off and had a good chunk of the final piece completed. There was only one problem, though—she had no answer to the Rachel thing, and she felt like she'd hit a wall.

Sharon walked past her cubicle and gave her a look. It was safe to say things around the office hadn't improved much since her work with Emerson was getting more and more attention. Sharon had decided to stop acknowledging her existence entirely—except to glare at her occasionally—which would have been fine all by itself if not for the continued character assault she was under by Drake. With every teaser piece released about Emerson by the *Sun*, he countered with something from Rachel's camp. It would appear Rachel had aligned herself with Drake. Just one more heaping complication to add to Hayley's already full plate.

C'mon, Hayley. You can do this. The devil is in the details. Think.

As she stared at the blinking cursor on the screen in front of her and she reminisced about their last meeting. It had been *a lot*. She and Emerson had discussed Emerson's dreams and her acting and the *Willow Path* project, but it'd also been intense. Intense in that Hayley was finding herself more and more attracted to Emerson and something told her Emerson knew it. Whether she felt the same way or not, Hayley wasn't sure. But the one thing she was sure of? She'd been having fitful dreams night after night of Emerson's voice-over performance. And it was incredibly distracting. And arousing. Which was distracting in and of itself.

Never in her life had she been so turned on by something. Emerson's timing was incredible—she didn't miss a single cue or struggle when a scene had to be reshot. Hayley saw one of the sound engineers fanning himself during the final scene, and she wanted more than anything to do the same. But she'd caught Tremont watching her reactions a few minutes before and she was trying—and probably failing—to seem unaffected. As if that was possible.

The zoomed-in, single-camera footage did nothing but enhance Emerson's moans and breathy additions. The scene was so real, Hayley had to remind herself that these were two highly paid and very talented actresses. And that the process of the filming was undoubtedly unsexy, with lots of pauses and reapplications of makeup, and people standing around with sound and video equipment…but still, movie magic was a damn thing and she had witnessed it happen firsthand. And then again in her dreams every night since.

The phone rang on her desk and Hayley was jarred from her reverie.

"Hayley Carpenter."

"Hayley." Jonathan's gruff voice filled the line. "I expect the final draft of your piece on my desk by the end of next week."

"Good afternoon, Jonathan. Why yes, I am having a lovely day. Thanks for asking."

Jonathan exhaled with a sigh. "Sorry. How's everything going?"

Hayley smiled at her small win. "Good. It's coming along nicely, thanks."

"Excellent. So, the deadline?" He was back to all business.

"You really don't mess around do you, Jonathan?" She couldn't help but tease a little.

"Not when it's the biggest story of the season, no," he replied, devoid of any sense of humor. Still.

"Way to set me up for failure…" His comment hit her like a punch to the gut. She didn't need any more pressure, thankyouverymuch.

Jonathan cleared his throat. "This is far from funny, Hayley. If it was up to me, a more seasoned writer would be on this project. But those little teasers you've been submitting are pretty decent."

Hayley frowned at the empty threat. She knew at this point that

Emerson wouldn't work with anyone else but her. They had been getting along well, and she felt like Emerson finally trusted her enough to start opening up. "Gee, thanks. I'll have it to you by deadline."

"Good." He disconnected before she could reply.

Hayley leaned back in her chair and examined the document on the screen in front of her. This felt hopeless.

Her phone rang, and she cursed under her breath. What more could Jonathan want?

"Yes?"

"Hayley?" The voice on the line was slightly distorted.

Hayley grimaced, realizing her phone etiquette was lacking. She'd been screening her calls of late since every single wannabe journalist and their mother had been calling to try to get the inside scoop. Drake's most recent article featured Hayley's direct line next to the label *Secret Sterling Source*. She really hated that guy. "Er, sorry, this is Hayley Carpenter. I'm not at liberty to discuss anything at this time. Please forward your comments, questions, and concerns to—"

"Hayley, it's Tremont." His connection must not be great. He sounded far away.

Well that was unexpected. "Oh, hey. What's up?"

"Something's come up. Are you available to meet with Emerson...?" A crackle on the line caused her to miss the last part.

"Meet Emerson when?"

"Tonight." He sounded impatient.

Hayley reached for her tablet and pulled up her schedule. She wasn't slated to see Emerson again until two days from now. She'd been counting on the off time to write. "Uh, sure. What time?"

"Well, now, actually. Can you leave work? I have a car waiting outside," he said, the line quality improving.

Hayley glanced around the mess of files and papers on her desk and nodded to no one in particular.

"Hayley? Time is of the essence." Tremont sounded annoyed and a little congested.

"Yes. Sorry. I just need like five minutes to pack up and I can be outside," she replied as she speed packed her belongings.

"Good. See you soon." She heard relief in his voice and wondered what all this was about.

As she hurriedly moved her tablet and notes into her messenger bag, Alison's voice sounded over her shoulder, "So, was that the famous movie star?"

Hayley nodded and looked up at Alison with a smile. "Mm-hmm. Well, the famous movie star's cranky assistant."

"I figured as much since I've only ever seen you move that fast to beat the line for half-price wings at Lilly's." Alison leaned against the edge of her cubicle. "Which happens to be tonight. Any interest on gossiping with me over wings and margaritas? You haven't told me anything interesting lately, and I need my Page Six fix."

Hayley felt oddly protective of the information Emerson gave her and hadn't shared much more than a few items that didn't make her weekly teaser. It wasn't that she didn't trust Alison, it was just that Emerson had shared so little with her—nothing of any seeming significance—that she wanted to ensure she wasn't cavalier with the information Emerson had shared. She had a feeling that the direction of their interviews together was about to change, and she was feeling a little superstitious. In fact, she had added some of her observations of Emerson and the things she felt were truly important to the *ES Musings* file on her desktop. Those things had yet to make it into her submissions to Jonathan. But all this hush-hush secretive shit was exhausting, and margs and wings with Alison sounded like heaven right about now. She frowned. "Seems like I'm needed on my night off. Let's hope it's for something good."

"Ooh, maybe it's the Rachel lead you've been hunting for all along." Alison rubbed her hands together with excitement. "Imagine if the unexpected and late-night beckoning of the complicated starlet was to tell you everything you wanted to know under the cover of darkness."

"You've been watching too many of those Lifetime mystery marathons," Hayley replied.

"Rob's been traveling. You're out fraternizing with the Hollywood elite. I've been bored." She shrugged.

Hayley felt awful. She'd been a shitty friend to Alison lately. It seemed like all her time was consumed with chasing Emerson to and from meetings or movie sets and trying to get a note in here or there. She'd had no life to begin with, but she had less of a life now.

"Let's have a movie weekend together. I'll come over on Friday and we can order Chinese food from that place with the awesome dumplings and I promise to watch all those horrible chick flicks you're obsessed with." Hayley gave Alison's shoulder a gentle squeeze. "Deal?"

Alison's eyes lit up. "Deal."

"Okay, there's supposedly a car waiting for me. I have to run," Hayley said and shook her head. "That sounds so ridiculous saying it out loud."

"I can't even handle how fancy you are these days," Alison teased, "but I meant what I said before, Hayley. This last-minute beckoning... feels like the start of something, doesn't it?"

"I won't hold my breath," she said. Even though she felt like she was making major ground with Emerson, she had a feeling that the Rachel bit would be as elusive as the white whale in this journey she was on. Every time she even got close to that line of questioning, Emerson shut it down. The reaction was almost like whiplash. One minute Emerson would be nodding and contributing little by little, and the next minute she would be stone silent and looking out at some far-off shape, closed off and lost. Hayley had struggled in the beginning when Emerson reacted that way. But over the last few weeks she had finally started to see the warning signs. Emerson had a few tells. Like, when she was uncomfortable with a line of questions, she would cross her left leg over her right and break eye contact. Or her smile would fade just a little and the light in her eyes would dim a bit. But perhaps the most significant change Hayley noticed was the way the usually confident and extroverted woman would shrink back into her seat—just a little—so infinitesimally that anyone who wasn't watching closely would miss it. But Hayley didn't miss it. She had learned to watch Emerson carefully, because she spoke more with her actions than with her words. And Emerson was practically a master at disguising her discomfort. Hayley supposed a life in the public eye hardened someone in that way. Discomfort was a sign of weakness. She understood that now more than ever.

She said her good-byes to Alison and exited the side of the building to find Tremont standing outside a black town car. He was rubbing his ear and opening and closing his jaw. His eyes were hidden behind large dark sunglasses, but Hayley could tell by his posture that something was wrong.

"Hey, Tremont."

"Hayley." He stepped back and opened the door. He motioned for her to climb in.

"Where are we headed to today? Makeup trailer? Back lot? Seedy hotel bar?" She started to unpack her tablet to take any necessary notes.

Tremont smiled as he sat next to her but grimaced immediately and held the side of his head again. "Not today, Hayley. Today we're headed to your place."

"My place?" Hayley panicked. She couldn't remember the last time she'd done laundry, or cleaned, or washed any of her dishes. The more she thought about it, the more she was positive her apartment looked as though it had been ransacked in a robbery and left untouched for crime scene investigation.

"Mm-hmm. Unless you plan on wearing that outfit for the next three days," he said as he pulled down his shades and surveyed her clothing with skeptical judgment.

Rude. "Wow, that was judgy. Three days? Where are we going that I need a change of clothes for three whole days?"

"Boston. Your flight leaves in three hours. That's just enough time for you to head home and pack a bag, get to the airport, and catch the next flight out. Oh, and grab a cell phone charger because your phone is dead. I called you like ten times before I had to look up your work number. Thank Gucci you were at your desk…" Tremont wiped his forehead dramatically.

"Oh, my bad." Hayley pulled her phone out of her bag to confirm it was indeed dead. Wait, did he say Boston? "Boston? Do I have any say in this?"

Tremont glanced over at her briefly before looking down at the phone in his hand and pulling up the airline's website. "Well, you have about two minutes to make up your mind—but, no, not really."

"Oh. Good to know," Hayley said as she leaned back into her seat and directed her attention to the window as the town car sped up on the expressway.

"It's warm in Boston, but not as warm as here," Tremont supplied from next to her. "You may want to pack some warmer clothes. And some more stylish shoes."

Hayley laughed and ignored his comment. This was another thing that had been happening lately, Tremont had been giving her unsolicited clothing and accessory advice. Emerson had assured her it was his way of opening up to her. She had mixed feelings about it. Even if he was always right.

❖

Hayley couldn't remember another time when she had packed so fast. She checked and double-checked her carry-on and small suitcase en route to the airport. She had the essentials: her ID, wallet, cell phone with charger, tablet, work stuff, clothes, toothbrush. Oh, and more stylish shoes. She knew this because Tremont gave her a brief nod of approval, so she figured they would do just fine. She supposed whatever she was missing she could pick up when she got there.

As they approached the airport, Tremont turned to her. "Okay, so let's debrief a bit."

Hayley nodded. That's what Tremont called her being updated on all things Emerson, *debriefing*.

He rubbed the area in front of his ear and opened and closed his jaw again before speaking. "I've recently taken up swimming and have developed a nasty ear infection." He held up his hand and shook his head. "Don't ask."

"I just assumed it was from the swim lessons Emerson told me you were taking on the side to impress Sebastian at your beach date this weekend," Hayley said. Emerson had been sharing more with her, just not a ton about herself.

"She told you that?" Tremont's expression was comical. Hayley tried not to laugh. "Ugh. Whatever. Anyway, I've been advised against flying, especially on a flight as long as the one from LA to Boston. So—until my symptoms resolve and these antibiotics kick in—I won't be able to accompany you and Emerson across the country. Her manager David had a death in the family and can't leave until tomorrow. And Emerson's schedule blew up and she has to be out there tonight for a photo shoot and interview and some location-specific scenes for the movie reshoots over the next couple days. None of the other people in her camp can swing the short notice—she has a lot of loose ends to tie up here that require their attention. So that leaves you."

"Glad to know I rank so highly on the list," Hayley added sarcastically as she shifted in her seat to face him more fully. She was pretending to be offended, when in fact, she was excited. There hadn't been many opportunities for her to be one-on-one with Emerson, let alone for any length of time. This was exactly what she'd been hoping for: a chance to have Emerson all to herself. That thought had her at the edge of her seat for a multitude of reasons. She'd had the sense that Emerson was flirting with her at the voice-over session, and the eye contact Emerson made with her during the sex scene had been on her mind constantly since that day. There had to be something behind those incredible eyes. Something she hoped existed for her and only her. But she wasn't foolish either. She knew that she could be completely in her own head about this, and her attraction to Emerson could be entirely one-sided...but *something* told her it wasn't. The same *something* that told her that Rachel and Emerson had a legitimate past when she first saw their backstage interaction so many weeks ago. So much had changed in that time, and yet she didn't know anything more than what her gut told her: there was something there. Of course, her gut told her something was there between her and Emerson as well, but she had little if any proof to support that theory. Only a hope and some really, really X-rated dreams.

"It was Emerson's idea, not mine," Tremont added with his eyebrow raised. "I suggested she take her mother, but she said she felt like it would be a better use of her time to have you accompany her. So you could work on your piece or whatever."

Hayley was pleased with this information. "I'm not complaining or anything, but—"

"This sounds like the start of a complaint." Tremont eyed her with clear annoyance.

"It's not"—Hayley paused—"but why does she need to be accompanied? I mean, she must make trips by herself once in a while, right?"

"Ha. I forget all your interactions with her have been in a controlled environment or in a private car," Tremont replied, giving her a curious expression.

Hayley looked at him, waiting for him to elaborate.

Tremont sighed. "So, I don't know if you've noticed or anything, but Emerson is a big deal. And any travel she undertakes requires either security or someone there to run interference on fans or paparazzi or whatever freaky shit is bound to happen. So she doesn't travel alone anymore."

"That makes sense, I guess. But I gotta be honest, Tremont, I'm not exactly deft at deflecting unwanted attention or large enough to wrestle some rabid fan away from her." The idea of having to fight off anything more than a fruit fly put Hayley on edge.

Tremont let a rare smile loose as he laughed. "Obviously not, Hayley. What is there, a hundred and fifteen pounds of you in that seat? Emerson is taller than you and has significantly more muscle. My money is on her, not you."

"Hey! I may look thin and weak, but I'll have you know I'm scrappy," Hayley said as she raised her fists, ready for combat.

"I bet." He looked amused. "We have security accompanying her on the flight and to and from the airport to the hotel. What we need is someone to sit with her and, uh, keep her occupied."

Hayley was lost. "What does that mean?"

"It means"—he paused for dramatic effect, lowering his voice and leaning in—"Emerson is afraid of flying and refuses to medicate like every other good little celebrity who flies all over the world, because she doesn't like the blunt feeling that comes with it. She's afraid someone will catch her off her A game and cause a ruckus. So she needs a distraction. A companion, if you will."

"And she feels like that companion should be me?" Hayley was shocked.

"No. She feels like that companion should be me," he added with a laugh, "or her hair stylist or her makeup team. But they're all busy. So, yes, that leaves you."

"I guess I'm, uh, honored?" Hayley tried not to feel insulted by Tremont's playful antagonism.

"You should be." His expression was unreadable as he added quietly, "I'm just teasing you. Like I said before, when she found out I couldn't fly, she asked for you personally."

"Cool." Hayley felt herself buzz with anticipation as they pulled up to the drop-off line for departures. This was going to be a very interesting few days.

CHAPTER ELEVEN

Emerson stirred the drink in front of her and adjusted the brim of the hat to rest lower on her forehead as she checked her phone for the time. Tremont had assured her he would get Hayley here with plenty of time before the flight, but they were cutting it close.

She was trying not to overthink anything, but she was failing miserably. Tremont's ear infection couldn't have come at a worse time. Well, that wasn't true…it could have been last weekend when she'd needed him with her in Colorado. Her stomach turned, and she felt nauseous. She hadn't been able to think of anything else since.

Deidre had had the forethought to talk with a child psychologist and had set up a plan for them all to follow when it was time to talk with Rory. Emerson had sat in on a session to prepare before they all got together and filled Rory in on the details. She'd found herself more nervous during that meeting than when the time had actually come to tell Rory the truth, partly because the actual reveal, thankfully, was handled by Deidre and the psychologist. It had been a tense discussion and there had been a lot of questions, but Emerson had walked out feeling hopeful.

Rory was strong, and Deidre, Tom, and Alex were three of the most loving people Emerson had ever known. This would be a lot for Rory and Alex to take in, but they could do it. In her heart, she felt like it would make them all stronger, but she realized there would be an adjustment period first. Because if Emerson was being honest with herself, she felt like a burden was being lifted from her shoulders by telling Rory the truth. But she also realized that that burden was now squarely resting on Deidre and her family's shoulders. This was far from ideal, but there was no way around it. And Emerson hated herself for that. This was her mess. This was her doing. This was just another example of how Emerson's mere involvement in other people's lives led to bad things. The dark cloud still ever present.

She'd stayed a few days to answer any of Rory's questions and attend a couple of psychologist sessions with Deidre and Rory, but in the end, it was decided by the family that they needed time and space to heal and figure things out. She'd talked at length with Deidre and Tom about her plan regarding Hayley and the interview they were working on together. She'd been dancing around the topic of Rachel and Rory because she hadn't been sure if her intuition had been right, but Deidre had agreed with her: They needed to take away Rachel's power by neutralizing her weapon. Emerson had to be the one to break the news about Rory to the media before Rachel had the chance to. She just had to tell Hayley and make sure the narrative was clean and uncomplicated. Which was ludicrous because there was nothing any more complicated than this. But she had a job to do, and that job was to stay away from the family and keep the press at bay until the time was right to tell the whole truth, before Rachel could ruin things any further.

Still, Emerson felt a little banished all the same. Part of her wanted to grieve with them—this affected her, too. But she couldn't make this about herself. Nor did she want to. That didn't make her feel any less alone, though it was making her usual life anxieties much worse. Which was one more reason why flying to Boston right now felt like walking right off a cliff.

She glanced up to give herself something to focus on besides her own screaming anxieties. From her place in the private lounge, she could see people passing through security for this wing of the airport. She exhaled in relief when Tremont's familiar fauxhawk passed into her line of sight. She could see that Tremont was saying something to Hayley and making her laugh. Emerson smiled at the exchange; she liked that they were getting along. Tremont could be a tough nut to crack, but he had warmed to Hayley in record time. She knew he meant well and had her best interests in mind, but he'd scared off more than his fair share of people—media and otherwise—with his protective and abrasive ways. Hayley seemed immune. That was just one more thing about her that Emerson liked more and more each day. Tremont was her family—it was important to her that they got along. That had been one of the dozens of red flags about Rachel—she and Tremont never got along. Ever. Another sign she'd ignored. She sighed.

"Yes, sir. We're expecting her." To her left, Francis—the muscled, plain-clothes-wearing security guy—spoke into his wrist microphone. Emerson assumed it was the announcement that Hayley was en route.

A few minutes later a similar-looking air marshal type escorted Hayley through the doors of the lounge and toward Emerson's seat by the window.

"Hey, there"—Emerson looked up, raising her glass—"welcome to the Presidential Lounge."

Hayley settled next to Emerson with a small wave. Emerson watched as she shuffled her messenger bag under her seat. "Hey, Em—er…you."

"Oh, yeah?" Emerson laughed. She'd missed her in the time they'd been apart. She'd thought about her a lot over these past five days. It felt like a lifetime since she'd had any lightness, but Hayley made her feel joy immediately.

"Well, it occurred to me that you might be doing an incognito thing, and I didn't want to blow up your spot," Hayley said.

Francis cast a concerned look over in their direction, and Hayley looked a little freaked out.

"Don't mind him. That's Francis. He's our security for the trip." Emerson tried to reassure her.

"Really? 'Cuz he's giving me a little side-eye," Hayley said as she gave her a skeptical look and pointed at Francis.

"That's probably because you said *blow up* before a flight," Emerson teased. "He's a very cautious man, that Francis."

Hayley's face relaxed. "Francis is into semantics. Got it. No joking with the hired gun—" She paused. "Shit. Can I say gun?"

Emerson laughed and flagged over a waitress in a black vest. She looked at Hayley expectantly. "Drink?"

Hayley glanced down at the drink in her hand and hesitated. "Sure. I'll have a Captain and Diet, with a lime, please."

The waitress nodded and handed her a glass of water before she walked back to the bar area.

"You're so polite." Emerson leaned back in her chair and took the opportunity to take in Hayley's appearance. She was dressed in tight black skinny jeans with chunky leather boots and a soft-looking white linen shirt. She had the top three buttons undone, and when she bent forward Emerson could see a hint of cleavage and the top of a camisole. She had to remind herself not to let her eyes linger, though she immediately betrayed herself by staring when Hayley leaned forward to retrieve something from her bag. She had to be careful. She found herself more emboldened the more time they spent together, and this weekend they would be spending *a lot* of time together.

Hayley shrugged. "Mama raised me right."

"Are you close with your mother?" Emerson asked. She really did care about the answer, but she also needed a distraction from the way Hayley's glasses slid up so perfectly into her hair, causing the waves of her hair to cascade around her face in the most delicious way.

"Yeah, we get along well." Hayley sipped her water. "We don't have that best friend kind of relationship, but we get each other. You know?"

Emerson nodded and considered the answer before she said anything else. "Sometimes I think that may be better."

"Are you close with your family?" Hayley took the cocktail the waitress brought with a polite nod, and she leaned back, relaxing into the chair. Emerson watched her fingers as she moved the ice around her glass.

"My sister and I are very close. We're different, but it works," Emerson replied with thoughts of Deidre and Rory fresh in her mind.

Hayley looked at her intently when she asked, "And your parents?"

"I never really knew my father." Emerson paused as Hayley wet the rim of the glass with her lime. Well, that was distracting. "My mother has always been there for me, maybe in a less than traditional way than most mothers, though. We see each other a few times a month, but it's more out of daughterly obligation than out of a burning desire to be in her presence."

"Another, miss?" The waitress returned and motioned toward Emerson's now empty glass.

"No thank you"—she checked her name tag to make sure she had her name right—"Sarah, two is my limit."

Hayley looked at the empty glass Emerson handed off as she sipped the final contents of her own.

"Hayley, a refill?" Emerson held her hand up, signaling for Sarah to wait.

"Ah, sure. Thanks." Hayley nodded toward Emerson's disappearing glass. "That's not the right glass for champagne. Are you breaking your own rules, Em?"

Emerson liked that Hayley remembered things about her and the way she used her nickname so freely, comfortably. She liked the way it sounded coming from Hayley's mouth. "Soda water and cranberry juice."

"No unnecessary depressants or stimulants. Noted." Hayley gave her that easy smile she loved.

"So, rum, huh?" Emerson closed her eyes as she rested her head back on the chair. She knew it was only a matter of time now before they had to board the plane. She was trying not to think about it.

She heard Sarah approach and Hayley politely accept another glass. That was an impressive turnaround for a new drink. Maybe this lounge area worked on a different time continuum than regular life. She made a mental note to make sure Sarah was tipped well.

"Yup," Hayley replied, her voice soothing, "wine makes me drowsy and beer makes me full. Martinis make me nauseous and tequila makes me naked. So, rum it is."

Emerson opened her eyes. That got her attention. "That's too bad. I like tequila. But not enough to drink it alone."

"No one said you had to drink it alone. I just said it made me less clothed," Hayley added as she sipped her drink. She paused seeming to realize what her statement implied. "Uh, I mean…I'm not saying…"

Emerson arched her eyebrow and smiled at the way Hayley squirmed with embarrassment. She was adorable. And now she was thinking about her naked. This was going to be an interesting few days.

"It's time, miss," Francis said as he leaned down between them. "We're ready for you now."

Emerson nodded and stretched before she stood. She looked back at Hayley, her heartbeat picking up as Hayley's gorgeous hazel eyes locked on hers in that way that took her breath away recently. She felt tongue-tied. Was she staring again? She should say something. Anything. "Ready to embark on our big adventure, buddy?" As soon as the words left her lips, she frowned. She should say anything but that.

Hayley cringed as she discarded the remainder of her drink. "Sure, as long as you promise to never call me buddy again."

Emerson had no idea what possessed her to say that in the first place. She couldn't remember an occasion in her entire life when she'd used *buddy* as a term of affection, endearment, or otherwise. She must be nervous about the flight. There was clearly no other explanation for that dorky slipup. Right?

"Got it. No more *buddy*. Check." Emerson gave her an enthusiastic thumbs-up because she was evidently possessed by the nerd devil and had no cool left in her system whatsoever. What was coming over her? And why was she feeling nervous around Hayley all of a sudden? Oh, maybe because she thought she was beautiful and smart and soon there would be no one there to run interference if she gave in to her desire to touch Hayley's skin and taste her lips. She was feeling off. Like she didn't trust herself. And that was a dangerous feeling to have right now. This was going to be a long flight.

❖

Emerson took the window seat with Hayley seated to her right along the aisle. She preferred first class for multiple reasons, but the chief one was that there were only two seats side by side and not more. That afforded her a little more privacy, even if only a little. Francis was positioned behind them to the right across the aisle from Hayley. Emerson had learned this was standard security protocol. He could watch the client and the surrounding passengers that way.

They boarded without any real commotion, which she was grateful for. A stewardess and one of the pilots stopped her for a picture and told her they appreciated her work, but otherwise it had been quiet. She'd learned that when flying commercially, it was best to board last to her first-class seat while someone blocked the aisle. That increased the odds of maintaining her anonymity, though it didn't always work out that way.

Emerson exhaled slowly as the captain spoke over the intercom and informed the passengers about the route they would be traveling, the speed, the weather, whatever. She ignored this information at all costs and avoided thinking about it. She kept her gaze directed out the window as the flight attendants walked through the emergency preparation protocol. She felt Hayley's eyes on her and she turned to look at her.

"If you could be any animal, what would you be?" Hayley asked.

"A domestic house cat," Emerson replied, without hesitation.

"Of all the animals in all the *world*—and you choose a domestic house cat?" Hayley looked at her skeptically.

Emerson shrugged. She tensed slightly as the plane moved forward on the runway. "Well, I like the idea of being a tiger or a lion or a panther, but I don't like the idea of being hunted as big game."

Emerson saw someone shift over Hayley's shoulder and suddenly her answer felt too real. A passenger two rows over was leaning forward, likely trying to get a better view of her. She sank back into the seat, trying to hide behind Hayley's slender frame.

"You mean like you are on a daily basis?" Hayley had followed Emerson's gaze and shrugged off her linen shirt as the young man pulled his cell phone out of his pocket. Emerson watched with relief as Hayley shifted in her seat and draped the now unbuttoned, open shirt over her head, effectively blocking the passenger's attempt at taking a picture.

"Precisely," Emerson said and laughed at Hayley's creative response to the intrusion. Hayley looked ridiculous. Emerson loved that she didn't seem bothered by it. "That's some impressive headgear you've got there."

"Didn't I tell you I'm secretly cotton royalty? This is my official headpiece, but I typically reserve it for formal occasions." Hayley's expression remained serious. Emerson laughed harder.

"My apologies, your royal linen-ness. I had no idea I was in the presence of such starchy greatness," Emerson said as she curtseyed in her seat.

"You're forgiven," Hayley replied and gave her a subtle nod. "We choose to remain as anonymous as possible, in order to best assimilate with the ordinary folk."

"You are too kind." Hayley didn't even crack a smile. Emerson was afraid if she laughed any harder she would pee.

Unperturbed by her near hysterics, Hayley pressed on, asking, "Why a cat, though?"

Emerson struggled to make a coherent sentence between bouts of laughter. "I like how free they are. They don't have any true masters—they sort of do their own thing, on their own terms. But they can climb and leap and sneak around like little furry ninjas if they so choose. Plus, they curl in those cute little warm balls and look so peaceful when they nap. Which takes up like twenty hours of their day—they are professional nappers. That sounds sort of heavenly." She nudged Hayley playfully. "What about you?"

"I'm definitely more of an eagle or bird kind of chick," Hayley replied. "I like the idea of being able to up and take off—fly wherever I want, whenever I want, migrate someplace warm. You know, get away."

Emerson did a double take when she realized their plane had taken off and hit cruising altitude while she and Hayley were talking. She hadn't noticed or needed to practice her deep breathing. It was a miracle. No, it was Hayley. "Thank you."

Hayley gave her a knowing smile. "Of course, anytime."

Hayley shivered, the coolness of the plane causing visible goose bumps on her skin. Emerson noted that Hayley's nipples were firmly pressing through the thin camisole as well. She gestured toward the flight attendants currently admonishing the amateur paparazzi over Hayley's shoulder. "I think we're safe for a bit, your royal fabric-ness. I thank you for your service."

"Glad to help. Damn, this plane is cold," Hayley said and she shivered once more as she pulled the shirt back over her shoulders and buttoned it, leaving the top three buttons open as before. Emerson noticed that as well.

Emerson reached into the seat back pocket in front of her and pulled out a neatly folded airplane blanket. She draped it across them both and gave Hayley a small smile. "I'm glad you're here."

Hayley pulled the blanket up to her chest and scooted closer, snugging under the warmth. "Me, too."

CHAPTER TWELVE

Hayley woke up with a serious case of dry mouth. She wasn't sure when she had fallen asleep, but she was suddenly very aware that Emerson's shoulder was currently acting as her pillow. She froze there for a moment in panic, trying to figure out how she could casually sit up and pretend none of that sloppiness had just occurred. She was silently cursing the rum and soda when Emerson shifted a little.

"I had them bring you a water—it's in the seat back pouch." Emerson's voice was melodious next to Hayley's ear. She let herself get lost in it and fantasize about the intimacy of it. Emerson, so close, talking just to her. Hayley had dreamed about this. The soft feminine scent of Emerson's perfume combined with what she assumed was Emerson's shampoo intoxicated her. This was better than anything she had dreamed about. As she willed the scents to memory, a thought occurred to her: she was only this close to Emerson because she'd obnoxiously fallen asleep on her. And now she was internally panicking. She carefully lifted her head from what was probably the most comfortable shoulder she had ever fallen asleep on and smiled shyly. "Thanks."

Emerson surveyed her with amused eyes as she parroted, "Of course, any time."

A quick bout of turbulence alerted Hayley that not only had she been pleasantly resting on Emerson's shoulder for God knew how long, but at some point, her hand had worked its way under the armrest and onto Emerson's lap. The reflexive hand squeeze from Emerson brought on by the turbulence comforted Hayley into thinking that maybe she hadn't overstepped in her sleep, intentionally or otherwise.

When Emerson made no attempt to shrug off her hand now that she was awake—and the turbulence was over—Hayley took it as a sign that they were making progress in their relationship and settled more comfortably into her seat.

❖

Hayley had concluded about three games of Uno ago that Emerson was rigging the deck. She was being absolutely destroyed by her. It didn't matter how many times she shuffled or cut the deck—somehow Emerson ended up with a clean sweep of her hand every time. It was sort of getting pathetic.

"I give up." Hayley exhaled dramatically and flopped back. "You are the undisputed Uno champion."

Emerson gave a little fist pump and clapped quietly before she shuffled the cards once for good measure. She slipped them back into the case and handed it back to Hayley. "I can't tell you the last time I played Uno."

Hayley gave her a challenging look and rolled her eyes. "I don't believe you for a second. That was some masterful skill displayed, Em. You've obviously been honing those talents in private."

"'Scuse me, Miss Emerson?" A small voice next to Hayley drew their attention.

The voice belonged to a little girl. Hayley estimated she couldn't be older than five or six years old. Her hair was in lopsided pigtails, and she was clutching a little book to her chest as she shifted back and forth nervously.

Emerson smiled and leaned over Hayley's lap to talk to her. "Hey there. What's your name?"

"Wendy Timmons." Her eyes were as big as saucers when Emerson reached out to shake her hand.

"Nice to meet you, Wendy Timmons." Emerson gestured toward the book the little girl was holding so tightly that her knuckles were white. "What have you got there?"

"It's the third book of the *Adventure Frog* series. It's my favorite." Wendy nodded enthusiastically and flashed a gap-toothed smile. "Zelda Frog is my hero."

Hayley laughed and looked back at Emerson. The gleeful look on her face melted Hayley's heart. Emerson had voiced Zelda in five installments of *Adventure Frog*. Alison's *Wikipedia* detective work had clued Hayley into a sixth one in the works for sometime next year. Then there was that full-length animated movie she'd mentioned. The *Adventure Frog* partnership was promising to be an enormous payoff for Emerson. It was a huge hit with the pre-adolescent crowd and showed no signs of slowing down. This was quite the departure from her much more adult and mature movie roles—she made a note to ask Emerson how she got into that later.

Emerson replied, "She's my hero, too. A *she*ro, even."

Wendy giggled and stepped forward, wedging herself in the space between Hayley's legs and the seat in front of her. She looked a little shy before thrusting her book toward Emerson and asking, "Will you read some to me?"

Emerson looked momentarily surprised before she glanced up. Hayley followed the direction of her gaze and saw a woman she presumed was the little girl's grandmother a few rows in front of them mouthing, "Sorry."

Emerson gave her a kind smile and shrugged. "Is that okay with you?"

The older woman nodded, and Emerson directed her attention to the flight attendant standing nearby. "All good?"

"As long as the seat belt sign is off, and the guardians on board are fine with it, that's okay by me." He gave her a quick thumbs-up and resumed taking the drink order of the person adjacent to them.

"Well then, I'd be happy to." Emerson put the armrest up separating her and Hayley and shifted so her back was angled toward the window. "Do you think you can fit between me and my friend Hayley here, so we can read quietly together?"

Wendy nodded and scampered between them in one quick motion. She cuddled close to Emerson and pulled her arm around her shoulder, and Hayley thought she might die from cuteness overload.

Emerson smiled and took the book. As she began to read, Wendy pulled Hayley's hand onto her lap and nodded encouragingly.

Hayley watched with amusement as Emerson acted out all the parts. She kept her volume low so as not to disturb the other passengers, and a few times Wendy's happy giggles drowned her out entirely. She tickled Wendy during one portion of the story, which caused Wendy to squirm and pull Hayley's hand up to her chest to protect herself. Hayley's fingers brushed against Emerson's in the tickle assault, and Hayley laced them together to help Wendy escape the Zelda-voiced tickle monster. Emerson squeezed her fingers and winked at Hayley when Wendy stopped squirming and pointed to the book for her to finish where they left off. Emerson nodded and repositioned her arm around Wendy's shoulders, keeping her right hand entwined with Hayley's. She ended the chapter and closed the book just as Wendy's adult approached them.

"That's enough now, Wendy. Let the nice ladies rest before the plane lands." The older woman had a kind face and an even kinder voice.

"Are you sure, Gramma?" Wendy pouted and wiggled closer to Emerson.

Her grandmother nodded as she gave them a soft smile. "Thank you for humoring her."

Emerson released Hayley's hand to help Wendy stand between the seats. "Thanks for being my reading partner, Wendy."

Wendy smiled—her missing front tooth on display again—as she leaned forward and gave Emerson a big hug and a sloppy kiss on her cheek.

Hayley was surprised when she too got a cheek nuzzle.

Wendy stage-whispered to her. "Thanks for saving me from the tickle monster, Hayley."

"Any time. Someone needs to stand up to those bullies," Hayley replied with a serious nod.

"C'mon, Wendy." Her grandmother took her hand and pulled her toward the aisle.

Hayley watched Wendy skip back to her seat as she chattered excitedly to her grandmother before she turned to Emerson and teased, "I think you just made a new best friend."

"Wendy has excellent taste in literature. She's good people. I'd be lucky to be a friend of hers." Emerson's eyes sparkled. Hayley was entranced.

"Do you have many friends?"

Emerson seemed to consider this. "It's hard to find people you can trust in this business, in this life. I have people I'm *friendly* with, but not as many friends as I'd probably like."

"I'll be your friend." Hayley was being playful, but she hoped Emerson knew she was also being sincere.

"You already are." Emerson's expression told her that her message was received. Hayley felt the butterflies in her stomach again.

"I'm very good at being a friend. The best, even." Hayley was more than aware she'd like to be more than friends with Emerson, something that was becoming glaringly obvious the more time she spent with her, but she could do this, too. She could be a friend to Emerson. She would be. She wanted to be.

"Oh, without a doubt." Emerson flashed her best red-carpet smile and replied in Zelda Frog's voice, "You're the bestest."

CHAPTER THIRTEEN

"Miss Sterling. We're ready for you on the mark," the photographer's assistant called from behind the video screen, and Hayley startled. She'd been trying—unsuccessfully—to organize the five thousand words Jonathan wanted by the end of the weekend. She was mostly unsuccessful because Emerson became less and less clothed as the minutes turned to hours.

It had been a whirlwind since they'd landed in Boston a few hours ago, at the crack of dawn. They were barely at the hotel for thirty minutes when the driver arrived to take Emerson to the photo shoot, which was supposed to be followed by an interview with *The Improper Bostonian*. The amount of schedule juggling this took made Hayley's head spin. But no more than having Emerson only ten feet away—practically naked—did. Hayley was having a hard time focusing on anything other than how Emerson looked under the flashing lights.

From what she understood, Emerson had contracted to be the face of a new and edgy lingerie and clothing line based out of Boston. A good portion of *Willow Path* was filmed on location here, and when reshoots meant Emerson had to head to the East Coast, Tremont and her team had scheduled this photo shoot and the *Improper* interview to overlap with the film obligations. It was a smart move schedule wise but was going to make for a very, very long day on next to no sleep. She was already feeling fatigued and she wasn't even really working. Well, not like Emerson was. And contrary to what she had believed, this photo shoot nonsense was work. Like, real work. It was a lot of hurry up and wait, hold that pose, reapply, appear still enthusiastic and charming even after it's been like a million hours. That kind of work. Emerson was really a pro. Hayley had gotten annoyed about fifteen minutes into this event, but Emerson smiled like it was her job. Probably because it was. Hayley didn't envy her.

The nice thing about this, though, was that with every new wardrobe or scene change, there was a delay in shooting. So they were able to chat on and off the record about stuff. It was mostly off the record, though, and a good amount of it was about Tremont and Sebastian, but Hayley loved it. She got to see Emerson's humor and playfulness, live and in action. She found those to be her favorite moments with Emerson—the ones where she didn't have to analyze anything and could just chat freely. Emerson felt like an old friend in a lot of ways, particularly in those instances.

She thought back to the plane ride and how easily she had bridged the gap of their working relationship and what she now considered their friendship. It had been far too easy to reach out and take Emerson's hand during story time with little Wendy. How fucking cute was Emerson reading to her in that frog voice? Like, seriously? It was magical. She could only imagine the kind of lasting impression she'd made on Wendy. Emerson surprised her often. But today, it wasn't her words or actions that had Hayley distracted. Today it was her apparent comfort wearing next to nothing.

"Okay. Whenever you're ready, Miss—"

"*Emerson* is fine," Emerson said as she dropped her robe and stepped out onto the marked spot. She took the photographer's cues to pose this way and that without any complaints. She would make an occasional observation or weigh in here or there, but she appeared to be agreeable to work with. This was a new departure for Hayley. She hadn't had the opportunity to be on this side of the lens before. There was so much going on behind the scenes, and it was amazing.

They took a break, and Hayley watched as a few assistants arranged a new scene for Emerson to be photographed in. This area had fake grass and a park bench. The background was filled with tall, deep green hedge-like things that appeared to be real. They looked real. But through the lens the scene looked as if it was summer and beautiful and outside, and they weren't actually in a rented warehouse space in downtown Boston on a rainy spring day.

Emerson glanced over to her in between outfit changes and gave her a wave. "Doing okay, Hayley?"

"Yeah. This is…interesting," Hayley replied. She was far from bored. Her mind spun as she tried to take in all the happenings around her. She was trying to make mental notes—she didn't want to miss a thing. If she planned to get to the heart of who Emerson was, she'd need to see as many angles of her life as possible. And Emerson had some really flattering angles. She looked back down at her tablet screen and frowned. She'd made no headway this afternoon at all.

"If you keep grimacing like that, you are going to give yourself brow lines." Emerson's voice sounded over her shoulder and she jumped.

"Jeez, you're like a ninja. I didn't even hear you come over here," she said as her eyes immediately went to Emerson's lingerie-clad body before they snapped back up to the perfectly applied eye shadow that accented Emerson's already showstopping eyes. She squirmed trying to cover up her unintentional leering. "Your makeup is beautiful."

"Thanks. The stylist team here in Boston didn't poke my eye out. It's a win-win, I suppose," Emerson said, her expression playful.

"Having working eyes is helpful." She had no idea why she said that.

Emerson gave her an amused look. "Indeed, the better to see you with."

Hayley laughed. She motioned around them. "I don't know how you do all this."

"Manage to be incredibly charming while prancing around naked with a bunch of strangers? You mean that?" Emerson replied, her tone teasing.

"Actually, yes." Hayley liked the playfulness of their banter now. They had settled into something comfortable. She was all for it. "You're very comfortable scantily clad, huh?"

"Asks the woman who took her shirt off in front of me." Emerson gave her a wink. She was flirting, right? That was a flirt.

Emerson draped her arm across Hayley's chair and traced her fingers along Hayley's keyboard with a shrug, her attention directed into the distance seemingly at nothing in particular. "I spend quite a bit of time wearing next to nothing at all. I wouldn't say I'm comfortable. I would say…I'm used to it. There's a difference."

Hayley lost herself in the delicate, dancing way Emerson's fingers moved along her keys, pressing lightly but not enough to engage a letter. She imagined it must be incredibly frustrating for the keyboard, almost getting keyed, but not. Or maybe it was just frustrating for her, wishing she was the keyboard under Emerson's unbelievably soft looking fingers. Okay, that was enough. *Reel it in, Hayley.*

Someone knocked over a clothing rack to their left, and the noise drew their attention. A few people scrambled to clean up the mess as one of the assistants held up two separate outfits and talked to famed Italian photographer Pasquale Marinello. They seemed to be in deep discussion over the choices.

Emerson nodded toward them. "Which do you prefer, Hayley?"

"Of the outfits?" They were talking about clothes, right?

Emerson looked at her, a glint of something in her eye. "Did you think I was talking about the woman holding the outfits?"

"I, uh…no," Hayley said, suddenly second-guessing herself. "Were you?"

"No."

Hayley felt herself blush. "Um, the black one."

Emerson nodded. "I agree. But I'm pretty into black, so I don't always trust myself."

"Well, don't use my judgment. I've been accused of being boring and uninspired in the clothing department."

"Oh?" Emerson took a step back and appraised her. "I like this look. It's very grunge chic."

Hayley pushed her dark-rimmed glasses into her hair and glanced down at herself. She was wearing the same dark jeans from the flight last night and the chunky leather boots that Tremont shamed her into bringing. She loved them, honestly, but still. There was shaming. She laughed when she noticed the shirt she was wearing over her basic black tank top. "See, though? This is what I mean."

She pulled the bottom of her favorite black and red flannel shirt away from her body and pointed. "My work girlfriend Alison is super stylish and chic and she thinks this shirt makes me look like a lumberjack."

Emerson raised an eyebrow at that. "Girlfriend?"

"Friend. Who's a girl. Named Alison. She has a boyfriend named Rob who's kind of a dickwad. We work together. She's in fashion." Hayley paused. "And I'm rambling. Sorry."

"Well, I don't know this Alison person, but I think you look great." She motioned toward her outfit. "This is a good look on you."

"Thanks," she replied. Wait until Alison heard about that. "You'd like her. Alison, I mean. You remind me of her a bit."

"Have you been friends long?" One of the PAs held up a glass of water to Emerson. She nodded and pulled out a metal straw from her purse. She'd told Hayley before that this was to limit smearing her lipstick. Hayley appreciated the environmentally friendly choice.

"About five years. We started working at the *Sun* around the same time. She's got a much clearer vision of her career than I do. She's got a real passion for fashion. It suits her," Hayley replied as she made a mental note to call Alison later. There was no way they were having their Chinese food date tomorrow night if she was in Boston.

"*Suits* her. That's cute."

Hayley face-palmed. "I wasn't even trying to be punny. I'm a word nerd. It's best you just accept that."

"No problems there." Emerson nudged her. "You *do* have a clear career vision, though, Hayley. You told me so in the car, remember? Hayley Carpenter, Screenwriter. I already ordered your business cards."

Hayley laughed. "Someday, maybe."

"Why not now?" Emerson asked. She was looking at Hayley intently again. She had a hard time focusing when Emerson looked at her that way. She decided to break up the tension with a little humor. That would help, right?

"Because right now," Hayley said as she pointed toward Emerson and pretended to thumb through some notes, "I'm interviewing the incredibly charming and scantily clad Emerson Sterling."

"Ha, there does seem to be that." Emerson paused. "Hey, you never talk about the screenplay. Tell me about it."

"It's more of a work in progress than a screenplay." Hayley felt exposed talking about her idea, which was ridiculous because Emerson was standing in front of her very literally exposed.

"Okay, so give me a brief synopsis. Is it current day? Does it feature a dragon? Is it bigger than a breadbox?"

Hayley laughed. "No dragons, but it's definitely bigger than a breadbox."

Emerson pretended to take Hayley's imaginary notes from before and add to them. "Got it. No dragons. Does it contain warm bread?"

"The story?"

"No, the box that contains *it*—whatever it is—that's bigger than your average breadbox."

"There's no box." Hayley chuckled.

Emerson made more pretend notes, her expression very serious. "No box. Got it. Is there bread, though? Because we haven't covered that angle."

Hayley thought about this. "There is a picnic scene by a lake."

"Aha! I knew it. Sandwiches happen at picnics. Most sandwiches contain bread." Emerson patted herself on the shoulder in congratulations. "Okay, your screenplay is about bread. Continue."

Hayley shook her head. "It's about a woman that goes off to college in NYC and has this torrid affair with her female professor that completely blows up in her face. She survives it—barely—and manages to carve out this whole amazing life in the city but has to give it all up to return home to her tiny little Maine town to fix some mistakes her family made. It's about her coming to terms with the life she had when she left and the life she's forced to live on her return. It fractures something inside her. She realizes she's compartmentalized so much of who she is that she's lost when among those things that are most familiar to her. It's kind of like a coming-of-age story about self-discovery amid tragedy and accepting the mistakes of the past that you can't avoid forever."

"Well, color me interested." Emerson's expression was sincere. "That sounds fantastic. When can I read it?"

"Read it?" Hayley had been trying to drink some water, but she nearly choked when she heard that. "Uh, it's not even done. I have loads of work to do on it still. It may never be done. Who knows? Maybe it's just a pipe dream."

Emerson frowned. "That is not an answer I can accept, sorry. Why haven't you been working on it? The idea is solid. It's exciting. I'm hooked. Don't leave me hanging here."

Hayley sighed. "Dreams don't pay bills, Em. I must work to afford the food which I must consume to live. One day, I'll finish it. Maybe."

Emerson shook her head. "You're too busy with work. That's what's stifling your creativity."

Hayley rolled her eyes. "Yup. Work is a real drag. You cracked the code."

Emerson looked at her seriously, the playfulness from before a distant memory. "Hayley, you're fired."

Hayley did choke this time.

Emerson patted her on the back as she gasped for air. "Fine, fine. You're not fired. Don't be so dramatic."

Through the tears in her eyes she could see Emerson's smile. Emerson kept her hand on Hayley's back when the coughing subsided, and even though Hayley was pretty sure she'd get pneumonia from all the water in her lungs, she appreciated the gentle, soothing circles Emerson was making between her shoulder blades.

"But I did mean what I said about the screenplay. You need to foster it. If there's anything I can do to help, let me know. I'm officially invested."

Hayley didn't know what to say. Anytime someone offered her encouragement, she felt grateful because it made her feel like she wasn't alone in this endeavor. She felt inspired by another person's belief in her. But Emerson's encouragement—and offer to help—made her feel unworthy. And at the same time, incredibly lucky. It was a confusing set of emotions made no clearer by the warm hand that now rested on her low back.

A PA entered through the side door of the room with a trash can, and Emerson shivered as a gust of cold air entered the studio. She glanced back at her abandoned robe and frowned. "I'm not sure why they keep these places so goddamned cold. They must spend all their time photoshopping out people's nipples."

Try as she might, Hayley could not stop the automatic trajectory of her eyes toward Emerson's chest. She shook her head and shrugged off her soft flannel shirt, then handed it to Emerson. "Here, let's not give those horny bastards any more fodder, eh?"

"Thanks." Emerson took the shirt with a grateful smile and pulled it on. She left it unbuttoned and loose as she sipped from the glass of water. Hayley watched as Emerson took the straw between her lips and closed her eyes. She leaned against Hayley's chair in the process.

"Tired?" Hayley asked. She closed her tablet and shuffled it back into her bag. There would be no words right now. It was a practice in futility.

"Always." A sad smile formed on Emerson's lips as the lead photographer interrupted them.

"Emerson! I love this." Pasquale reached out and ran his fingers along her shoulder. "Take off the bra and let's have the lapels hang over your chest—it'll make those boy shorts look fantastic. Great idea, Emerson. The execs are going to love this. It's very—"

"Grunge chic?" Emerson said.

"Precisely. It will really tie in to that movie role you are working on, too. This just screams Willow, doesn't it? Come, come," Pasquale said as he clapped enthusiastically.

Emerson put down her glass and looked at Hayley. "Hay, what size shoes do you wear?"

"Um, an eight and a half," Hayley replied, unsure of what to expect next.

"Good. Let me borrow your boots." Emerson held out her hand and waited as she called over her shoulder. "Get Amy in here. Tell her to bring the kit."

"The kit?" Hayley was feeling a little naked without her boots or trusty shirt.

"Well if we're going to do this, we're going to do it right. Time to play the part." Emerson winked and took Hayley's glasses off her face as she slipped them into her hair.

Thirty minutes later, Hayley gaped at the digital shots that flooded the screen in front of her. "Whoa."

"She's such a beauty. I love this look on her—it brings her back to her bad girl roots, you know?" Pasquale dragged the stylus over the screen and highlighted his favorite shots. From time to time he would circle particular angles that he liked and chatter to himself. "Look here, her cheekbones are perfect with that tuck of her chin. She's such a natural. Always a pleasure…"

Hayley tried to ignore his rambling, but she could see what he was talking about, albeit for a markedly different reason. Try as she might, she couldn't get over how freaking perfect Emerson looked in her clothes. The tone of the photo shoot had changed completely when Emerson donned Hayley's shirt. She was posed on the park bench, dressed only in Hayley's chunky black boots and plaid shirt. She tried on a few different black bottoms before they chose a cheeky high-cut boy short from the lingerie line. Emerson had Hayley's reading glasses tucked up into her hair, letting wisps fall randomly as Amy from makeup put on a deep red lipstick. The smoky eye, red lips, and gentle nibble she occasionally applied to the end of the glasses were captivating. Emerson had everyone's attention in the room—particularly Hayley's—a fact that made Hayley a little uncomfortable. She was developing a pretty significant crush on Emerson. And seeing Emerson in her clothes was doing nothing to help that. At all. Not even a little.

"This is the one, this is the cover piece." Pasquale tapped the glass and nodded.

He had circled a series of Emerson reclining on the bench. She was stretched out on her side, with one knee bent while the other boot rested on the wrought-iron armrest. Her toned, flat stomach was on display, and her ample chest was just barely concealed by Hayley's shirt lapels as she arched her back. She had propped herself up on her elbow and had Hayley's glasses hanging loosely from her blood-red lips while her right hand settled at the waistband of the boy shorts. Pasquale's favorite of the series was a picture in which Emerson's thumb had slipped beneath the material just enough to make the already suggestive photo straddle the line of X-rated.

Hayley had to agree—the shot was gorgeous. Emerson was glorious, all lean muscle and flawless tanned skin. With her light eyes and dark makeup and her hair impeccably coifed to look effortless, she every bit personified a cover girl and movie star. And she did it all without breathing a word. That was something Hayley had noticed over their weeks together. When Emerson spoke to another interviewer or reporter, she only spoke when asked a question and she didn't elaborate unless it was necessary. Her interactions with Hayley had been vastly different to the exchanges Haley'd witnessed with other press. That was what she had been trying to put into words when Emerson interrupted her earlier and starting stripping Hayley of her clothes.

Emerson reemerged in the clothes she had arrived in, with her hair pulled up into a loose ponytail. And just like that, she looked like a regular person again. Well, a perfectly gorgeous regular person, but a regular person nonetheless.

"Incredible, Emerson," Pasquale said, and the rest of the people in the room clapped as she bowed her head. There was a lot of clapping around here, it seemed.

"Thanks, Pasquale." Emerson stepped in to give him an air kiss. "I'm excited to see the final product."

"Go, go, look at the monitor. I need to make some calls, this changes some things." Pasquale wandered off, snatching up a PA and barking off orders as he went.

Emerson walked over to Hayley with a shy grin as she handed back Hayley's belongings. "Thanks."

Hayley pulled on the shirt, grateful for its warmth in the cold room, and slipped her feet into the unbuckled boots. As she tucked her glasses into the shirt pocket, she got a whiff of Emerson's perfume on the fabric. "If I had known that my clothes would be such a vital part of this trip, I would have let Tremont into my closet like he asked."

"Oh God. Don't do that," Emerson warned. "He's been known to keep scissors hidden on his person. The next thing you know, your favorite pajama shirt is a midriff-baring sex outfit. Bad news."

Hayley pulled the shirt tighter around herself and blew out a sigh of relief. "Thanks for the warning. He almost breached the threshold for this trip. My intramural Yale broomball shirt would never have made it."

Emerson let out a low whistle. "You dodged a bullet there."

"Or scissors, as it were," Hayley replied.

Emerson laughed and walked to the monitor to examine the photos. Hayley watched as she scrolled through the dozens of images and read the notes made in the margins. She touched the screen to enhance a shot of her looking off set. Hayley remembered when it was taken because it had been eerily quiet at the time. Emerson had been between poses, and they had just touched up her makeup. Before the next background was complete, Hayley had heard the soft click of a smartphone camera to her right. In the silence of the moment, it sounded like an echo in the room, and Emerson's head had whipped its direction. She appeared to breathe out a sigh of relief when she saw it was Amy taking a picture of the lipstick combinations on her hand and not of Emerson. She'd glanced at Hayley before returning her attention to the camera. The exchange had settled like a stone in Hayley's stomach. There was something so incredibly sad about it.

"You look a little haunted there." Hayley joined her at the monitor and added softly from behind Emerson's shoulder, "Almost vulnerable."

Emerson nodded and was quiet for a few moments. "It's a beautifully candid shot." She seemed lost in thought.

"What are you thinking about?" Hayley had an increasing desire to reach out and touch her.

Emerson turned her head and caught Hayley's gaze. They were so close, she could feel the heat of Emerson's body radiating onto her own. Her eyes were drawn to Emerson's lips.

"That I have no doubt this will make the final spread, and I was contemplating vetoing it," Emerson replied.

"Why?" Hayley asked but she had a feeling she already knew the answer. "Because of the rawness, right?"

"Mm." Emerson gave her a tiny nod before she motioned between them. "But that's what we're here for, isn't it? The naked truth."

"It is." Her eyes flicked back to Emerson's lips again. They looked delicious.

"And what are *you* thinking about?" Emerson's voice was barely a whisper when she turned Hayley's question back to her.

Hayley bit her lip in response. The question caught her off guard. She was aware of the way Emerson's eyes traced her face, as if watching to see her expression, taking stock of her reaction. "I…uh."

"Mm-hmm." Emerson gave her a knowing smile and Hayley stepped back. She needed to regain a little control.

"So, do you get to keep any of the clothes?" Hayley looked for something—anything—to busy her hands with. She picked up an empty water bottle near the monitor and fiddled with the label.

"Well, most of the wardrobe was yours this time around, so no. I did swipe a pair of those boy shorts, though." She tapped her butt playfully. "But only because I'm pretty sure that bench gave me an ass splinter, and it was easier to leave them on than try to do surgery with fifteen people standing around back there."

"Never in my life would I have anticipated spending my day knowing what kind of underwear you had on." Hayley's eyes widened when she realized that comment was said out loud.

"Let's just call it even, then, since I find you taking off your shirt in my presence to be terribly distracting." Emerson leaned close and took the glasses from Hayley's pocket. She carefully slid them into position on Hayley's face and grazed Hayley's chin with her thumbs as she lowered her hands. "Now you don't have to subtly check out my ass when I walk out of the room because you already know." She paused and added, "Thanks again for the shirt."

By the time Hayley realized she had crushed the bottle in her hands, Emerson was already gone. That didn't just happen, right? There was no way Emerson was flirting with her. Not possible. She was obviously still jet-lagged.

She tossed the mangled plastic into the recycle bin nearby and exhaled slowly. "What am I getting myself into?"

CHAPTER FOURTEEN

The photo shoot had been long, but that didn't bother Emerson as she'd thought it might. Maybe because Hayley was there to keep her company. And Hayley was good company. Very good. And a delicious distraction as well. She never got tired of being in Hayley's presence, it seemed. She helped her feel relaxed and at ease, which was impossible these days given all that was going on with Rory.

Rory had FaceTimed her when she was changing out of Hayley's clothes at the end of the shoot. The call had come at just the right time since it was really the only time she'd been alone at all that day. The conversation was short, but sweet. Rory had been really transparent about her feelings. Her biggest concern was that Emerson didn't want her, and that's why she gave up custody to Deidre. Emerson did her best to assure her that was as far from the truth as possible. She wanted Rory to have the best life, and that would only be possible with someone else. She seemed to understand, but Emerson had a feeling they would be discussing that again sometime soon, and she welcomed that.

The truth was, Rory had been at the forefront of her mind since her interaction with Wendy on the plane earlier. She'd been on her mind constantly anyway, but her heart had hurt watching Wendy walk away. It made her think of the relationship she had given up when she agreed to relinquish parental rights almost twelve years ago. She'd pushed those feelings aside for a long time, but now that the wound had been reopened, she realized she had some healing to do on her own still.

And that healing would come only with doing the one thing that she feared most: revealing the truth about Rory to the world and exposing her to its harsh scrutiny. Her only hope was to do as much damage control in the beginning as possible, and that would only happen if someone could help ease the narrative into the world. That person was Hayley. She just knew it in her gut. Hayley would be able to tell her story, she had to. Emerson needed her to. But first, Emerson had to tell her. And that made Emerson nervous because somewhere over the past several weeks, Hayley had become more than just a confidant. And she was quickly becoming more than just a friend. Because you didn't have crushes on friends, right? And she was definitely crushing on Hayley these days. Big time.

Her mind was buzzing with thoughts of Rory and Hayley as she keyed into her hotel room, exhausted and ready for bed. Too bad her day was far from over.

Emerson hadn't been in the hotel room more than fifteen minutes when her cell phone rang. She contemplated letting it go to voicemail. She was enjoying the quiet and knew she wouldn't have it for much longer. She glanced at the clock. Her time was ticking away—the interviewer from *The Improper Bostonian* would be here any minute. The phone stopped buzzing and she smiled. The caller had made the decision for her. That was a relief. But it was short-lived, because the phone buzzed insistently again. She reached for it. Tremont was calling.

"Hello, darling," she said as she looked in the backlit mirror of her bathroom vanity. This was great lighting. And her brief collapse on the bed for the ten seconds she had to herself revealed the incredibly comfortable bed. She made a note to mention that to Tremont. They should stay here every time they were in Boston. The concierge desk had signs all over it boasting that it was the preferred hotel of Boston's Miss Match, whoever that was. She made another note to investigate this woman.

"Did the flight go okay?" He had genuine concern in his voice. She appreciated that.

"Actually, yes." The flight had been fine, easy even. Hayley had been a great companion and Emerson had found the time flying— literally—in every sense of the word. She got the same safe feeling from Hayley that she got from Tremont. Well, sort of the same. But different, too. She'd had years to foster her relationship and trust with

Tremont, but she could tell that it wouldn't take as long with Hayley. She'd felt a connection to her, right off the bat. That's why she took a chance on her. That's why she was taking the risk.

"Good. Hayley didn't do anything stupid, right? Because I like her, and I'd hate to have to have her killed," Tremont said dramatically.

"No, she was perfect." She thought back to when Hayley had fallen asleep on her shoulder and reached for her hand while she slept. Emerson hadn't given a second thought to holding her hand and sinking lower in the seat to make sure she was comfortable. Nor had she felt the need to release her hand when she awoke. Something she'd been grateful for when the turbulence hit, and Hayley gently stroked her thigh to comfort her. She had felt comforted. And truthfully, a little turned on, too. Which was unexpected. So later, when Hayley's fingers found hers during the tickle fight, she held them because it felt right. And because she missed the physical contact of another person. With everything that was going on in her head and in her life lately, she wanted more than anything to curl up with someone and feel loved. To feel important. To feel like she was more than a headline or a payday. Maybe that was asking too much. Maybe she was looking for something she couldn't have.

"Perfect, huh?" Tremont asked.

"Yeah, perfect," she replied without elaborating. She wasn't ready to talk about those thoughts yet.

"And the photo shoot?" he asked.

"Long, boring, unreasonably cold and nipple-y. The usual. We did something a little different last minute—tried a different look. I think you'll like it." She was sure he would approve. This was the kind of thing he encouraged in her, to take fashion risks. He was always right, even if she hated to admit it.

Tremont hummed. "I should get the preliminary prints in the next day or so. We can go over them together."

"Great." She loved talking to him, but she doubted he'd called to chitchat. "So, besides the fact that you missed me desperately and can't live without being in my presence, I assume you called for a reason."

"No flies on you, Em," he teased. "Your interviewer is there. He's waiting in the lobby."

She dropped her head. It was time to go to work again. "You know, technically this ear infection is giving you some time off. You don't need to man the phones and assist me from the left coast. I can manage myself for the day or two it takes for me to wrap up here."

Tremont laughed. "No, you can't. And absolutely not. The doctor cleared me to fly tomorrow. I'll be there by midafternoon—"

"Tremont," she argued, "I'm fine. Stay there. Rest. Get better. I'll manage."

"I love you, Emerson Sterling. I do. But you cannot manage yourself out there. You just can't," he replied.

Emerson was offended. "I can, too."

"Do me a favor?"

"After that insult?" She was half teasing. Half.

"Go to the front door of your suite." He paused. "Go on, I'll wait."

She sighed and walked back through the large bedroom toward the designated living room area. "Okay, I'm here. What now?"

"You're at the door?" Tremont sounded skeptical.

She was by the coffee table but that was close enough. "I am."

"You're lying. I can tell by your voice." He clearly had a spy camera set up. Or he was clairvoyant.

She pulled the phone away from her face and scoffed at it. "That's creepy."

"Go to the door, please."

"Fine." She walked to it and waited. "Now what?"

"Is the security bolt on?" She could tell by the sound of the smile in his voice that he already knew the answer.

"Shut up, Tremont." She slid the security lock closed and turned back toward the living room area.

"Someone could have stolen you, and I would be forced to sell my gorgeous body to pay rent. You need me to remember things like locking the door and your credit card information if you want to buy lady porn after hours."

"I'll just charge all that to the room, duh." She flopped on the couch and dropped her head back onto the cushion. They both knew that Francis was on the job, somewhere out there, and would ensure no one would break into her room, but the lady porn thing was a valid point.

"I expect nothing less," Tremont said. "Do you feel ready for the interview? Or do you want me to cancel?"

She closed her eyes and breathed out slowly. "Canceling was an option all along? Yes. I choose that option."

"It's not an option. I was just trying to give you the chance to make the right decision." He added, "You failed."

"Drat. Foiled again." She yawned. "I'll be fine. I've done this about ninety thousand times before. Smile. Answer their questions. Be charming and polite but a little evasive to keep the mystery alive. Boom. Someone hand me an award, I'm awesome."

"You're *extra*, that's what you are," he said. "And if he brings up Rachel and her cray-cray?"

"I make with the flirty eyes and laugh before telling him that only Hayley gets that inside scoop, so he can suck it."

"Right, except maybe leave out the sucking part. That seems crass," Tremont teased.

Emerson nodded. "I'll consider it."

"I gave him your approved list of talking points"—Tremont was back to being all business...buzzkill—"but expect him to push the boundaries. They all do."

She was prepared for that. "Duly noted."

"Okay, I'll tell them to send him up with security. I assume Hayley is going to observe this."

"Sure. Why should she get the night off?" Emerson was joking, but in truth she wanted Hayley there as a safety blanket, like before. And because she missed her. Which was weird, right?

Tremont agreed. "Damn skippy. I'll call her and send her over."

"Can't I just call her?" Emerson felt like she could manage that.

"Sure. Just give her a ring."

She nodded before a thought occurred to her. "I don't have her number. You always communicate with her."

"Yup."

Dammit. Why was she so sheltered and useless? "You were testing me again."

"Yup."

"Fine. I need you. I'm lost without you," she whined. "Now can you please text me her number."

Her phone buzzed against her ear.

"I already forwarded her contact to you." She checked, it was there. "Okay, I'll send him up in say, fifteen minutes? Is that enough time?"

"Yes sir, Captain, sir." She sat up at the edge of the couch and saluted to no one.

"You're a nut. Good luck. Call me after it's over."

"Will do."

Emerson disconnected and added Hayley's contact into her phone. She sat there for a moment wondering what to say. "Why are you being so weird about this? Just text her and tell her the guy is here. Stop making this a big thing." Great. Now she was talking to herself. She sighed.

Hey, it's Emerson. The magazine guy is coming up. Do you want to sit in on it?

There was a pause before some text bubbles appeared.

how do I kno this is really U? What if this is a trap? I'll need a clue or something

Emerson smiled.

You suck at Uno. So bad. You're the worst.

More bubbles.

Nope. This is an imposter. Bc clearly you were cheating.

I was not cheating. You're just terrible. And you kept showing me your cards. That was true. Hayley really needed to perfect her card holding technique.

An admission! I knew it. More bubbles. *Headed UR way now. U R in the fancy suite at the end of the hall, right?*

Maybe I am. Maybe not. We should have a secret knock, just so I know it's you.

Hayley wrote back immediately: *Shave and a haircut?*

Emerson nodded. *Two bits.*

Hayley replied with a fist emoji and some musical notes.

See? She could totally handle herself. Tremont was overreacting. This was no big deal.

❖

Emerson hated being wrong. Like, really hated it. She especially hated being wrong when it involved Tremont.

Hayley closed the door to her suite and turned before leaning against it. "Well, that happened."

Emerson hung her head and sighed. "How bad was that? Be honest. I can take it."

Hayley ran her hand through her hair and shrugged. "It could have been worse. You could have forgotten your name or room number. Oh, wait, you did."

Emerson collapsed onto the couch and buried her head under a cushion. She emerged and said, "You're going to put that in your article, aren't you?"

Hayley pushed the room service cart farther into the room and poured two water glasses before handing one to Emerson. "Oh, yeah. I'm probably going to lead with it."

Emerson took the glass and sipped its contents. "Judas."

Hayley feigned offense. "Hey, I'm not the one who can't order room service correctly."

Emerson sat up and flapped her arms around. "I panicked. There were so many choices. How was I supposed to pick a dinner when breakfast is available all day. All day, Hayley. That means pancakes for dinner and—"

"Crepes. And fruit cup. And two different bran muffins. A Greek yogurt parfait, an egg white and spinach omelet with goat cheese, and steel-cut oatmeal." Hayley uncovered each dish and pointed to the second shelf of trays below. "And also a burger, fries, two different milkshakes, and a mixed-greens salad with honey mustard dressing *on the side.*"

"Dressing always on the side," she pointed out. "There's no reason to be unhealthy, Hayley."

Hayley pushed the coffee table aside and moved the room service cart into the now open space. "You know, they would have assembled this for you and let you choose the fancy utensils and folded napkins if you asked."

"Asked? I nearly ordered everything on the menu because I couldn't make up my mind. You think if they gave me any other choices, I would have been successful?" Emerson's mouth was watering. The buffet she ordered smelled fantastic.

"All I'm saying is that you managed to make it through that

interview no problem at all. But when you were tasked with picking something to eat, you *crumbled*." Hayley pointed a french fry at her before popping it into her mouth.

"Har, har. A food reference. Funny." She swiped a strawberry off the top of the crepe and moaned in ecstasy. "Yassss."

Hayley gave her a raised eyebrow.

"What? I'm passionate about food." Emerson shrugged and forked the corner of the small pancake.

"I'm learning so much about you." Hayley picked up a milkshake and pointed to it. "Please explain this."

"Well, it's ice cream and milk, and ice, blended to make something spectacular." Emerson took the milkshake from her and sipped it. "This is ridiculously good."

Hayley accepted it when she offered it and tried it herself. "Agreed. Stupendous, really. And I know what a milkshake is. I just wanted to know what possessed you to have them combine these flavors. Why peanut butter and almond? Why not chocolate or vanilla or—?"

"Oreo? Because I got an Oreo one—it's over there." She pointed toward the overflowing food cart. "That one's for you, but I'm willing to share this because it's life changing."

"I can get down with Oreo." Hayley picked up the other shake and smiled.

"And to answer your awfully judgmental question, peanut butter has a high protein count in addition to its deliciousness. And almond milk is fortified with vitamins and minerals."

"There was a method to all this madness?" Hayley waved her hand dramatically at the food cart. "Now you're just lying to me."

Emerson scoffed, "Allow me to educate you, Ms. Carpenter."

Hayley leaned back on the couch and crossed her legs. "I'm all ears, Professor Sterling."

"I like the way that sounds. Very academic and in charge." Emerson considered this a moment. "Isn't there a professor in your screenplay? Tell me about that. We never talk about that."

Hayley waved her off. "Don't try to change the subject. You were about to give me a lesson on the major food groups and how pancakes play a part in them."

"As you wish." She bowed her head and curtsied in her seat. "I shall start with the most important food group: breakfast."

"That's not a food group, Em. That's a meal that occurs at a certain time of day," she pointed out.

"Au contraire. Breakfast can happen anytime. And in this lesson, breakfast is a category of foods."

"Says who?" Hayley was smiling broadly. Emerson liked that she was playing along.

"Me. It's my class." She shook her finger at Hayley. "Don't argue with the teacher or you'll get five demerits."

Hayley's eyebrows rose. She brought her finger and thumb across her closed lips in a zipping motion.

"Right. So, breakfast is the most important meal—"

"And food group." Hayley snapped her mouth shut and covered it with her hand.

Emerson gave her a look. "Of the day. And in that category, we have the essentials: proteins, fiber, natural sugars, dairy, and essential vitamins."

Hayley nodded.

"So we'll start with the obvious ones. Steel-cut oats are loaded with fiber and overflowing with protein. They also have plenty of magnesium and potassium, too. Which everyone knows helps maintain a normal blood pressure and limit muscle cramping, among other things."

"Obviously."

Emerson ignored her. "Onto the omelet. Egg whites are protein heavy and spinach is packed with vitamin A. The goat cheese is full of good fat and more protein. It's filling and delicious. The salad is dark greens laden with fiber and vitamins. The bran muffin is—"

"Full of fiber. And vitamins," Hayley added.

"Exactly. Plus, there are cranberries in there, and who doesn't love cranberries?"

"Agreed. I'm an East Coaster. We love us some cranberries around here."

Emerson gave her a high five. "Cranberries are great for cocktails and dried snacks and are one of the few major fruits that are native to North America. They have vitamin C and good, natural sugars. Basically, cranberries are the bomb."

"Okay, this is all well and good and I'm sure you could wax poetic about all the food on the cart, but I really want to know about the pancakes. Where do pancakes fall in all this?"

"Oh." Emerson felt a little shy. "I got those for you."

Hayley looked surprised. "For me?"

"Yeah." Emerson scooted closer to Hayley and forked the edge of the pancake. She collected some syrup with the edge of the fork and brought it to Hayley's mouth. "The menu said they contain blueberries from Maine. I remembered you saying that your favorite memory growing up was at your grandmother's cabin on the lake. I figured you'd like a reminder of that."

Hayley took a bite and closed her eyes. Emerson was careful to remove the fork delicately, her attention drawn to the way Hayley's lips hugged the metal. Hayley hummed happily, and Emerson was glad she'd added the pancakes to the dinner list.

Hayley opened her eyes and Emerson realized she was still hovering with the fork. She started to move away when Hayley took her hand and held her there. She watched as Hayley took the fork from her and gathered some of the large, lush blueberries from atop the pancake stack. She twirled them in the whipped cream and brought them to Emerson's lips.

"This is my favorite dessert." Hayley's voice was soft. "Wild Maine blueberries picked from the backyard and freshly whipped heavy cream from the farm just down the road. This is the taste of summer and my childhood. This is the memory I search for when I'm having a bad day."

Emerson opened her mouth and accepted Hayley's offering. The bursting sweetness of the blueberries was delightful as it combined with the richness of the cream. This was a perfect dish all by itself. "Wow."

Hayley nodded and handed the fork back to Emerson. "That whipped cream is good. But it's not as good as the cream from Boudreaux's Farm."

"I'd like to try it." Emerson was aware of how close they were sitting. And of how close they were speaking.

"I'll take you there sometime." Hayley had the most expressive hazel eyes. They shone with a brightness that captivated Emerson. Her long dark lashes fluttered, and Emerson felt mesmerized. Hayley gave her a small smile. Her lips looked so soft and inviting. Shit. This impromptu dinner was giving her all kinds of impromptu thoughts.

She placed the fork back on the pancake plate—safely out of reach of her hormones and libido—and tried not to think about how badly she wanted Hayley to take her to the quiet Maine farm. Or to her bedroom fifteen feet away. Either or.

CHAPTER FIFTEEN

Hayley couldn't quite believe what was happening. She was lounging on the couch with Emerson having *all* the food and she'd just offered to take Emerson to the funky little milk farm next to her grandmother's cabin. After she fed her whipped cream. Directly to her lips. She must be dreaming. There was a lot of silence. Was it quiet in here? *Say something, Hayley.*

"Have you always been into food this way?" *That's what you decided to lead with? Cool.*

Emerson smiled and seemed relaxed. It occurred to Hayley that this might be the most relaxed she'd ever seen her. Maybe the food question wasn't lame after all. She mentally fist pumped.

"Yes and no. I love food. I love flavors and tastes and the experience of eating. I love the socialness of it. And the intimacy of it. But I have a very specific job with very specific requirements. And I have to be smart about what kind of food I put into my body. My profession depends on it."

"So ordering all this food the night before a reshoot and costume fitting for the movie isn't an issue for you?" Hayley teased.

"I like to taste things." Emerson reached out and swiped her finger through the hazelnut and chocolate drizzled on the crepe. She brought it to her mouth and slipped it past her lips. "Mm. That's what I mean. I could never consume all that food. But I can taste it. Little bites of all of it, or medium bites, or all the bites. That's my choice. But I try to make smart choices about the things I put in front of me. So, yes, there's protein in my milkshake. But it's still a milkshake. And it's delicious."

Are. You. Freaking. Kidding. Me? Hayley was sure she was dead.

She'd died, and her family was going to think it was from eating every breakfast food imaginable. But it was actually from Emerson licking Nutella off her finger. Her life was not lost in vain. She had seen it all.

A miracle happened. Hayley found words from the afterlife. "Is that something you learned from being in the spotlight?"

Emerson picked up the Greek yogurt parfait and shifted on the couch. She angled herself toward Hayley while resting her back on the armrest. "Yes. The fuel you put in your body helps to keep you going. The cleaner the fuel, the longer you can run. It's a basic principle." Emerson shrugged. "But I allow myself to live. I work out hard, so I can enjoy food and drink as much as I'd like. It's not always easy, but I think it's worth it."

"It's definitely working. You look amazing." And out the window went the miracle. And her career. Hayley couldn't believe she'd actually said that.

Emerson rested her head on the back of the couch. "Thank you." She abandoned the parfait and slid down a little, stretching out her legs and rolling her neck. Hayley mirrored her position to give her more space. Emerson gave her an appreciative nod and crossed her ankles next to Hayley's hip.

"It's dangerous talking to you, Hayley. It feels too easy." Emerson's voice was soft, like a purr.

Hayley knew what she meant. "That's kind of the point, isn't it?"

Emerson shrugged. "Maybe."

Hayley thought about the interview from before the feast arrived. "You were different with the *Improper Bostonian* guy."

"Different from now?" Emerson leaned forward to exchange her milkshake for a water, and in the process her legs brushed against Hayley's side. Hayley was aware of their warmth. And her desire to rest her hands on them.

"You were polite in that you answered all his questions, but you didn't really *share* anything with him." She motioned between them. "I feel like you share things with me."

Emerson rested her head on her hand. "I do." She paused. "I have a hard time remembering I'm supposed to be working around you. I have a hard time reminding myself to remain guarded. I seem to lose time with you."

Hayley wasn't expecting Emerson to be so honest. Nor was she expecting to be so flattered. But she felt it, too. Being with Emerson like this, on the couch, sharing things about herself—it felt totally normal. And right. And that was ridiculous, right? "I know what you mean."

Emerson nodded. "I know you do. That's why it's so tricky with you. Because it's not. It's just too damn easy."

"Can I ask you something?" Hayley had been thinking about something Emerson didn't answer from earlier. Clearly this guy had been given talking points and advised away from some questions, but he'd asked something that had caused Emerson to pause. One of her tells appeared—she crossed her left leg over her right and broke eye contact to take a sip of water. He'd asked her if she was happy. She'd said yes, but her eyes had dimmed. She was lying.

"I'm always afraid you will." She smiled with a sigh.

"Because you're afraid you won't want to tell me?" Hayley gave in to her desire and dropped her hand to Emerson's leg.

Emerson's eyes went to her hand and she massaged the skin softly. "No, because I'm afraid I will."

"Are you happy, Emerson?" Hayley rubbed her thumb along Emerson's shin. She wanted to slip under the cuff of her pants and feel her skin. She'd bet her life it was the softest skin she'd ever felt.

"In this moment I am. Here, with my milkshakes. Talking with you." Emerson looked up at her with those incredible eyes, and she could swear she saw want reflected back in them.

She slipped her hand under the bottom of Emerson's pants and smiled. She was as soft as she'd hoped. She continued to massage Emerson's calf as she asked again, "And outside of this room? Outside of this vacuum? What about then?"

Emerson closed her eyes and shifted lower. Hayley pulled Emerson's feet up onto her lap and attended to her other leg. Emerson's breath was so quiet and even, that she thought she'd fallen asleep.

"There's a lot of expectation and chaos outside these walls." She was surprised when Emerson spoke. "Someone always wants something from me. An endorsement, or an affirmation, a headline…They want my picture. They want me to be perfect, but they pay a handsome price to catch me in the most imperfect positions. People hang from trees to get a glimpse of my life and publish it for all to see. Out there it feels like someone is always around the next corner, waiting to take it all away. And sometimes I think that's okay. Sometimes I think I'd give it up without a fight."

Hayley moved lower and took Emerson's right foot in her hands. Her skin was flawless, impossibly soft and smooth. Her toenails were painted a deep red with one tiny daisy on each big toe. She caressed the skin on the top of her foot. "You mean people like Rachel?"

Emerson didn't move. She didn't breathe. She just lay there, still. Hayley worried that she'd pushed too hard. But they'd danced around this for long enough. If Emerson wanted Hayley to get the naked truth, she'd have to share it with her.

When Emerson opened her eyes, she looked tired. She looked… defeated. "Exactly people like that."

"Emerson." Hayley was at a crossroads. She thought she wanted to know what happened between them more than anything. And she had a feeling that if she asked, Emerson would tell her. But as she brushed against her skin and felt her warmth, she didn't think she could do it. She didn't think she could ask the hard questions. She didn't *want* to.

Emerson seemed to understand. She sat up and pulled her legs from Hayley's hands. She tucked her knees under her chin and braced herself. "Ask me, Hayley. I'll tell you."

Hayley sighed. "I know you will."

Emerson blinked. Her eyes welled with tears and something broke in Hayley.

Before she realized what she was doing, she'd moved forward and knelt in front of Emerson. Emerson looked up at her and she saw it again, the want. The need. She felt it, too. She dipped her head and Emerson's hands cupped her face as she pulled their lips together.

The kiss was earth-shattering. The softness of Emerson's lips was more than she could ever have imagined, and the electricity she felt was almost too much to handle. Emerson held her close, clutching at her jaw, and Hayley gasped because she had wanted this for so long, so badly, that it didn't feel real. But it was. And Emerson's lips moved against hers in a way that felt too good to be true. Too much and not enough at the same time.

Emerson leaned back and pulled Hayley down on top of her, and Hayley's hand threaded into Emerson's hair to keep her mouth close. Emerson kissed her hard and deep, and Hayley lost her breath because she had never been kissed with such *want* before. She moaned into Emerson's mouth and was rewarded with Emerson's tongue against hers. Emerson's hand slid up her side under her shirt and settled at her back. She made little circles against her skin and Hayley shuddered. She felt dizzy. Breathing was clearly on the back burner to the kissing. So much kissing. She gasped and pulled back.

Emerson ran her hand along Hayley's cheek and through her hair. She looked up at her with a smile. "I've wanted to kiss you all day."

"Just today? Because I've wanted to kiss you for weeks. But I'm glad you finally came around—"

Emerson's lips were on hers again, and she forgot what she was saying. Emerson sucked her bottom lip between her teeth, and Hayley felt her insides ignite. Emerson licked her lip and held her mouth close as she breathed out, "No one said anything about coming yet. Just kissing."

"Fuck." Hayley felt like she might explode.

"Maybe if you're lucky." Emerson was hell-bent on killing her. It was decided.

Hayley didn't know what to say. Emerson laughed and pecked her lips. She shifted out from under Hayley to reach her nearby water. She sipped it before offering it to Hayley, who accepted with a shaky hand, the energy of their kiss still pulsing through her.

The water felt cool on her lips. It was refreshing but in a different way than the way Emerson's lips felt. That was refreshing, too. Like it had been exactly what she needed and didn't know it, except she sort of did, or hoped for, anyway.

She put the water aside and ran her thumb against Emerson's bottom lip. It was cold from the water. Damp, too. She closed the distance between them and held her lips against Emerson's. She savored the sensation.

After a few moments, Emerson broke the kiss and rested her forehead against Hayley's. "Ask me."

"Marry me?"

Emerson laughed and shook her head. "I have too much baggage to answer that question right now."

Hayley tried again. "Do you want to get married? Ever? Is that something you see yourself doing?"

Emerson reached out and entwined their hands. "Sure. The idea doesn't scare me, if that's what you're asking. But I don't know that I'm ready for that yet, sorry."

Hayley gave her an exaggerated pout. "It was worth a shot."

Emerson nodded. "Mm-hmm."

Hayley took a deep breath. She knew what Emerson was getting at before, but she realized she didn't need to know. She'd had an epiphany: it didn't matter. "You don't have to tell me, Emerson. I have enough information about you to write the piece without that."

Emerson looked at her and she got the impression Emerson really *saw* her in that moment.

Still, she wanted to make sure she understood. "I told you before that I was working on my screenplay a bit, remember?"

"I do." Her expression was thoughtful.

"Well the truth is, I have. I found my muse. And it's you." Hayley exhaled. "The thing is, Emerson, I could have written that entire piece about you after you interrogated me on that balcony."

Emerson winced. "I'm sorry about that. In hindsight it seems a little harsh."

"It wasn't. It was exactly what I needed to check my privilege and understand the depth and complexity of what you were asking of me. You needed me to see you for who you really were, not some circus animal that the media salivates over. You aren't here for other people's enjoyment. You aren't obligated to give anyone anything, information or otherwise. And I needed to see that from your perspective. Which required me being a little uncomfortable for a short while." She paused. "But that's all it was—a short while. It wasn't my whole life or every waking minute of my existence. I'm not chased or pursued or *hunted*. I'm free to exist in the world in any way I see fit, and that's just fucking fine because I'm nobody."

"Hayley, you're not." Emerson took her hand.

She entwined their fingers together. "I'm okay with being nobody. I'm more than happy to be sitting behind my laptop and writing stories for people like you to bring to life on the big screen. That's what I want in this world, Emerson. To write and play and be creative."

She took a breath. "So like I said before, I have more than enough to finish your article. And if I'm being honest? It's basically already done. Selfishly, I've been enjoying my time with you and dragging the process out for as long as possible. But in that bag—and in the cloud, because I've learned that horrible lesson more than once—is the skeleton of the entire article. Soup to nuts. Complete and requiring only a fresh set of eyes to edit and few big words to make me sound smarter than I am. But the content is essentially done. I wrote your story, Emerson. You gave me everything I needed to understand you and what you represent. Anything more you give me from this point on is just because you want to, not because I need you to."

Emerson's face was unreadable. She looked almost confused, which Hayley hated, because she was pretty sure she'd just used way too many words to say what she'd been trying to say.

"Hayley, if you don't mention Rachel or her accusations in that article, you're going to be dragged by the masses. People are counting on you to unearth the dark secrets that Rachel has been implying exist. Or at least, they expect you to counter those insinuations with my side of the story." She paused. "A story that I asked you to write for me. I knew what I was getting into."

She rubbed her thumb along the back of Emerson's hand. "That's entirely the point, Emerson. You don't owe anyone an explanation. So what if you did have an affair with Rachel? You're both consenting adults, right? It doesn't matter. And it shouldn't detract from *Willow Path* and what you hope it will represent for audiences. It's all distraction and noise obscuring the bigger picture."

"That's all fine and good but…" Emerson looked pained. "Hayley, you have to write about the Rachel angle, or you'll be ruined."

Hayley felt like that should concern her more than it did. She was feeling a lot of things right now, but concern for her career was not one of them. "Emerson, I don't care. I'm happy to have you weigh in, but I don't want anything from you."

She motioned between them. "Except this. Whatever this is, this friendship with the unexpected awesomeness of kissing or just a regular run-of-the-mill friendship without kissing, that's fine, too. Less awesome, but still awesome."

Emerson laughed, and Hayley pressed on. "I care about this. I care about you. I don't care about anything outside this room and this vacuum. If I've learned anything over the time I've spent with you, it's that there is no controlling the uncontrollable. I don't care to try."

"I've never met anyone like you." Emerson kissed her and held her close.

"The kissing implies that's a good thing, right?" Hayley smiled against Emerson's lips and stopped worrying when Emerson's tongue slid along hers.

"It's a very good thing." Emerson kissed away from her lips to suck on her pulse point and Hayley's sex throbbed. Emerson shifted her flat on her back again and lowered her mouth to Hayley's collarbone, licking and sucking as she went.

Hayley closed her eyes at the sensation and threaded her hands into Emerson's hair. The weight of Emerson's body held her in place but her hips begged to cant up. She missed Emerson's mouth on hers, but she loved the sensation of her lips caressing the skin of her chest and neck. "You feel so good."

Emerson unbuttoned Hayley's plaid shirt and pushed it off her shoulders, trapping her arms by her side. She lowered her mouth to the swell of Hayley's breast under the edge of the tank top and dragged her tongue along the curve of the fabric.

"Do you have any idea how long I've wanted to do this with you? To taste your skin and feel my lips on you?" Emerson's fingers skimmed along her chest, palming over her breast, and settled just below her navel before moving lower. She stroked along the seam over the crotch of Hayley's jeans and asked, "Do you have any idea how long I've wanted to feel your lips around me?"

"God." Hayley panted. "You have no idea how badly I've wanted you to. Please."

Emerson moaned and pressed harder against her crotch. Hayley rolled her hips up, seeking Emerson's friction. She wriggled her arms out of the shirt and discarded it on the floor, as she pulled Emerson on top of her and held her there with one hand at her low back, while the other gripped Emerson's jaw.

Emerson kissed her hard and ground her hips against Hayley's, her hand still trapped between them over the fabric of Hayley's jeans. Hayley's hand left Emerson's back to flick open the button and unzip her fly. "Please, Emerson."

Emerson nodded and deepened the kiss, and Hayley saw stars when Emerson's free hand traced circles over her nipple through her bra before twisting and pulling at the erect flesh. Hayley felt herself climbing. She wouldn't last long at this pace. She begged, "Emerson."

Emerson pulled back and Hayley looked up into the dark, wanting eyes above her. "I'm not ready for this to end." Emerson seemed as short of breath as Hayley felt.

"Make me come and I promise I'll come for you again and again." Hayley had no doubt she'd carry her end of the bargain.

Emerson's mouth dropped open and she licked her lips. She shifted her hips to straddle Hayley's leg and pressed her center down on it. Hayley could feel the heat of Emerson's cunt through her jeans and she twitched. Emerson lowered her lips to Hayley's ear and slipped her hand beneath the offending fabric that kept them apart. As she glided along Hayley's lips and collected her wetness, she breathed out, "That is the single sexiest thing anyone has ever said to me."

She slid inside Hayley and ground her hips down along Hayley's leg and that was all Hayley could take. She bucked up against Emerson's hand and the delicious weight of her body with a blinding climax that left her breathless. Her body tremored and shook with each thrust and rub of Emerson's hand against her sex. She clutched at Emerson's hips, encouraging her motion, and palmed at Emerson's breast through her shirt.

Emerson ducked her head and let out short sharp breaths as her rhythm got more and more erratic. Hayley struggled to keep her thigh still against Emerson's movements while her clit continued to throb with Emerson's fingers still firmly inside her, moving in and out just enough to prevent the blissful shock waves from subsiding.

"Kiss me while you come, Emerson." Hayley nudged her nose along Emerson's jaw in an effort to reach her lips. "I want to taste your release on your lips. I dream about those lips, Emerson. Kiss me."

Emerson turned her head and connected their lips as she trembled against Hayley's leg. She moaned into Hayley's mouth and shuddered as Hayley slipped her hand under Emerson's shirt and under her bra to cup her naked breast. The weight and swell of the tissue in her hand gave Hayley the boost of energy she needed to drive her thigh up against Emerson on her next thrust, and Emerson called out as she came hard and fast against Hayley's leg. "Fuck."

Hayley held their lips together as Emerson slid out of her. She kissed her slowly and deeply as Emerson caught her breath, her body stretched out on top of her like the warmest and sexiest blanket she'd ever had. She released Emerson's breast only long enough to help her out of her shirt. She sat up on her elbows as Emerson unhooked her bra and dropped it to the floor next to Hayley's forgotten shirt. Hayley shrugged off her bra and settled back on her elbows.

Without anything between them now, Hayley was able to see Emerson's chest for the first time. It was everything she'd expected and more. She bent forward and took one of Emerson's nipples between her lips. She stroked her tongue along it while she sucked gently. "You're so beautiful, Emerson."

"You are unreal." Emerson's hand was in her hair, holding her lips in place as she purred above her. "Hayley?"

Hayley moved to the other breast and massaged the flesh with her lips. "Yeah?"

Emerson gripped her chin and pulled her up until they were eye level. "I hope you meant what you said before because I have every intention to make you come like that all night."

Hayley kissed Emerson because she could. "What are you waiting for, then?"

CHAPTER SIXTEEN

You never called me back last night," Tremont said.

"Oh?" She'd had more important things to tend to. Namely, making Hayley scream as often as possible. Hayley had more than kept to her promise last night. It was glorious.

"There's a picture of you in this gossip rag," Tremont added dully from behind the magazine as he lounged on his couch. He had FaceTimed Emerson a few minutes ago to catch up with her and help her navigate her day at the movie studio while she was doing reshoots. She'd popped back into her trailer to review some script edits and enjoy some downtime while they set up the next few scenes. Tremont's FaceTime call was a happy surprise but also a nerve-inducing one, considering the events of last night. She wasn't sure she wanted to tell him about that yet. She had some things she wanted to figure out first.

Emerson didn't bother looking up from the script rewrites. "And that's new and different because?"

The sound of Tremont yawning in the background made her yawn as well. She hadn't gotten much sleep last night. Not that she had any regrets about that. "Because this one is bound to stir up some trouble."

That got Emerson's attention. "Why? What did I do this time?"

Tremont cleared his throat and read the headline. "*Emerson Sterling seen cuddling with mystery brunette and tiny fan on flight.*" He turned the magazine and showed her a picture of her tickling Wendy on the flight to Boston. Hayley was seated to her right but turned in such a way that her face was hidden.

"Her hair is auburn. Not brunette." Emerson returned to her script review. "I don't see what the big deal is. That could be anyone."

Tremont looked at her silently until she looked back up at him. "What?"

He pointed to the picture again, holding his finger in place until she noticed what he was focused on: she was holding Hayley's hand. The photo had been snapped during the tickle fight.

Tremont spun the magazine and read on. "Emerson appeared more than comfortable with her seatmate, who is rumored by insiders to be the woman Emerson was spotted looking cozy with last week on the studio lot. Over the six-hour flight they could be seen snuggling close and laughing while playing cards. No news yet on this mystery woman, but if the smile on Emerson's face was any indication, this lady is special."

Emerson cringed at that last part. The picture was innocent enough, albeit out of context. But she couldn't dismiss the other information that had been true. She *had* enjoyed her time with Hayley. And that was before the time she'd enjoyed with Hayley between the sheets, all night long. Which was enjoyable in a much more significant and memorable way than the flight. She crossed her legs and smiled at the gentle ache from their play last night. She became acutely aware of how little clothing she had on. She'd had so many outfit changes on set today already, she'd decided the robe and her undergarments were enough for her downtime between takes. "It's nothing, Tremont. You and I both know that people see what they want to see."

"This is coming right on the heels of Rachel's most recent dish session, Em."

This was true. Rachel had leaked a little more of her side of the story last night while doing some press for a new movie she was working on. She was on *Extra*, flirting with the reporter, when he brought up *Willow Path* at the end of the interview. Rachel danced around it a bit before telling him that Emerson had seduced her by asking her to practice their kissing scene behind closed doors, to help set the tone for when they were in front of the camera. She made it a point to cry and blubber that she'd felt like they'd had a real connection, and he handed her a tissue, which of course made her cry harder. It was all hearsay—and total garbage—but damn, that woman could act devastated better than anyone she knew.

Emerson scowled and pushed the script aside. "I can't seem to get out from under that bitch, can I? Not everything comes back to who people think I am or am not sleeping with. Speculation is what got me in this mess to begin with. Ignore it."

"Funny, I always imagined you the top in that particular dance," Tremont teased.

Emerson just glared at him.

"You know David is going to want to make a statement or pose you with someone at next week's fund-raiser," Tremont added.

"Let him try and see where that gets him." She focused her attention to the script in her hand.

"What's your plan with him?"

Emerson raised her eyebrow but didn't look up from her rewrites. "I haven't figured that out yet. Right now, I need him to be a part of the team."

"And then? What happens when you don't need him anymore?"

Emerson sighed. "Then we go our separate ways. I can't forgive him, Tremont. I tried."

"Fine by me. I never liked the little weasel." He laughed. That was true. David and Tremont never got along. Just like Tremont and Rachel. But Hayley, on the other hand...No. She needed to focus.

Emerson looked back at the page in front of her and willed the words to settle in her brain. They had finished filming so long ago she'd forgotten about the energy and the emotion in this scene. Reshoots this late in the game were unusual, but then again, firing one of the leads more than halfway through filming was also unusual. She and Johnny had other contract obligations, and trying to get everyone in the same place again had been near impossible. The last thing she wanted to be doing right now was reshooting a scene in Boston when her attention was needed elsewhere.

"You know what I meant before about the headline causing an issue, right?" Tremont's tone was gentle. That was all she needed to hear from him. She knew. How could she forget. She needed to call Deidre and see how Rory was doing from her perspective. She fired off a quick text to her sister while they talked.

"I was hoping you were just worried about my image and bad press," she said, hoping to deflect, but knowing it wouldn't work. It was worth the try, she supposed.

"Em."

She pushed the script away. This was hopeless. "That picture is going to piss Rachel off. We both know that." Deidre and Rory were fresh in her mind, and she'd be lying if she said she wasn't a little nervous about Rachel being provoked into shaming her family. She was wary of Rachel's power and influence in the press. This was uncharted territory, and the privacy of her sister and her niece was at stake. The thought made her sick.

Tremont nodded, his expression bleak.

"Hey, T?" Emerson hadn't broached this topic with him yet, but it was now or never.

"What?"

"I'm going to tell Hayley about Rory. I want her to include it in the article."

Tremont sat up taller. There was a pause. "Are you sure about that? It's one thing to tell her about Rachel and have her write a little ditty about how great you are behind the scenes, but it's a whole 'nother animal to tell her about Rory. David doesn't even know about Rory. No one does."

Emerson sighed. "I know. But we need to make the first move. We need to be bold to limit the backlash. We need to—"

"Thrust Rory into the spotlight?" Tremont seemed unconvinced.

She closed her eyes to gather her thoughts. "I talked it over with Deidre and Tom, and I think it's the best choice. It's been my plan all along, I just wasn't sure it would be necessary. But you said so yourself, Rachel is escalating. We need to act now. I don't want her to take this from me. She's taken so much already, but she can't take my truth. I won't allow it."

Tremont looked stunned. And Emerson felt the same way. She hadn't meant to be so candid. She didn't even realize that was how she felt until the words had left her mouth.

"Okay." Tremont nodded and let out a long exhale. "Shit is gonna get super complicated."

Emerson laughed. "Truth."

"Are you sure Hayley's up to the challenge? Do you really trust her that much, Em?"

"I do." Emerson didn't hesitate in her reply. She didn't have to. She knew it in her soul that Hayley was the right person for the job.

Hayley had the talent. She had lots of talents, actually, particularly a slew of new ones Emerson had just discovered last night, but none of those had to be mentioned to Tremont in this exact moment.

"This is heavy stuff, Emerson. Are you sure you don't want me there now? I could be there by midnight."

"I'm fine. Stay there, get better. I'm going to need you well." She appreciated his concern, but she felt like she needed to have this conversation with Hayley alone. There were lots of things she wanted to do with Hayley alone…

"Oh, I see, you've replaced me with Hayley." He teased her and pointed to the photograph, tapping it. "You two do look awfully cozy."

"Don't even start." Cozy seemed to be the word of the day. She'd been awfully cozy in her bed this morning with Hayley. Hayley had stayed with her until the very last second because the bed was perfect, and Hayley was incredible and why not? By the time they reconvened and got down to the waiting car, Emerson was running forty minutes late. Hayley was adorably shy in the car ride with her to the movie lot. They sat close in the back of the hired car but didn't have much time to talk since Emerson had to field a call from the studio during the ride. She'd peeked over Hayley's shoulder and seen that she was working on something, but she couldn't tell what it was. She'd reached out and stroked Hayley's cheek while she typed because she'd wanted to. Hayley had nuzzled against her, and she felt like they had an understanding. She didn't want Hayley to feel like last night was a one-off. To feel like she wasn't important. Emerson had given in to her lust, that was for sure, but she cared about Hayley, too. "I don't need you encouraging me to make any bad decisions. I do that plenty well on my own, thanks."

Tremont clucked. "Well, now. Bad decisions, you say? That sounds like there's been something on your mind to make a decision about."

Shit. So much for keeping things to herself. She decided to try and play it cool. Share but not share too much. She did it with the media all the time. She could do it with Tremont, right?

"Ooh, girl. You like her, don't you? It's because she's sassy, isn't it?" Tremont clapped and held up his hand. "It's her butt. She's got a great butt. I noticed. I'm a butt guy."

Emerson nodded. That was a fair assessment. Hayley had a really fantastic ass. She'd gotten more than a handful last night. Stop. *Stop thinking about Hayley naked, or he's going to figure it out.* "Wait, you've been looking at her butt?"

"No. But that nod tells me that you have."

He was so sneaky. She loved it. "Maybe a little." More than looked. She crossed her legs again as she felt herself flush from last night's memories. She was glad he was on the phone and not in person.

"Okay. Progress. Tell me more. What it is about Lois Lane that's got you holding her hand on an airplane of all things? The flying metal coffin of doom isn't exactly what I would have picked as your most romantic first date preference."

She'd been sorting through some of this on her own for the last few hours, so when Tremont opened the door, she stepped through it. "She's different. It's like she knows we're in this bubble, right? Like we're in this very fragile existence and any outside or inside force can cause it to burst so she savors the moments in it. I never feel like she's distracted around me—"

"So, you're saying she's obsessed," Tremont joked.

"Not even. That's the thing. I really get the impression that she doesn't give a crap about my celebrity or my presence or what other people think of me. I don't know how to explain it." This was all true, not just intuition on her part—Hayley had confirmed these beliefs last night. Her gut told her this was a fact. Time would tell, she supposed.

"It's like…" She paused. She was normally so well-spoken. So rehearsed. So practiced. "It's like when we're alone, talking about the movie or nothing at all, I feel free. Like I can just be a person who exists on this planet, talking to a pretty girl with an enormous brain who is smart and funny and sarcastic, and for a few blissful minutes I'm not Emerson Sterling. I'm not Willow Path, and I'm not being head-hunted by my crazy ex-girlfriend for her fifteen minutes of fame."

Tremont just looked at her with big eyes. "Well, damn."

"What? I said a lot of things there. You'll need to be a little more specific."

"That's the first time you've ever called Rachel your ex-girlfriend. Ever."

She gaped at him. "Seriously? That's where you went with all that? Back to Rachel?"

He shrugged. "It seemed relevant to mention."

She huffed. "Rachel is a complicated mess. Hayley isn't."

Tremont crossed his arms and raised his eyebrow at her. "Oh, sure. Falling for the one person who's supposed to give a clear and unbiased account of you as a person and a media personality sounds as uncomplicated as possible. No complications there. None."

She gave him a look.

"I'm just saying, maybe give this a little space. You've got some heavy lifting to do in the family department. Maybe focus your energies there while we wait for Rachel's next bombshell." Tremont looked pained. "I hate having to say that."

"I hate hearing it." Emerson pouted. "But we aren't going to just wait around, Tremont. We have a plan. We just have to implement it."

He nodded. "All kidding aside, I really do like her, though. Hayley. She's good people. And I think you two would be cute together if that ever happened."

She smiled, seeming to have convinced him it was just a crush and not already a bedroom encounter. A knock at her trailer door distracted her from replying. "Come in."

Hayley popped her head up from the stairs. Emerson turned the screen toward Hayley and she waved. "Hey, Scoobies. Having a meeting?"

"That all depends. Where are your glasses, Velma?" Tremont asked.

Hayley stuck her tongue out at him and settled into the bench next Emerson, so they could talk to him together. "They're reading glasses, Tremont. Not investigation glasses."

Emerson snorted. She was happy to see Hayley. She was hoping to use the downtime today to discuss last night's events.

"You're smiley." Tremont gave Hayley a suspicious look.

"It's sunny. And I'm caffeinated. Plus, doughnuts are in abundance at the craft service table, which—conveniently—is immediately outside Emerson's trailer." Hayley patted her belly and sighed. "Delicious, delicious doughnuts."

Tremont frowned. "Don't remind me."

"Missing those old sugar days, Montie?" Emerson teased. She'd been surprised how loyal Tremont had been to Sebastian's diet and exercise plan. Doughnuts were a serious weakness for him. Something she'd mentioned to Hayley when they were gossiping the other day.

If the glint in Hayley's eye was any indication, she'd mentioned the doughnuts on purpose.

"You're evil." He pointed at Emerson and his image vibrated. He smiled at the screen.

"Speaking of the devil," Hayley said. "Tremont smiling and a vibrating phone screen mean one and only one thing."

Emerson nodded. "Text from Sebastian."

"It's like he knows we're talking about glazed sugary goodness." Hayley tapped her bottom lip and Emerson tried not to think naughty thoughts.

Tremont covered the camera with his hand briefly before he glared at Emerson. "You need to stop gossiping about me to Velma. It's rude."

Emerson merely shrugged. "It gets boring talking about myself all day."

"Yeah, see, calling me Velma is totally a compliment. She was the only smart one of the bunch. Like, genius," Hayley said.

"Mm-hmm. Terrible fashion sense, though." Tremont's image paused, and Emerson assumed he was firing off a text. When he came back to real time, he gave Hayley a teasing once-over.

"That's a matter of opinion. I think she made bold color choices." Hayley stretched. "Some people look good in orange."

Tremont laughed. "No one looks good in orange. No. One."

Hayley feigned offense. "Agree to disagree."

Tremont's screen vibrated again, and his picture froze momentarily. "When's your next teaser due to run?"

Hayley glanced at her naked wrist and her eyebrows rose. "Uh, about two hours, Pacific time."

"Have you finished it?" Tremont asked.

Hayley clasped her hands behind her head and leaned back. Emerson decided she was adorable. "Why? You nervous?"

Tremont scoffed. "Someone is getting comfortable."

"You two fight like siblings," Emerson observed as Tremont's phone buzzed again. "Tremont, go answer your phone. I want to go over some of these script changes with Hayley."

Tremont looked between the two of them. "Why with Hayley?"

Hayley cleared her throat. "We were talking about the movie on the flight. I was curious about the process." That was a total lie, but Emerson was turned on by how quickly Hayley thought on her feet.

She reached under the table and ran her fingers along Hayley's thigh. Hayley smiled, and Emerson took that as a good sign.

"Fine. I'll check in with my temporary replacement over there and find out how much time until they need you on set. I'll be back in a bit." Hayley's fingers found hers under the table and she massaged Emerson's hand.

"Tell Sebastian I said hi," Emerson called out, and Tremont flipped her off as he ended the call.

Hayley turned in the seat so she was facing Emerson. She ran her hand through her hair, and it fell in soft looking waves around her face. "So…"

"So?" Emerson replied.

Hayley blushed and pointed to her wrist. "Any chance you stumbled upon a watch in your suite this morning?"

Emerson cocked her head to the side and gave Hayley her best lazy smile. "What does it look like?"

Hayley leaned back and motioned with her hands. "Oh, you know, it's about yea big, black leather strap. It has little hands that move in a clockwise fashion."

"Silver face?" Emerson narrowed her eyes at Hayley. "Little hands, you say?"

Hayley nodded.

Emerson reached into the pocket of her robe and pulled out the watch, examining it closely. "I'm not totally sure, but could this be it?"

"That's the one." Hayley sounded relieved.

"It's important to you." Emerson traced her fingers along the watch face. It was simple but elegant. She hadn't noticed it before. The leather straps were worn but remained in good condition—Hayley obviously took care of this.

"Very." Hayley added, "It was a gift."

Emerson turned the watch over and read the inscription on the back. *There's no time to waste, Love GG.*

"Who is GG?" Emerson held it out and motioned for Hayley to extend her wrist to her.

"Grandma Ginny." Hayley obliged, and Emerson took her time slipping the watch over Hayley's delicate wrist. She adjusted the strap to the stretched hole indicating Hayley's desired fit. She marveled at the smoothness of the stitching along the leather.

"What's she like?" She abandoned the watch strap in favor of making circles on the skin on the underside of Hayley's wrist.

"Was like." She looked up to see sadness in Hayley's eyes. "She passed away right after I moved to LA. This was the gift she gave me before I left. She told me that I'd wasted so much time and talent running from my own dreams that I had to take the leap and head to Hollyweird, as she called it. She told me time was precious and I shouldn't squander it."

Emerson took her hand and squeezed it. "I'm sorry for your loss. She sounds like a very smart lady."

Hayley traced her thumb along Emerson's as she spoke. "She was smart all right. A smart-ass, a smart aleck—you name it, she had it in spades. That woman could slap you with sarcasm so effectively it left your head spinning." She gave Emerson an impish look. "She taught me all kinds of amazing things. My grandfather died young, so she raised my father and his siblings alone for most of their childhood. She was resourceful like no one I've ever met."

"Is she the one with the cabin in Maine?" Emerson asked.

"You remember that?" Hayley looked surprised.

"I pay attention to the important things." Emerson gave her a wink and Hayley entwined their fingers.

"Something tells me you pay attention to *all* the things." Hayley held her gaze before she spoke again. "My grandmother was Maine through and through. She cut her own lumber, drank moonshine from a growler, and cursed like a sailor. She was the best." Emerson liked seeing the happiness return to Hayley's eyes as she spoke of her grandmother. She could tell there were endless stories behind those eyes. She wanted to hear them all.

"Tell me about one of those amazing things she taught you. Can you throw an axe from across the room and split an apple with it?"

"Sadly, no. Although I can fish with just a stick, some fishing line, and a hook." Hayley separated their hands enough so that she could play with Emerson's fingertips. It felt magical.

"That's useful, I guess." She watched their fingers dance along each other.

Hayley paused her movements and Emerson looked up at her. "She did teach me one thing of note."

"What's that?" Emerson wished more of Hayley was touching her.

Although she enjoyed the opportunity to sit next to her, it wasn't enough. She missed the closeness they'd had last night and this morning. She couldn't remember another time in her life when she'd felt so drawn to someone. So needy for their touch. It frightened her a bit.

"She taught me how to whistle."

Emerson thought back to the night on the red carpet, the night they sort of met. "That whistle nearly got you blacklisted from my entire existence."

Hayley frowned and took Emerson's hand between both of hers. "Because you thought I was working with James Drake."

Emerson nodded. She had. She'd even cursed her for it.

"I knew it the moment I saw your face." Hayley looked remorseful. "If it's any consolation, I felt awful that I silenced the crowd enough for him to grill you like that."

Emerson winced. "It wasn't my best poker face, huh?"

Hayley shook her head. "Still a beautiful face, though."

"Ha. Thanks, Hay." She thought about their near conversation about Rachel last night and the pictures in today's celebrity newsreel. They had to talk about the elephant in the room, no matter how much Emerson wanted to avoid it. She owed that to Hayley, and Hayley would need it to properly write her piece. Even if she fought her about it. Hayley's respect for her privacy was noble, but it was foolish. "We should talk."

Hayley's shoulders sagged, and she released Emerson's hand. Emerson missed her touch immediately. "I figured."

"Have you seen today's gossip columns?" Emerson kept her voice light. She didn't want to alarm Hayley.

"I saw your name pop up on *E!* and *TMZ* and my notifications have been buzzing all day. Is there one in particular you were talking about?"

Emerson pulled up the link Tremont had texted her. "The one you're in."

Hayley looked at the image. "This is that amateur paparazzi jerk from the other side of the plane, huh?"

Emerson shrugged. "Hard to tell without the image of the linen queen standing guard."

"It was a valiant attempt."

"It was." Emerson smiled at the memory.

"Are you mad?" Hayley looked sheepish.

"That your cotton blockade didn't work? I thought it was genius. And very chivalrous, I might add."

"Ha-ha. Thanks." Hayley sighed. "I meant, were you mad that someone snapped a pic of us together again. That's twice in as many days. And this one has us holding hands."

Emerson leaned back in her seat. "Better an innocent picture like that than one of the not-so-innocent activities of last night."

Hayley blushed. "Yeah. So, about that…"

Emerson's confidence wilted. "Do you regret that?"

Hayley looked caught off guard. "No. Not for a second. Never." She face-palmed. "That wasn't nearly as overeager sounding in my head. Let me try that again." She closed her eyes and took a breath before opening them. "No, Emerson. I don't regret last night. I had a lovely time, thanks for asking."

Emerson burst out laughing. She needed that. "You're one of a kind, Hayley Carpenter."

"That's a good thing, right?"

"The best." Emerson reached out to cup her cheek. Hayley leaned in to connect their lips, and those familiar butterflies from last night reappeared. Emerson closed her eyes and savored the feeling of Hayley's lips on hers. She felt an unexpected safety through Hayley's touch.

Hayley pulled back and gave her a broad smile. "I'm all for you telling me how great and wonderful I am, but I feel like we got sidetracked from a more serious conversation."

Emerson frowned. "I've been watching Drake take the offensive with you more and more lately. And Tremont told me that Drake gave out your work number recently. Is that true?"

Hayley pursed her lips in frustration. "That guy is a first-rate asshole."

"I've also noticed that he seems to be working with Rachel these days." Emerson hating even saying Rachel's name.

"If she is anything like him, they deserve each other." Hayley crossed her arms and huffed. Her expression softened. "I saw her *Extra* interview last night."

Emerson nodded. She figured that was inevitable. "We should probably talk about that, too."

When Hayley didn't say anything, Emerson slipped past her out of the booth and began pacing her trailer. She felt like she had to be moving to drum up the courage to talk about this. "We need to talk about Rachel and what happened between us."

"There's more to the story than what she's been telling." Emerson found herself vibrating with anxiety. She wanted to tell Hayley everything, to protect her, because she knew the photo on the plane was a tipping point, that Hayley's loss of privacy because of the proximity to Emerson's celebrity was only beginning. She could just feel it. And she needed to talk about Rachel, so she could talk about the more important issue of Rory. "I'm not a bad person, Hayley. Contrary to what Rachel might say, I'm not."

On the fourth trip through the trailer, Hayley intercepted her.

"Hey. You don't have to tread a hole in the carpet." Hayley loosely gripped her arms and held her still. "And you don't need to tell me you're not a bad person. I already know that."

Emerson didn't feel like that, though. She felt like she'd made a lot of bad decisions that led her to this moment in her life, and although she felt the need to verbalize her good intentions, she realized that was because she had such staggering guilt, guilt that had more to do with Rory than Rachel. She had to own those bad decisions, even if Rachel had blown them way out of proportion. But she was afraid of coming off as an ass, all the same. She sighed. "I'm not a good person, Hayley. I've made mistakes. And Rachel Blanche was one of them."

Hayley had been rubbing up and down her arms up to that moment. She stopped and pulled her hands back from Emerson's skin, and Emerson felt the rejection like a punch in the stomach. "You had a sexual relationship with her."

"Yes." Emerson tried to steady the hands at her side that were threatening to shake. "I did."

"And what she said about you, her accusations—they're entirely false?" Hayley was close, but not touching her, and it killed her a little.

Emerson sighed. "Not exactly."

Chapter Seventeen

Hayley didn't say anything because a part of her was in denial. She'd been listening to Rachel bad-mouth vaguely about Emerson for weeks and weeks. But over that time, she'd decided that even if there was a relationship between them, there couldn't be any truth to the villainous personality Rachel described. The Emerson she had gotten to know in that time was not vindictive or duplicitous like Rachel claimed. The Emerson she had gotten to know was wary of the limelight, fearful of being caught off guard, and vulnerable. She was on the defensive, not the attack. Rachel's narrative didn't match up. It couldn't be true. Could it?

The silence seemed to make Emerson jittery. She started pacing again. "It started really casually at first. She'd come by more and more between scenes and lounge around the trailer. We'd run lines and talk about the characters and their quirks in hopes of perfecting the performances and to really understand the nuances of Willow and Rhea. Honestly, I didn't think anything of it. She was so aggressively flirtatious with Johnny—and everyone with a heartbeat—I guess I missed the signals. I thought flirting was just her...voice. Nothing personal.

"What she said last night on *Extra* was partially true. The shift in our relationship *did* occur in my trailer and we *were* rehearsing an emotionally difficult scene that eventually leads to Willow and Rhea kissing for the first time but—I promise you—we weren't rehearsing the kiss. That was all Rachel."

Hayley leaned her hip against the counter and waited. "Go on."

Emerson ran her hand through her hair. "She kissed me at the end of the scene, and I went with it. I assumed she just wanted to work out some nerves before we were in front of the camera, but that wasn't the case. In the film Rhea makes the first move but backtracks after Willow reciprocates, but Rachel never backed off." She stopped pacing and dropped her hands by her sides. "And I don't know what happened next. I know I stopped her and told her I wasn't sure what she wanted, and she told me she wanted me. And then suddenly there it was, like it had been there all along. We were more than costars on *Willow Path*. We were so much more than that."

The disappointment Hayley felt must have been all over her face, because Emerson looked as distressed as she felt. Hayley hated feeling that way, but a tiny part of her had hoped it was all just Rachel spouting off at the mouth. She was...jealous. Which felt stupid because she was just in bed with Emerson last night. Which suddenly made this seem so much more embarrassing...because who else had Emerson fallen into bed with? Anyone that spent any significant amount of time with her? No, that didn't seem like her. But did she really know her? She thought she did. Now she wasn't so sure.

Emerson stepped forward and took Hayley's hands. "Hayley, you see what my life is like. You see how incredibly lonely it can be. Behind the flashing cameras and the television interviews, there's this exhausting sprint of the Hollywood machine. And I made a bad decision. Because even though I knew in my heart that Rachel's motives were for her own gain, I ignored them."

"What does that mean, Emerson? What motives?" Hayley's head felt foggy. All Emerson had done up to this point was confirm Rachel's story. What had she gotten herself into? "I think I need to sit to hear this."

Emerson frowned but nodded. She pulled Hayley back to the bench they'd shared and sat next to her. She turned to face her but left space between them. More space than was there before. But things were different now. How quickly things had changed. That space helped Hayley clear her head. She needed that space to breathe and think. And—most importantly—to listen.

"Rachel is used to being on top, in every sense of the word. She's used to being the prettiest and the highest paid and the most successful and whatever other bullshit she needs to make her ego feel stroked.

What she wasn't used to was not getting her way." Emerson pointed toward the script. "This film is different for a lot of reasons, but one of those reasons is that a female director is at the helm."

"Paige Montgomery," Hayley replied.

"Exactly. And the script was adapted by the original author—"

"Kate Stanton."

"Precisely." Emerson worried her lip before continuing. "Rachel is used to dealing with men—seducing them, playing to their egos to get what she wants, manipulating them...It worked wonderfully with Johnny—she had that moron eating out of her hand—but it didn't work with Kate and Paige. In fact, her little shenanigans backfired in a big way."

"What shenanigans?"

"At first it was little stuff, like she showed up later and later, which cost the already strapped production time and money. And then she wanted rewrites to elevate Rhea's character. She wanted to change the narrative to be more flattering because she felt like the writing didn't portray Rhea in the light she was hoping."

"Which was how, exactly?" Hayley had read the novel. Rhea's character was flawed—that's what had been so appealing to her about the novel and the prospective film. Rhea started out as every bi-curious straight girl Hayley had learned to fear and hate. But her character arc was well done. She was fleshed out and the reader could feel empathetic to her confusion and subsequent struggle. Rhea's character development showed an important and valuable example of sexual fluidity and self-acceptance, even though in the end—spoiler alert!— she denied her true feelings. Hayley had expected the movie version to line up with the book.

Emerson shook her head. "Rachel doesn't live in the same world as the rest of us." She paused. "I know how that sounds coming from me. Let me clarify."

"Please do." Hayley was joking. She felt like they needed levity. Emerson's small smile told her that she'd succeeded.

"Willow and I are not that different. I've been in meaningful relationships with both men and women, but I've chosen women most times." Emerson continued, "But I've been Rhea, too. I fought with myself and my perception of what was allowed and acceptable. In this business, you don't want to pigeonhole yourself. You don't want to be typecast for life because—let's face it—the careers of actresses are shorter than our male counterparts'. When things show any sign of wrinkling or sagging, our expiration date gets moved up."

Hayley tried not to revisit the naked images of Emerson from last night since this was a serious discussion. There was no sagging anywhere there, but she felt like it was inappropriate to mention that at this moment. "You feel like you're expendable."

"A dime a dozen around here in the Land of Beautiful People." Emerson sighed.

Hayley considered the truth of that statement. She was very well aware Rachel was stunningly attractive. And she knew, by society's standards, she couldn't hold a candle to her. But for some reason Emerson seemed to like her—why? That she wasn't sure of. "Okay, so you're like Willow. And Rachel's not?"

Emerson's expression was devoid of emotion. "I'm not going to say that Rachel doesn't have legitimate feelings for any one person, regardless of their sex or sexual identity, but I will say that Rachel loves herself first and above all else. It wouldn't surprise me if she ends up marrying a real-life Disney Prince Charming after all this hoopla, and our short tryst together becomes a talking point for her to propel or enhance some project or movie. I didn't matter to Rachel in the grand scheme of things. I was a means to an end. A stepping stone for world domination. But she didn't count on the director and the screenwriter being gay women who could smell her fraudulence better than I could. I was too close to it. Or too foolish to accept it."

Hayley hadn't seen Emerson so detached and cold like this before. It made her uncomfortable. "Paige and Kate knew?"

"Not exactly. I think they suspected it. But I tried hard to keep it under wraps. I knew what it would look like in the media. I wanted to feel it out a bit before I made any grand statements or gestures."

Hayley could have done without that word choice, but she didn't mention that either.

"Her on-set antics started to piss everyone off, and when she tried to change the direction of the storyline, Kate nearly killed her." Emerson laughed. "Rachel has a volatile, at times violent, temper. That was something I learned about her behind the scenes. She was the jealous type, but it was more than about relationships or affection from someone else. She was the jealous type about fame and esteem as well. Rachel was used to casting shadows, not being in one."

Hayley considered this. She'd read interviews from Paige and Kate regarding the movie and the filming process and both women had gushed praise after praise about Emerson's work. They talked about her professionalism, her work ethic, her raw intensity and authenticity. Kate said she'd written this role with Emerson in mind but hadn't told Emerson that until after she'd signed on. She'd said an interview Emerson gave while still in her teens just stuck with her for years and years. Their affection and respect for Emerson was clear as day. Hayley got the impression they had a different take on Rachel. "You cast the shadow this time."

Emerson looked shy. "This is the role of my lifetime and I know it. I knew it the day I saw the script. To leave anything on the table would be a disservice to myself and this story. I ate, drank, and slept this role."

"Interesting word choice." Hayley couldn't help herself. She was a little jealous, okay?

"Ouch." Emerson feigned a dramatically wounded look before getting serious again. "I didn't seduce Rachel. I let myself get fooled into thinking there might be something there when there most definitely wasn't. I'm guilty of being a fool. And naïve. And I hate myself for that. But I'm not some evil seductress out to ruin Rachel's career. She did that all on her own. I won't take the blame for that."

Hayley didn't know how to feel. The disbelief was fading away, in its place the cold, hard truth. Emerson and Rachel had had a relationship. She might as well start there. "How long did it go on?"

"A few months. Three, tops. The film was shot quickly and on a tight schedule. We got involved after the first quarter of filming was completed."

Emerson was giving her that direct answer thing from last night, the one she'd used with the *Improper Bostonian* guy. Hayley didn't like it. She wanted *her* Emerson back. The thought made her sad all over again. As if she was privy to anything or had any ownership over this thing between them. If it was anything at all. Her insecurity flared. "Why didn't you tell me earlier?"

Emerson looked surprised. "I offered to—"

"Last night." Hayley pointed out, "I've asked you directly and indirectly nearly a dozen times and you shut me down. Why now?"

Emerson's tone was soft. "Things are different now."

"And why's that? Because we slept together?" Hayley could hear the trepidation in her voice and willed it to stop.

"Yes." Emerson blinked.

Ouch. She was telling her out of pity. Or—worse—out of a feeling of obligation. Ugh.

"But that's not the only reason." Emerson reached for her hand but hesitated, instead stopping just short. "Hayley, what I said before was true."

"The part about falling into bed with Rachel and keeping it a secret?" Hayley hated herself for saying that because she could tell that Emerson was struggling here.

Emerson's eyes flashed with hurt and Hayley hated herself a little more. "Hayley. Don't. I…"

Hayley kept her mouth shut because Emerson was trying to tell her something and all she could do was insult her.

"Last night was important to me. It is important to me, in the present tense, as in *in this moment*. I don't share myself, Hayley. I don't give myself to people. I can't. I get hurt and used and discarded. I'm—"

"Expendable." Hayley softened. She could see it now. A little of it. She thought she could anyway.

Emerson nodded. "I'm a cover story. A payday. A headline. I'm everything Rachel thought I was and more. I'm ashamed of how easy I made it for her."

Hayley could see the regret etched across Emerson's face, and she felt guilty all over again. "Do you love her?"

"What?" Emerson looked shocked. "No. God, no. Not even a little. We had a brief relationship, completely devoid of emotion or sentimentality. Or sincerity, for that matter. It was the Rachel show through and through. And deep down, I knew that all along. I just ignored it until it was too late."

"And now?" Hayley traced the outline of Emerson's face with her eyes. Her mind was racing, and her heart was, too. Emerson had gone out of her way to tell her that last night was important. She wanted to talk about that some more, but she needed more answers.

Emerson shrugged and deflated against the cushion behind them. "And now I'm fighting a losing battle in the court of public opinion and I'm exhausted."

"Is that why you don't fight back?" Hayley had been wondering that all along. "Is it really such a big deal that you two were in a relationship?"

Emerson's expression as unreadable and Hayley was confused all over again. "It's more complicated than that."

"Why?" she challenged. "Why not just cop to it and tell your side of the story?"

Emerson looked away. A tell. She wasn't being entirely honest.

"Emerson."

Emerson blinked and took a breath. "There's a lot of moving pieces in this puzzle, Hayley. The studio, the financial backers of the film, the film itself, my career, all of it. There are more reasons to stay quiet and let Rachel self-destruct than there are to stand up and fight back." Emerson paused. "But I am fighting back. I have you. You are going to set the record straight, lay it all out there. The good, the bad, the ugly. I'm trusting you to do just that. That was always the plan."

Emerson looked at her and the vulnerability from before reappeared. The softness from last night, the need. It was there on her face, in her eyes, so loud that Hayley could feel it.

"You're unlike anyone I've ever met, Hayley. You're different. Things are different because you're different. Not because we slept together—which I already told you meant something to me. No. It's more than that. I can't quite find the words, but it's more. *You are more.* More than I'm used to, more than I can comprehend. More. And it's wonderful and scary and palpable."

Emerson reached out again, but this time she didn't stop. She caressed Hayley's cheek and Hayley didn't have any insecurities anymore. She was brought back to last night on that couch and her impulse was to protect Emerson. To shield her and care for her. She cared for Emerson and it was undeniable. And the look in Emerson's eyes told her the feeling was mutual.

Emerson leaned forward and rested her forehead against Hayley's and Hayley was glad to have her close again. She decided she didn't need the space after all. She had a lot to unpack about this conversation, but she knew the end result would be the same. Emerson was here—in this moment, in front of her, open and exposed—and she wouldn't turn away from that. She couldn't. "Last night was important to me, too."

Emerson leaned back and studied her face. She gave Hayley an almost imperceptible nod before saying, "I've been thinking about it all morning. I can't focus on anything else. Every time I close my eyes, I see you and I want to touch you and feel you. And I probably shouldn't, but I do. And it's all I can think about—"

Hayley closed the distance between them and pressed her lips to Emerson's. She couldn't talk about it anymore. She needed to feel it. To taste it. Because she'd felt the same way Emerson described. Last night had been incredible for a million different reasons, but Emerson was reason numero uno.

Chapter Eighteen

Emerson closed her eyes at the feeling of Hayley's lips on hers, and she forgot about all the stress and anxiety that conversation had stirred up in her. They had more to talk about, but now didn't seem like the time. Right now she wanted to be in the moment with Hayley. Maybe everything would be okay. Maybe she could have this—this happiness, this closeness—with Hayley and still juggle the rest of life's chaos. Maybe she could make this work. She wanted it so badly.

"Has anyone told you you're an amazing kisser?" Hayley spoke across her lips before kissing her harder. Emerson opened her mouth to let Hayley's tongue in. Hayley purred, and Emerson felt herself warm all over. That was a noise she could hear all day and not get tired of.

"Not like that, they haven't." She kissed away from Hayley's lips to suck on her jaw. Hayley's arms settled around her shoulders, holding her close.

"Like what?" Hayley dipped her chin to kiss Emerson again and Emerson laughed against her lips.

"Like they were grateful about it." Emerson pulled back to look at Hayley.

Hayley bit her lip and Emerson leaned forward to soothe it with her tongue. Hayley pulled back at the last second to add, "Well, I am grateful about it."

Emerson reconnected their mouths and danced her tongue across Hayley's bottom lip, sucking it between hers and massaging the flesh with her tongue. Hayley's thumb stroked behind her ear and she let out a contented sigh. "Kissing you, Hayley, is something to be grateful for. I'm just glad you think I'm good at it."

Hayley leaned back and shook her head. "You are everything and nothing like I expected you to be."

Emerson leaned her head on the back of the cushioned bench they shared and rested her chin on her hand. "Oh?"

Hayley brushed a loose strand of hair behind Emerson's ear and her eyes sparkled as she answered. "You're tender and soft. And sweet. I don't think I expected you to be so sweet."

Emerson warmed at the compliment. "I like to consider myself pretty versatile in the romance department, but I'll accept that observation," she teased.

Hayley gave her a mischievous look. "That was not in any way an attempt to put you in a box, Emerson. If last night was a glimpse of even a fraction of what you are capable of—"

Emerson reached out and pressed her finger to Hayley's lips, quieting her. "I have to read over these script changes, but the more you speak and the more those lips move, the more I want to taste them…and you. So I need you to be really sexy and brilliant over there for a few minutes, so I can get some work done."

Hayley opened her mouth and licked Emerson's finger and Emerson about died.

"Fuck the script, they can give me the lines as needed." She pushed the papers away and pulled Hayley to her by her shirt.

Hayley's hand slipped between the lapels of her robe and grazed her stomach and Emerson wondered if there was a way she could lock her trailer door from up here. Hayley's hand moved south and soothed the top of her thigh and Emerson needed to be free of the small dining table and bench arrangement.

"Hayley." She accepted Hayley's kiss with enthusiasm.

Hayley untied her robe and pushed apart the plush fabric, resulting in a rush of cool air that made Emerson's skin prickle. "Yeah, Em?"

Emerson pushed Hayley toward the end of the bench and stumbled out after her. "This bench is intimate as fuck and all, but there's a bed right through that door and I need to be on it and under you, okay?"

Hayley's eyes were dark as she nodded in understanding. They only made it two steps toward their destination when Emerson's phone rang. Tremont was trying to FaceTime.

Emerson let out an exasperated noise. "The fucking timing around here, seriously."

She was careful to ignore his call and not accept it. The last thing she needed was for Tremont to get an eyeful of Hayley's hands all over her near-naked chest. She closed her eyes at the sensation and forgot what she had been doing.

"Bed, Emerson." Hayley palmed her breasts over her bra and licked along the lace of the cup.

Oh, right. Emerson nodded and moved toward the slightly ajar door to the bedroom again, when Tremont's face reappeared on her phone screen. The FaceTime ringtone taunted her. "Motherfucker," she whined and silenced it again.

Hayley dropped to her knees and kissed across Emerson's stomach. "He's going to keep calling, Em. You'd better just answer and get it over with."

Emerson's mouth dropped open as Hayley's tongue slid along the waistband of her panties. She wouldn't dare, would she?

Tremont called for a third time and Hayley pulled Emerson's panties off with her teeth. Hayley pushed Emerson's hips back against the kitchenette counter and pressed her hand flat against Emerson's stomach, holding her in place as she eased her legs apart and lowered her mouth to Emerson's center.

"Oh God." Emerson's breath caught in her throat when Hayley's mouth met her lips. Hayley teased and licked along her sex in the most maddeningly delicious way. Emerson felt sure that in that moment she would do just about anything to feel Hayley's tongue on her clit.

"You're so wet." Hayley's voice vibrated against her and her knees buckled. Hayley's hand pressed against her abdomen to stabilize her. "Don't go anywhere just yet."

Emerson looked down and caught Hayley watching her. Her chest tightened at the sight. Hayley had some sort of power over her, and it had nothing to do with the incredible things she was doing with her tongue at the moment. Although, that was awfully powerful, too. Her phone vibrated again, and she tossed it on the counter behind her, preferring to run her hands through Hayley's hair instead. "I'm all yours, Hay."

Hayley closed her eyes and dipped her head. Her tongue slid into Emerson with a practiced ease that Emerson was beyond grateful for. She hooked behind Emerson's knee and guided Emerson's leg to her shoulder, and Emerson saw stars.

Emerson loved the way Hayley was so confident with her, like she knew what she wanted and needed. And right now, she needed to feel Hayley's tongue deeper inside her. "Please, Hayley."

Hayley looked up at her again, and she moved her hands from Hayley's hair to stroke along her cheek. Hayley turned her head to kiss Emerson's fingertips and Emerson froze—she wasn't used to such intimacy. It was giving her all kinds of feelings she wasn't ready to process. Before her brain could sabotage the moment, Hayley sucked two of her fingers into her mouth and redirected Emerson's lust to the task at hand—or mouth, as it were.

The sound of a pinball machine coming from Hayley's hip broke them apart, making Emerson painfully aware of how close she was to climax.

Hayley pulled her phone out and held the screen up to Emerson. Tremont was calling.

"Your ringtone for him is a pinball machine?" Emerson was breathless.

Hayley silenced her phone and slipped it back into her pocket. She shrugged and gripped Emerson's leg closer to her shoulder, which brought her mouth inches from Emerson's sex. "Is that what you're thinking about right now?"

"No." Emerson shook her head so hard she got dizzy. "Not at all."

Hayley moved closer, but not close enough. "You sure?"

"Positive."

"What are you thinking about?" Hayley bumped her nose against Emerson's clit and a tremor shot through her.

"Nothing innocent or clean, that's for sure." She threaded her fingers through Hayley's hair again and pulled her head back a bit. "Mostly I'm thinking about how badly I want to come on your face, but I don't know how to politely say that."

Hayley raised her eyebrow and licked her lips. "That was plenty polite."

"Yeah?" Emerson didn't have a chance to say anything else because Hayley went to work making sure she was speechless. And she was. Twice.

CHAPTER NINETEEN

Hayley felt like she was having an out of body experience. Or that she was in someone else's body and living a life she could never have dreamed of. Maybe she had died and gone to heaven. That would make more sense. Because these last two days with Emerson had turned out to be heavenly. In every sense of the word.

Not that they had discussed what this was or anything. Or if it would be anything more than an unchaperoned trip to Boston where evidently nothing was off-limits, including Hayley's full-frontal access to everything Emerson. Everything. All of her. But still, this had to have an expiration date, right? Emerson hadn't hinted to that or said anything along those lines, but Hayley knew this bubble had to burst. This couldn't last, could it? She tried not to think about it.

After their brief encounter in the trailer, Emerson had gone back to work on set. But not before being thoroughly chastised by Tremont for missing his calls. Hayley had tried not to laugh in the background, but it had been near impossible. Emerson had thrown a pillow at her to quiet her down, but that only made her laugh harder. Her punishment from Emerson was an intense make-out session and a quick and dirty climax up against the interior of Emerson's trailer door, so she vowed to do that a million times more.

"Great, Emerson. That was perfect." Paige Montgomery stood from her director's chair and clapped.

"Thanks, Paige." Emerson accepted the towel from the wardrobe assistant and patted her face. They were shooting the final good-bye scene between Willow and Rhea, but scheduling issues were going to force them to edit some shots in after the fact. Piper couldn't be here today, so Emerson was acting in front of a stand-in who was wearing a funny outfit with headgear that had tiny little balls all over it. Hayley was informed that these would act as markers for Piper's face and body to be added in after the fact. This was the only scene left for Emerson for the day, but it had been a long one. And an emotional one. And that was just from Hayley's perspective. She couldn't imagine where Emerson's headspace was, but she had successfully pulled off being devastated and heartbroken as was needed for her character. She'd inquire about where she found that emotional inspiration later.

"I think that's enough for us, Em." Paige turned and called out through a loudspeaker, "That's a wrap on Emerson."

The crew applauded, and someone hooted, causing them all to laugh. Emerson went over and thanked each crew member as the set was broken down. Hayley watched in awe of how easily Emerson chatted with these people. Some of them were local hires, but a majority of them had been with the production all along. They'd weathered this storm with Emerson and the rest of the production team.

Hayley's pocket buzzed, and she fished out her phone. It was Tremont. "Hey, what's up?"

"Someone is taking pictures of her and sneaking video. There are livestreamed images going up online by the minute. What's going on there?"

The anxious tone in his voice hit Hayley square in the gut. "Shit."

"Get her out of there." That wasn't a request.

She noticed Francis off to the side. She'd completely forgotten about him. He seemed to be alerted to this information, too. His brow with pinched in focus and his hand was at his hip.

Hayley looked left and right to find the culprit. Emerson was posing for selfies with a bunch of the crew and people were moving around everywhere—she didn't see anything out of the ordinary. Not that she'd trust herself to notice. This was all out of the ordinary for her.

"I'll get her."

"Be quick about it." Tremont ended the call.

Her phone buzzed again, and she checked it—Tremont had sent her a link. She clicked it and the headline read: *Starlet Unfazed by Brokenhearted Ex: Sterling flirts and canoodles with crew and director while Blanche falls apart.*

An image of Emerson embracing Paige filled the screen. Hayley had been there when it happened, a few moments ago. The photo was juxtaposed with one of Rachel in frozen hysterics from her interview the other night. A second image of Emerson leaning to accept a towel followed the first, and Emerson's hand resting on the assistant's shoulder in gratitude looked like something more. It was completely out of context. This one was paired with one of the grainy photos Rachel's camp had released of Emerson and Rachel between takes during filming. It was the most intimate-looking exchange between them to date. Hayley had been annoyed when it showed up before their flight together. But knowing what she did now, it did more than annoy her. She was straight up mad about it because she knew Emerson would be upset, and that was the last thing she wanted to happen.

Her phone buzzed again, and this time Tremont sent her a link to another media outlet, this one featured Emerson kissing one of the female crew members on the cheek during a selfie. From the vantage of the picture, the person taking these pictures must have been just a few feet away. Hayley scanned the crowd again and thought she saw someone holding a phone against their chest. He was moving away from the group. She waved to Francis and pointed. Francis took off after him and she made a beeline to Emerson.

She dashed forward, nearly knocking down Paige in the process. "Sorry."

"No worries." Paige put her hand on Hayley's shoulder to steady herself. "You all right?"

Hayley looked back at Emerson. "Someone is livestreaming the set and filming Emerson. LA called. I need to get her out of here."

"Not on my set." Paige looked pissed. She reached for the walkie-talkie on her hip and called for security. She called out to the crowd that had gathered, "This is a closed set. No more photos. If I catch you with a camera, you're fired."

Everyone froze, including Emerson. She looked at Hayley and Hayley pointed to her phone mouthing, "We need to go."

Emerson didn't hesitate. She said a quick good-bye and blocked her face with the towel as she raced toward Hayley and off in the direction of her trailer.

"What happened?" Emerson's pace was frantic.

"Someone is taking pictures." Hayley had to hustle to keep up.

"Someone is always taking pictures, Hayley. I'm a zoo animal.

Roar." Emerson held open the door and ushered Hayley inside before joining her.

Hayley would have laughed but her heart was beating too fast. She felt like they were under attack. Emerson's phone chimed, and she answered it on speaker.

"Emerson? Are you in your trailer?" Tremont sounded worried.

"I am." She walked to the kitchenette and grabbed a bottle of water. She sipped it casually before offering it to Hayley.

"Are you okay?"

"I'm fine." Emerson hopped up onto the counter and looked at Hayley. "Why is everyone freaking out?" Her phone buzzed on the counter and she opened the photo Tremont sent over.

Hayley put the bottle down and gaped. The photo was of Hayley and Emerson inside Emerson's trailer, and from the looks of it, this was taken about a minute before things got X-rated.

"Someone is staking out your trailer, Emerson." Tremont voice was flat.

Emerson's face dropped, the gravity of the situation becoming apparent. "Are there any more like this?"

There was a shuffling from Tremont's end of the line. "A few of you and Hayley leaving the hotel this morning, getting into the car. One of you on set working with makeup. One of Hayley watching you run through your lines."

Emerson let out a slow breath. "That's it?"

"Isn't that enough?" Tremont raised his voice. "I don't like this, Emerson. That picture of you and Hayley looks like it was taken from inside the trailer. What were you doing in that picture, anyway?"

Emerson looked up at Hayley and raised her eyebrow. "Running lines."

Tremont was quiet for a moment. "Must have been some dialogue you were working on."

Hayley felt her eyes bug and Emerson rolled hers in response but said nothing.

"Check the windows in there," he said, though it was more of a command.

Hayley walked through the trailer and noticed nothing. Emerson nodded toward the bedroom and Hayley peeked behind the nearly closed door. Right above the bed, the blinds were pulled back. "Son of a bitch."

She turned and saw Emerson in the doorway. She had positioned herself so the door obstructed her from the opening in the blinds. "Well, then. There you have it."

"Have what?" Tremont asked across the line.

"The blinds were open in the bedroom." Emerson turned and walked back toward the dining area.

Hayley closed the door and followed her. That feeling of being violated was heavy in the pit of her stomach.

"How much filming do you have left?" Hayley could hear Tremont's fingers on a keyboard.

"We're done. I'm a wrap." Emerson's face was unreadable. She picked up the bottle Hayley had discarded and drank from it.

"Great. You can fly out tonight. Commercial or private?" Tremont's question sounded more like a statement.

Hayley's alert sounded on her phone and Emerson motioned for her to show her. It was a tweet from Rachel tagging Hayley and Emerson. The picture of Hayley and Emerson from the trailer was split screen next to the one with Emerson's hand on the assistant's shoulder. Rachel's tweet read, *Emerson's favorite four letter word: next.*

Emerson scowled and pushed the phone away. "LAX is going to be crawling with paps, but at least I know what to expect there. Evidently Boston is littered with amateur ninja photogs."

"Logan might be too open for you." Tremont hummed in agreement. "You'll need to come back private."

Emerson looked panicked. Hayley remembered what she'd said before, that the smaller planes made her more nervous than the large commercial airliners. Hayley reached for her. She lowered her voice to afford them some privacy. "I'll help you take your mind off the flight."

Emerson gave her a tight smile and accepted her hand, but only briefly. "Okay."

"I can't hear you. Are we in agreement?" Tremont asked.

"Private. Fine." Emerson sounded as weary as she looked. "But not tonight. I need to rest."

"Tomorrow?" he asked.

"Maybe. I'll get back to you." Emerson gave Hayley a curious expression. "I have an idea of a way to get out of the public eye for a bit. Maybe let things simmer down."

"What does that mean?" Tremont asked. Hayley was wondering the same thing.

"I'll call you later." Emerson disconnected the call and turned to her. "How far from here is it to your grandma's place in Maine?"

"A couple of hours, why?"

Emerson gave her a shaky smile. "I've never been to Maine. I hear it's beautiful. Care to show me?"

Hayley wanted nothing more than to kiss Emerson in that moment, to try to soothe the palpable nerves and stress vibrating off her. But she thought better of it. Maybe getting out of town was the perfect idea. And her grandmother's remote cabin would certainly offer them some privacy and give Emerson a place to rest without someone spying through a window.

She nodded. "I'd love to."

Chapter Twenty

Emerson looked out the window of Hayley's rental car and let herself zone out. They went back to the hotel to gather their stuff but didn't formally check out. Emerson hoped they could sneak out before someone caught wind. Against Tremont's advice, she brushed off Francis and told him she'd see him when they flew out. No one was thrilled by this idea, but she needed a break from everyone who wasn't Hayley.

Hayley offered to rent a car in her name and drive, since she knew the way. Emerson was grateful not to have to think about any of the details. She hadn't been a front seat passenger in so long, she'd forgotten how enjoyable it could be. She was letting herself soak it up.

Hayley glanced over at her from time to time but otherwise kept her eyes on the road. She had been beyond patient, not asking too much of Emerson since Tremont's call in the trailer. Emerson would be lying if she said she wasn't a little unnerved by the whole thing. That picture of her with Hayley could have been much worse. Part of her wondered if there were more scandalous pictures waiting to come out. She worried about Hayley. She worried about her sister. She worried about Rory.

She checked her phone. Deidre had texted back and said they were doing okay. She told Deidre about the newest pictures and let her know that she planned to lay out the truth to Hayley as soon as they were at the cabin. She encouraged Deidre to take the kids out of town for the weekend to let things blow over. She wanted them as far away from the internet as possible. If Rachel chose this weekend to drop any bombs, she was too far away to do damage control. And she was doing plenty of damage on her own out here. Hayley turned the dial on the radio and she felt a pang of guilt. She'd dragged Hayley into this. This was all her fault.

She should have told Hayley about Rory in the trailer earlier, but she knew she had to be on set in a short time. She'd told herself that she didn't want to rush that reveal, but she knew a part of her was being a total coward. She chose to be selfish and Rachel's video, tweets, and photo leak caught her unawares. Which was precisely what she was trying to avoid. But she let her feelings for Hayley cloud her judgment in that moment. In all the moments.

"Everything okay?" Hayley checked in before shifting in her seat a bit. She looked uncomfortable. Emerson wanted to ask why.

"Uh, yeah. Just checking in on my sister." Emerson hadn't planned to be so forthcoming.

Hayley nodded but kept her eyes on the road. "Is she okay?"

That was a loaded question. "She's worried about me. That's all."

Hayley hummed. Emerson could tell Hayley was worried, too.

"I'm sorry about all this, Hayley."

Hayley looked at her. "Why are you sorry?"

Emerson ran her hand through her hair and turned in her seat to face Hayley. "Because this is what I do. I manage to fuck things up by just existing. That's what you should put in your story, Hay, that my existence in this world is a black hole that sucks in innocent bystanders. And I'm sorry."

Hayley gave her a look. "That's the most dramatic thing I've heard from you yet, and today you did a convincing job acting devastated about being dumped by a woman in a bright green full body onesie with tennis balls Velcroed to her head. So that's saying something."

Emerson laughed.

"Seriously, I was totally convinced she'd broken your heart."

"Thanks." Emerson turned back toward the window and watched the trees as they passed by. They'd been on the road for a little over two hours now and the night sky glittered with stars. There was no smog here, no pollution-clouded sky. Emerson looked up and she could see the endless forever. It was humbling.

"What's your sister like?" Hayley's question caught her off guard.

"Deidre? She's steady and calm and hilarious," Emerson replied.

"She's reliable and has always been my greatest support. She's great. I couldn't have asked for a better sister."

"And she has kids? You mentioned you have a niece and nephew."

Another pang of guilt and another complicated question. "Rory and Alex. Dee's a great mom."

"Are you three close?" Hayley flipped on a blinker and Emerson strained to see a path in front of them. The road was shifting from pavement to dirt, and the visibility—although the night was clear—was limited to the length of the headlights. They were off the beaten track, that was for sure.

"The four of us are. Dee's husband Tom is pretty fantastic, too." He was a great dad. The thought made her sad all over again. Poor Tom.

"I meant to ask you before how you started working on the Zelda Frog series. Did it have anything to do with your sister's kids?" Hayley slowed the car as they climbed up a steep hill to the left. Emerson's eyes were glued to the road. Hayley had put her on moose watch about an hour ago. She'd thought she was kidding. Suddenly she wasn't so sure.

"Yes. I felt like there weren't enough positive female role models out there for little girls. When Rory was born, I was suddenly more aware of that than ever. I felt like there needed to be some sort of character that could help teach morals through tough lessons while still remaining innocent enough to be generally accepted." This was true. Except the thought had occurred to her during labor when she was walking through the hospital gift shop during contractions and only saw pink, frilly things for girls while boys had action figures and adventure-themed toys and clothes as gifts.

"And adorable. Because Zelda Frog is freaking too cute," Hayley supplied.

"That she is."

"I did a little research into the book series and show. There isn't much out there about Rafaela Silver. How did you two get connected? Did you hear about her in your travels? She's a mystery." Hayley flicked on her high beams as the road they traveled on shifted to one entirely made of dirt.

"You could say we're intimately acquainted." Emerson mused. Hayley could be taking her off into the woods to kill her and she'd never know it. The thought amused her.

"Seriously?"

Emerson nodded. "She is I, I am she. We are one and the same."

"Are you freaking kidding me?" Hayley gaped at her.

"I needed to distance myself from acting a bit and wanted to try my hand at some of my own storytelling. The idea for Zelda came after a rather sleepless night helping with Rory...I think I was hallucinating. It worked out for the best." That was true. She left out the part where she was way over her head and had nearly had a breakdown in the process. If not for Deidre, she wasn't sure either she or Rory would have made it through the night. Those were dark days in Emerson's life. It was a miracle something good like Zelda Frog—or her relationship with her sister and Rory—had come out of it.

"I was in a creative slump and needed a change of pace. I could retreat into Zelda's world and hide from my problems. The couple of years out of the limelight helped me heal some parts that had been broken a long time."

"Oh, this was after you set that guy's car on fire," Hayley said.

"Allegedly." Emerson gave her a small smile and looked back out the window.

"How did you settle on the pen name of Rafaela Silver?"

Emerson chuckled. "I'm named after Ralph Waldo Emerson and my last name is Sterling."

Hayley shook her head and laughed. "I can't believe you've been the Zelda Frog mastermind this whole time, and you let me believe you'd only voiced the character. You're so..."

"I'm so what?" Emerson looked back at her.

"Incredible. And complex. And multilayered. And a—"

"Moose."

"What? That was definitely not where I was going with that," Hayley replied.

"No. Moose! Hayley, moose." Emerson pointed ahead of them and Hayley slammed on the brakes, launching them both forward in their seats.

Emerson's hand flew to her chest as she took in the sight. She had never seen such a magnificent creature in all her life. He was positively huge and standing very, very still. Which made Emerson's already rapidly beating heart crawl up into her throat at the thought that he might charge them. Did moose charge? They should back up. Now.

But Hayley didn't seem to share her concern. Instead, she started hysterically laughing.

"Hayley…" Emerson whispered. "Maybe we should back up."

That only made Hayley's laughter increase until tears rolled down her cheeks. Great. Now she was crying. They were in a crisis and Hayley was going to laugh them both into a stampede death. Perfect.

"He's, he's—" Hayley rubbed her eyes as she struggled to speak through hiccups. "Wood."

"What?" Emerson was trying not to make any sudden movements, since Bullwinkle over there was staring right at them. No reason to poke the bear, er, moose.

"He's made of wood. He's fake. It's a carving. My grandmother made it to designate the start of her property." Hayley gasped for breath.

Emerson leaned forward to get a better look at the mammoth. No way. "You're lying."

Hayley burst into a fit of giggles and eased the car forward. Emerson clutched at the dashboard and leaned back. Fresh tears sprang from Hayley's eyes as the laughter started back up.

Hayley pulled closer to the moose and trained the car's high beams on him. Emerson couldn't believe her eyes—the moose was a fake. An enormously real looking behemoth, but a fake.

"You've got to be kidding me." She didn't know what to say.

Hayley let out a giggly sigh. "Emerson, meet Stan. Stan, Emerson."

"Wow."

"I told you, my grandma had a wicked sense of humor. This was her way of making sure tourists and would-be campers didn't show up on her property looking to hunt or hike. She liked her privacy, and this is how she ensured she got it." Hayley drove past Stan with a wave. "It's not nearly as impressive in the daylight. Stan was her first real woodcarving endeavor. He was a learning trial."

"She did that with a knife?" Emerson spun in her seat to watch Stan as they drove away, part of her still unbelieving.

"Stan? Oh God. That would have taken years." Hayley shook her head. "No, no. She used a chainsaw. And a hatchet."

Well, that was unexpected. Emerson shook her head in awe. "Wow. Just, wow."

"I told you, she was quite the character." Hayley pointed through the glass. "And we're here."

Emerson followed the path of her finger and saw a dimly lit, beautiful single-story log cabin at the end of the muddy gravel driveway. Hayley pulled up in front of the old wraparound porch and parked to the right of the front steps. A motion-sensor light over the detached garage to their left shone brightly and Emerson shielded her eyes.

"Home sweet home." Hayley was out of the car before Emerson had a chance to blink out the circles of light in her eyes.

When she could see again, she saw Hayley twirling on the front porch. She looked angelic.

Hayley bounded back down the stairs and pulled open her car door. She tugged her out and gestured to the house in front of them. "This house, this yard, this place…this is where the best memories of my life took place. I know it's not much, but—"

"It's perfect." Hayley's smile was contagious. Even after the long day of shooting and the invasion of privacy and the unexpected road trip, Emerson felt surprisingly relaxed and happy. Hayley had a way of making her feel better about everything. This was no different. Hayley was happy to be here. Emerson was happy, too.

"I just need a second to grab the spare key out back. I'll help you unpack the car in a few." Hayley didn't wait for an answer. She disappeared around the side of the house into the darkness beyond.

Emerson could hear lapping water nearby. She assumed this was the lake Hayley had told her about. The air smelled clean and crisp. It was cool out here—not cold, but cool enough that you would want a sweater. Her skin had thinned in her years of LA living. Location shoots in colder climates always chilled her to the bone. But this wasn't uncomfortably cool, more of an awakening coolness. She felt *alive*.

She looked up at the clear night sky and marveled at the speckles of light above her. Thousands of stars shone and blinked, the sky uninhibited by buildings or monuments here. Only treetops stood between her and the heavens.

"It's unlike anything you've ever seen, right?" Hayley's voice was soft and reverent. "I've traveled a lot in my lifetime, but I've never found a sky like this. Not quite like this. Not as peaceful, or as—"

"Endless." Emerson completed Hayley's sentence. The sky seemed endless. They were such a small, insignificant part to this world when you saw the vastness above you. It was humbling. Emerson shivered, and Hayley ran her hand along her arm.

"Come inside. I'll start a fire to warm you up." Hayley extended her hand toward Emerson and she took it.

Hayley led them up the front steps to the large wooden door. Emerson peeked through the stained-glass window of the door and tried to catch a glimpse of what was inside. She didn't have to wait long. Hayley put a key into the lock and the door groaned in brief protest before opening with a push.

Hayley flicked on a switch and flooded the room with light. She walked through the living room area to the kitchen and turned lights on as she went. The cabin was more spacious than it appeared outside. The furniture was plush and comfortable looking with heavy wooden frames. The couch was facing a fireplace with a mantel made of ornately carved wood. Two overstuffed sitting chairs flanked the couch and a warm but worn looking rug connected the three pieces with a sturdy wooden coffee table anchoring it down. The exposed brick of the chimney was aged and beautiful. The contrast of light and dark woods in this room was lovely. Emerson was excited to see how it looked in the daylight. She wandered into the open concept kitchen area and stepped up to the sink. Through the large bay window over the counter she could see glinting light in the darkness. The lake. It was only a stone's throw from where she stood.

"The sunrise on the lake is incredible. You're in for a treat tomorrow morning." Hayley dropped the small grocery bag they'd picked up on the ride here on the counter and unpacked the fruit and salads. She'd had the forethought to stop and grab some food. Emerson was grateful. She hadn't realized she was hungry until now.

"This place is way bigger than I was expecting." Emerson leaned against the sink and watched Hayley settle in.

"Yeah, I hear that a lot. People assume that since it's one story it's some tiny shoebox inside, but the house is a decent length. And truthfully, you end up spending most of your time on the back deck by the lake. The indoor living space is irrelevant most of the time."

Hayley fiddled with the fireplace and grabbed some wood from behind the front door that Emerson hadn't noticed was there. She poked at something in the base of the fireplace and starting shoving paper and small logs into the metal rack thingy. Hayley struck a match and dropped it onto the woodpile, which simmered and crackled as the flames grew. It occurred to Emerson that she couldn't recall ever seeing someone start a fire in a fireplace. Most of her fire exposure was of the pit variety or inset gas type.

"Do you get to come here often?" Emerson kept her eyes on the flames. The flickering orange and yellow drew her in. The room warmed quickly, another thing she was grateful for.

"No." Hayley stood back and admired her handiwork; the flames were bold and vibrant. She added a few larger logs, placed the safety grate in front of the fireplace, and walked back toward the kitchen. "I wish I did, but Maine is about as far from LA as you can get."

"Good," Emerson mumbled.

Hayley gave her a soft frown. "Do you want to talk about earlier? The pictures?"

"Maybe later." Emerson shrugged. "Or never." She accepted the water bottle Hayley handed her and opened it. "Someone must be here often to keep everything up and running, though, right? It's way too clean and dust-free to be idle for a long time."

"We rent the cabin out for a majority of the year. The family only uses it for summers and some select weeks here or there. But as my cousins, aunts, and uncles have grown older and moved away, fewer and fewer of them show interest in coming back here. It's mostly just my parents and my brother that use it. I stay here for a few weeks at the end of the summer if I can." She tapped her bottle to Emerson's in a celebratory cheer. "We happened to catch it on a free weekend—that was lucky."

Hayley pulled out plates from the white-faced wood cabinets above the sink and went to wash and cut the fruit. Emerson unpacked the rest of the bag's contents onto the large butcher's block countertop of the island. She traced her fingers along the grain of the wood. It was smooth and silky.

Hayley folded a few paper towels in half and placed forks on them. "We've kept as much of the original charm as possible, but there have been some improvements. The original kitchen was a galley type with tiny windows, and it faced the woodshed. My parents updated the layout to allow for better flow and give it an open, entertaining feel. I think they did a good job keeping the rustic charm of the house while pairing it with some modern conveniences."

She tapped the counter. "This is my favorite part of the house, though. This is from a tree that used to be on the edge of the property.

Over the years it started to sag and wither from the harsh storms. My grandmother had it taken down for our safety, since it was in the primo hide-and-go-seek part of her property. She salvaged as much wood as possible and this piece was her dining room table for a long time. As the house changed and the needs of the renters and our family changed, it became the center of the kitchen. The heart of the house. I love it."

"It's beautiful." Emerson was looking at Hayley and talking about the counter. But about Hayley, too. She was glowing here. It was like this place breathed new life into her.

"Thank you." Hayley looked at her and she thought that maybe, just maybe, she knew that Emerson meant that about her as well. She should tell her that she was beautiful. Because she was. Hayley handed her a plate with salad. "Hungry?"

"Famished." Emerson followed her to the couch and sat next to her. She pulled her legs onto the plush cushions, tucking them beneath herself.

Hayley placed the plate of fruit on the coffee table in front of them and grabbed a small throw blanket off the armchair to her right. "Here." She handed it to Emerson. "The fire will get the room pretty hot eventually, but there's no reason to be uncomfortable while you wait."

Emerson draped it over her shoulders and looked at Hayley.

Hayley stopped midchew. "What? Is there something on my face?"

Emerson laughed and took a bite of salad. "No. I was just thinking about something."

Hayley looked relieved and continued eating. "Anything specific?"

Emerson ate a little more to take the edge off the hunger. "I'm really thankful I met you. I was just thinking about the night we first crossed paths."

"The night of Grandma Ginny's famed wolf whistle." Hayley nodded.

"Right." Emerson took a bite of the grilled chicken. It was delicious. "You know, I almost didn't go that night. I nearly backed out of the presenting gig."

"Really?" Hayley asked.

"Really. Rachel's statement nearly spooked me off. I didn't think I could face the media." She finished her plate and set it aside. "But if

I hadn't gone that night, we wouldn't be sitting here right now. And I wouldn't trade this for anything."

Hayley blinked.

"What I'm saying is, I'm glad things worked out the way they did. And I guess that surprises me a little. That's what I was thinking about when you asked me."

Hayley put her plate aside and turned toward Emerson. "You're surprised that you're enjoying your time with me?"

"What? No." Emerson leaned forward to touch Hayley's hand. "Not at all. No, I'm surprised because this"—she motioned between them—"makes all that seem less daunting. I didn't expect to find peace in myself with you. But I do. I feel whole and happy and I know that I probably shouldn't because of the mess that exists outside this door, lurking in LA, waiting to pounce on me when I return. But I'm not worried about it for some reason. And you lit a fire and gave me a blanket and you're kind of perfect."

Hayley gave her a shy smile. "Sometimes I think this is all a dream."

Emerson reached out to touch her cheek. "It's not. But I know what you mean."

Hayley leaned forward and kissed her, and Emerson was grateful again.

As much as it pained her to stifle the moment, Emerson knew she had to take the courage she felt in that instant to talk to Hayley. Really talk to her. It was time.

She pulled back and closed her eyes with a sigh. "I wasn't entirely honest with you earlier."

She heard Hayley shift on the couch in front of her. "Oh?"

Emerson opened her eyes to see Hayley regarding her curiously. "Before, when I said things were complicated and that I wasn't fighting back against Rachel and the media because of the movie and the studio and whatever, well, that's all true, but that's not the real reason I haven't engaged her."

"It's not?" Hayley leaned back and positioned herself against the armrest of the couch. "Then why?"

Emerson reached for her phone and opened her photos. She picked her favorite picture of her sister and her family. She handed the phone to Hayley and pointed to the smiling faces. "This is my sister Dee and her husband Tom. This little guy is Alex, he's a total charmer and schmoozer, the world isn't gonna be able to handle him when he's older. And this"—her finger hovered over Rory—"this is my daughter, Rory."

CHAPTER TWENTY-ONE

Hayley wasn't sure she'd heard Emerson right. Her eyes jumped from the preteen on the screen up to Emerson's face and back again. Did Emerson just say she had a daughter? She could see the clear resemblance, right down to the stunning color of Rory's eyes, but that couldn't be, could it? Was Emerson even old enough to have…"A daughter?"

Emerson nodded. "A daughter. Who is also my niece but was my daughter first."

Hayley was shocked. No, that wasn't right. She was completely blindsided. And hot. Was it hot in here? She felt a little faint. She glanced at the fireplace and realized it was blazing too strongly for her to handle with this new information. "Hold on a second."

She strode over to the fireplace and partly closed the flue, keeping the fire low but still alive so that the room wasn't so warm. When she rejoined Emerson on the couch, she made it a point to put some space between them. She didn't want any distractions for this next part. "I'm going to need you to explain a bit."

Emerson looked at the space between them and a sadness settled across her face. "Yeah. That's fair." She ran her hand through her hair.

"I was fifteen when I had too much to drink at a party and had unprotected sex with my then boyfriend. He drove home drunk from the party and got into a bad one-car accident. He didn't survive. Luckily, I didn't get into the car that night. Unluckily, I got pregnant." She frowned.

Hayley nodded because she didn't know what else to do or say. Nodding felt safe.

Emerson continued, "I was too young to be a good parent, but I found out too late to make the decision to terminate. Not that I think I could have, but the choice wasn't mine any longer. So I had Rory and I was just shy of sixteen. I struggled in those days. I was in the peak of my juvenile television and movie career and I'd kept my pregnancy and delivery a secret in hopes of not derailing what I'd worked for my entire childhood: my fame. But I was miserable and out of control. Later we found out I had postpartum depression, but at the time everyone thought I was just an angry teenager lashing out. My manager, at the time, insisted I get into anger management therapy—you saw how that turned out."

"Ah, the burning car thing." Hayley remembered their conversation earlier.

Emerson shrugged. "I had rage." She continued, "I was a mess. Deidre took me in and helped me take care of Rory. When it became apparent that I couldn't take care of myself, let alone a child, we started looking into adoption options. And we almost went through with it, until Deidre sat me down and asked me to give Rory to her. She was seven years older and she had a normal life and a normal job and a fiancé, Tom, I'd known for years. It seemed like the perfect solution. We could keep Rory in the family and make sure she was cared for and raised by someone that loved her, but I wouldn't have to be the burden of a terrible parent to a kid who had the chance at a better life with someone else. Anyone who wasn't me."

Emerson sighed. "I was selfish and young, and I'd made bad decision after bad decision. But having Rory and giving custody of her to Deidre was the best decision I'd ever made. She had a real chance at happiness with Deidre. We all did."

Hayley was stunned. She tried to picture herself at sixteen. She'd been a rebellious mess with no direction and a penchant for heavy, dark eyeliner. She wasn't fit to be a parent. She wasn't even fit to pass her driver's test—that took four tries. She couldn't fathom the difficulty of having to choose a path for someone so small and so helpless when Emerson was still very much a child herself. "I had no idea."

Emerson watched the dwindling fire for a bit before responding. "I made a promise to Deidre on the day I relinquished custody that I would never interfere with her raising Rory. I had such immense relief on that day. A relief that I wasn't the sole provider for Rory, and a relief that Deidre didn't want me to be anything more than a fun aunt." She looked at Hayley and her expression was pained. "Deidre and I look enough alike that we thought we'd never have to address the issue of biology. We agreed to never tell Rory, unless it was medically necessary or a question of life or death.

"Deidre and Tom got married shortly after Rory was born. Tom had been supportive of the idea all along, and he's raised Hayley as his own. After a few years of trying, they had Alex, but not without difficulty." She frowned and looked away. "For eleven and a half wonderful years, Rory had the best family she could ask for. She had two amazingly loving and supportive parents, an annoying little brother, and a famous aunt who spoiled her rotten but kept her out of the public eye. All that changed when Rachel figured out the connection. The bubble burst and nothing has been the same since."

A million thoughts raced through her head in that moment, but the urge to comfort Emerson was undeniable. Hayley reached out and placed her hand on Emerson's thigh.

Emerson looked up at her and gave her a small smile. She traced the skin on the back of Hayley's hand and she exhaled slowly. "We made the decision to tell Rory the truth before she read about it on *TMZ*. That's why I had to go out of town before this trip to Boston. Having that conversation with her and my sister's family was the hardest thing I've ever had to do. It was awful. And devastating. And life altering. She took it better than I expected, but it's far from over. There's still much to be done and said."

Hayley wondered if that was why Emerson had seemed so stressed at the ADR session and why she was so emotional about talking about Rachel in the hotel last night. That show of vulnerability was what had moved Hayley to kiss her. She had felt so honored to be able to see that side of Emerson, a side she knew didn't see the light of day very often. A part of her felt hurt that Emerson had waited until now to share this with her, but maybe she'd given her as much as she could.

"Rachel and I were never meant to be anything more than what we were. It was short and fast and passionate, and the relationship should have fizzled out with time, but Rachel napalmed it instead. What I said to you all along was true—Rachel's jealousy over celebrity and her perception that I was more liked than her led to the end of our relationship. What I didn't mention to you was that Rachel got David drunk one night and needled him for information about me, and he said something about how important my niece was to me and focused her attention on the topic. Then, a little while later, Rory and Deidre visited me on set during school vacation, and Rachel saw Rory's resemblance to me when she was fooling around with some of Willow's character makeup. I didn't even know she'd made the connection or had the conversation with David until after we'd broken up and she threatened to tell the world about it. I was so stunned that she'd unearthed our secret that I didn't deny it fast enough and Rachel claimed victory."

"That's why you haven't responded to the rumors about your breakup." Hayley finally realized why Emerson never fought back against Rachel in the media.

"She's building a case to make herself appear to be the victim, but I know she's intending to drop the bomb about Rory any day now. Part of me assumed she would do it closer to the release of the film, as a way to attempt to ruin my career and the movie's release. But she's been escalating in her attacks lately."

"So she's blackmailing you to keep quiet." Hayley was working this out as they went.

"She's a peach, isn't she?" Emerson said sarcastically. "She knows I want to keep it a secret, but she also had gambled and lost. By losing her role in *Willow Path*, she was on the rebound and needed a boost to bring her back to relevance. Her tell-all about our relationship is exactly the boost she needed. She can ride the buzz of the film and reinvigorate the rumors surrounding her departure while still managing to look like a victim in the whole scenario. She knows I won't fight with her or defend myself because Rory's privacy is at stake. No amount of potential vindication in the press was worth it to me to ruin Rory's life."

"Jesus." Hayley had no idea the Emerson and Rachel thing was so complicated. "Can I just say that I feel like a total ass for challenging you and arguing with you about your relationship with Rachel?"

"How were you to know?" Emerson said. "I told you it was complicated."

"Understatement of the century." Hayley felt awful. Her mind was a storm of questions and emotions. But something Emerson just said stuck with her. "What did you mean when you said Rachel was escalating? Were you talking about the *Extra* interview?"

"No." Emerson shook her head. "I think she's responsible for the pictures. I think she's becoming more aggressive because she's not happy enough with the response to her mudslinging."

Hayley's immediate reaction was anger. She hadn't been able to shake that feeling of being violated since that picture of her and Emerson in the trailer surfaced. She'd been silently worrying that more was coming. This new information from Emerson made that seem inevitable. She was afraid of what that meant for her. And for Emerson.

Hayley took the hand Emerson had been cradling on her lap and reached out to stroke along Emerson's cheek. Emerson was being honest and vulnerable with her, and she felt like she should match it. "I've never felt as violated in my life as I did when that picture came out today. It scared me a little."

Emerson nodded and pressed Hayley's hand to her face. "I know. I'm so sorry about that."

Hayley rubbed her thumb along Emerson's cheekbone. "It wasn't your fault."

Emerson leaned back, and Hayley missed touching her skin. "It is, though. This is the life, Hayley. There are casualties in this business, and privacy and, sometimes, security are some of them. Rory deserved to be whoever she wanted to be without anyone telling her otherwise. But her relationship to me means she's a target. And you are, too. I can't protect you from anything outside these walls, Hayley. I can't."

"You don't have to." Hayley was no damsel in distress. She didn't need a handler.

Emerson gave her a sad smile. "But I do. That's the hard part. I kinda do. Because without me, this wouldn't be happening to you. That's the theme here. I bring bad things to people's lives."

Hayley disagreed with her, but she didn't see the point in arguing right now. She had more important things to work out. "So, what now?"

Emerson's shoulders drooped, and she looked a little lost. "Now we pull the trigger and cut Rachel off at the pass. I need you to write about Rachel in the piece about me. And I need you to talk about Rory."

Hayley blinked. "You want me to talk about Rory? Are you sure?"

Emerson shrugged. "She's part of the narrative, Hay. She's the most important part. She always has been. My family and I can't live in fear of Rachel pulling the rug out from under us. We need to get on the offensive. I need to tell my side of the story, all of it. And I need you to write it for me."

There it was. All of it. Emerson needed her. She needed her to clear the air and break what would probably be the biggest story of Hayley's career. She should have been more stressed out by that, but her mind went back to last night.

Her face must have shown her feelings because Emerson's response was tentative. "Are you okay with that?"

"Uh, yeah." Hayley hadn't begun to process her feelings about that just yet. "About last night…"

Emerson gave her a knowing frown. "You're second-guessing last night."

"Should I?" Hayley didn't want to. She didn't want to second-guess last night or earlier today or tonight on the couch when Emerson kissed her and this all felt too good to be true. She didn't want any of this to be too good to be true. Not the part where she and Emerson had a connection that felt electric. She hadn't felt this way about someone, well, ever. And she wasn't ready to give that up just yet.

Emerson scooted toward her and cupped her face with her hands. "No. You shouldn't. Hayley, I can be free and vulnerable with you in a way I've never been with anyone before. I'm not sure what this information will do once it's out in the world, but I can promise you that I'm willing to take the leap if you're with me. I don't just want you to write this article, Hay. I want you. Just you. And if that's too much to handle, then I totally get it but—"

Hayley kissed her because words seemed too hard and not enough. "It's not too much to handle"—she motioned between them—"but this space is."

Emerson smiled and slid into her arms, cuddling close. Hayley was relieved to see joy return to her face. That beautiful face. The face she dreamed about and couldn't believe shone brightly for her, like it had over and over these past few months. She didn't know what the future held, but if that beautiful face smiled at her that way, then she could figure it out.

CHAPTER TWENTY-TWO

Waking up next to Hayley felt like coming home. Hayley slept soundly on her side, her breathing a gentle rhythmic lull that kept Emerson in bed longer than her body wanted to stay. The lingering jet lag and time change pulled at her mind and made her body want to be restless, but Hayley's warmth and her soft exhales of slumber made her snuggle closer and ignore her momentary discomfort. Soon she dozed, her arms wrapped around Hayley, keeping her close. Only when she awoke hours later, with the undeniable urge to pee, did she leave the bed. And that was a freaking emergency. But she was greeted with the most incredible day just waiting for her. The sun was shining, the trees were a vibrant green, and the lake, God, that lake, it spoke to her. She had to go to it.

She tiptoed back to the bedroom to find some pants and a robe or something, but when she saw Hayley's plaid shirt poking out from her suitcase, she took it. It was her favorite shirt after all.

She stepped out onto the porch and breathed in deeply. The air was clean and fresh. The sky was blue and cloudless, and the lake was calm, save for a few ripples at the small wooden wharf at the edge of the cabin's yard. She walked across the soft grass and stepped gingerly on bare feet to the end of the pier. A few houses spotted the lake's edge, but for the most part it was empty and untouched. The nearest neighboring wharf was far enough away that Emerson couldn't even see the house it belonged to, just a faint dark blob in the distance. She wondered if any of those belonged to the dairy farm Hayley had mentioned before. Could dairy farms be on lakes? She had no idea, but she knew Hayley would tell her if she asked. Hayley would tell her anything.

And she knew she could do the same, which was evidenced by how surprisingly easy it had been to tell her about Rory last night. Still, she was a little scared about the unknown that awaited their future. Both hers and Rory's and hers and Hayley's. This was a big burden to put on someone. She knew that.

She lowered herself to the edge of the pier and dipped her feet into the cool, clear water below. She had some guilt about being here. About running from her responsibilities. She knew there was a shitstorm brewing back in LA and was confident that *TMZ* or *Buzzfeed* had run pictures of her and Hayley doing more than just talking. That picture of them was set off to the right, so her only hope was the partially closed bedroom door had afforded them some privacy since they'd never made it into the bedroom. Not that she even knew what privacy was anymore, but Hayley still did. And she was worried about what this would do to her. She'd been following Hayley's career closely since they'd met and agreed to work together. Drake was dragging her every chance he got, even going as far as calling her a no-talent hack who only got this job interviewing Emerson because something was going on between them. He'd said that before anything *was* going on between them.

Emerson had inquired about the harassment and how she was doing, but Hayley dismissed her concerns. That photo all but guaranteed she'd be an ongoing target for the paparazzi now. Emerson didn't think she realized that just yet. She didn't want to be the one who broke it to her. But she had to, right? Since this was her fault and all.

She closed her eyes in that moment and tried to shut out the noise in her head. She thought of Deidre and Rory and felt guilty all over again. She was hiding, but they were sitting ducks. She blinked her eyes open and looked out at the water in front of her. It would be easy to slip in and drift away. She wouldn't, but it would be easy. She couldn't do that to them, though. Or to Hayley.

Hayley. Somewhere along the way Hayley had come to be so much more to her than a reporter or a friend. Somewhere she had become *everything*, and Emerson hadn't even realized it had happened. And suddenly, Hayley was there, and she was acutely aware of how much she missed her when she was gone or how much she looked forward to her arriving someplace. And now she was in this perfect paradise and Hayley was just a few hundred feet away, sleeping soundly in the bed they'd shared last night. A night they'd shared that was intimate and wonderful and everything Emerson had needed. Hayley was everything that Emerson needed. Hayley. She was everything.

Emerson sighed. This wasn't supposed to happen like this. This wasn't supposed to be so complicated. But then there was kissing and so many feelings and Hayley's laugh was contagious, and the way she focused when she wrote just consumed Emerson's thoughts. And then she was naked and soft and perfect. And Emerson fell into her arms like she was pulled by an irresistible and powerful magnet.

She was drawn to Hayley and the pull was getting stronger by the minute. And she liked it. She didn't want to fight it. She wanted to be happy. She wanted something that she had convinced herself she couldn't have because of who she was or what people thought they could gain from her. But what she wanted was messy. There was no way around that. It was messy and passionate and life changing, and it was upon her. She was in the midst of it and she wasn't sure how that made her feel.

She looked out at the lake and let herself get lost in its beauty. She could see why Hayley loved it here. She stayed there for a few moments until her stomach growled. As she walked back toward the house, she noticed the porch furniture for the first time. Breakfast on the porch with one of the many books she'd noticed in the bookcase by the fireplace last night sounded like the perfect way to relax and wait for Hayley to wake up. She could figure out all the big, looming questions and uncertainties later. Right now, she wanted to soak up some of Hayley's favorite sun, breathe in Hayley's favorite air, and wait for her favorite, Hayley's kiss.

Hayley rolled to her side and blinked as the sunlight shone through the windows. She sighed. It had all been a dream. She'd known it in her soul, but she hadn't wanted to accept it. But now that she was awake, facing the pending day, there was no hiding from the truth. She'd dreamed it all and as magnificent as it was, it was a figment of her imagination.

She rubbed her eyes and flopped onto her back. She stared up at the slow-moving fan above her and let it ease her into the morning. She slid her hand in along the side of the bed Emerson would have been sleeping on were this not all an amazing hallucination. She found it empty. As was to be expected. But what wasn't expected was the sheets were in such disarray as to imply that side of the bed had been recently occupied.

She sat up with a start and the sheets fell away from her chest. The coolness of the air caused her nipples to harden under the soft cotton T-shirt she wore over a pair of boy shorts and nothing else. She glanced down to the floor and saw her discarded pants next to Emerson's impossibly stylish and expensive boots. It wasn't a dream after all.

She stumbled out of bed toward her suitcase, which sat open on the floor. After a few seconds of digging, she found the comfortable gray sweatpants that she'd packed for her nights in the Boston hotel room. These were her writing pants. She wore them when she had a deadline. They were sort of good luck and a warm hug, all wrapped up into one. She pulled them on and found some socks before she headed out in search of Emerson.

It was early but not too early. She'd missed sunrise on the lake, which saddened her since she wasn't sure when she'd be back here to experience it again. Being here right now was an unexpected gift. For a multitude of reasons. She knew that.

She exited the bedroom and headed toward the kitchen, pausing to check her hair in the bathroom mirror and freshen up a bit. It was warmer today—she could feel it already by the warmth of the floorboards and the heat coming from off the glass. She doubted it was warm enough to swim, but maybe they could sit outside and soak up some sun. *They.* What was she doing? What even was all this?

She stopped by the hallway closet and rummaged through some of the clothes she left here for her stays in the cabin. There was no point hefting all these warm winter clothes with her to the City of Angels where it barely got near freezing. She snatched an old sweatshirt off one of the hangers and thanked her overzealous and neurotic mother for washing it recently—it smelled like fresh linen, even though Hayley couldn't remember the last time she'd worn it.

She slipped it on and padded out to the living room. Still no Emerson in sight. She raked the fireplace to make sure everything was extinguished and made the short trip to the kitchen. That's where she stood when she second-guessed her level of lucidity again. If this wasn't a dream, then she never wanted to sleep again because outside the kitchen window sat the most beautiful sight she had ever seen.

Emerson was stretched out across a lounge chair, her head reclined back and her hair a gorgeous, flowing mass over her shoulders. She was wearing Hayley's plaid shirt again, with a light gray tank top and low-rise jeans that hugged her hips in a way that should be illegal. Her eyes were hidden by dark glasses, but her lips formed a small smile as she read from a book in one hand while holding a cup of something in the other.

Hayley stood there appreciating the peacefulness of the moment. Emerson's image against the lake and forest in the background was positively stunning. Emerson alone was stunning. But seeing her in the place that held Hayley's heart? That made her feel something she wasn't expecting. It made her feel…like Emerson held a piece of her heart as well. Oh, shit. She was falling for Emerson, and somehow, she had foolishly combined her happy place with the mysterious and magnetic woman that was also sort of her happy place, now that she thought of it. Two worlds had collided, and here she was, standing in her grandmother's kitchen looking out at her two favorite views.

She was so fucked.

She thought about yesterday. Things had shifted from one extreme to the other in seemingly no time at all, and the Rachel revelation was only a blip on the radar. She'd started her day waking up next to Emerson after what very well might have been an incredibly hot one-night stand. But it wasn't, not really anyway. And a part of her had known that as soon as they were together again in the car on the way to the shoot location. Emerson had been free with her affection, and something about it took the nerves that Hayley had been feeling and released them. She'd felt at ease. So much so that making out with and hooking up with Emerson just a short while later in the trailer didn't faze her. It felt right. She had the sense that they had both been on the same page for a while now, and that first night in Boston had just opened the door to seemingly endless opportunities.

As she looked out at Emerson now, her heartbeat picked up. She didn't want to close that door again. She wanted this for a long time. She wanted what was brewing between them to blossom into something more. They should talk. She should make sure Emerson was feeling the same way she did. Last night told her that she was.

After they'd talked about Rory, Emerson had settled against her in an almost vulnerable, fragile way. Hayley did her best to soothe her, to comfort her while her mind tried to unpack all the new information. Emerson leaned back after a long while and looked at her. She said nothing, but her eyes spoke volumes. And when she answered Emerson's gaze with a kiss, Emerson kissed her like she *needed* her. That's how all the kissing felt, but last night it was so much more. Last night it was breathtaking. Emerson had stolen her breath on that couch. She couldn't seem to get enough air, and Emerson seemed unquenchable. But it wasn't for sex. Emerson appeared to want Hayley's closeness. It was like she wanted her affection. Hayley had tried to make her feel safe and protected. She'd wrapped her in blankets and pressed kiss after kiss to her face, her eyelids, her lips. They'd cuddled on the couch until Emerson fell asleep, and Hayley lay there with the weight of Emerson against her chest, as she watched the embers in the fireplace die out. She stayed like that for a long time until at some point she dozed off herself. When Emerson stirred in her arms, she moved them both to the master bedroom down the hall. She was barely out of her pants before Emerson pulled her under the covers and wrapped herself around her. It felt incredible to be so needed. She savored it. She hoped Emerson could feel how much she had grown to mean to Hayley.

Hayley thought about that now. This feeling wasn't what she'd felt the day she blocked Drake from filming Emerson. That had been moral obligation. About fairness and justice. That had been a defense of right and wrong, and she'd done it without thinking. But this feeling, the one she had right now looking out at Emerson by the lake and the one she had the first night they kissed? It was the same feeling she had last night when Emerson couldn't be held or kissed enough. She knew what that feeling was. That feeling was the momentous soul-shaking kind of thing that couldn't be undone, couldn't be turned off, and couldn't be ignored. She was in love with Emerson Sterling and there was no way around it.

"I'm so fucking fucked, aren't I?" Hayley said to herself. She half expected the ghost of her grandmother to slap her upside the back of her head. She needed it.

She looked down at the counter just to break the spell of staring at Emerson—which she seemed to have no problem doing, like a total creeper—and she noticed coffee in the coffeepot. Emerson had made her coffee and laid out a saucer and a mug with a spoon. Because of course she did. That woman was perfect. Ignoring that fact was hopeless.

Hayley could see Emerson's smile broaden at the sound of the screen door opening. She walked toward her slowly, cradling her hot coffee so as not to spill it.

"I wasn't sure if you were ever going to wake up." Emerson slid the dark glasses up into her hair, and Hayley was lost in those incredible eyes of hers.

"It's a pretty comfy bed." Hayley shrugged and sat at the foot of Emerson's lounge chair.

Emerson nodded. "It is. Surprisingly more so than that couch." She rubbed her neck with a smile.

"I take personal offense at that statement. I'll have you know you were mostly on me, not the couch, and I happen to have on good authority that I'm amazingly comfortable." Hayley sipped the coffee and winced.

"Too strong? It's too strong isn't it?" Emerson leaned forward with her mouth pulled to one side in a worried expression. "I don't drink coffee, so I never know how many scoops or how much water or why it can't be easier to make…There are a lot of coffee rules I've come to find out. *A lot.*"

Hayley patted her hand and coughed. "It's good. Really. It's fine. Thank you."

Emerson frowned. "It's terrible."

"It's terrible."

Emerson huffed, and it was adorable.

"But it's the thought that counts. It was very, very thoughtful." Hayley traced her fingers along the back of Emerson's hand and squeezed when Emerson touched her back. "How's your warm water and honey?"

Emerson sipped her cup and frowned again. "Cold now."

Hayley reached for it. "Here, let me have it."

Emerson gave her a curious look but handed Hayley the cup. Hayley poured out some of her coffee between the wooden slats of the porch and poured the remainder of Emerson's cup into hers. She stirred it with the spoon and took another sip. "There. Much better."

Emerson looked unconvinced. "You don't need to humor me."

Hayley took a bigger sip. This was a significant improvement. She could totally drink this now. "I'm not. It's delicious. Care to try?"

Emerson held up her hand and shook her head. "Oh no, I'm good."

"You sure?" Hayley leaned closer and teased her. "It's good and strong. You might find the taste rather enjoyable."

Emerson leaned forward, and her eyes sparkled. "I'm not opposed to tasting it. I'd just rather it not be from the cup."

Hayley was confused. "How do you plan to do that exactly?"

Emerson took the hot coffee and placed it on the table next to her. She pulled Hayley to her by her sweatshirt and placed a slow, lingering kiss to her lips.

Hayley melted into her.

"Like that." Emerson leaned back and dragged her thumb over her bottom lip and Hayley suddenly had a desire for something much tastier than coffee.

"Well, damn."

Emerson laughed and stretched in the chair.

Hayley pulled at the bottom of Emerson's shirt, her shirt. "This looks good on you."

"Thank you. Speaking of that"—Emerson cocked her head to the side—"I bet the preliminary shots are in from that photo shoot. We can check them out." She reached next to Hayley's mug for her cell phone, but Hayley stopped her hand.

"Wait." Her thoughts from before came rushing back to her. She knew this blissful quiet couldn't last forever, but she was in no rush to have it end either. "No phones."

Emerson raised an eyebrow at her. "No phones?"

Hayley shook her head. "No. Just for a bit. Just until we can't avoid it any longer. Can we just have some time? Just today?"

Emerson seemed to consider this, and her expression softened. "I'd like that."

Hayley breathed out a sigh of relief, but the words she was trying to stifle came spilling out. "I just, I just want to freeze time a little, you know? We can have this here." She motioned between them and to the lake behind her. "This can be ours for a while. Just us. Here. Without life getting in the way. Is that okay?"

Emerson blinked at her and she thought maybe she'd sounded crazy. She'd said too much. "You'd like that? To freeze time with me, here in your happy place?"

Hayley nodded, but she didn't have the courage to tell Emerson that somewhere along the way *she* had become Hayley's happy place. "I would."

Emerson smiled and cupped her jaw. "I think it's a fantastic idea. And I'm honored you want to share this space with me. And I'm grateful you brought me here. You're kind of my hero."

Hayley turned her head and kissed Emerson's palm. "There's no one else I'd rather be with."

The look in Emerson's eyes told her that she hadn't said too much, even if she felt like she'd betrayed herself with that last bit.

Chapter Twenty-three

Emerson was tired, but it was the good kind of tired. It was the kind of tired that came from a long day of being in the sun and lounging by the lake. It was the kind of tired that followed a dinner of grilled hot dogs and burgers on the patio where Hayley regaled her with stories of her childhood. She and Hayley talked for hours about all the good and the bad and the in between. They talked about Rory and what that had been like for Emerson then, and how she felt about it now. They talked about whether they wanted families and kids. No one had ever asked Emerson if she planned on settling down and having kids one day. She'd never given it much thought because she never truly expected to find someone she could share her life with. But she had a feeling that might be changing. Hayley wanted a big family: kids, a dog, maybe some birds. She loved hearing about that. She wanted that for her. So the tiredness of today didn't matter because it was the kind of tired that came from staying up too late eating s'mores after dinner and learning about the constellations from Hayley. It was a vacation kind of tired. And she loved it.

Emerson couldn't remember another time in her life when she had felt so free and so unencumbered. The past twenty-four hours had been some of the best in her life and she had Hayley to thank for them. But all good things must come to an end, and she needed to get back to the life she'd been avoiding. So this little extra bit of tired she felt this morning—a morning when she was up extra early to make sure she could try to give back to Hayley a little of the magic that she had given her—this tired was entirely worth it.

She kissed Hayley's ear and nibbled on her earlobe. "Hayley, it's time to get up."

Hayley groaned but snuggled closer. "Too early. Shh, sleeping."

Emerson looked down at Hayley. She was gorgeous. She lay there, naked from their night together, wrapped only in sheets and a light blanket. The weather had been so unseasonably warm yesterday and into last night that they'd discarded the duvet. They'd made plenty of their own heat without it.

"Baby. C'mon. I want to show you something." Emerson pulled the sheet away from Hayley's chest and traced the skin along her shoulder to her clavicle. She lowered her lips to the side of Hayley's neck and left warm, openmouthed kisses along the skin.

Hayley hummed and peeked open an eye. She reached up and patted Emerson on the cheek. "You're very convincing. But the sun isn't even up yet."

"I know." Emerson held Hayley's hand against her face briefly before she entwined their fingers. "I want to watch the day begin with you."

Hayley's eyes blinked open and the realization set in. "You remembered."

"You told me it wasn't to be missed. I don't want to miss a thing with you." Emerson was being honest. They'd shared something last night, something she hadn't expected but she was grateful for. Last night they'd made love. It wasn't just lusty fucking or a desperate need to climax. No. Last night had been slow and sensual and endless. It had been emotional, so emotional. She knew it was different than before, and she could tell by the look in Hayley's eyes when she came undone that she'd felt the same way. By telling her about Rory, by trusting her to keep them both safe and do right by them, Emerson felt like she'd opened herself up to a new level of vulnerability than she'd ever had before. They'd ventured into new territory, and she had no intention of turning back. "Watch the sunrise with me, Hayley Carpenter. Be the best part of my morning." She already was.

"As if I could say no to that." Hayley smiled up at her and her heart fluttered in her chest.

"Come on." She pressed a quick kiss to Hayley's lips before she pulled her out of bed. "I'm going to grab some blankets from the couch. Meet me on the porch."

"Yes, ma'am."

Well, that did unexpected things to her clit. She filed that away for the future. Authoritative title use was evidently something she enjoyed hearing from Hayley's mouth. One of many things. She had to leave this room right now, or they would miss all the sunrises.

She hurried to the living room to gather supplies while Hayley got dressed. It was too cool to be out there without any clothes on, although Emerson would be lying if she said she hadn't checked first in hopes of being pleasantly surprised that yesterday's heat wave had continued. She was in no rush to cover up Hayley's beautiful body. Though selfishly she was hoping Hayley would want to snuggle with her to stay warm. So there was that plus side pending.

As she headed toward the porch, she noticed her phone charging on the kitchen island. They'd remained phone free for the day and it had been blissful. During a trip into the kitchen to retrieve some water a little after midnight, she'd shot off a text to Tremont to calm his ass down. He'd left her like a million texts and calls. He'd tried to FaceTime her immediately once she'd sent the text, but she didn't feel like explaining her nudity to him, so she'd ignored it and texted him back instead.

He'd booked them a red-eye out of Boston tonight back to LA. They were flying privately to avoid unwanted attention. Emerson's stomach had flipped at the prospect, but he assured her that it had been absolute chaos while she was offline. She told him that she'd rather not know the details until she was home. If she had to know them at all. She didn't want to taint her last few hours in paradise if she didn't have to.

She placed the phone back on the counter and moved around the kitchen, rushing to finish everything before Hayley came out. She wanted this to be perfect. She hoped it would be.

"Whoa." Hayley stepped out of the screen door with her mouth open in surprise.

Hayley's timing was impeccable. Emerson had just finished setting up their little viewing area. She'd taken a few blankets from the living room and grabbed all the spare pillows she could find and built them a little bed on the back patio facing the lake. "Come on. You're going to miss it."

Hayley shuffled toward her and Emerson thought she was adorable. She was barefoot, wearing a Yale hoodie and those gray sweatpants she'd told Emerson were her lucky writing pants. But Emerson had come to find out that they were just her lucky *everything* pants. And to be fair, they were incredibly comfortable. She'd slipped them on last night during their s'mores date out here. Although she much preferred them on Hayley.

Emerson sat on the sunrise bed and patted the space next to her as she pulled the chilled prosecco from the little cooler she'd found under the sink. She'd smiled when Hayley had grabbed the bubbly at the overpriced little convenience store they'd stopped at to get the food for the weekend. Emerson was touched she'd thought of her.

As she unwrapped the fruit she'd cut up last night, she became aware of Hayley's eyes on her in the darkness. "What?"

Hayley pointed to the little makeshift fruit platter and little plastic cups. "When did you have time to do all this?"

Emerson filled the cups with prosecco and dropped a strawberry into each one. "Sometime between rounds three and four. You were napping. I was surprisingly awake."

Hayley gave her a sated grin. "Round three was particularly fantastic. And exhausting." She paused, her expression changing to one of worry. "You weren't tired? Was it not go—"

Emerson kissed her to silence her unfounded concerns. "Don't think that for even a second. I was just on an endorphin high and needed some water. Because you dehydrate me in the best possible way."

"I will take the compliment and the suggestive nature of said dehydration and wear it as a badge of honor." Hayley made a swirling sign over her heart and Emerson wanted to kiss her again.

She handed her a plastic cup and clinked hers with it. "To sunrises in paradise."

"To sunrises in paradise with you." Hayley's version made Emerson swoon.

She held Hayley's gaze and thought about what Hayley had said. Could this be something that happened again? Ever? Would they be able to weather the shitstorm that awaited them back in LA? Was it even feasible to hope for?

The sky was lightening by the second, and Hayley's hazel eyes sparkled a dazzling green-brown as the light burned behind the trees. Emerson felt like she could look into Hayley's eyes all day and never get tired. She would try to make this work. She'd do whatever it took. She wanted more sunrises in paradise with Hayley.

"It's time." Hayley gave her a small smile and pointed in front of them.

The sun broke through the trees like a fireball emerging from the earth. All around them sounds of nature waking up stirred and amplified. Birds chirped, a distant bullfrog croaked, and crickets played their song as the darkness receded and the day was born before them. But the lake, God, that lake. It shimmered and glistened as though lit from beneath. As the sun rose and cast its orange and pink hues across the sky, the lake came to life. Little ripples formed in elegant circular patterns and spread, dancing farther and farther out until they reached the lake's edge. And in those few moments—in those incredibly humbling minutes when Mother Nature stole her breath and floored her with its untouched beauty—Emerson looked to Hayley and found her watching her again.

"It's…"

Hayley nodded. "I know."

Hayley placed her head on Emerson's shoulder and exhaled. Content. Emerson felt the same way.

"Come here." She shifted back and leaned against the pillows. She spread her legs and pulled Hayley between them, positioning Hayley's back to her front. She pulled Hayley close and rested her chin on Hayley's shoulder as Hayley reclined into her body. Emerson slipped her hands into Hayley's hoodie pocket and held Hayley's hands in hers. It was a sweet and intimate embrace, holding Hayley and watching the sunrise break over the horizon. This was paradise. Holding Hayley, being in the quiet, and seeing the world for what it could really, truly be. Perfect.

"I'm so glad you asked me to take you here, Emerson." Hayley rested her head against her.

"I'm so glad you didn't just take me into the woods and kill me."

"You did sort of blindly follow me."

"I know, right? I was practically asking to be kidnapped and sacrificed to Stan."

"No one would be any the wiser. Stan is a good secret keeper."

"No one *wood* be any the wiser, you mean."

Hayley squeezed her hands and groaned. "That was terrible."

"I've been waiting to say that all weekend. Legit, my time here *wood*'nt be complete without it."

Hayley face-palmed and shook her head. "You're so much dorkier in real life. It's unbelievable that the amazingly sexy woman who wore my shirt and nothing else at that photo shoot the other day is the same woman who just made a series of dreadful lumber jokes."

"And kicked your ass at Uno. Don't forget that part." Emerson squeezed Hayley tight.

"Yup. You're the total package—"

"*Wood* you say I'm really someone to *pine* over?" Emerson huffed as Hayley gave her an elbow jab to the stomach.

"It's a good thing you're gorgeous and great in bed. I'm willing to overlook the other stuff." Hayley snuggled into her embrace and Emerson kissed her temple.

"At least I have that going for me."

"At least."

After a few minutes of comfortable silence, Hayley said, "I meant what I said, Em. I'm so glad you're here with me." Hayley turned her head to look at Emerson and she saw it again. That look from last night. The one that told her they were both in deeper than they'd planned.

"I know." Emerson connected their lips and whispered, "I never want to forget this moment, Hayley. Being here with you feels right."

Hayley pressed their lips together and Emerson slid her hands out of Hayley's pocket to slip under her sweatshirt. She was pleasantly surprised to find that Hayley wasn't wearing anything under this hoodie, and she'd bet the same was true under those pants.

"I love touching you, Hay." She kept their lips connected as she made lazy patterns on Hayley's stomach before she dipped and swirled her fingers around her navel.

"Don't stop." Hayley's tongue was in her mouth and she slid her hands up to cup Hayley's breasts. Feeling the fullness of their weight and how quickly Hayley's nipples reacted to her touch made her wet.

Hayley whined when she teased her nipples between her fingers. "Emerson."

Hayley's hips bucked forward, and Emerson dropped one hand to grip the front of her hip and pull her back against her again.

"You keep saying my name like that, and I'll do anything you ask." Hayley's breaths were getting shorter by the second and Emerson moved under the waistband of her pants to find Hayley naked and waiting for her.

She massaged Hayley's breast as she caressed the inside of Hayley's thigh before moving to her center. Hayley's hand slid up into her hair, holding their mouths tight together, and she bucked her hips again at one particularly bold swipe from Emerson against her clit.

"Ask me. Ask me, Hayley."

"Emerson." Hayley was panting, and she strained under Emerson's touch. "Please. Touch me."

Emerson slipped between her lips and stroked two confident fingers against her opening. "Just touch, Hay?"

Hayley dropped her head back and Emerson licked along the column of her neck. The little desperate noises Hayley made were driving her crazy.

"Fuck me, Emerson. Please, just—" Hayley's hand scratched at the one cupping her breast and she moaned when Emerson slipped inside her. "Yes, there. Don't stop."

Emerson pinched and twisted Hayley's nipple as she held Hayley tightly against her. She angled the heel of her hand against Hayley's clit as she slid in and out of Hayley, harder and faster with every one of Hayley's breathy pants.

Hayley shuddered, and Emerson redoubled her efforts. Hayley climaxed with her kiss-plump lips apart in a silent moan, and Emerson decided she'd never seen anything so beautiful. She kissed her as the last of the darkness receded and the sun shone above them brightly, refusing to be ignored.

"You are perfect, Hayley." Emerson was surprised by the emotion in her voice.

Hayley turned in her lap, shifting forward and draping her legs across Emerson's so they were chest to chest and lips to lips. Her breaths were still short and ragged, but her hands were in Emerson's hair and her eyes were brilliant and sparkling. "Stay with me here forever, Emerson. Stay here with me and start every day like that."

Emerson smiled against her lips. "Just like that?"

"I'm flexible on the positions and the order of things, but basically, yeah, just like that."

"Well, you're definitely flexible, I'll give you that." Emerson kissed her and ran her hand though Hayley's hair.

"Does that sound so bad?" Hayley wrapped her arms around Emerson's neck and leaned forward.

When Hayley's tongue teased across her bottom lip, she shook her head. "It sounds heavenly." It did. Having sex with Hayley was easily her new favorite activity.

"Agreed." Hayley rested her forehead against hers and Emerson breathed in the familiar and comforting smell of Hayley and her fading perfume from the day before. "How much longer do we have?"

Emerson frowned. She lost time around Hayley. She had no idea how long they had been out here, but the sun was bright in the sky above them, marking the end of their escape together. She couldn't keep putting off the inevitable. "A few hours before we have to worry about it. Tremont secured a night flight back to LA. He seems to think it's safer for everyone if we arrive under the cover of darkness."

Hayley leaned back and brushed a hair off Emerson's face. "So we have some time."

"We do."

"Good." Hayley shifted out of Emerson's lap and climbed over her as she pressed her back to the makeshift bed below. "Then let's put it to good use."

Emerson pulled Hayley's lips down to hers and purred. "There's no time to waste."

Chapter Twenty-four

The drive back to Boston had been mostly quiet—not unpleasant, but quiet. Hayley got the feeling that Emerson was more anxious about their return to the left coast than she was. As soon as they'd entered a steady cellular zone, she realized why. Both of their phones started vibrating and pinging with notifications. It appeared that Rachel had been busy with her smear campaign against Emerson while they were off the grid. And if the look on Emerson's face was any indication, she wasn't surprised in the least.

Pictures of Rachel and Emerson in more intimate embraces and kissing in dimly lit rooms flooded the screen of her phone, and blog after blog full of conspiracies clogged her browser alerts. Her work voicemail box was full, and her unread emails had quadrupled since she'd last logged in. Everyone and their mother it seemed wanted her take on the pictures or information regarding Emerson or her reaction. It puzzled Hayley why they wouldn't just reach out to Emerson's camp, but Emerson noted that they might have thought Hayley was a weak link. That just made her annoyed.

Hayley watched as all that calm, carefree energy Emerson had had at the cabin seemed to drain out of her by the minute. By the time they pulled up to the small private airfield, her foot was tapping, and she was restless. Now Hayley was restless, too.

The airport was set off from the road along well-paved and well-lit pathways. Security met them at the gate, and they were instructed to follow a guard on a golf cart toward the tarmac.

"This is out of control. We just drive right up?" Hayley felt like she was in a movie.

"Mm-hmm. Someone will unload the car and we'll meet the pilots and then we take off when air traffic control gives them the okay." Emerson continued to look out the passenger window when she spoke. She'd been like that for the last fifteen minutes, quietly staring off into the distance.

"That's it? No bomb sniffing dogs or pat downs by busty women with latex gloves?" That got Emerson's attention.

"Busty women? With latex gloves?" Emerson raised her eyebrow in amusement.

"You know, the security ladies at the airport. The ones that skim their gloved hands between your breasts and ask you to let your hair down, so they can check you for drugs or weapons or whatever." Hayley put on her blinker out of habit, not because there was anyone else on the tarmac besides the golf cart guy. She tried not to follow him too closely. Could you tailgate a golf cart?

"You've been groped by airport security?" Emerson looked skeptical.

Hayley feigned offense. "Are you trying to say I'm not gropeworthy? Because I totally am. I bet some people would really like to grope me. In fact, I bet people would line up to do it."

"With latex gloves on, no doubt."

"Or non-latex. I'm not picky. No allergies here." Hayley thumbed toward her chest a little too hard and jabbed herself.

Emerson laughed but it was short-lived. They'd reached their destination. The G5 Tremont had rented for them was only about thirty feet away. The runway was quiet except for some people that Hayley assumed were crew and some guy in a mechanic's outfit who came to get their bags. She held on to her messenger bag, but Emerson stepped toward the plane with only her phone, sunglasses, and the outfit she was wearing. She looked so elegant and practiced as she walked toward the stairs of the plane. This was not new territory to Emerson. That thought still boggled Hayley's mind.

"Welcome aboard, Ms. Sterling." An attractive young flight attendant greeted them at the base of the stairs. "My name is Stephanie and I'll be traveling with you this evening."

"Hi, Stephanie." Emerson was polite, but Hayley could see the stress on her face. She waved to the hulking suit standing behind Stephanie.

Hayley waved when she recognized Francis, the security detail from their flight into Boston. "Hey, Frank."

He didn't even crack a smile. Typical Francis, all work and no play.

"Still got that winning personality, huh, Frank?" Emerson elbowed her in the ribs and she laughed. "What?"

"No bomb talk this time, 'kay, Hayley?" That was the first genuine smile she'd seen on Emerson's face in about three hours. She'd take it any way she could get it.

"Whatever you say. You're the boss lady with the fancy plane."

Emerson gave her a look, but a smile tugged at her lips, so she was totally winning still.

They boarded and Stephanie gave them a quick tour. The pilots came out and shook Emerson's hand before they disappeared behind the door of the cockpit. The plane was long and narrow but plenty roomy. Stephanie explained to them that it had seating for up to eight passengers with a queen-sized bed in the back. A bench to the right when they first stepped on converted to a twin bed, and all the remaining seats were of the fancy leather recliner variety that did all sorts of cool things by touch screen. Hayley tried not to fuss over the awesomeness of this plane. She could tell that Emerson was eager to get into the air, probably to get this over with.

She thanked Stephanie for the glass of cold water and sat across from Emerson with a small dining table between them. This plane was easily as big as Emerson's trailer. It was all light colors and streamlined elegance. Emerson looked very much the part, sitting across from her with her fancy LA clothes and the uninterested look on her face. This fit her. But the woman who'd lounged with her by the lake in cutoff jeans she'd found in the closet, wearing Hayley's plaid shirt, also fit. Emerson was complicated and multifaceted that way.

"What are you thinking?" Emerson caught her off guard.

"Oh. Um. Just that you look like you belong here. Like this suits you." She motioned to the space around them.

Emerson leaned back against the large, comfy seat and brought a knee up to her chest. "There are definite perks to celebrity. It's nice to fly in luxury. But it's still flying."

"I know." Hayley frowned. "But it's fancy as fuck. I mean, this water is in a crystal glass. Crystal. Glass. And it's already chilled."

Emerson chuckled and teased. "I love that you appreciate the simple things in life, Hayley."

"I like to think I have a rather refined taste for a woodsy Maine girl at heart."

"You are delicious, I'll give you that." Emerson winked at her.

Hayley had been reaching into her messenger bag when Emerson's word choice stopped her from finding what she was looking for. "Did you just turn a very innocent statement into something sexual, Emerson? Because that's what it sounded like. Are you objectifying me?"

"I totally was. Sorry." Emerson gave her an exaggerated pout. "Still like me?"

"I suppose I have to at least pretend to like you since we're on this extravagant jet adventure together." She made a flying motion with her hand.

Emerson looked out the window and gasped. "We're in the air."

Hayley nodded. "As planes tend to do."

"You did it again." Emerson looked back at her with a grateful expression. "Thank you for distracting me from the takeoff."

Hayley shrugged. "It's the least I could do." She pointed toward Francis, who was sitting up by the cockpit and talking to Stephanie. "You don't need my master fabric cloaking skills on this flight. I need to make myself useful."

Emerson reached across the table and patted her hand. "You are the most useful."

Hayley brushed imaginary lint off her shoulder. "All in a day's work, m'lady."

Emerson nodded toward her bag. "What's in the bag of tricks today?"

Hayley pulled out the two little boxes she'd picked up from the gas station on their way to the airport. "We now have Skip-Bo and a deck of cards, in addition to Uno. But I'm telling you right now, if I catch you cheating at Uno, I'm going to sit with Frank up there and you'll have to entertain yourself."

"So many threats." Emerson's flashed her those perfect Hollywood teeth. "I'll be on my best behavior."

"You do that." Hayley was all bark. She'd let Emerson cheat at Uno all day and the wink Emerson gave her let her know she knew it, too.

❖

After Emerson yawned for the dozenth time, she finally consented to sleeping. The bed was in a separate section of the plane, in the rear opposite the bathroom and tiny kitchenette. There was another recliner in there, with a small table and a privacy door that closed off the bedroom area from the rest of the plane. It wasn't exactly Fort Knox, but it would give Emerson a chance to rest and some privacy, which Hayley could tell was something she desired.

Even though Stephanie and Francis stayed at the front of the plane and only ventured back occasionally, Emerson seemed wary. It was like she expected one of them to be spying on her or something. Hayley wondered if Emerson felt violated by the images of her and Rachel sharing what clearly were intended to be private moments together that now flooded the interwebs. She imagined the various gossip networks were probably having a field day with this. Emerson's face was definitely on loop by now.

Hayley had followed her into the bedroom space at her request. She wasn't sure where they stood exactly now that they were out of the sanctity of the lake house. Emerson had seemed so stressed by the media overexposure and then the flight that she hadn't wanted to ask.

Emerson sat at the edge of the bed and kicked off her boots. She motioned for Hayley to close and lock the door.

Hayley dropped her messenger bag onto the nearby recliner and stretched, unsure of what to do next.

Emerson patted the space next to her on the bed and Hayley sat down beside her.

"You seem anxious around them." Hayley thumbed toward the door. "You okay?"

Emerson sighed and leaned into Hayley before pressing their lips together. "I miss the lake house. I miss the quiet."

Hayley savored the feeling of Emerson's lips on her own. She wasn't sure how many more times this would happen. "I miss kissing you whenever I want."

Emerson pulled back and looked at her. She hadn't meant to say that out loud. Goddamn broken filter. She blamed Emerson's full, pouty lips. They were incredibly distracting.

"I want to. Can we just…" Emerson frowned. "I want you to kiss me whenever you want. And I want to see what happens here." She motioned between them before her frown deepened. "But it's not going to be easy, Hay. It's going to be hard and frustrating and—"

"And worth it." Hayley kissed her forehead and pulled back the comforter. "We'll figure it out. Let's get you some sleep and we can worry about all the big crazy later on."

Emerson looked disappointed. "You're not coming to bed?"

"Oh." That hadn't occurred to her. She was planning to work on her piece for the *Sun*. She had quite a bit of info to add and polish since she'd last worked on it. She had a ton of new information, like all the Rachel and Rory stuff and the firsthand knowledge of what Emerson looked like when her head was thrown back in ecstasy in bed. Not that she'd ever write about *that*, but…Great, now she was thinking about Emerson in bed while sitting with Emerson on a bed.

"I lost you, didn't I?" Emerson slipped under the comforter and extended her hand to Hayley.

Hayley allowed herself to be pulled down next to Emerson and wrapped her up in her arms. "No, I'm right here. I was going to do a little work, but I'd much rather be your personal pillow and space heater."

Emerson rolled on her side and Hayley spooned up behind her. She laced their fingers together and Emerson sighed. "You have to finish your piece."

"I do." She placed a kiss behind Emerson's ear and breathed in the smell of the lake house's shampoo in her hair. It gave her all kinds of feelings, the melding of Maine and Emerson. She decided it was her new favorite scent.

Emerson turned in her arms to face her. She traced her finger along Hayley's lips. "What will you say about…"

"Rory?" Hayley kissed her fingertip.

Emerson nodded. She looked nervous again.

"Just what I need to tell the narrative of your life, Emerson. It can be nothing or everything or something in between. It's to be determined, really."

Emerson nodded but said nothing.

Hayley hesitated. "Do you want me to leave it out? I will. I told you that before—"

Emerson pressed her finger to Hayley's lips again. "Write what needs to be written, Hayley. I trust you to do what you think is best. Tell my story. It's what we set out to do here."

Hayley reached out and stroked Emerson's cheek. She was mesmerized by those incredible eyes. "Is that all we're doing here? Telling your story?"

"I hope not." Emerson's voice was soft. She looked as exposed as Hayley felt. After a beat she asked, "Stay with me until I fall asleep?"

"Of course." Hayley decided she would stay with her forever, if she'd have her. "There's no place else I'd rather be." That was true.

Hayley dozed with Emerson for a bit before some turbulence woke her up. Luckily, Emerson didn't seem to notice and slept soundly next to her. After lying there for some time, she decided she couldn't fall back asleep. She slipped out of bed and tucked the pillows and blankets around Emerson to keep her comfortable.

She walked toward the recliner in the corner and settled into the seat. Although the plane was quiet, it was still a plane. And it still hummed loud enough that Hayley was confident she could work on her laptop over here without disturbing Emerson's sleep.

She powered up her laptop and signed into the Wi-Fi with the code Stephanie had given her when they'd boarded. She opened her web browser and checked on the alerts icon in the corner. Within seconds, her screen was filled with images of Emerson, old and new, standing next to various celebrities and nobodies posing this way and that. A picture of her standing with Johnny and Rachel caught Hayley's eye. Johnny was smiling, and Rachel was midlaugh. Emerson was looking at Rachel. There was an affection there. Or at least there appeared to be some. Hayley couldn't help but wonder if they'd been sleeping together at the time this was taken. She tried to ignore the tug of jealousy that bubbled up.

She loaded a new search bar and typed in Rachel's name. Although she'd done some preliminary research at the beginning of this process, she'd mostly ignored Rachel in lieu of focusing on Emerson. But she had a feeling that she needed to have a better idea about Rachel and her background to really process all the information she'd learned from

Emerson over the weekend. Could this woman really be threatening to ruin a child's life to get back at an ex-lover? What made Rachel tick?

She thought about the look on Emerson's face that first night she'd seen Rachel interact with her backstage. She'd seen that same face earlier when Emerson fled the red carpet and again when Tremont had sent them the link with the picture of Emerson and Hayley in the trailer talking—it was a look of fear. Carnal and raw. Emerson had appeared afraid of Rachel. And now knowing what she did about Rory, she could see why. Still, a part of her was curious about Rachel's side of the story. Could this really all be about ego and fame? Or did Emerson mean more to Rachel than Emerson thought she did? Hayley wasn't sure she'd ever get those answers.

She loaded her piece and skimmed it over. She was proud of this. It was some of her best work and she knew it. She could feel the passion in the words. She had poured herself into this and it showed. She thought about Emerson and Rachel and Rory and what they meant to the narrative in front of her. Could she do the story justice by leaving Rachel out? She wasn't thrilled about giving this woman any more media attention. But she knew that, no, she couldn't leave her out, either, since she was the reason Emerson had to reveal the truth about Rory in the first place. Could she protect Emerson and Rory and shine light on Rachel's fucked-up behavior without putting too much of a spotlight on either of them? Was there a way that anyone would end up unscathed by this? Or was she just about to make things worse for everyone involved? She wasn't sure about that. There had to be a way she could get the truth out there without devastating Emerson's career or her family's privacy in the process.

She sighed and leaned back in her chair. Her decision to mindlessly cruise Twitter failed epically when she found that she had hundreds of mentions, notifications, and direct messages. She had never been so popular. On a whim she skimmed through the DMs to see if anyone of interest had reached out to her. There were a few fellow reporters. Anna Mae Teslan from *LA Life* had been messaging her furiously over the weekend. A couple of threats by some Rachel fans, it seemed. And, shut the front door, a message from Rachel herself: *we should talk. lets meet.*

Suddenly the already complicated mess in front of her just got a little messier. Wait until Alison got wind of this. OMG, she had totally stood up Alison for dumpling night. "Shit. Alison."

"You know, someone with a little less confidence would be worried that you were saying another woman's name with such passion," Emerson said from behind her.

She turned and winced. "Did I wake you?"

"No. You did a fantastic pillow stacking job. I was convinced you were still the big spoon. Nice work." Emerson stretched out on her side and yawned.

Hayley exited her DMs and closed her laptop. She wanted to think about the Rachel thing before she told Emerson. If she told Emerson. She should, shouldn't she?

"So why are we shitting Alison?"

"What?"

"You said, *Shit. Alison.* I want to make sure I know why we're shitting her." Emerson yawned again.

Hayley rubbed her eyes and walked toward her, letting herself be pulled to bed by Emerson. She flopped back on the pillow and Emerson snuggled into the crook of her arm. "We had a tentative date watching chick flicks and having dumplings. Not only did I miss it, I didn't even text or call her. I stood her up." Hayley felt awful.

"Well, I did whisk you to the East Coast with next to no warning," Emerson pointed out.

"And seduced me with your feminine wiles."

"That's fair. But who's to say you didn't seduce me first?" Emerson kissed under her jaw and she closed her eyes at the sensation.

"You're right. That's what I'll tell our kids when they ask who made the first move. I'll tell them it was me. I seduced you. Full stop."

Emerson's laugh vibrated against her chest. "Well, you and that flannel shirt. Which I'm keeping, by the way."

"No way. That's my lucky shirt." Hayley dipped her head to connect their lips.

"You can keep your lucky pants." Emerson slid her hand along Hayley's stomach and slipped beneath the fabric. "I prefer you out of them anyway."

"I do love those pants." Hayley's mind was on the current pair that Emerson was helping off her.

"Mm. I like this compromise." Emerson climbed over her and nuzzled her nose. "Why don't we celebrate our mutually agreed upon custody of your clothes by taking off the ones we're wearing?"

Hayley shrugged off her shirt and pulled Emerson back down on top of her. "I never agreed to relinquishing ownership of my shirt, just FYI."

Emerson kissed her hard and she forgot what she had been saying. "I can be very persuasive."

"Yeah?"

Emerson leaned back and licked her lips as she palmed Hayley's breasts and ground her hips against Hayley's. Hayley moaned at the sensation. All the sensations. So many sensations. "Let me show you just how persuasive I can be."

As Emerson took her nipple between her lips, Hayley decided Emerson would give her shirt a good home. As long as she got regular visitation of Emerson in it—or out of it—that would be just fine by her.

Chapter Twenty-five

W e need to talk." Tremont stood over her and blocked the light she had been soaking up.

"Can you stand over there and chastise me without casting such an epic shadow over my existence? That's eerie as fuck." Emerson waved him away and closed her eyes again. This was the first time she'd been back home in months. Once they'd landed from Boston, it became painfully clear that her rental home anonymity had been compromised. No less than thirty paparazzi were at the house when she pulled up, and another fifteen were at her actual residence. She might as well be back home as be caged in someone else's house. At least she knew where the extra towels were here. She swore she'd spent half of her time at that rental house in search of clean towels. They were as elusive as her privacy as of late.

"Emerson, I'm serious." He sounded serious. He was doing a good job of *serious*.

"You're *seriously* blocking my sun. Move." She tossed a lemon wedge from her water at him and he huffed.

"Fine. Drama queen." He dropped his man purse and plopped next to her on the plush chaise by her infinity pool and took a sip of her water. "It's hot as hades out here."

"I'm in love. Don't talk about it." She flapped her arms and clasped them behind her head to help get an even tan across her chest.

"That's what I want to talk about."

She slid the sunglasses up into her hair and looked at him. "Oh? Do you know something I don't?"

"Probably not." He crossed his legs and leaned back. "Something tells me you've known for a lot longer than I did."

"I don't know what you're talking about." She slid her glasses back over her eyes and closed them.

"Don't be a rude bitch right now. Glasses off, Emerson. Eyes here," Tremont snipped.

She gave him a look. "Rude bitch, huh?"

Tremont laughed. "Too harsh? I'll try again." He cleared his throat. "Emerson, darling. Stop ignoring me like a nasty twat and talk to me. Better?"

"Much." She took off her glasses and smiled at him. "You were saying?"

He playfully shoved her and replied, "I want to know what's going on between you and Hayley."

Emerson nodded. She figured she owed him that much. "When did you figure it out?"

"That picture while you were *running lines*"—he made air quotes—"in Boston. I know that look. I've seen that look on your face before when you were doing that predatory seductive thing you do. And on hers, when she was watching you do the voice-over work. Those were faces that were up to no good."

"It's creepy when you say things like that. Like the faces in question are their own entities."

"The word *titty* is in entity," Tremont said.

"Is not. Not enough *t*'s," she corrected.

"You'd know better than I would since you've been groping Hayley's."

"Again. That sounds creepy. I didn't grope them. I'll accept *fondled* or *massaged*. But not *groped*. Unless she says it. Then I am all for groping."

Tremont just stared at her.

"What? Did you expect me to deny it?"

"Kinda. A little. This feels too easy." He gave her a suspicious look. "Are you just trying to throw me off the topic by lying and being really blunt to make it seem like you did fondle her breasts when in fact you didn't?"

This conversation was making Emerson dizzy. "No?"

"I'm confused." Tremont pouted.

"Me, too." Emerson took back her water and sipped it through the metal straw.

"Did you sleep with Hayley?"

Emerson considered this before answering. "There was sleeping. Yes."

"Emerson. You're driving me crazy." Tremont threw his hands up. "Did you two have sex, yes or no?"

"With each other? Or just in general? Because that's a little vague."

"For fuck's sake," he cried.

"Lower your voice. You're making a scene." She shushed him.

"We're in your massive backyard. Alone. Just you, me, and this uncomfortably tepid water." He snatched her glass away and sipped the contents with a grimace. "It's warm. Gross."

"Yes."

"Yes, what?"

"Yes, we slept together. And had sex. Together. With each other."

He stared at her again.

"You need to stop staring at me, it's—"

"Creepy. I know." He sighed. "When did you two first start hooking up?"

"It sounds so cheap when you say it like that." Emerson looked out at the pool and missed the lake. "Boston. It happened sort of by accident."

"And how does that happen exactly? By accident, I mean?" Tremont didn't look convinced.

She shrugged.

"I knew I shouldn't have left you two alone." He shook his head.

"Why do you say that?"

Tremont looked at her like she had ten heads. "You're joking, right?"

Emerson shook her head.

"You two have been making moon eyes at each other for, like, a month. I figured it was only a matter of time. I just thought you'd be smart enough to keep it in your pants until after the article was released. You know, to cut down on some of the scandalousness of all this."

Emerson was offended. "Well it wasn't exactly planned, Tremont."

"Mm-hmm. First time you're alone without a chaperone and you get all handsy with your reporter girlfriend. Not planned at all. Yup."

"It wasn't." She frowned. "I just...we were talking and then she was so sweet and incredible and then there was kissing. So much kissing."

Tremont softened. "What were you talking about?"

"Rachel."

His expression soured. "And that got you all hot and bothered? You two need therapy."

Emerson laughed. "No. She offered to publish the piece without including anything about Rachel. It was sweet."

"And dumb."

"Tremont."

"Okay. Or sweet. We'll go with sweet." He rolled his eyes. "And you told her about Rory?"

"I did." Emerson regretted nothing.

"So, what now?"

"We publish the article with the whole story." Emerson shrugged. "And then we wait."

"Wait for what?"

"The other shoe to drop." Emerson sat up and moved to the edge of the chaise, perching on the end.

"It already has." Tremont frowned and pulled an envelope from his murse. "These showed up at my condo this morning. No note. Just these."

Emerson took the envelope and pulled out the three eight-and-a-half-by-eleven photographs. They were of her and Hayley kissing in the trailer. And they were scandalous. "Fuck."

❖

Hayley looked at her watch and exhaled. Rachel was late. Like, super late. If she was even coming at all. It hadn't been easy to find a time when they could meet, and finding a semiprivate location was near impossible. Hayley had been under paparazzi surveillance since her arrival home, and someone was always nearby snapping a photo. Didn't they know she was a nobody?

She sighed and checked her reflection in the mirror. She smiled as a card tumbled out from the visor. When she'd gotten home from

Boston, she'd found a box of designer business cards at her doorstep. They read *Hayley Carpenter, Screenwriter.* Emerson had really ordered them after all. She had slipped them into her messenger bag and put one in her car to remind her of her long-term goal and of Emerson. Not that she needed the reminder about Emerson. She thought about her constantly, it seemed.

But even though they were in the same city, she hadn't seen Emerson in person since they'd landed. Although they talked daily—and often—it wasn't the same. Emerson had been all over the place doing press for the movie release. The reshoot editing process had been fast-tracked and *Willow Path* was scheduled to be screened for critics in mere weeks. Her drop-dead deadline for the final draft of the article was looming, and everything she'd been hemming and hawing over since Rachel's message needed to be smoothed out and put into action. Which was proving to be an impossible task.

Hayley was about to give up when a flashy red convertible pulled up. Subtle. Great.

"Wanna ride?" Rachel's eyes were hidden by her sunglasses, but her smile was unmistakable. Hayley had seen it in dozens of movies and on scores of magazine covers. It was blindingly perfect.

"Not really." Hayley didn't like the idea of being trapped in a moving vehicle with Rachel. Emerson's warning about Rachel's violent temper was fresh in her mind. Plus, the blackmail thing was pretty shady as fuck, too, so she was set against getting too close.

"Fine. Have it your way." Rachel pulled over and stepped out. She moved with a gracefulness unlike anything Hayley had ever seen. She appeared to float as she walked. It was otherworldly.

"I thought we agreed that we would meet under the condition that you wouldn't make a scene. Or call unnecessary attention to yourself." Hayley stepped closer to the building and tried to hide herself from sight.

"Oh, honey. There's no such thing as me not drawing attention to myself. It's in my blood." Rachel was completely serious.

Hayley gave Rachel her best side-eye. "Okay. I'm outta here. Nice to meet you, Rachel."

"Wait. Sorry." Rachel stepped closer, lowered her voice, and said, "I rented out the café for the hour. We can sit in the back."

She followed Rachel into the small coffee shop and found Rachel's statement to be true. It was the middle of the day and completely empty. Well, except for a tall hulking black guy by the back door.

"That's Bernard. He's with me." Rachel walked to the back of the café and sat at one of the tables. Bernard brought her a cup of coffee, saucer and little spoon and all. "Coffee?"

"Uh, no. Thanks." Hayley surveyed Bernard suspiciously. "You needed security for this?"

Rachel took off her glasses and sparkling blue eyes shone back at her. She was even more beautiful in person. Hayley was suddenly feeling self-conscious. "Who knows if Emerson poisoned your mind? You might be dangerous. Are you dangerous, Hayley?"

"No." She turned the question back on Rachel. "Are you?"

Rachel laughed. She sipped her coffee and pushed it aside. "That depends on what you mean by dangerous."

Hayley waited for her to elaborate.

"Look. I asked you to meet because I think we could help each other out."

"And how's that?"

"You're writing a story. But you've only heard one side of it. Don't you think it's worthwhile to hear my version of the events?" Rachel's tone was polite. And her posture was relaxed and welcoming. Hayley, on the other hand, felt everything but. A voice in her head was screaming that this was a bad idea.

"Okay. I'm all ears." Hayley decided to commit to it. She had already made the decision to be here. Now she might as well *be* here.

"Well, first of all. I'm not a bad person." Rachel reached forward and took her hand. She gave Hayley an exaggerated pout. "I'm misunderstood."

Hayley doubted that greatly, but the familiarity of the phrase wasn't lost on her. She patted Rachel's hand and pulled hers away, preferring as little contact with this woman as possible. "Okay."

"You know Emerson. She's…she's just so enigmatic and beautiful. She sucks you in. When you're with her, it's like the whole world is all butterflies and rainbows. She's magical."

Hayley was careful to maintain a blank expression. She was in full agreement with Rachel's statement, but this felt like a trap. "She's quite something."

"Right? Anyway. Truth is, I developed a little crush on her and things got a little hot and heavy for a bit, and then they fell apart." Rachel shrugged and reached for her coffee. "But that's where the narrative gets tricky."

"What do you mean?"

Rachel smiled at her and she felt dirty. "Emerson has a habit of keeping secrets. She's a liar. Our relationship ended because I caught her lying. Then she turned the director and screenwriter against me. Then the studio. She seduced me and then tossed me out on my ass. And that's not acceptable. You shouldn't toy with someone's emotions like that. Or screw with someone's career."

"Yeah, see...that's not the story I heard." Hayley didn't like the way this conversation was playing out. She assumed that Rachel's statement about Emerson's lies had something to do with Rory's existence in the world. But she knew better than to show her hand and let on that she was privy to that information. She decided to lead with what she had planned to all along, Rachel's obsession with fame. "I heard you got a little too big for your britches and ran into some interference from the studio and that you self-combusted."

Rachel's smile was gone in a flash. "Drake was right about you. You're a sneaky bitch. You and Emerson are made for each other."

She stood, and Bernard stepped forward. "Listen, clearly I'm not going to change your mind, but you should know that the Emerson you've been chasing around with your little tape recorder is a fake. And you're going to be made a fool of by her like I was. Unless of course you scrap the story and write mine instead."

"You're joking." What the hell was happening?

"I'm not."

"And what exactly would I even write about you?"

"The truth." Rachel crossed her arms and looked like a petulant child. "What Emerson did was unforgivable. Why anyone is listening to her story over mine is beyond me. I worked my ass off for my success, and I'm not going to let some tramp drag me through the mud on her quest for fame."

Hayley wasn't sure if she was talking about Emerson or herself. But either way she wasn't having any of it. "You're the only one I see dragging anyone here."

Rachel's nostrils flared. "You'll go down with the ship then, too.

It's a pity. I've read some of your work. It's quite good. Rumor has it you want to write a movie someday. Too bad you aligned yourself with the wrong side on this one. I'd hate for that to be the end to your little pipe dream."

Rachel headed toward the door but paused. "Have you met the family yet, Hayley?"

"What? No." She hadn't meant to answer truthfully.

Rachel's smirk was menacing. "I guess I'll give Drake my scoop instead. Let Emerson know she'll be headline news soon enough. And tell her she has you to thank for it."

Rachel and Bernard exited the café, and Hayley was left in eerie silence. Well, except for the fact that her brain was screaming profanities at her. What was she thinking when she set up this meeting? What good did she think would come of it?

There would be no more extensions on her deadline. And suddenly she was no better off than she was when she'd first started. Scratch that. She was legions behind where she first started because now Rachel had threatened Hayley's future in Hollywood and was putting a ticking clock on Emerson all because she'd poked the bear. She never should have met with her. Ever.

"What did I do?" Hayley dropped her head to the table and wished she could disappear.

CHAPTER TWENTY-SIX

E merson! Over here!" Voices called from every direction. It was disorienting.

She ducked into the waiting car and gave the driver the directions to Hayley's apartment. She'd never been there, but she was hoping Hayley wouldn't mind the unexpected company. She hadn't seen her in almost two weeks.

After the envelope arrived, a note followed telling her to stay away from Hayley or the pictures would be leaked. She was still keeping her distance from Deidre and Rory so as not to draw attention to them until Hayley's piece came out, and now someone was threatening to leak photos of her and Hayley making out. And so far, the pictures didn't include the activities by the kitchenette, which was good. But still, these photos were damning on the brink of Hayley's publication. Privacy and all. Those fuckers.

So she had been lying low. They'd talked every day, but she had been so busy with movie press and interviews that they'd only had time for nightly phone calls or stolen FaceTime sessions. It wasn't the same. She missed her.

Her anxious excitement turned to dread when they pulled up to Hayley's building. It was crawling with paps. Crawling. Literally, she could see one of them in the trees. Her stomach turned as she surveyed the seriousness of the situation. Hayley had mentioned there were some people following her and taking photos, but she had majorly downplayed the situation. This paired with the threatening note and photographs made Emerson panic. What had she gotten Hayley into?

After taking a minute to talk herself off the ledge, she video called Hayley.

"Hey. This is an unexpected surprise." Hayley smiled broadly at her and her heart skipped a beat. "As were the incredibly obnoxious and beautiful flowers you sent me this morning. Thank you."

"I'm glad you like them." Emerson had sent her flowers every other day since Boston. She might have physically kept her distance, but she had no intention of emotionally separating from Hayley as well. At this point, she wasn't sure if she could. She certainly didn't want to. Although the paparazzi swarming around her car gave her pause. She sank lower in the seat and ducked her head.

"I do." Hayley rested her hand on her chin and gave her a lazy smile. "I like you, too."

"This call is good for my ego." Emerson looked forward to talking with Hayley. Always. Even if chaos circled around them, Hayley was her happy place. "Are you home? Please say yes."

"I am." Hayley looked amused. "Yes."

"How do you feel about blondes?"

Hayley gave her a curious look. "In general?"

Emerson pulled a wig out of her bag and put it on.

"Oh, on you. Well, I like everything on you. And off you. If that was your next question."

Emerson laughed. "And how do you feel about unexpected guests?"

Hayley paused. Her face lit up. "Tell me you're here and this is like that moment in *Pretty Woman* when Richard Gere shows up at Julia Roberts's fire escape."

"It is. Except I'm going to be incognito and I'm going to need you to let me in to the front door of your building. Or better yet, send someone else. Because it's like a red-carpet premiere out here."

Hayley squealed and clapped. "I know the perfect unassuming old lady for the job. I'll be right down. Or, rather, she will."

"Great." Emerson was giddy. She tried to ignore the panicky sensation all the photographers outside Hayley's building gave her.

True to Hayley's word, a cute hunched-over older woman opened the door to her building and looked around. The paparazzi's cameras flashed but once they realized it wasn't someone of interest, they abandoned their posts. Emerson ducked out of the rear passenger door of the car and knocked the glass. Her driver took off and blared his horn, distracting the lingering paps enough for her to run into the open door.

Hayley was waiting inside, hidden behind a large shrub in the lobby.

"Hayley." Emerson felt like the weight of the world was off her shoulders. She went to her with the full intention to kiss her silly but stopped at the last second when she realized they had an audience. "Oh, hello. Thank you for your help."

"This is Greta, she lives next door," Hayley supplied.

The old woman smiled. "Sure. I'm all for young love." She gave Hayley a stern look and pointed at her. "Don't forget our agreement. Keep it down and no more singing off-key to that Swords woman. It's annoying."

"Spears. And I'm never off-key," Hayley replied.

Greta took out one of her hearing aids and fiddled with it. "You're always off-key. I shut off this little guy every morning because your bathroom is next to my bedroom. It's a good thing I'm deaf in the other ear."

"Oh, like that ear is any better," Hayley mumbled.

"What?" Greta barked.

Emerson intervened. "She'll be on her best behavior. We'll get her singing lessons, or better yet, she'll take a vow of Britney Spears shower silence."

"Hey." Hayley frowned.

"It's only fair." Emerson nudged her with her elbow. "Greta did save the day."

Hayley pouted. "Fine."

Greta put her hearing aid back in and smiled. "I like you—you're nice. You look familiar. Have we met before?"

"Bye, Greta." Hayley tugged Emerson around the corner and up the stairs to her apartment.

Once they arrived, Hayley pulled her into her apartment and kissed her against the closed door. Emerson had waited for this moment for what seemed like forever. "Hi."

"Hi." Hayley kissed her again and her hands found their way into Hayley's hair. Hayley scratched at her back and Emerson pulled at the lapels of her shirt, unbuttoning the top two buttons to free the skin beneath. She wanted to kiss across Hayley's chest and smell her perfume.

Hayley moaned when her lips connected with her collarbone. "I missed you." She caressed Emerson's cheek and her hand bumped into Emerson's wig.

Emerson reached up and pulled it off, tossing it to the side. "These things are hot."

"I thought that was just you." Hayley took her hand and led her into the apartment.

"I accept that compliment." Emerson looked around. "This place is cute. Very Hayley."

"Thank you." Hayley led them to the living room and closed the blinds before plunking down next to Emerson on the soft brown couch. She hadn't noticed it at first, probably because she was so happy to see her, but upon closer inspection, Emerson could see the stress on Hayley's face. And the exhaustion. She wondered how she was sleeping, if at all.

Emerson took her hand, a wave of guilt washing over her. "How long have they been staked out like that?"

"Oh, my new fan club? Since Boston. But it's tripled since yesterday." Hayley looked annoyed. "I figured it was because of Rachel's most recent play for attention."

Two nights ago, Rachel did a filmed interview with James Drake. She was supposed to be promoting a new project, but it was a blatant bash session against Emerson and the studio. She'd brought up Hayley and said they were colluding to paint a bad picture of her. Drake asked her about the leaked pictures of Rachel and Emerson kissing, and she started that sob story again about how Emerson had duped her into thinking they were in a committed relationship only to leverage that relationship to get Rachel booted from the film, as if Rachel needed any help from her in that department. That woman was a ticking time bomb.

Up to this point, Emerson hadn't replied to any of the attacks. Nor did she intend to. Her response would come in the form of Hayley's article. She was sure that Rachel was behind the photos, which was one of the reasons she'd taken the risk to come here today. That interview had gone viral, and Rachel had managed to overshadow the movie's hype just as it was about to be screened for critics. The studio was pissed. Emerson's stomach was in knots. Hayley's story was supposed to come out tomorrow and all eyes were on her now. That made Emerson even more nervous, because she hadn't mentioned the photos that showed up at Tremont's to Hayley yet.

She'd hired a private detective to try to identify the sender, but so far, he'd been unsuccessful. She'd come here today with the intention of warning Hayley in person. Which right now felt like an impossible task considering how stressed Hayley looked. She had no desire to makes things worse. She frowned. "I think this is going to get worse before it gets better."

Hayley looked defeated. "Yeah. About that. I need to tell you something."

"Is this about the pictures?" Emerson had hoped she could suffer the burden of this alone, but it had occurred to her that maybe Hayley had gotten the same threat.

"What pictures? The old ones of you and Rachel kissing in the dark?"

Well, that answered that question. "No." Emerson's heart was heavy as she reached for her purse. "These pictures."

Hayley took the envelope from her and pulled out the contents. Her mouth dropped open and she sat there without saying anything for a long time. Her voice was soft, almost inaudible, when she said, "Where did you get these?"

Emerson ran her hand through her hair and sighed. "They showed up at Tremont's apartment with a note that told me to keep my distance from you, otherwise they would be leaked. Which would be—"

"Very, very bad." Hayley looked up at her. "For a multitude of reasons."

"Right. Because your article is coming out tomorrow and the movie is being screened for critics and you could—"

"Get fired." Hayley was staring off into the distance, her eyes not seemingly focused on anything.

"Well, yeah, there's that, I guess." This was what Emerson had agonized over. It was one thing for Hayley to lose her privacy. It was another thing for Hayley to lose her career entirely. "I'm trying to find out where they came from, but it's more complicated than I thought. But we're working on it."

"I think I know who sent them." Hayley looked pale.

Emerson felt sick. "Who?"

"I did something maybe a little stupid." Hayley was wringing her hands.

Emerson reached out to stop them. "Go on."

"I met with Rachel."

Emerson pulled her hands back like they'd been burned. "You did what?"

Hayley stood up and began to pace. "She messaged me and told me she wanted to meet. Said she wanted to tell me her side of the story."

Emerson was in shock. "And what side is that?"

Hayley rubbed the back of her neck. "She just said more of what she'd said before. That you seduced her and turned the studio against her. She blames you for her firing."

"Okay?" The panic that Emerson had barely been keeping at bay was bubbling over. Rachel was a master manipulator. She hadn't thought to tell Hayley to be careful of her. She never thought they'd cross paths. How stupid and naïve that had been.

Hayley sighed. "She didn't say much actually. Except to threaten me and basically tell me she'd make sure I never worked in this town again. Which seemed a little dramatic, if you ask me, but I'll admit she's a bit scary when she loses her temper…I see what you meant before about her being volatile."

"She threatened you?" Emerson saw red. She couldn't believe what she was hearing.

"Sort of. In a roundabout way. She wanted me to drop your article and write her story instead. I refused, obviously. She didn't like that." Hayley frowned. "She also said to tell you that she was going to make you headline news and to tell you it was my fault. But I didn't take her too seriously, until the other night. When she made you headline news. And I think it *was* my fault."

Emerson felt like the walls were closing in around her. She could see their best-laid plans unraveling in front of her eyes. If Hayley had in any way antagonized Rachel, she could beat them to the reveal or leak those pictures if she was behind it. Then all their work, all the work she did with Rory and Deidre to try to minimize the damage, would be for naught. And Hayley would look biased. "When did you meet with her?"

Hayley looked ashamed. "A few days ago."

Emerson's head was spinning. She started running dates in her mind. Rachel didn't expose the truth about Rory to Drake on TV the other night, why? "What did you tell her? Did you say anything about Rory?"

"What? No." Hayley looked offended. "I wouldn't...I didn't say anything. It was mostly just her monologuing in my direction while her beefy bodyguard looked on."

"Bernard?" Emerson already knew the answer, but she was biding her time, trying to scale back the bile that was building up in her throat. She was most definitely going to vomit. Or have a breakdown. Or both.

"Yeah, actually. Not as chatty as your guy, Francis." Hayley gave her a small smile, but Emerson couldn't return it.

Hayley sighed again. "We didn't talk about Rory, but as she was leaving, around the time she threatened to make you front page news, she asked me if I'd met your family yet. I told her I hadn't. She sort of smirked and told me she was giving the story to Drake and that I was going to go down like the *Titanic* or something nautical like that."

That was about all she could take. Rachel had basically confirmed to Hayley that she was going to ruin Emerson's life by way of exposing Rory. And she was promising to make sure Hayley's career and life spiraled out with Emerson's. This had been her greatest fear this whole time, that she was her own worst enemy, that she couldn't risk having any sort of intimate relationship with anyone. Ever. Her celebrity had already hurt Deidre and Rory, and now Hayley's privacy and career were on the line as well. For what? For Emerson to have an iota of happiness? If it meant so much pain for the people she loved? She couldn't do this to anyone else. Hayley deserved better than to be dragged through the mud. "Hayley, I—"

A knock at Hayley's door caused them both to jump. Neither one of them moved. A second knock, this one louder and more determined.

"Hayley? Are you home?" A female voice sounded from the other side of the door.

"Alison?" Hayley looked as flustered as Emerson felt. She mumbled, "Your timing could not be worse, Ali."

Hayley strode to the door and opened it. Alison fell through the doorway and staggered into the foyer, clutching two bottles of wine and a bag of something.

"Hayley, did you know there are like a million people with

cameras outside your apartment building? There were a bunch looking for you at the office too, and by Lilly's—that place is so good. One of them offered to buy me a drink the other day for intel on you. I told him to go screw. You're so fucking famous now, I can't take it," she slurred. "Anyway the guys outside asked me if I knew you. I told them I did, because, duh, you're like a celebrity now, and then they wanted to know if you and Emerson were dating because of that picture of you two from last week, and the one where she was touching that director lady. Is she really handsy? Anyway, I told them no way. But maybe you wanted to be. Do you want to be?" Alison put her hand over her mouth. "I don't think I said that out loud. Maybe I did. Do you want to be dating her? I would. She's gorgeous. Is she single?"

"Alison, are you drunk?" Hayley lunged forward to save a bowl from crashing to the floor as Alison stumbled into it. Emerson would have been impressed by her catlike reflexes if she wasn't convinced they were in the twilight zone.

"A little bit." Alison hiccupped. "Okay, a lot bit. Long story short, Rob's been cheating on me and I threw him out and I'm going to be alone forever, and you owe me a dumpling date, so I brought the dumplings and the bar to you." She held up the wine and the greasy food bag as she swayed in place.

"Rob cheated on you? I'm so sorry, Ali." Hayley walked over to her friend and took the bottles from her before she gave her a hug.

"I know, right?" Alison dramatically flailed her arms and Emerson was glad Hayley had removed the potentially injurious wine from her. "His loss. I'm a total catch."

She started sobbing and Hayley patted her back before giving an apologetic look to Emerson. Alison wiped her eyes and finally noticed Emerson's presence. "Oh. You have company."

A look of realization crossed her face and she took a shaky step forward. "OMG. You're Emerson fucking Sterling."

"Hi." Emerson gave her a weak wave because what was she supposed to do?

"Hayley is totally in love with you. Like, totally. She's all head over heels about how smart and funny you are. She kept going on and on about how your trip to Boston was life changing and she learned so much about you and…" Alison did this weird laugh-cry combination thing and muttered, "Emerson fucking Sterling…unbelievable."

"Right. Sorry. Ali, this is Emerson." Hayley took Alison's hand and tried to lead her to the couch, but Alison stopped and pulled her hand back.

"Wait." She hiccupped and seemed to sober for a moment. Her eyes got big and she pointed between them. "You're fucking Emerson Sterling."

"*Emerson* is fine." Emerson gave Alison her warmest smile. Alison was someone Hayley had talked about a lot. She'd been looking forward to meeting her—under different circumstances, but still.

"Yeah, no. That's not what I meant." Alison squinted and pointed to Hayley's shirt. The top two buttons were still undone from their brief make out session at the door. She turned to Hayley. "You're fucking Emerson fucking Sterling. That's what I meant."

Hayley's mouth dropped open and she looked to Emerson for some guidance.

Emerson merely shrugged. What else could she do?

Alison slapped her forehead and stumbled back a bit. "I totally lied to those camera guys, then. Oops. You are dating. Good for you." She looked at Emerson. "Did I tell you you're really pretty? Because you are. And taller than I expected. You look shorter on the movie screen, which seems silly because you're much larger on the screen since it's so big. I'm rambling. Hi."

Emerson accepted her extended hand and gave it a shake. "Hi. I'm sorry about Rob. Hayley tells me he's a total ass."

Alison nodded. "He is. I hate him."

Emerson nodded. "Me, too. Fuck that guy."

Alison cheered. "Fuck him!" She turned to Hayley. "I like her. Can she stay for dumpling night?"

Hayley looked caught off guard. "We, uh, we were sort of in the middle of something."

"Sex." Alison nodded and frowned. "I miss sex."

"No." Hayley put her hands up. "Not sex. Just talking."

"With your shirt undone?" Alison sounded skeptical. She was struggling to stand still with her hand on her hip. Emerson would feel a lot more comfortable if she sat down.

"Two buttons, Ali. It was hot in here."

"Yeah, because you were hooking up with her." Alison raised her hand for a high five. "Don't leave me hanging, Hay."

Hayley begrudgingly gave her a high five and Alison finally sat. Emerson was relieved.

Alison yawned and stretched out on the couch. "Don't mind me. Finish your love sonnets to each other or whatever. I'm just going to take a little napsy until you're ready for dumplings."

"Ali—" Hayley's objection was halted by the soft snores of her friend. "Okay. Good talk."

Emerson grabbed her bag and picked up the wig from the floor. "I'm going to head out."

"Emerson, we have more to talk about." Hayley met her at the door, a frustrated look on her face.

"Hayley, you're being stalked. At your home, at your office, at your favorite watering hole. Your best friend is getting propositioned for information about you and me and this insanity." She gestured to the space around them. "You're a prisoner here. Your shades are drawn, and you look like you haven't slept in days. This is madness."

Hayley blinked. "What are you trying to say, Emerson?"

She felt her eyes well with tears. "I'm saying that the people who mean the most to me, the people I love, are the ones hurt the most by my relationship with them. I brought a dark cloud into your life that night, backstage at that awards show, you just didn't realize it. But I did. Because it's what I do. I ruin people who get too close to me. Rachel and Drake are going to make sure you pay for helping me. And there's nothing I can do about it. Because I let it go too far. I got too deep into my feelings for you, and I forgot who I was for a few blissful, perfect days."

"Wait." Hayley reached for her as she pulled open the door. "Don't do this. Don't go. Don't just walk away from this."

She felt that familiar tightness in her chest and throat. If she stayed any longer she'd lose it. "I know your article drops tomorrow. I look forward to reading it. I know it's incredible and full of heart and humor and amazingness. Because you are all those things, Hayley. And I never deserved you sharing them with me. I'm so sorry, Hay…" Hayley was crying now, and Emerson hated that this was the last expression she'd see on that beautiful face.

"Emerson, wait—"

Emerson stepped into the hall and jogged to the stairwell, so Hayley couldn't stop her. She made it down to the first floor before the stream of tears made it too blurry for her to see. She crumpled in a heap on the bottom step and dropped her head into her hands. How did everything go so wrong so fast?

She looked down at the wig in her purse and her heart broke a little more. She was walking out into the lion's den with no plan, no direction, and no Hayley to seek comfort in. This day go could straight to hell.

CHAPTER TWENTY-SEVEN

Pictures of her and Rachel outside the café flashed across the screen and Hayley wanted to throw the remote at the TV.

"Turn it up." Alison croaked from the couch beside her. She'd stayed over last night because she was a mess and because Hayley was a mess and they could be a sad, crying mess together.

"I don't want to." Hayley went to click it off when Alison stole the remote from her. "Hey."

"Shh." Alison turned up the volume and the talking head host of the entertainment mag addressed the camera.

"Things are heating up in the gossip department for the cast of *The Willow Path Convergence*. With the movie about to drop and today's publication of the *Hollywood Sun*'s exclusive one-on-one interview with starlet Emerson Sterling, things could not be messier on the Boulevard." Video clips of Emerson and Rachel on the red carpet were juxtaposed and the now infamous grainy kiss photos from the set filled the screen.

The talking head continued, as photos flashed. "Rumors were circulating that Sterling and Blanche had a torrid love affair both on and off screen during the filming, and those rumors were confirmed by Blanche herself after she separated from the project and her role was recast with up-and-coming actress Piper Sanderson. Blanche hasn't shied away from opening up about some of the hottest questions of the hour."

A clip of her interview with Drake was cued up and Rachel wiped tears from her eyes as she described feeling discarded and manipulated by Emerson. Hayley groaned.

"Shh." Alison elbowed her in the ribs.

"Sterling's camp has been quiet about her alleged involvement with Blanche, but she's been generating some buzz of her own—she was seen in intimate proximity to the *Sun*'s Hayley Carpenter." Pictures of Hayley with Emerson at the ADR studio and holding hands on the plane popped up. "An insider confirms Sterling is very fond of Carpenter, and if this picture is any indication, the feeling appears to be mutual." The picture from inside Emerson's trailer filled the screen and Hayley felt violated. They were only talking, but they were very close, and she knew what had taken place moments after this picture was taken.

"Carpenter's exclusive interview with Sterling—including the bombshell revelation that the actress had a child in her teens that she gave up for adoption—has received positive feedback since its release earlier today, but calls to her camp for comment have remained unanswered. The identity of the child and the circumstances surrounding the adoption remain private."

Hayley looked at the cell phone she had turned off after it started ringing nonstop. Alison had taken the house phone off the hook, and they'd avoided as much technology as possible. She wished they'd kept it up.

Alison muted the show as they moved onto Kardashian news. "Holy shit. You were on *E!*"

Hayley dropped her head. "Ugh."

"I read your piece this morning. It was incredible. Really. You nailed it, Hayley." Alison gave her a one-armed hug, but she felt no comfort or pride.

"I lied." Hayley stared at the floor.

"About what?"

"Rachel."

Alison sat up straighter next to her. "What do you mean exactly?"

She looked at Alison and felt so defeated by admitting this. "Rachel—if I'm being frank—is a fucking super bitch who was blackmailing Emerson about her daughter so she wouldn't fight back in the press. I softened the edges for both of them so as to limit the negative backlash for either camp. Or myself." That part was what she was most ashamed of. Rachel had frightened her at the café. Her thinly veiled threats had settled heavily on Hayley's shoulders. She wanted to do right by Emerson, but she wasn't particularly eager to highlight the target on her back. She felt weak and cowardly.

She sighed. Emerson. She had been so hurt yesterday when Hayley had told her about Rachel and about how Rachel had threatened her. She had looked devastated. It wasn't something Hayley ever wanted to see on Emerson's face. That image haunted her last night during her restless sleep. She had met with Rachel to better understand where some of her anger might be coming from, where her desire to hurt Emerson and Rory originated. But all she did was make everything worse, for Emerson and herself.

"Oh. So you just fudged the truth a little." Alison patted her on the shoulder. "Love is the worst."

"Sure is." Hayley was emotionally exhausted. She should be doing cartwheels because her story was generating so much buzz. But the only person she wanted to talk to about this wasn't going to call or text or stop by. There was a finality to how Emerson walked out last night, and she knew it. Still, she hoped Emerson would read the article and find peace in it. She hoped she would be pleased. She hoped she would laugh and smile at the parts Hayley had put in there just for her. And she hoped, more than anything, Emerson could see that she wrote it with love in her heart and the best intentions in mind.

"I'm going to go out and buy us the biggest ice cream sundaes possible, and you are going to shower and change into something less tear soaked and comfier, and we're going to watch bad buddy comedies and avoid the world for one more day. Then we can face it." Alison stood and grabbed the Tylenol off the table. "After I medicate. Because my head is swimming."

Hayley laughed and settled into the couch, resigned to remaining under house arrest for another day. She had no intention of stepping outside and into the flashing camera lights. She hoped that now that the story was out, she'd get some privacy back.

The thought made her sad because she might be able to get back to normal, but Emerson and her family wouldn't. The movie premiere was in two days, and this was just the beginning for her, and for them. The secret was out, but Hayley hoped Emerson felt like she had done right by her and that it was on her terms. Hayley closed her eyes and tried to remember the image of Emerson in her shirt at the lake. That was her favorite memory of them together. She hoped Emerson could find some semblance of that tranquility as the weekend thundered on. But Hayley wished more than anything that she would have been able to find it with her.

❖

Emerson had read Hayley's piece about four times since it came out. Each time she found something she'd missed the first time, when she'd raced through it to see what topics and points Hayley had expounded upon. Only then did she read through it again more slowly, to truly appreciate the content.

The write-up was funny and sweet and at times hard to read. She wasn't used to seeing herself from someone else's perspective. Hayley's perceptions of her were honest and sincere. But *honest*. Some of Emerson's hardened Hollywood side was represented, like how she interviewed with people who weren't Hayley, and how she shied away from phones and cameras. Hayley did an amazing job of humanizing Emerson's celebrity and making it seem almost tangible to the reader. Emerson appreciated her interpretation of the world Emerson lived in. Hayley described her akin to a prima ballerina, performing night after night for demanding and unforgiving audiences, with no room for error or injury. There was no place for a misstep or imperfection. Emerson could picture the delicate porcelain ballerina in the ornate jewelry box that Hayley described—spinning perfectly and eternally without ever moving forward or back. That's how Hayley explained celebrity in this article. Unrealistic, brutal, exacting, and never ending. An impossible façade for a flawed, imperfect human to uphold.

Most importantly, though, Hayley was gentle with the Rory reveal. She was careful to limit the facts disclosed while bringing attention to the emotional journeys. Hayley described the challenges posed by Emerson's age and her inability to properly care for Rory in a way that was honest but kind. Hayley wrote about how giving up a child was an impossible decision made by a person who was a child herself, but that the decision had been made selflessly and with a maturity that Hayley did not have at that age. Emerson smiled at that, because she had always felt like she did the best with what she had at the time, but that never felt like enough. Hayley's narrative told her it was. She wanted to believe it.

She found the bit about Rachel particularly interesting. Hayley had told the truth, but she'd softened it. She'd rounded the edges and removed the sharpness. And she didn't mention Rachel was a blackmailing monster. Emerson wondered if this had anything to do with the meeting she'd had with Rachel. Part of her thought it was a smart move to preserve whatever career Hayley would have in this town moving forward, although she hated that that was even a thing to consider. But another part of her felt like Rachel was getting off scot-free. Both parts made Emerson feel like shit.

She pushed away her tablet and looked up at the ceiling fan. The premiere was tonight but she didn't feel like celebrating. In fact, she didn't feel like ever leaving this bed. But the vast emptiness of it made her heart hurt.

Tremont and her team were still working hard to find the origin of those photographs, and Hayley's revelation about meeting with Rachel didn't help minimize their suspect list at all. But something about it seemed off. Emerson's gut was telling her that Rachel, though probably involved, wasn't likely to be the mastermind here. This person had intimate knowledge of where Emerson would be and when, and the move was calculated in a way that Rachel wasn't. Rachel was more explosive and dramatic and, well, *Rachel*. Emerson was glad she'd had the chance to give Hayley some forewarning, but she hoped, for Hayley's sake, that now that the article was public, some of the threat was neutralized.

She'd wanted nothing more than to call Hayley and congratulate her on the article's release and the good buzz it was garnering so far. But she couldn't bring herself to do it. She'd done enough damage to Hayley's life already. And this attention, although positive for now, wasn't going to go away anytime soon. As long as *Willow Path* was relevant in the media, Hayley's article would be mentioned. She was along for the ride whether she wanted to be or not. Emerson wondered if Hayley regretted ever meeting her.

She felt bad about that. Because even though she'd walked away from Hayley, she did it for Hayley's own good, not for her own. She didn't regret anything that happened between them, except for the part where Hayley was getting hurt. She just hoped not too much of that hurt was directly from her. Because she was in love with Hayley. So much. And she couldn't imagine hurting Hayley intentionally or otherwise. That's why it was better that she leave, to shield Hayley from replays of this episode for the rest of her life.

But this was the worst—watching Hayley's genius and talent recognized and celebrated and not being able to share that with her. Because that's all she wanted, time with Hayley. She just wanted Hayley.

Her cell phone rang beside her. She had every intention to ignore it, but at the last second, she scooped it up and was glad she did. It was Deidre.

"Dee. Hi."

"Hey, Em." Her sister sounded tired. "So, I read the article…"

"What'd you think?" Emerson hadn't realized she would be nervous about Deidre's opinion until now. But she was. So nervous.

"I think this Hayley woman is a total catch." Deidre laughed softly.

"Oh, why do you say that?" Emerson's heart hurt because it was true, but she wanted to hear why Deidre thought so.

"She's got your number, Em. She pulled no punches. She did a great job describing you and all your little idiosyncrasies, and she made you seem lovable and gorgeous and smart, and best of all? She handled Rory's story with a delicacy that I never could have expected. She managed to tell your story, without telling too much, and she gave us a real shot at preserving our family's privacy. So that's what I mean when I say she's a total catch. Because she is."

Emerson started crying and she couldn't stop. She was crying because she felt relief. She was crying because she felt regret. She was crying because her sister, like always, was right. Hayley was a total catch and Emerson had to live the rest of her life knowing that and not being able to be with her.

"Emerson? Why are you crying?" Deidre sounded worried. "We'll figure it out, Em. We'll find a new normal. You saved us from a tidal wave. Your intuition was dead right—you took the narrative from Rachel, and Hayley delivered. It all worked out, Em. The best it could have. We'll figure it out. It's going to be okay."

"I hope you're right." Emerson was glad to hear the relief in her sister's voice, but her concerns were selfishly rooted in her own broken heart at the moment. She knew Deidre and her family would be fine. They had each other to lean on for support. Emerson was alone. Again. And it had never felt more devastating.

CHAPTER TWENTY-EIGHT

Rachel's face fell momentarily when Emerson walked into the soundstage where her current project was based, and Emerson took an inordinate amount of pleasure from that. Rachel rebounded quickly, a tight smile forming as she dismissed whatever minion was nearby. Emerson didn't really care who was around to hear what she had to say.

"Emerson. This is a pleasant surprise." The flash of anger in her eyes told her that was a lie.

"Rachel." She matched the sweet tone Rachel was feigning and took it a step further, leaning in for an embrace and kissing her on the cheek.

Rachel was rigid in her arms. Emerson noticed Bernard in the corner, but he didn't move. She imagined Rachel must had signaled for him to stand down. She had it on good authority that Bernard liked her, anyway. She wasn't worried about that big teddy bear. She didn't have any beef with him.

"We should catch up." She leaned back but stayed close.

Rachel looked uncomfortable. "We should. I'm a little busy at the moment. Another time, perhaps."

Rachel made as though she was going to take a step to the side, but Emerson matched her move.

Rachel's eyes widened, and she opened her mouth to say something, but Emerson cut her off.

"Don't you fucking dare call Bernard over here. I swear to you—I will make you pay for every bad fucking thing you have ever done, you selfish, narcissistic monster. Smile and come for a walk with me, or

I'll air your dirty laundry on every major media outlet within the next fifteen minutes."

Rachel snarled. "You have nothing on me. I'm the victim here."

Emerson laughed but kept a perma-smile on her face to keep up appearances. Her voice was a near whisper. "You think I've been lying low all these months and just taking your hits without building an arsenal of my own? You're foolish if that's the case. I'm sure America would love to hear how you threatened the life and safety of an eleven-year-old girl to get back at your ex."

"I never threatened her."

"Like hell you didn't."

Rachel looked panicked. "I didn't do anything."

"Walk, now."

She nodded and collected herself. "I'll be right back, Bernard. Emerson and I need to have a chat."

Bernard looked suspicious but didn't move. He gave Emerson a nod as they passed. She'd always liked him.

Emerson led them to a quiet area and asked for the room. A few techs scattered when they realized who was asking. No one made direct eye contact. Clearly, Rachel had flexed her muscle here, and people were afraid of her. Good. That benefited Emerson.

Once the room was clear and the door closed, Rachel raged, "How fucking dare you show up here and act like you have any authority over me."

That was the Rachel she was used to. Not the sad, pathetic crybaby who'd been in the media lately. Her Rachel was a fiery beast, and at the moment, she was fuming.

Emerson strode up to her and walked her back against the wall behind her. She crowded her to the point just before touching. "I don't know which one of your two faces to say this to, so I'll try both. I'm done with your bullshit. We both know what went down, and I have no apologies for the mess you made for yourself. But you came after my family. You want the fame and the praise and the love? It's yours. I never fought you, I never fought back. But you came for Rory and now I'm done with your games. So help me God, Rachel, if she gets hurt or is harmed in any way, I will make it my life's work to ruin you and everything you hold dear."

Rachel's eyes were wide, and she sagged under Emerson's gaze.

"I never meant for this to get out of hand, Emerson. I wouldn't have said anything. I was just angry. I thought it would bait you into...I'm sorry."

Emerson could tell by Rachel's face that she was telling the truth. She stepped back, and the fury that fueled her began to fade. "I never meant to make you feel like you didn't matter to me, Rachel. I've heard what you said, over and over. You weren't insignificant to me. I'm sorry about the way things worked out, if I ever made you feel unwanted or—"

"You didn't." Rachel sighed. "The truth is, you were great. And you're right. I made this mess myself and I need to sort it out."

Emerson appreciated her honesty and stepped back to give her some space. "I was actually going to call your friend Hayley and thank her. She did a nice job of not making me out to be the bad guy—"

"Even though you are, and you totally deserve it." She still had a little rage. She wasn't perfect, okay?

"Even if I deserved it." Rachel's face softened, and Emerson saw the woman she had developed true feelings for when they were together. This Rachel was kind and more caring than the one who graced movie screens and the pages of magazines. But she was fleeting. This Rachel could not survive in the harsh world that Hollywood forced upon them. And Emerson understood that better than anyone. "She took the high road and I'm grateful for that."

Emerson nodded. What Hayley did had been noble. She didn't have to paint such a pretty picture of Rachel, or of Emerson, for that matter. She'd taken a risk and from Emerson's standpoint, it'd paid off.

Rachel extended her hand toward Emerson. "Truce? I'll stop stirring up the past as long as we agree to let Hayley's version of the story live on in the media. Both of us accepting of what happened and agreeing to leave it behind us."

Emerson was wary but also weary. "Fine. No more mudslinging. No more threatening the people in my life, including Hayley and anyone else. And above all, Rory stays out of the media. She didn't do anything to invite this scrutiny and she deserves her privacy. Agreed?"

Rachel nodded. "Agreed."

"Did you tell anyone else about her?" Emerson had to know.

Rachel shook her head. "I never intended to say anything, ever. I was trying to hurt you. That was wrong."

"You succeeded." Emerson felt herself deflate.

"I'm sorry. I mean that." Rachel's expression was sincere.

"Me, too." Emerson sighed. "I didn't mean to be so forceful with you before, either."

Rachel smiled. "It was all kinds of hot. In retrospect, I mean—in real time it was terrifying. But also hot."

Emerson laughed. "Thanks, I think."

"That was totally a compliment." Rachel looked at the clock on the wall. "I should probably get back before Bernard thinks you murdered me."

Emerson glanced at the time as well. She had to get ready for tonight's event. "Hey, did you stake someone out to take pictures of me?"

"You mean besides the usual hyena pap horde? No. No need. You generate enough front-page news and interest that I didn't need to." Rachel held open the door and Emerson walked through with her.

"Yeah, the more I thought about it, the less and less I thought it was your style. But I wasn't sure." Emerson's mind raced. "Thank you for walking with me."

Rachel gave her a look. "You didn't give me much of a choice."

"I wouldn't hurt you. You know that, right?"

"I do." Rachel gave her a genuine smile. "Maybe we can be friends after all this, Em."

Emerson walked her the rest of the way back to Bernard and gave him a wave. She hugged Rachel and stepped back. "I don't think that's ever going to be possible, Rachel. But I'm willing to hold up my end of the bargain if you are."

Rachel looked a little sad, but she nodded. "I will."

And for once, Emerson believed Rachel's words matched her intentions.

❖

"You're going. Stop overthinking it," Alison called out from behind a clothing rack in the fashion department at the *Sun*.

"I can't. What will I say to her? What if she isn't happy to see me? This is a big night for her. I should just have Sharon go. Or anyone else.

They can get the story and interview or whatever and I can stay on my couch and cry into my ice cream sundae." Hayley was beyond nervous.

Alison reemerged holding three very expensive- and extravagant-looking dresses. "Stop that. You love her, right?"

Hayley nodded. She'd known for a while now, but watching Emerson walk out the other night had made it impossible to ignore.

"Then go. Just look gorgeous and go." Alison pointed to the dresses. "I'm thinking dark green. It'll pull out the color in your eyes."

Hayley wasn't so sure about this. The *Sun* had gotten tickets to the *Willow Path* screening and she'd plan to attend as media, but that was long before everything that had transpired between her and Emerson. And Rachel. Alison had nearly had to kidnap her kicking and screaming to agree to come here and get dressed in the best couture they had on site. "Alison, what if something happens to the dress?"

"It won't. Plus, it's insured." Alison gave her an encouraging nod. "It's a loaner. I'm loaning it to you for the night. You'll look incredible, and the dress will get to go out for a night on the town. No one will be any the wiser."

"Unless there's pictures," Hayley pointed out. She'd come to find out there were always pictures. Always.

"Meh, let me worry about that." She checked the time on her phone. "We need to hustle. Your car will be here shortly."

Hayley accepted the dress Alison selected and stepped behind the screen to change. "Okay, let's go over it once more."

"Right. Tina and Cari will be here in five to do your hair and makeup. You owe them big-time, but I think two nights of happy hour at Lilly's will cover it. Then the car will take you to the venue, and you'll enter through the media entrance in the back and meet up with Scotty. You'll watch the movie and stay for the actor Q and A, and then you'll see Emerson and blow her away with your Hollywood transformation, she'll realize she can't live without you, and you'll ride off into the sunset together. And have really, really attractive babies."

Hayley had gone over and over the events of the other night and she felt a mix of anger, confusion, and frustration, but her overwhelming sensation was sadness. A part of her felt responsible for the photo leak, like she'd unleashed a heap of trouble for all of them by contacting and meeting with Rachel, but something Emerson said wouldn't leave her.

She said that she ruined Hayley's life and that she was a black cloud. That was as far from Hayley's perception as possible. Sure, they'd run into some…drama, but didn't the positive outweigh the negative? Her heart told her it did. Her brain told her she should be terrified about being jobless and consequently homeless if those pictures ever got out, but her heart didn't care. Her heart was with Emerson, and she wanted to be there, supporting her tonight, because even if this didn't work out between them, she felt like she owed her that. She owed herself that.

"You make it sound so easy." She took a deep breath and stepped out from behind the screen, pointing to her back. "A little zipper help?"

Alison nodded and complied. "It is that easy."

"Nothing is easy, Alison." Hayley stepped back and looked at herself in the gown. "Whoa."

"Whoa is right. You look amazing. I'm so good at my job." Alison fist pumped. She put her hands on Hayley's shoulders and gave her a squeeze. "You've got this. I'm rooting for you."

She reached up and covered Alison's hand with hers. "I really appreciate this, Ali. I know you've got your own stuff going on, and this can't be easy."

Alison shrugged. "It's a nice distraction. You deserve to be happy. So do I. I realize I wasn't happy with Rob. And I think I knew it all along. It sucks—don't get me wrong—but I'll survive."

Hayley turned and gave her a hug as Tina and Cari arrived with a wave. "You know, I know a strapping ginger with a great sense of humor who has an amazing eye for lighting and flattering camera angles."

Alison considered this. "Scotty?"

"One and the same." Hayley added, "I'll put in a good word tonight. Maybe you two can talk shop and nerd out over camera stuff."

"You do that, and I'll buy the first round of drinks at Lilly's." Alison extended her hand for a shake.

"Deal."

"Great. Now go get gorgeous and get your girl back."

Hayley exhaled and sat in the makeup chair. She had nothing to lose and everything to gain, right?

CHAPTER TWENTY-NINE

Tell me you have some good news for me." Emerson looked at Tremont and held her breath.

"Yes and no."

"I don't like the *no* part." Emerson looked out the window of the limo. They were third in line to unload on the red carpet. Try as she might to get excited about tonight's movie premiere, she couldn't seem to garner the enthusiasm. She hated the way things had ended with Hayley and she wanted more than anything to see her tonight and share this with her. She hoped Hayley might show up, but she could understand why she would stay away, especially if they hadn't figured out who was threatening to leak those photos. She was still at risk and that made Emerson queasy.

"Your private investigator's been busy. We found out who snapped the pictures." Tremont's brow was furrowed in concentration while he scanned his phone screen.

"Who is it?" She had to resist the urge to snatch the phone from him to see for herself.

"Some pap named Gerard Foreman who contracts for a few celebrity tabloid sites. He picked it up as a side gig, cash payout."

"Who hired him?"

"We're working on that. I'm told we'll have an answer shortly." He typed something, then put his phone on his lap, screen side up.

"How much is that going to cost me?"

Tremont gave her a look. "How much is it worth to you?"

They both knew she didn't care. She wanted to know who was

hunting her more than she cared about how much the information cost her.

"And Hayley?" Okay, so maybe she'd asked Tremont to see if she would be there tonight, you know, in a professional capacity.

Tremont frowned, his expression sympathetic. "Nothing yet."

"Dammit." She felt like crying, but they'd already redone her makeup twice. She bit the inside of her cheek to quell the urge. The car moved forward. It was time to go.

Tremont leaned forward and took her hands. "You're going to do fine. The advance buzz has been amazing. Tonight is all pomp and circumstance for the studio. Just smile for the cameras. Then go in, and we can go over some of the possible Q and A topics while the audience watches the film." He paused. "I assume you don't want to watch it again."

"No." Emerson had had her fill of seeing herself as Willow Path on the screen. This movie had brought more struggles and pain than she had ever imagined possible. She had anxiously anticipated this day, but now that it was here, she was dreading it.

Tremont picked up his phone and answered a call. He held the phone to his ear and spoke to Emerson. "I'm being told by Chandra that you're going to walk with Kate and Paige. They're ready for you."

Emerson nodded. She'd asked Tremont to arrange for her to walk the carpet with someone else to take the scrutiny off her. She wasn't feeling as sharp or focused as usual, and she wanted a wingperson to help distract as much as possible. Kate and Paige were the perfect people. They could talk about the movie and she could stand in the background, fulfilling her requirements but not carrying the conversation. This was the best option possible.

A knock on the glass told them it was go time.

Emerson went to slide toward the door, but Tremont stopped her.

"You worked hard for this, Em. This is for all the beans. Try to enjoy it as best you can. I'll keep working on my end, and I'll update you with everything as it comes. We'll figure this all out, and at the end of the day we'll look back at this fondly and reminisce about all the alcohol we had to consume to get through it."

Emerson laughed. "I couldn't do this without you, you know that?"

"I love you, too." Tremont gave her hand a squeeze. He pointed to the overpriced watch that she'd gifted him. "And as much as I love this guy, he needs a friend. Just remember that when it's bonus time."

"I'll take it under consideration."

The door opened, and Chandra's head popped in. "We good?"

"All good." Emerson stepped out and smiled toward the shouts of her name.

❖

"The early reviews have been great, Paige. Congrats." Emerson slid her arm around Paige's waist and posed for another picture.

"There'd be no *Willow Path* without you." Paige gave her a broad smile and her spiky blond hair bounced with her nod. "Or Kate, for that matter. You done good, Kate."

Kate Stanton laughed. "Everyone always thanks the writer last. As if either of you would have a job without me."

They chuckled and posed together before waiting on their mark until it was time to move to the next section of carpet.

"Hey, I read that write-up about you. It was well done." Paige turned to her and spoke privately. "I had no idea you had to make such a difficult choice in your youth. Kudos to you, Emerson, you endured something that could have wrecked you and managed to succeed in spite of it. I hope everything has worked out in that department for you."

"I couldn't have said that better myself." Kate nodded. "Hayley did a great job navigating the difficult Rachel situation. She really kept the focus on you and the complexities of the business without making it sound too whiny or overly flattering. It was a good balance."

"Yeah," Emerson agreed, "and thank you."

"Is Hayley here tonight?" Paige looked out at the media behind the gates in front of them. "I'd like to thank her for that last day of shooting."

"Thank her for what?" Emerson asked.

Paige turned her back to the media and brought their conversation circle in closer. "She was the one who alerted me that there was someone secretly filming our last shots. Security caught the guy. Someone from Celebrity Dish Network or something. Turns out he was hired by—"

"James Drake." Tremont appeared behind Emerson, out of breath and panting. He held up his phone to show her an image of two men exchanging something. "Drake hired the photographer. He's trying to set you up."

Paige nodded. "Yeah. That guy. I didn't think to mention it before."

"I hate that guy." Kate scowled. "He's such a—"

"Parasite. Waste of air. Festering, septic wound," Tremont supplied.

"I was going to say opportunist. But those work," Kate said.

Emerson looked up the carpet to see if Drake was anywhere in sight. She didn't see him. That was probably better for everyone.

Chandra approached and told them it was time to move to the next mark.

"Well, damn." Tremont let out a low whistle.

Emerson looked back at him. "What are we whistling about?"

"Did someone say whistle?" A piercing shriek came from a few feet away.

"Hayley." Emerson searched for the familiar sound and her jaw dropped. "Oh."

"Yeah. That's what I was talking about." Tremont patted her on the butt and pushed her forward. "I'll take Kate and Paige to the mark. Meet us when you're ready."

Emerson stepped forward and Hayley gave her a shy smile. "Hayley."

"Hi."

Emerson felt like a weight had been lifted off her shoulders. She hadn't expected the first feeling the next time she'd see Hayley to be one of relief, but it was. And Hayley, well, Hayley looked incredible. "You look great. Like, really great."

"Thanks." More shy smiling. It was adorable.

"I read your piece. I meant to call you but—"

Hayley raised her hand and motioned around them. "Maybe we can talk about it later. In private?"

Emerson nodded. "Right. Yeah." Something occurred to her. "You need a sound bite, right?"

Hayley shrugged. "Not really why I'm here."

"And why's that?" Emerson didn't care who was around. She wanted to talk to Hayley. She needed to.

"I'm here for you. To support you. To show you that none of this was about a story or a job. It was for you. All of it." Hayley's eyes sparkled, and Emerson swooned.

"Watch the movie with me."

"What?" Hayley looked confused.

"Be my guest. Get your sound bite or whatever and sit with me for the showing. Then we can talk, more privately." Emerson needed Hayley to make her feel grounded and in control. She wanted to warn her about Drake, and she selfishly just wanted her for, well, her. She needed just a few minutes to feel whole again. "Please."

"I'd love to." Hayley seemed a little emotional. Emerson felt the same way.

She called over her shoulder to Kate and Paige, then asked Hayley, "Have you met Kate yet?"

"No, I haven't had the opportunity." Hayley stood a little taller and introduced herself.

"Ah, you wrote the article on Em here. It was well done. I was talking about it earlier to them." Kate motioned to Paige and Emerson.

"Oh? Thank you."

Emerson leaned in. "Kate, did you know Hayley's a screenwriter? She's moonlighting as a reporter for the moment, but she's been working on something that sounds really exciting."

Hayley's eyes bulged.

"Oh, really? I'd like to hear about it sometime." Kate smiled to someone calling her name and waved. "Are you going to be inside for the premiere?"

Hayley looked at Emerson and smiled. "I am."

"Great. Let's chat over drinks before the show. I might know a director who could use some decent material to work with."

"You don't say?" Paige chimed in, and Emerson thought she might be flirting with Kate a little. They would be a cute couple, she decided. "Drinks on Kate. But count me in to the convo, too."

Hayley looked floored. "I'll nervously work on my pitch when you walk away. No worries there."

Kate laughed and nodded toward the man with the camera standing behind Hayley. "Quick shot before we move on?"

"Absolutely." Hayley waved for him to shoot. "Ladies, the critics have been fawning over your work together. Was there any one thing that made you feel like this trio worked so well?"

Emerson answered, "Hard work. And sticking together. There were lots of challenges that came up during the filming and editing process, but Kate and Paige were consummate professionals and made every attempt to make us as actors feel welcomed and appreciated. This was an—at times—difficult process, in part because the story requires so much emotional vulnerability to be believable. That can take its toll on a person. But in the end, being vulnerable is worth the reward that awaits you. That's something I learned during filming. I'm grateful for them both. I don't think *Willow Path* would have come out the way it did without them. They're a real dream team to work with."

"Well, there's no way I'm topping that." Kate laughed.

Paige dabbed away invisible tears. "I just love you ladies so much."

The crowd around them laughed, and they had a brief break before the next mark. Paige and Kate stepped forward to answer some more questions, but Emerson trailed behind to talk to Hayley some more.

"How much longer do you need to stick around out here?" she asked Hayley.

Hayley looked up at camera guy behind her. Man, he was tall. "What do you think, Scotty?"

"All good here. I can get some background shots without you." He acknowledged Emerson's presence. "Nice to meet you, ma'am."

"*Emerson* is fine." She gave him a warm smile.

Hayley raised her eyebrow. "You know, I was just telling Scotty how great my friend Alison is."

"She's a hot ticket, that one. A real catch," Emerson said to Scotty.

"Oh, okay, good to know." He blushed and fiddled with the camera settings.

She turned back to Hayley. "I'll send Tremont to bring you inside. See you soon?"

"Definitely."

Chapter Thirty

Y ou look fantastic. Did I tell you that already?" Emerson looked at Hayley with those eyes she thought about all the time, and she felt truly beautiful in that moment.

"You mentioned it once or twice, but feel free to continue." Hayley felt like she was in a dream again. She'd had the chance to socialize with Kate and Paige before the movie, and God, the movie. The movie was incredible. The previews didn't do it justice. Emerson was unbelievable as Willow Path. She laughed, she cried, she squirmed at the sex scenes, and she wasn't sure she'd ever be the same again. But what really made it special was that Emerson sat beside her the whole time, holding her hand in the dark. She shared this moment with her. It was something she thought she'd never get over or forget. Emerson had changed her life in so many ways. She wasn't sure how to thank her.

Emerson reached out and touched her hand, but the touch was far too brief for Hayley's liking. "I'll tell you all day long if it makes you glow like that. It's true, after all."

"You're sweet-talking me and I'm supposed to be here sweet-talking you." Hayley had come here to win Emerson back, but she was too busy being swept off her feet.

Emerson gave her a small smile. "Your piece was great, Hay." Her voice was tentative. "It was perfect. I couldn't have asked for a more honest and sincere depiction of myself. You don't need to sweet-talk me, Hay. You already won me over."

Hayley stepped a little closer. "Oh, yeah? And when did I do that?"

Emerson's eyes flicked down to her lips, so she licked them for good measure. "Somewhere between LA and Maine."

"You can't get much farther in the US from LA than Maine." Hayley thought of their time together at the lake house daily. She revisited it when she needed to remember the bigger picture. The relationship she had formed with Emerson was the bigger picture.

"I want to kiss you right now," Emerson said. Emerson was close enough to touch her, but she didn't. Hayley figured that was because they were in public...or because she was second-guessing asking Hayley to be her guest tonight.

She frowned. "The feeling is mutual. But something tells me you haven't because—"

"I'm sorry." Emerson shook her head and looked around them. When she looked back at her, Hayley could see a sadness that wasn't there a moment ago. And just like that, the elation she had felt mere minutes before was gone.

Hayley took a step back in preparation for what she expected would be rejection. She'd seen that look on Emerson's face the other night. It was one of regret and remorse. Hayley hated that look.

Emerson said in a near whisper, "I found out who's behind the pictures."

Hayley froze. "Who is it?"

"It was James Drake." Emerson lip curled, her anger palpable.

Hayley looked around. Just hearing his name made her skin crawl. His attacks on her had escalated to the point that she had seriously entertained the idea of quitting the *Sun* after the release of Emerson's piece. His reach was far and wide, and his fans were as unscrupulous as he was. "Are you sure?"

"Positive," Emerson replied.

Hayley wasn't sure she'd ever hated someone as much as she hated Drake in that moment. "I'll kill him."

Emerson gave her a sad smile. "That's not how it works in this town, Hay. Plus, I'm pretty sure that slime isn't killable. He'll get his, I'll make sure of it."

"How?" Hayley hoped it involved sharp pins and electric shocks to his genitals, but she kept that to herself.

Tremont jogged to them and gave Hayley a smile. "You clean up nice, Velma."

"Gee, thanks, Montie."

He smiled in response, but it was short-lived. He turned to Emerson and frowned before looking back to her. "I'm glad you're here, Hayley. We need to talk. There's been a development."

"What kind of development?" Emerson looked a little unnerved.

He looked back at Hayley but didn't say anything at first. He pulled his phone out of his pocket and handed it directly to her. "I'm so sorry, Hayley. The pictures are live. And there's more of them."

"Oh my God." Hayley took the phone and nearly dropped it. On the screen in front of her were the three photos Emerson had shown her the other night. But the real stomach punch came when she scrolled a little farther, and the next image showed her hand in Emerson's robe, while her mouth was on Emerson's neck. She had sort of half-heartedly rehearsed a defense speech in case she got fired for the kissing pictures, but this was something else. There was no talking her way out of this one. She didn't dare scroll any farther, not in public anyway.

"Fuck." Emerson's voice was a harsh whisper over her shoulder. She glanced up in time to catch the panicked expression on Emerson's face, and her knees nearly buckled as a wave of nausea swept over her.

"Hayley." Emerson grabbed her elbow and steadied her, but just as the room stopped spinning, Hayley noticed the people standing around her were all staring. At her. Some were pointing, all were whispering, and that devastating feeling of violation was present again, this time a thousandfold.

"We need to go. We have to get her out of here." Emerson's voice sounded distant, but Hayley was aware of her hand still guiding her elbow.

"The car's outside waiting," Tremont replied. She vaguely heard him get on the phone with someone and tell them that Emerson wouldn't be at the Q and A, but she missed his reasoning. They were moving quickly, and she was doing her best to keep up, but her head felt foggy and like it wasn't attached to her body.

They flew down the stairs to the first floor and slipped down another near empty corridor toward the rear exit of the building. Tremont jogged ahead and ushered people out of the way, but for the most part the halls were empty. The distant sounds of laughing and clapping could be heard behind them. It was business as usual for everyone else.

"The car's out here." Tremont was out of breath by the time they reached the back door. He pushed it open with a grunt.

A heavy rain fell outside the doors and blanketed the back lot of the auditorium in sheets of water. Steam rose from the hot LA pavement as the rain pelted the ground and splashed back into the air. This would have been a fantastic image—the rain and the darkness with the rising mist—if this was a movie and not real life. But it was very, very real. And so was James Drake, standing there with a film crew and a microphone, blocking their way out.

❖

Emerson took one look at Drake and reeled. That fucking bloodsucker. She made eye contact with Tremont and he used his bag to shield Hayley's face as he ushered her into the waiting car. With the two of them safely stowed away, Emerson was free to handle this. And oh, how she would enjoy it.

She charged forward, catching Drake off guard. "Looking to get the inside scoop, Drake?"

"Emerson. What do you have to say about the pictures of you hooking up with Hayley Carpenter of the *Sun*?" Drake held up his phone and one of the images that had arrived in that envelope filled the screen.

"I suppose you're the person to ask about that, Drake." The rain beat down on her shoulders, but she barely felt it. Her hair and makeup were probably way past ruined, but she didn't care.

"I don't follow," he called out.

"Oh, but you do. You do follow, don't you?" Emerson turned to the camera and spoke directly to it. "James Drake hired a freelance photographer to follow me and take pictures for the purpose of promoting a smear campaign he's been carrying out against Hayley Carpenter. A campaign that he has freely championed in his daily, weekly, and monthly contributing columns, blogs, and vlogs through his paid work through the *Hollywood Daily Mail*." She turned back to Drake. "What do you think the people at the *Mail* are going to say when they find out you were stalking the very people you are supposed to report on? While using their contacts and their resources? Haven't you already been slapped with a restraining order? I bet this type of activity violates the terms, but I'm no lawyer. Perhaps some of your fans are. Care to weigh in, America?"

"You have no proof of these accusations, Ms. Sterling. This is grounds for a lawsuit." Drake sneered back at her.

"Is that so?" Emerson stepped into his space and Drake backed up, nearly knocking the cameraman off his feet. "And you think you're the only one who can hire someone to take pictures of people? What would you say if I told you I have evidence of you exchanging money and information with a Gerard Foreman? That name ring a bell? I hear he does some contractor work through *TMZ* and Celebrity Dish Network, among other places. What do you think they'll do with that information? Look into it a bit? Or blackball you? Sounds like there might be a lot of angry people out there, Drake."

Drake's smug expression faded, and he motioned for the filming to stop. The light from the camera flicked off and they were in near total darkness as the storm raged on.

"Stay away from me and my family, Drake. All of them. Ms. Carpenter included. Or we're not done here." Emerson strode toward the waiting car and got inside. What was done was done. There was no going back now.

❖

By the time they'd gotten onto the 105 it was late and Hayley hadn't spoken a word to her. Emerson had tried—unsuccessfully—to talk to her, but Hayley just gave her a blank stare until they were near the exit for her house. She banged on the dividing glass and asked the driver to take her home first.

"Hayley, are you okay?" Emerson kept her voice low, because something told her that if she used her usual volume, Hayley would spook. Because she already *looked* spooked. Emerson couldn't imagine what kinds of things might be going through her head right now, but she didn't think she should be alone with those thoughts. "Come home with me tonight. It's late. We should talk—"

"I just…" Hayley looked at Emerson before looking past her, looking through her. "I think I just need to be alone right now."

Hayley looked out the window and banged on the divider glass again. This time she told the driver to stop and let her out. "This is close enough."

"It's pouring, Hayley. At least let me take you to your door," Emerson pleaded. She didn't want Hayley to go. Not like this.

"You know, I didn't believe you when you said you brought a dark cloud into my life. I thought you were being overly dramatic and that you'd been through storms in the past that made you feel nervous or insecure or whatever, but I thought we could weather any storm that came our way, together." The car stopped, and Hayley opened the door. She motioned to the monsoon outside as she said, "But maybe you *were* right all along. Maybe I'm not cut out for these kinds of conditions. I just…I just need a little space right now."

"Wait. Hayley."

"Good-bye, Emerson." And with that, Hayley stepped out into the torrential downpour that was her life.

Chapter Thirty-one

Hayley was grateful the premiere was over the weekend because it gave her a few days to stay home and recover—or cry—about how things had turned out. Alison had been sweet and stopped by with some food, but Hayley had no interest in eating. Or in anything, really.

The media was abuzz with praise for *Willow Path* and Hayley's name came up often. Some of it was in reference to her months-long research with Emerson and the completion of their article, but most of it circled back to the photos of them in the trailer. There were two more that were much the same as the one she had seen on Tremont's phone, the series of which were now being called the "Hands-On Reporting." So far nothing else had come out. She had a feeling if there was anything worse, it'd be headline news by now.

Her Monday morning was filled with avoiding the stares of her coworkers and not answering any phone calls or emails. People from all over the world were calling for her comments on the photographs or asking to interview her about her time with Emerson. She was too numb from this weekend's disaster to be of use to anyone. She barely remembered her commute to work today. There was no way she could string coherent words together. She was a shell of a person today and she knew it.

An ad for *Willow Path* played on the edge of her Facebook wall, and she sighed. She'd replayed the events about a million times over the weekend. The high from her article release was what motivated her to take a chance and attend the premiere, in hopes of reconnecting with Emerson. And the opportunity to chat with Kate and Paige had made an already unbelievable night hit interstellar levels of amazing.

And the movie. Sigh. Seeing the completed film—something she and Emerson had spend literally hundreds of hours discussing—was such a magical experience for her. She'd seen the work that went into the behind-the-scenes stuff that made the movie possible. She'd gained a new appreciation for all the moving parts required to bring the final product to fruition, and yet it was her time with Emerson that had been the most significant.

Emerson. It always came back to Emerson.

She closed the web browser and stared at the wallpaper on her laptop screen. It was a view of the lake in Maine from the cabin's back deck. The weather would be warm enough soon that you could swim in the lake every day. All day. Even into the night. Night swimming was one of her favorite things. That was something she hadn't been able to try with Emerson; the water had been too cold when they were there. *They*, she lamented. As if there was ever a *they*.

Hayley felt her eyes fill with tears as she considered what could have been with Emerson. All of it had felt so real to her. She loved Emerson. She loved her deep and fierce and her heart ached at the way things had played out. She was beyond sad, but also angry. Though she was proud of the way she'd handled the Rory situation, she was angry because she'd put her concerns for Emerson's well-being ahead of her own. She was angry because Rachel warned her, much like Emerson had, that there were consequences to her relationship with Emerson, but she didn't heed those warnings. Maybe she had been too blinded by love to see what was right in front of her face all along, that she had put herself in real danger. And that made her angry, too.

Her office phone rang, and she startled. She could tell by the caller ID that it was Jonathan.

"Hayley. My office." His voice was flat. She'd been waiting for this.

She wiped her eyes and took a deep breath. There was no use putting off the inevitable.

Jonathan didn't stand when she entered the room. His brow was furrowed in concentration as he motioned for her to close the door.

She sat and waited.

"Hayley, your article has gotten a lot of great feedback." He made eye contact with her and a fatigued expression looked back at her.

"Thanks, Jonathan."

He sighed. "We need to talk about the pictures."

"I figured." Hayley shifted in her chair. Discussing this with him made her uncomfortable.

Jonathan stood and walked to the front of his desk. He leaned against it and crossed his arms over his chest. "Do you remember what we talked about when you first took the assignment to work with Emerson Sterling?"

"I do."

"Then you remember me telling you that if there was any way you might be compromised or found to be colluding with Emerson or her team, I wouldn't be able to help you, right?"

Hayley set her jaw. "I didn't collude with anyone. But to answer your question—yes, I recall you mentioning something about throwing me to the wolves."

Jonathan bristled. "What happened? Tell me what happened and help me understand."

Hayley shrugged. She couldn't answer that for herself, let alone for her boss. "Nothing and everything. I don't know. I did the job I was asked to do. I got to the bottom of the story and reported my findings to the best of my ability."

"And at some point along the way you fell onto Sterling's lips and compromised the entire project, is that what you're saying?" Jonathan looked none too thrilled.

Hayley sighed. "They're just photographs, Jonathan. You have no idea the context of what was occurring before, after, or during that photograph."

He laughed. "I've been doing this a long time, Hayley. A picture is worth a thousand words. I don't care if you were choking and she saved your life, with or without her tongue. I also don't care if she was having a heart attack and your hand inside her robe was there to check to see if her heart was still beating. Those pictures depict you two in an intimate exchange. You crossed the line with her, Hayley. And the other media outlets are crying foul."

"Let them." Hayley stood and mirrored his position, her arms crossed in defiance. "Drake crossed the line by hiring someone to stalk me, but no one seems to be concerned about that."

Jonathan pinched the bridge of his nose and shook his head. "Not the best example, Hayley. Drake's been fired and there's murmurings of legal action."

This was news to Hayley. "Oh."

Jonathan nodded and frowned. "Hayley, I'm sorry. This is causing too much negative attention. I've been putting out fires since Friday night. We can't continue like this."

"What are you trying to say?" Hayley knew what he was saying, but she wanted to make him say it.

"You're fired."

And just like that, a bad few days turned into the worst week of her life.

Chapter Thirty-two

Emerson nervously tapped the steering wheel of her rental car. She'd tried listening to music, but she couldn't find a station that didn't keep cutting out on her. So she was driving in silence, which gave her too much time to think. She would have used her phone to cue up Pandora, but she'd foolishly left her charger at home and she was afraid of running out of battery. A battery she desperately needed to keep her GPS going, not that that seemed to be much help. The little car on the GPS app occasionally spun in circles.

She sighed. Tremont would have a field day if she told him she forgot something as important as a cell phone charger. She was grateful that was all she'd forgotten. This was the first time she'd packed anything for herself—without any help from him or his snide-ass Post-it reminders—in as long as she could remember. But this was a trip she wanted to take on her own. She'd even taken the flight by herself, which took a lot more mental preparedness than packing. But she'd survived it. If she survived that, she could survive anything, right?

The little GPS car did a do-si-do, and Emerson tried not to panic. Was she supposed to turn here? She relaxed her hands when her knuckles started to throb. She hadn't realized she was clutching the wheel so tightly. This looked familiar. Well, everything looked the same, but this looked more familiar than the other green trees and unpaved roads. Or was she about to drive off into the woods and never be found with no way to charge her cell phone or call for help? That was also a possibility. Fuck it. Take the turn, Emerson.

She eased onto the path and tried not to overthink it. She'd chosen a modest rental car, but the agent at the car center was more interested in taking a selfie with her than helping her choose the right vehicle, something that was suddenly very important to her when she saw the grooved mud tracks from what appeared to be a recent storm. She doubted this car had all-wheel drive, not that she'd know how to engage it if it wasn't automatic anyway. She vowed to learn to be more independent if she survived this trek.

The last two months had been a whirlwind. The general release of the movie was received with open arms and award buzz had already started. It looked like the studio would get their *Titanic* after all. She was getting praise after praise for her performance, but somehow none of it mattered the way she'd expected it to. She'd been spending a lot of time in Colorado in between her studio and press obligations. She'd put a hold on any future acting projects and had focused on working on some new Zelda Frog stuff. That way she could spend time with Deidre and her family more, since she could do that work remotely.

Things with Rory were improving every day. They'd started to go to therapy as a family. And Emerson had started doing her own therapy on the side as well. She liked talking about her stress and what was expected of her. And what she expected of herself. She felt like the therapy had had a positive impact on her fear of flying, too. That was an unexpected and added bonus.

But therapy also helped her identify what was truly lacking in her life. She couldn't get excited about *Willow Path*—or anything, really— because what she wanted most was Hayley. And Hayley had packed up and disappeared. She'd left town. She was just gone. Emerson looked for her and she'd tried to reach her. Hayley didn't seem to want to be found. But deep down, she knew where to find Hayley. She just had to work up the nerve to put herself out there and take the risk. Hayley was worth it. She had always been worth it.

The road seemed to go on forever and everything was lush and green and dense, so she had no idea if she was going in the right direction since her GPS had effectively told her to fuck off about twenty minutes ago. Was this road this long last time? She couldn't remember.

The road veered toward the right and it narrowed. The

overgrowth made it feel like the forest was closing in on her, and she felt momentarily claustrophobic. She squinted through her tinted sunglasses to try to see if she was getting close.

"These are so fucking dark." She pushed them up onto her head just in time to see the moose dart out in front of her. "Sonofabitch!"

She slammed on the brakes and jolted forward as the car fishtailed in the muddy grooves of the road. She tried to throw the car into reverse to get away from the animal, but the wheels spun and whined in a useless and pathetic show of force.

Emerson looked back up at the moose and tried to decide the best course of action, since she seemed to be stuck. Then something occurred to her.

"You bastard." She laughed and yelled out the window in triumph. "That's a hell of a welcome, Stan."

Standing before her with a goofy, smug expression was Stan the marker moose identifying the edge of Hayley's Maine cabin property. And she had never been so glad to see his ugly mug.

She gave her heart a minute to slow down before she put the car in drive and prayed it would move. It didn't. Because of course. She looked down at her cell phone and swallowed thickly. She had less than 10 percent battery left. She dropped her head to the steering wheel and exhaled.

"You can do this, Emerson. You were named for a nature-loving transcendentalist. You have been in a dozen stunt car accidents, and you played a fucking badass jungle explorer." She looked down at her designer shoes and sighed. "Just accept that you are totally going to ruin your fucking shoes. That will help ease the sorrow later on when you have to sacrifice them to make a flare when you can't get out of here anyway."

She stepped out of the car and the sludgy road swallowed her left foot. "See? You were totally expecting that. It's good to be prepared." She looked up at Stan and shook her fist at him. "You're kind of an asshole, Stan. I'm just putting that out into the universe."

She swore Stan winked at her, so she flipped him off.

"So much for unexpected romantic gestures à la *Pretty Woman*," she grumbled. "Richard Gere's car would totally have survived this kind of murky roadway."

She paused. "He had a driver. Of course he did. You're right, Stan." She looked up at the carving and nodded. "Next time I'll stick with a driver. Then I wouldn't have to worry about digging out the wheels and trying to find a nice flat board to help get my car out of the mud. You make a good point. I see you have some redeeming qualities."

She sighed and asked with a smile. "Any chance you've got a shovel up your ass?"

❖

Hayley stood up from her desk and stretched. The cell phone alarm sounded to remind her to step away from the computer and hydrate or walk or pee. Whatever. She needed to be reminded because all her days ran into each other since she'd moved here from LA.

After the photos were leaked and she was fired—both of which sucked, by the way—she'd gotten the hell outta Dodge, so to speak. Except it was LA and she doubted anyone would miss her now that she was the reporter that hooked up with a celebrity to get the inside scoop. Okay, maybe she was being a little harsh on herself, but those photos of her and Emerson kissing popped up every time she googled her own name. So she was *that* kind of internet famous, it seemed.

But she knew that some people missed her. Like Alison. They talked every few days. Alison had started dating Scotty after she introduced them, and they were making plans to come out in the next few weeks to stay a few days with her before the fall entertainment season picked up and they both got too busy to travel. Being as the lake was at its peak temperature and beauty, she really wanted to share this with someone. Anyone.

She frowned because the person she wanted to share this with was the same person she had actively been trying not to think about for the last two months. Emerson. She knew that Emerson had missed her too, since she'd tried to reach her about a thousand times. But Hayley ignored every call and text and email and even a few handwritten letters that were really beautiful, and Emerson had such gorgeous script, but that was beside the point because she wasn't going to answer them, ever.

She didn't know if Emerson had tried to find her at her old apartment since she'd moved out immediately after she was fired, but the forwarded mail told her she'd at least tried to write her there. But the sixty days of mail forwarding ended earlier this week, so any further correspondence seemed unlikely. Especially since she'd canceled and permanently signed out of every social media forum in an effort to purge her obsessive checking of Emerson's whereabouts and her own faux celebrity gossip status. Because how many times could she look at that picture of Emerson leaving that Starbucks wearing *her* plaid shirt? She needed to live more simply. She needed to get back to her roots. She needed her Grandma Ginny. But she'd settle for her essence and her cabin. Her happy place. Or at least, what used to be her happy place.

Try as she might to forget the weekend she'd spent here with Emerson, it was absolutely impossible. Even though numerous others had stayed in the cabin since they'd stayed here, she still found little reminders of Emerson tucked here or there.

Her first night in the cabin had been the most difficult. She swore she could smell Emerson's perfume on the sheets in the master bedroom. So she slept on the couch. But there she was haunted by how comfortable Emerson had been sleeping on her chest, in front of the fireplace. After a fitful night she washed all the linens, the couch cover, and all the pillows in an effort to purge Emerson's phantom scent from the fabric. It didn't help. She still smelled her everywhere.

And then there was the book. She'd had a particularly good two weeks of not missing Emerson when she'd gone to the bookcase next to the fireplace for something to read and distract herself from the quiet. She blindly reached for a book and pulled one out without looking at it. As she settled onto the couch, the book opened to a dog-eared page. Hayley rolled her eyes initially because who damages a book like that? But then she noticed the pretty, slanting script along the edge of the page. It was Emerson's handwriting. She had taken notes. She thumbed through the book and read all the passages Emerson highlighted or little anecdotes she scribbled in the margin. Most of it was humorous commentary regarding the main character's actions or inactions. But some of it was very, very poignant, too, like the stuff she had kept in that *ES Musings* file on her desktop that she wasn't supposed to look at, ever. And that made Hayley's heart hurt because she had seen the silly *and* the deep sides of Emerson. And she loved them both. Or she thought she'd seen both sides, but she didn't trust herself regarding Emerson anymore. Sometimes she thought she must have dreamed her version of Emerson up entirely, because she seemed too good to be true all the time. Because evidently, she was. Which was why Hayley was here, alone. She'd shelved the book after a while and hadn't gone back to the bookcase since, for fear of finding something else there to remind her of Emerson.

"Stop thinking about her," she mumbled to herself as she headed out of the guest room toward the kitchen. She padded across the warm wooden floor on bare feet as she looked out toward the lake from the kitchen window. The late day sun strained through the trees to give the lake its last bit of light before the sunset lit it on fire with orange and red hues. The sounds of the forest around the cabin would start to get louder soon. The crickets and bullfrogs would start their symphony and the fireflies would dance their mating dance as dusk fell. These were the comforts that helped her sleep at night. The consistent dependableness of the woods around her had helped her heal here. She'd started to feel whole again, but just started. She had a long way to go and she knew it, but she was on the right path.

She rinsed her cup out and dropped some ice into the glass before pouring in some water from the filtered pitcher by the sink. Her grandmother believed that all water should be drunk at room temperature, but Hayley wasn't uncivilized. Although she abided by her grandmother's routine of leaving the water out, she also added ice, because duh. But she wasn't paying attention and she overfilled the cup and it runneth over. All over her pants and onto her bare feet.

She jumped back at the wetness and sent more of the cup's contents spilling onto the kitchen floor. "Dammit."

She put the cup on the counter and grabbed a dish towel to clean up the mess. After she'd patted down her pants and tidied the kitchen, she went about the task of refilling her cup. Ice first, then water. As she dropped a few cubes in the glass, she thought she heard what sounded like a knock at the front door. But that was impossible since there was no one around here who would visit without calling, and her parents were in Italy for the summer, which was why she had the cabin to herself.

She poured some water into the cup and heard the noise again. That was definitely a knock. She turned to look at the front door and dropped her cup because the ghost of Emerson Sterling was peering through her window, and she looked like she'd just crawled out of a grave.

CHAPTER THIRTY-THREE

Emerson flinched as the sound of the breaking porcelain echoed through the open screened windows of the cabin. She hadn't meant to startle Hayley, but she was glad to find her here all the same.

Hayley gaped at her for a moment before disappearing from view behind the butcher-block top of the kitchen island. What felt like an eternity passed before her head popped back up and then her body. She had a look of disbelief in her eyes and a pile of ceramic shards in her hands.

Emerson gave her a weak wave and an apologetic smile.

Hayley just blinked at her.

Well, at least she didn't throw anything at her, right?

Hayley blinked again and then discarded the broken whatever into the wastebin and walked slowly toward the door. Like, really slowly. Emerson was practically vibrating with anticipation when Hayley finally opened the door.

"Hi." Emerson waved again because she was nervous and because Hayley looked incredible. She had a light summer tan and her hair was swept up into a messy bun on the top of her head. She looked fit and strong, like she'd been hiking or cutting wood or doing really sexy woodsy related things by the lake. Or maybe she'd been rowing and swimming a lot. That could totally be why her collarbone looked so delicious as it peeked above the loose V-neck collar of her shirt, because she'd been swinging an ax or practicing her freestyle swimming technique or just being Hayley. Because that was sexy enough. God, how badly she wanted to rip open this screen door and touch her.

"Emerson. What are you…why are you—" Hayley opened the door with a look of confusion and disbelief.

"Covered in mud?" Emerson had given herself a quick once-over in the car's rearview before she'd gathered up enough courage to walk up the front steps of the cabin. She was splattered in mud. Her pants, her shirt, her beyond ruined Louboutins…She'd even managed to get some mud in her hair. It was masterful, really. But she'd made it. She'd dug out those fucking useless wheels and found enough small sticks to wedge under the tires to get traction to drive out of the mud. And although the car looked like it had been in a demolition derby at the bottom of a mud pit, she'd arrived alive, before sunset, with 3 percent cell phone battery to spare.

"It's a long story that involves a wooden moose with a holier-than-thou attitude, a somewhat improperly dressed city slicker, and an ill-informed choice regarding vehicle selection for an off-roading adventure on a series of unpaved roads after a storm or six."

"Wow. That sounds—"

"Dirty. And far-fetched. I know." Emerson leaned against the door and motioned up and down her body. "But I can assure you, this time fact is stranger than fiction."

Hayley handed her the dishcloth she had draped over her shoulder and Emerson bowed her head in appreciation.

"Thanks."

Hayley nodded but said nothing.

"So. You're, uh, a hard lady to find." Emerson wiped off her face and hands with the cloth and grimaced. The cloth appeared to be ruined. She folded it neatly and held it in her hand to give herself something to do. "Sorry about the cloth."

Hayley eyed it for a moment before looking back up at her. "Don't worry about it. I have about fifty more. And I wasn't hiding. But I wasn't looking to be found either."

Ouch.

Hayley turned and walked into the cabin, leaving Emerson standing in the doorway.

Emerson wasn't sure if that was an outright dismissal or what, so she hovered in place, unsure of what to do.

Hayley walked to the back of the cabin and started to go out through the back door before she stopped and turned back to her. "Maybe leave the shoes on the porch to dry out. There's fresh linens in the hall closet. You know where the bathroom is. Feel free to freshen up. But maybe use the darkish towels, just to be safe."

She didn't wait for Emerson to reply. Instead she slipped out the rear door and disappeared.

Emerson stepped out of her mud-caked shoes and tiptoed through the house, trying to limit as much dirt castoff as possible. That wasn't exactly the welcome she'd been hoping for, but it wasn't an outright door to the face, either. She could use a shower or five. And it would give her some time to prepare what she wanted to say. Or rather, prepare how she wanted to beg.

She walked to the hall closet and pulled out some towels. She lingered there and ran her hand along the soft sleeve of the sweatshirt Hayley had worn when they were here together, so many months ago. It was as soft and welcoming as she remembered. She pulled it off the hanger and took it with her into the bathroom. It only occurred to her that she didn't have pants once the shower ended and she was naked from the waist down. She popped her head into the hallway and called out to Hayley, but there was no answer.

She took the short walk to the master bedroom and found it was a little different than how she remembered it. It was more cluttered now. There were clearly things of Hayley's strewn about the room in an organized chaos. The room was a mix of simplistic nondescript furniture akin to a rental space, with splashes of Hayley's personality and favorite things draped here and there. Hayley's messenger bag sat on the chair next to the dresser, and a few pictures of LA's most famous landmarks speckled the dresser's surface. Emerson saw the corner of a movie ticket under a small stack of notebooks, and she pulled it out.

It was a souvenir ticket from the premiere of *Willow Path*. That had been an impossibly emotional night for her. She wondered if Hayley felt the same. She placed it back where she found it and opened a few drawers until she found a pair of pants to borrow.

When she made it to the back porch, she found Hayley lounging on one of the chairs. Her eyes were closed, and her knees were tucked under her chin. Emerson sat on the chair next to her and waited.

After forever, Hayley spoke. "Why did you come here?"

Emerson turned to look at her, but Hayley's eyes remained closed. "My heart is here."

Hayley's eyes shot open and she shook her head. "Don't do that."

"Do what?"

Hayley turned her body toward Emerson, but she kept her knees tight against her chest. "Don't sit here in my clothes telling me I'm important to you in that perfect voice that makes me want to melt into your arms and forget all the fucked-up shit that happened to me after meeting you. That. Don't do *that*."

"Fine." Emerson grabbed the hem of her borrowed sweatshirt and started to pull it over her head.

"Whoa. What are you doing?" Hayley's hands were on hers, stopping her from pulling the shirt off.

"I'm giving you back your sweatshirt."

Hayley huffed. "That's not what I meant."

"What did you mean then?" Emerson reached for Hayley's hand, but Hayley pulled back from her touch.

"Emerson." Hayley didn't look amused.

Emerson nodded. "I get it. You hate me. That's fair. I brought unbelievable chaos to your life, that's true, but I never—"

"Meant for me to be so incredibly embarrassed on a global scale that I had to flee to the woods and obscurity just to find some peace?" Hayley asked. "Is that what you were about to say?"

Emerson took a breath and tried again. "Actually, I was going to say that I never expected to fall in love with you and I wasn't ready for the ramifications that it had on my soul. On my entire being." She paused. "Hayley, these last two months without you have been the most miserable time of my entire life and I wanted to tell you that to your face."

Hayley only blinked at her. She took that as a win.

"Now, I drove a good while to get here, and I nearly drowned in mud in the process, so I'm going to go to my garbage rental car and pull out the groceries I picked up on the way, and I'm going to make us both dinner. And if you still can't stand the sight of me in the morning, then I'll be on the road and out of your hair forever." Emerson stood over Hayley and added, "But I left my cell phone charger home because I'm incapable of being a responsible adult, so I'm going to borrow yours.

While I make risotto. You're welcome to help me cut veggies if you'd like."

She turned to go when she felt Hayley's fingers tug at her sleeve. "What kind of risotto are we talking about?"

She smiled and bent down, bringing her face level with Hayley's. "It's wild mushroom and I plan to be heavy-handed with the sauvignon blanc."

Hayley raised an eyebrow at her and nodded almost imperceptibly.

Emerson took a chance and leaned forward, pressing a tentative kiss to Hayley's cheek. "I'll see you inside."

Chapter Thirty-four

Hayley watched in amazement as Emerson glided around the kitchen like a seasoned pro. She realized that in all their time together, she'd never seen her cook a real meal. They'd barbecued and had salads, or someone brought them dishes through room service or craft services or whatever, but she'd never seen Emerson cook. It was a thing of beauty.

Emerson mixed and folded, stirred and simmered with a practiced ease that hypnotized her. The wineglass in Hayley's hand was nearly empty. This was her second. She was feeling less and less inhibited from asking the questions that swirled around in her head.

"Okay. I think it's done. Ready to eat?" Emerson wiped her hands on the apron she'd borrowed and swept a hand through her dark hair, brushing a strand behind her ear in that lovely way she did when she was focused. Hayley tried to ignore the familiarity of it.

"Yup. I'm starving." Damn wine was breaking down her resistance.

Emerson gave her a genuine smile of relief. "Good. Go sit, I'll bring everything to you."

Hayley left her near-empty glass on the island and moved to the couch. It was cool away from the stovetop. An unseasonable chill had settled outside, and a steady breeze was coming off the lake. Even though she'd closed the windows a while ago, it still hadn't warmed up yet. She would have to start a fire at some point.

Emerson brought over two heaping plates and two small salad bowls. She carried over the water pitcher and two cups, one with ice, one without. Hayley smiled when Emerson handed her the cup with ice, but she didn't miss the way Emerson's fingers danced along hers in the transfer.

Emerson held up her water glass and offered a toast. "To a warm meal and good company."

Hayley didn't trust herself with words right now, so she merely nodded and sipped from her glass. The coolness was refreshing. Her stomach growled. She was hungry.

Emerson gave her a nervous smile and waited as she tasted the risotto on her plate. The flavors were delightful, a mix of creamy and robust with a subtle earthy, nutty flavor. "This is amazing."

Emerson beamed and tried some of her food. She smiled as she ate. "Good. I worked up a legit appetite after the ditch-digging mud fight with the car. I was really worried I'd overcooked this and we'd have to share the few granola bars I did pack in lieu of my cell phone charger."

Hayley laughed and ate some more. "It's not overcooked at all. It's delicious."

"Good." Emerson settled into the couch next to her and they ate in amiable silence for a bit, until Emerson put down her dish and walked back to the kitchen.

Hayley watched as she refilled their wineglasses and sat next to her again. But this time, she sat at the edge of the cushion, like she couldn't relax. Like she had something she wanted to say. Hayley put down the rest of her plate, her appetite having faded.

She took the wineglass Emerson offered her and sipped it slowly, savoring the taste on the back of her tongue. It'd been a while since she'd had a nice cold glass of wine. A thought occurred to her. "I've never seen you drink wine."

Emerson took a hearty sip of her glass before she placed it on the coffee table in front of them. "I don't often drink it."

"Champagne. Or seltzer water with cranberry. Or warm water with honey." Hayley listed the drinks she'd recalled Emerson partaking in.

"Or milkshakes." Emerson brought up the night of their first kiss. Their first night of passion. The night everything changed.

"Why did you come here, Emerson?" Hayley placed her glass on the table next to Emerson's and faced her.

"I told you. I came here for you."

Hayley shook her head. That was exactly what she wanted to hear, so it must be a figment of her imagination. "I don't believe you."

Emerson reached out to touch her cheek and Hayley leaned back. She wasn't ready for that yet. Emerson pulled her hand back into her lap and nodded. "I want to tell you something. I want to talk about Rachel. And Rory. And my life before I met you. Is that okay?"

Hayley wanted to hear what Emerson had to say, but part of her wanted to storm out of the room and go cry on her bed, too. She settled for nodding.

Emerson exhaled. "Okay. Good. Great." She shivered, and Hayley held up a hand.

"Hold on." Hayley walked to the fireplace and started a fire. By the time she sat back next to Emerson, Emerson had reclined on the arm of the sofa and put a little more distance between them. "Okay."

Emerson took in a breath. "My life has been lonely, for a long time. So lonely, I'd gotten used to it. Which was all fine and good until you saved me from Drake that day. You were selfless and unafraid and absolutely magnificent. And I felt seen for the first time in a long time. Because even though I didn't know you then, I knew that somehow you were going to change my life for the better. I just knew it. I knew it in my gut, but more than that, I knew it in my soul."

She continued, "Fast-forward a bit, and I'm spending all this time with you, learning about myself through your questions, seeing myself through your eyes. Feeling not so alone for the first time since I was fifteen and making the decision to give up custody of *my daughter*. I realized I hadn't felt whole, I hadn't felt not alone, since that day. And I'd been living a numb existence and completely oblivious to it.

"Rachel, for all her faults, opened a new door for me. She exposed a passion and a fear in me that I had been hiding from for a long time. I am so grateful for the misery that woman put me through, because if not for her, I wouldn't have met you. And I wouldn't have the relationship with Deidre and Rory that I have now. A relationship of open communication and feelings and no secrets. And it's hard sometimes and it's sad sometimes to think of what could have been or ask myself what would be different if I did this or didn't do that in regard to Rory and her life, but it's no longer a secret. And that's a burden I didn't realize was sitting so heavily on my heart"—she paused—"that is, until my heart found another reason to beat and be happy. My heart found you, Hayley."

Emerson moved a little closer and took Hayley's hand. She didn't pull back this time. She didn't resist at all. She was tired of resisting.

"My greatest regret in all this, Hayley, is you got hurt. So incredibly hurt. And I can't imagine the depth of that pain because I've spent the better part of my life as the focus of someone's camera lens, and I haven't had a private moment in a long time, definitely not one that I would have wanted to protect as fiercely as I wish I could have protected our private moments. The ones that were shown for all to see. But I can tell you I'm sorry. I am so, so sorry that my presence in your life brought you pain. Because I am. I am, and if there was anything I could have done or can do to make it better, I will. I would. I'll never stop trying." Emerson brought Hayley's hand to her lips and kissed her knuckles. "Because at the end of the day, you are the best thing that ever happened to me, and I don't want to lose you. Ever."

Hayley felt like her heart was going to beat out of her chest. She couldn't believe this was happening right now. She couldn't believe Emerson was here, in person, telling her all the things she wanted to hear. She couldn't believe it, because if she did, then she could have it taken from her. Like her sense of privacy. Like her dignity. She sighed.

"You didn't lose me, Emerson." Hayley turned her palm over and stroked Emerson's cheek.

Emerson pressed Hayley's hand to her face and gave her a sad smile. "You left, Hayley."

Well, that was true. "I did."

"Why?" Emerson's eyes searched her face. She looked beautiful in the glow of the fireplace. She always looked beautiful.

Hayley left for a multitude of reasons, but she would be lying if she said that having people camped outside her apartment building and favorite smoothie place wasn't one of them. "Okay. Fair point. I didn't love all the stalking stuff. Or the endless phone calls and tweets from trolls. Or the hate mail from the BlancheHards. Plus, I got fired and that was sort of the cherry on top."

"Yeah. I know. It's a lot."

"It wasn't just *a lot*, Emerson. It was devastating. I've never felt more embarrassed or more violated than I did when Drake leaked those pictures that night. I felt like everywhere I went, people were staring at me, taking pictures…there's a meme out there of us. A meme. You must have seen it, right?"

Emerson sighed. "I have."

"Exactly. That's why I left, Emerson. Because you broke up with me because you were worried something bad would happen, and I tried to convince you it wouldn't by wearing an overly priced, borrowed dress that later got ruined in a rainstorm, and then something bad did happen anyway and just proved us both wrong. Or right." She shook her head. "It doesn't matter. What matters is I don't think I can ever be in the public eye again and definitely not LA, and you being here telling me you love me and want to be with me is very overwhelming and confusing because I love you." She huffed.

Emerson's eyes were filled with tears, but a broad smile spread on her face. "I can't promise you any of that stuff will change. Over time it will wax and wane, but there's always a chance that someone will pay a hefty price for a photo of you blowing your nose after a spicy dinner."

Hayley laughed, and Emerson moved closer. She cupped Hayley's jaw and looked at her with such raw intensity that she was hypnotized.

"I came here for you, Hayley. I came here to tell you these last two months without you have been some of the worst of my whole life and it has nothing to do with my current family drama or my work obligations. It was you. It was always you." Emerson dragged her thumb along Hayley's bottom lip. "I love you, Hayley. I've known for a long time, but I was afraid to say it out loud because the thought of losing you was far too much for me to handle. But then you were gone, and I thought I'd lost my chance. So I'm here, telling you I love you, because I can't think of anything else, ever. I love you, Hayley Carpenter. I love you and the only thing I want to do in this whole world is tell you how much you mean to me every day and kiss you to sleep every night."

Hayley felt like her heart tripled in size. Her chest felt too small to contain the emotions she was currently feeling. "Just *kiss* me?"

Emerson licked her lips and purred. "Well, to start anyway."

The last of her inhibitions vanished at the sight of Emerson's tongue on her lips, and she leaned forward. "Then why wait? There's no time to waste."

Emerson didn't hesitate before connecting their lips, and Hayley didn't bother trying to fight her feelings anymore. She loved Emerson right back and having her here—in this moment—was exactly what she'd wanted all along.

CHAPTER THIRTY-FIVE

Emerson wasn't sure how things would play out, and she didn't have a backup plan if things blew up in her face. But she didn't waste any time thinking about that when Hayley's lips connected with hers. This was what she had been missing. This was what she wanted to feel. This was where her heart had been all along.

"I love you." She kissed Hayley with everything she had. She slid her hands into Hayley's hair and pulled her mouth closer. Always closer. She couldn't get enough of Hayley's lips, her tongue, those soft wanting murmurs...all of it. She loved them. She loved *her*.

Hayley's tongue massaged against hers, and Hayley pulled at the sweatshirt Emerson had hastily thrown on after her shower. She sat back against the couch and tugged Emerson up onto her lap. "Come here."

Emerson spread her legs and lowered herself onto Hayley's lap. Hayley rewarded her with a dominant kiss and her hands under Emerson's shirt. One soothed up her back and made delicate patterns on the skin there, while the other cupped her naked breast and kneaded the tissue with affection. Hayley licked across her lips. "I like this no underwear thing."

Emerson moaned when Hayley teased at her nipple. "It wasn't planned, but I regret nothing."

"Good. Neither do I." Hayley let go of her breast only long enough to remove Emerson's shirt. "I love you in my clothes. Like, it does things to me. But I really need you out of them."

Emerson lifted off Hayley's lap enough for Hayley to work her pants off her hips. She maneuvered them off her legs and let Hayley guide her back to her original position, straddling Hayley's hips. The look Hayley gave her floored her. Emerson had never felt sexier than she did right now.

"I'm feeling a little underdressed at the moment." Emerson dragged a finger along Hayley's collarbone before hooking it into the V-neck of her T-shirt and pulling down to expose Hayley's bra. Hayley gripped at her hip and pulled Emerson's naked sex against the fabric of her jeans. It felt heavenly. Emerson rocked into the sensation.

"Really? Because I don't think you've ever been more beautiful." Hayley leaned forward and licked the underside of Emerson's breast before closing her lips around her nipple and sucking at the firm nub. Suddenly the blazing fire behind Emerson that was keeping her comfortably warm in her nudity felt much, much too hot.

Emerson threaded her hand into Hayley's hair and pressed her breast against Hayley's lips and tongue. She wanted to feel more. She wanted more of Hayley on her body. "Hayley."

Hayley looked up at her and released her nipple as she licked her lips. She moved her hand from Emerson's hip and zigzagged her index finger along her abdomen and under her navel. Emerson shuddered as she dipped lower and teased through her wetness. This was just enough to drive her crazy but not enough for her to come. Though Hayley's fingers were dancing a fine line. She'd wanted this for so long, she didn't know whether she could hold out with all the teasing. She didn't trust herself not to climax the moment Hayley slipped inside her. Oh, how badly she wanted that.

"I missed you, Emerson." Emerson wanted to hear her name said like that for the rest of her life. Hayley abandoned her teasing to grip both of Emerson's hips. She lifted Emerson off her and slipped out from underneath her, and she had to bite her lip to keep from whining at the loss of contact.

Emerson watched as she pulled the blanket off the back of the couch and laid it on the floor in front of the fire. She stripped out of her clothes and knelt before Emerson, kissing along the front of her thighs and licking everywhere but where Emerson needed her most.

Emerson stroked Hayley's hair and lifted her chin, bending to kiss her lips. "Lie down, Hay."

Hayley's eyes were dark, her pupils dilated, and her lips kiss-plump and waiting. Emerson needed to feel Hayley against her skin. All of her. She guided Hayley to the floor and crawled over her, stretching her body on top of her and moaning at the delicious friction. She entwined their fingers and pressed both of Hayley's hands to the floor above her head. She rolled her hips against Hayley's and lifted her chest, separating their skin only enough to look down at Hayley. She'd had many lovers in her life, but none of them had the effect on her that Hayley did. None of them got her this wet or this turned on or this close, just from looking at her. "You feel so good. You always feel so good."

Hayley lifted her head and kissed her lips. "Make love to me, Emerson. Love me like I have loved you every night in my dreams since the weekend we shared here. Love me like I love you, with everything I have. Can you do that?"

Emerson quivered above her and nodded. "I will spend my whole life trying to do just that."

"Good. Now more kissing and fucking, please, because I have been missing you something serious, and I intend to love you until this fire burns itself out." Hayley rolled up against her and shifted to slip her leg between Emerson's thighs, while grinding against the leg now positioned between hers.

"And then?" Emerson saw stars as Hayley released one of her hands only to pull her hips against her leg. Hayley moved her in circles against her muscled thigh, and her clit sent a shock wave through her abdomen. "Fuck."

Hayley pushed Emerson off her leg and slipped two fingers into her, guiding her back down into her palm and curling inside her. Emerson's insides clenched and pulled at Hayley's fingers. She was so wound up, so turned on. So, so wet. She wasn't going to last. She didn't want to. "And then I'll take you into the bedroom and lick you until you faint. Only to revive you to do it all over again. Is that okay with you?"

"More than okay." Emerson directed Hayley's free hand to her chest and dropped down, so her elbows settled on either side of Hayley's face. She panted against her mouth and rocked her hips to the rhythm of Hayley's thrusting and rubbing. "Yes, Hayley. Yes. Make me come. Please, please. Harder."

Hayley spread her fingers on the next thrust and Emerson came hard and fast against her hand. Her cries of pleasure were swallowed by Hayley's lips, and the tremors that echoed though her body intensified when Hayley's tongue found hers.

Emerson enjoyed Hayley's affections, but she didn't wait to catch her breath. She eased Hayley out of her and shifted to her side. She could tell by the wetness on her leg that Hayley was plenty turned on, and she had no intention of letting that go to waste.

She sucked Hayley's earlobe into her mouth as she stroked the swollen tissue of her sex and rubbed against Hayley's clit. When Hayley moaned and bucked up against her hand, she slipped inside her, making slow and deliberate movements to draw out Hayley's pleasure.

When Hayley's insides tightened almost painfully around her fingers, she pressed her thumb to Hayley's clit and whispered, "I love you," into her ear as she came undone. And as they lay there, recovering and out of breath on the floor in front of the fire, Emerson had never felt so wanted, so needed, or so in love as she did in that moment.

She curled up next to Hayley and draped her leg across Hayley's center. She loved the heat she felt coming off Hayley's body. It made her sleepy and sticky at the same time.

Hayley rubbed along her arm and pressed gentle kiss after kiss to the side of her face. "Thank you for enduring the mud pits to come find me."

Emerson laughed. That seemed an eternity ago. "Stan was no fucking help, let me tell you."

Hayley nuzzled her cheek. "That doesn't surprise me. He's a bit of a stiff."

Emerson gave her a playful shove before snuggling closer again. "You're hilarious."

"Hilariously in love with you. Forgive me?"

Emerson looked at her and shook her head. "No forgiveness necessary. I accept you for your flaws and encourage them."

Hayley pecked her lips and smiled. "Good. I didn't really have any intention of changing."

"Don't." Emerson propped her head up on her hand and looked down at Hayley's gorgeous body. She danced her fingers along Hayley's arm and took her hand. "What have you been doing while holed up in the woods?"

Hayley smiled, and her heart melted some more. "Writing. I've been doing some really great angsty screenplay writing. It's fantastically dark and romantic."

Emerson was excited Hayley was working on her craft, but she felt bad that she might have contributed to some of those angsty feelings. "I'm sorry about you losing your job and being driven out of town by the overzealous paps. But I'm sorrier that I thought distancing myself from you would somehow make everything better. For me, it made everything much, much worse. I thought I could save you by walking away, but I couldn't walk away, not really anyway. You deserved a more honest conversation about my fears, Hayley. I was wrong to make a decision and act on it without talking to you first. I'm sorry about that."

Hayley seemed to consider this before she said anything. "It worked wonderfully in the inspiration department, but I much prefer this kind of motivation and muse-provoking activity."

"Agreed on all fronts."

"And you? What were you up to?" Hayley looked a little sheepish. "I sort of, kind of, totally deleted my entire social media existence when I became a professional woods-woman, so I'm kind of out of the loop."

Emerson kissed her because she could. "I noticed that. It's hard to keep tabs on you when you go dark like that, Hayley." She brushed a lock of hair off Hayley's forehead and tucked it behind her ear. "I spent a lot of the time thinking about you and how all the best things in my life started with you. And then I spent a lot of time thinking about myself and the person I'd become and the parts of me that felt lost or undernurtured. I spent some time with Rory and Deidre and the family, reconnecting. Oh, and I fired David because he's a backstabbing snake."

Hayley's mouth dropped open in surprise. "Really?"

"Really." Emerson nodded and sighed. "When I found out that Rachel wasn't involved in the photo thing, I got to thinking about it: For Drake to get the shots he did in the way he did, he'd need to have some inside scoop as to my whereabouts. The only person who had that intel outside of Tremont was David. And we both know Tremont wouldn't sell me out."

"Most certainly not. He likes the finer things in life, and without you, there are no finer things." Hayley winked, and Emerson loved that she knew her bestie as well as she did.

"Exactly. So out went the trash." Emerson was glad to have David off her payroll. She'd lost respect and trust for him over the Rachel thing, but their relationship had started to unravel years before. It was time for her to move on, but she never would have guessed he'd make it so easy for her.

"So basically, I pined for you and went to work on myself and reconnected with Rory a bit, and then I booked a flight for myself to Maine, because this is my happy place. With you."

"Naked on the floor in front of the fireplace."

"It's poetic, isn't it?" Emerson let herself get lost in Hayley's eyes, the flickering flames reflected in them. She was so, so happy in this moment.

Hayley gave her a contented smile, but it was short-lived. "What happens now?"

Emerson wrapped her arm around Hayley's waist and hugged her. "I was hoping for a little mushy snuggling and cuddling before some less wholesome activities and maybe some role play. But I'm open to suggestions."

Hayley chuckled and shook her head. "That's not what I meant."

"I know." Emerson gave her a lingering kiss. "But you're thinking about it now, aren't you?"

Hayley nodded. "Yup. You got me."

"I already had you," Emerson replied confidently.

"That's true, you did." Hayley stretched.

Emerson lowered her head to Hayley's chest and answered her previous question. "I hope *this* happens. Lots more of this and things like this."

"How long until you have to leave?" Hayley's voice sounded sad.

Emerson lifted her head and looked at her. "I don't."

Hayley sat up on her elbows and unceremoniously dumped Emerson on the floor in the process. "What do you mean you *don't?*"

Emerson rubbed her shoulder and mirrored Hayley's position. "I mean, I fired my manager and I canceled all my upcoming projects to focus on my family and you. So I don't have to leave unless you want me to."

"I don't want that."

"Me to leave or me to be around?" Emerson was confused.

"You to leave. I want you to stay. I want to try to make this work." Hayley motioned between them and Emerson couldn't agree more.

"Then I'm here to stay."

Hayley beamed, and Emerson vowed to make her that happy forever and ever.

"And what about future work projects and your family?" Hayley gave her a concerned look.

Emerson nodded. "I've been spending a lot of time with Deidre and Rory, trying to figure out our new normal. And it's work, but it's working. I'll have to fly out there a bit over the next months, years, whatever it takes to make sure Rory and Deidre and their family feel comfortable. But I need to respect their need for distance and space, too." Emerson sighed. "And as far as work goes, I might have to take some meetings or be in LA for short periods, but I'm happy to work with you on a schedule or a plan if you want to stay out here permanently. I'm pretty fond of this place—and you—so it's worth my time commuting."

"So in other words, we'll figure it out," Hayley said.

"Right. We'll figure it out. But there's no rush."

"Okay."

"Plus, who knows? Maybe this screenplay of yours will drag you back to LA, and we can coast hop while you become Hollywood's next media darling, and I can just sit back and bask in the awesomeness of my girlfriend." Emerson accepted Hayley's kiss and smiled.

"Media darling, huh?" Hayley rolled her eyes and pulled Emerson back on top of her.

Emerson bit her lip at the delightful arousal this position evoked. "Stranger things have happened."

Hayley's eyes sparkled as she looked up at her. "Like a movie star falling in love with a reporter from a gossip rag?"

Emerson closed her eyes as Hayley's hands wandered back to places that still ached from their previous play. "Mm-hmm. Just like that."

EPILOGUE

Six Months Later

Hayley ran her hand through her still-wet hair as she looked at the two dresses laid out on the bed in front of her. She was completely stumped as to which direction to go. The dark green one really complemented her eye color, but it was decidedly sexier than the understated yet elegant dark blue one. Either would look fabulous, and she knew she couldn't go wrong since Tremont and Alison had chosen these options together. She loved how well they got along. It made board game night so much more fun, especially since Sebastian and Scotty bonded over fitness and a love for cage fighting, which, Hayley admitted, surprised her since they were both so mild mannered and sweet. And she was able to secretly work on her Uno skills with Scotty, in preparation for Rory staying with them in Maine for a part of the summer. She needed to up her game if she hoped to stand a chance against Emerson's wily, if somewhat suspect, skills.

"You know my preference." Emerson stepped up behind her and kissed the side of her neck. Her hands skimmed along Hayley's sides and played with the lace cups along the sides of her breasts. She was grateful she hadn't finished getting dressed, if only to feel Emerson's fingers on her skin again.

She closed her eyes at the sensation and dropped her hands to Emerson's, now draped around her waist. She could tell by the fabric that pressed against her back that Emerson was still in just her silk robe from earlier. "Naked isn't an option, love."

"Not just naked. That's so boring." Emerson worked her way up to her ear and sucked the lobe between her teeth. "Naked, wet, willing..."

Hayley moaned. "Em, if you keep that up, we aren't going to make it to the red carpet at all. This is a big night for you. We don't want to miss it."

Emerson's lips moved to her jaw. "There is nothing more important in my life than making you scream my name over and over again. It's my favorite song. I could literally listen to it on loop forever and ever."

"God, you're good at that." Hayley breathed out, trying to slow her heart rate.

Emerson turned her in her arms and placed a hot, lingering kiss to her mouth. "Kissing?"

"Well, yes. But I meant distracting me. You're very good at that, too." Hayley massaged the back of Emerson's neck and smiled as Emerson picked her up and deposited her on the bed.

"As long as you think I'm a good kisser, then all other compliments are icing on the cake." Emerson separated the lapels of the robe and crawled over her, looking down at her with a smile. "So, about that kissing part..."

Hayley connected their lips and marveled at the sensations Emerson provoked in her. Even after all these months, Emerson could get her from zero to sixty with that talented mouth, in no time flat. Kissing Emerson was her favorite pastime, second only to making love with and cuddling with Emerson, which were equally amazing.

"I love you," Emerson murmured against her lips before she nibbled Hayley's bottom lip between her own.

Hayley slid her hands greedily over the naked skin of Emerson's back and sides, opening her mouth to deepen the kiss, and Emerson slipped in easily, her tongue dancing along Hayley's in a practiced ease that she knew Emerson was employing to relax her nerves about tonight.

"We should really keep getting ready." Hayley's protests were half-hearted and foolish. They both knew they had time to play a bit, but she felt the need to voice her concerns anyway. For good measure.

Emerson pulled back and looked down at her, her eyes dark and her pupils large. "We are getting ready, Hayley. This is called foreplay. It's the play before the play. It's the warm-up. Some would say it's the best part, but I would say those people have never felt your touch. Because that, my love, is the best part. The part when"—Emerson took Hayley's hand and guided it inside the open robe, pressing her fingers into the wetness between her legs—"you touch me for the first time, after I beg for it. That's the best part. When you can feel how wet I am for you, always."

"Fuck." Hayley felt her body flush as Emerson spread her legs and guided Hayley inside her. She didn't need any direction. Emerson was everything she had said she liked best: naked, wet, willing. Hayley slipped into her and angled her fingers to hit Emerson's favorite spots. Her favorite spots now, too.

"Yes. Hayley, mm, like that." Emerson's mouth was by her ear, panting and moaning as Hayley increased her thrusts. "I want you so badly. Make me come, baby. Make me come."

Hayley arched up against Emerson and pressed her thumb against her clit, propelling Emerson into a climax that rocked them both.

Emerson rolled to her side and laughed softly, between gasps for breath.

"Oh, yeah?" Hayley turned on her side to face her, cupping Emerson's cheek as she placed a kiss on her lips. "Something funny?"

"Not at all." Emerson burst into another fit of giggles, and Hayley rolled on top of her, tickling her sides before pinning her hands above her head. Emerson arched her back in an attempt to get away, but Hayley was having no part of it.

"You were saying?" Hayley nipped at the skin under Emerson's jaw and Emerson's wiggling slowed to a stop.

"Mm." Emerson tucked her chin to connect their lips. "I was just thinking about how incredible it is that this time last year you were catching my attention with a whistle on the red carpet. But now"— Emerson's expression turned sincere—"you're catching my attention with those beautiful eyes and that perfect smile and—"

"My hand between your legs?" Hayley reached down and pressed against Emerson, her actions rewarded with a deep, throaty moan.

"Well, that, yes." Emerson inched backward, taking Hayley's hand in hers and kissing her fingertips. "What an incredible year it has been, Hay. I never would have expected to be this happy, this blissfully in love, one year ago. I wasn't even sure I'd make it down the carpet that night. So much has changed."

Hayley warmed at Emerson's words and the sensation of Emerson's lips on her fingers. "I know what you mean."

Emerson's eyes sparkled, and she sucked two of Hayley's fingers into her mouth.

"No, no way." Hayley shook her head. "Hair and makeup are going to be here any minute. We still have to get into our dresses and get debriefed by Tremont and—"

All attempts at forming a sentence ceased when Emerson pressed Hayley on her back and licked her way down her body.

"Don't worry, Hay." Emerson glanced up, her mouth just millimeters from Hayley's sex. "There will be plenty of debriefing. As much as you can take. At least a mouthful."

Hayley would have rolled her eyes at Emerson's joke if her eyes weren't so busy rolling into the back of her head. The things that woman could do with her mouth...

❖

"Hayley! Over here!" Anna Mae Teslan from *LA Life* called out from the spot in front of them on the red carpet, a metal barrier separating her and her camera crew from Hayley and Emerson. "Can you give us a sound bite, for old time's sake?"

Emerson gave her a wink and stepped toward the railing to take an interview with another media outlet nearby.

Hayley took a deep breath and stepped forward. She'd known this moment would come eventually.

"Hi, Anna Mae." She flashed her best Hollywood smile that she'd been practicing for weeks. She hoped it would suffice.

"Hayley Carpenter, it's great to see you again. Tell us, are you excited to be here today?" Anna Mae put the microphone in her face and she second-guessed herself for a moment.

"I'm thrilled. Thank you for asking." That was safe enough, right?

"Great to hear. So your girlfriend, Emerson Sterling, is up for Best Actress tonight. That must be exciting, right?"

Hayley smiled and meant it this time. "Emerson worked very hard on *Willow Path*, and she deserves this win. But I'm sure she'd tell you that the nomination is honor enough. I'm biased, though. I want her to take home the little gold bald guy."

"Oh, Hayley, you are too much." Anna Mae laughed and clapped her hand against the microphone. "Now, this past year has been challenging for you, Hayley. We all know about the photographs and the disappearing act you pulled. Tell us, how are you doing?"

Even though Hayley was expecting the next part, she still paused when Anna Mae's tone changed. "Truthfully? I'm grateful. I'm grateful to have learned some valuable lessons about this business and still managed to keep my sanity. It's been a slow transition back, but I do my best to go back to my happy place as often as possible." She stole a glance at Emerson, who was standing nearby, looking proud.

"You two are just *too* cute." Anna Mae was laying it on thick, but Hayley had expected that as well. "Don't think you're going to get away without giving me the scoop, Hayley."

"Oh, what scoop is that?" Hayley smiled as Emerson walked over to her and whispered something sweet in her ear.

"Well, rumor has it you left LA and wrote one hell of a screenplay. Our sources say that it's been fast-tracked, and Kate Stanton and Paige Montgomery, who are both nominated tonight as well, have both committed to bring it to the big screen. Care to comment at all?"

Hayley laughed and shook her head. "You'll have to wait and see on that one, Anna Mae. It was great seeing you again."

Anna Mae gave her a nod and waved her hand, stopping the crew from filming. She leaned across the barrier and spoke directly to Hayley. "You surprised us all, Carpenter. I hope that rumor is a thousand percent true. Find me when you want to tell the story of your ascent into Hollywood royalty."

Hayley laughed and let herself be led by Emerson toward the next mark.

"So how was your first red carpet interview?" Emerson looked gleeful.

"Surprisingly...fine." Hayley was on cloud nine.

"I knew you'd do great." Emerson kissed her, and a few dozen flashes erupted to her right. And though Hayley was still getting used to the attention and all the pictures, she didn't pay them any mind, because Emerson was looking at her like she was the most beautiful woman in the world, and she felt like she was.

"Have I told you I love you in green?" Emerson asked.

"Once or twice," Hayley replied.

"Great. Because I do." Emerson gave her a cheeky grin. "It's an acceptable alternative to my first suggestion. Which, just for the record, I think would have gone over well, too."

"Mm-hmm." Hayley shook her head. "There'll be plenty of time for that later."

"Good, because I was thinking if we must put a timeframe on it, forever would be acceptable."

"Forever sounds perfect."

About the Author

Fiona Riley was born and raised in New England, where she is a medical professional and part-time professor when she isn't bonding with her laptop over words. She went to college in Boston and never left, starting a small business that takes up all of her free time, much to the dismay of her ever patient and lovely wife. When she pulls herself away from her work, she likes to catch up on the contents of her ever-growing DVR or spend time by the ocean with her favorite people.

Fiona's love for writing started at a young age and blossomed after she was published in a poetry competition at the ripe old age of twelve. She wrote lots of short stories and poetry for many years until it was time for college and a "real job." Fiona found herself with a bachelor's, a doctorate, and a day job but felt like she had stopped nurturing the one relationship that had always made her feel the most complete: artist, dreamer, writer.

A series of bizarre events afforded her with some unexpected extra time and she found herself reaching for her favorite blue notebook to write, never looking back.

Contact Fiona and check for updates on all her new adventures at:

Twitter: @fionarileyfic
Facebook: "Fiona Riley Fiction"
Website: http://www.fionarileyfiction.com/
Email: fionarileyfiction@gmail.com

Books Available From Bold Strokes Books

All of Me by Emily Smith. When chief surgical resident Galen Burgess meets her new intern, Rowan Duncan, she may finally discover that doing what you've always done will only give you what you've always had. (978-1-163555-321-5)

As the Crow Flies by Karen F. Williams. Romance seems to be blooming all around, but problems arise when a restless ghost emerges from the ether to roam the dark corners of this haunting tale. (978-1-163555-285-0)

Both Ways by Ileandra Young. SPEAR agent Danika Karson races to protect the city from a supernatural threat and must rely on the woman she's trained to despise: Rayne, an achingly beautiful vampire. (978-1-163555-298-0)

Calendar Girl by Georgia Beers. Forced to work together, Addison Fairchild and Kate Cooper discover that opposites really do attract. (978-1-163555-333-8)

Cash and the Sorority Girl by Ashley Bartlett. Cash Braddock doesn't want to deal with morality, drugs, or people. Unfortunately, she's going to have to. (978-1-163555-310-9)

Lovebirds by Lisa Moreau. Two women from different worlds collide in a small California mountain town, each with a mission that doesn't include falling in love. (978-1-163555-213-3)

Media Darling by Fiona Riley. Can Hollywood bad girl Emerson and reluctant celebrity gossip reporter Hayley work together to make each other's dreams come true? Or will Emerson's secrets ruin not one career, but two? (978-1-163555-278-2)

Stroke of Fate by Renee Roman. Can Sean Moore live up to her reputation and save Jade Rivers from the stalker determined to end Jade's career and, ultimately, her life? (978-1-163555-162-4)

The Rise of the Resistance by Jackie D. The soul of America has been lost for almost a century. A few people may be the difference between a phoenix rising to save the masses or permanent destruction. (978-1-163555-259-1)

The Sex Therapist Next Door by Meghan O'Brien. At the intersection of sex and intimacy, anything is possible. Even love. (978-1-163555-296-6)

Unexpected Lightning by Cass Sellars. Lightning strikes once more when Sydney and Parker fight a dangerous stranger who threatens the peace they both desperately want. (978-1-163555-276-8)

Unforgettable by Elle Spencer. When one night changes a lifetime... Two romance novellas from best-selling author Elle Spencer. (978-1-63555-429-8)

Against All Odds by Kris Bryant, Maggie Cummings, and M. Ullrich. Peyton and Tory escaped death once, but will they survive when Bradley's determined to make his kill rate 100 percent? (978-1-163555-193-8)

Autumn's Light by Aurora Rey. Casual hookups aren't supposed to include romantic dinners and meeting the family. Can Mat Pero see beyond the heartbreak that led her to keep her worlds so separate, and will Graham Connor be waiting if she does? (978-1-163555-272-0)

Breaking the Rules by Larkin Rose. When Virginia and Carmen are thrown together by an embarrassing mistake, they find out their stubborn determination isn't so heroic after all. (978-1-163555-261-4)

Broad Awakening by Mickey Brent. In the sequel to *Underwater Vibes*, Hélène and Sylvie find ruts in their road to eternal bliss. (978-1-163555-270-6)

Broken Vows by MJ Williamz. Sister Mary Margaret must reconcile her divided heart or risk losing a love that just might be heaven sent. (978-1-163555-022-1)

Flesh and Gold by Ann Aptaker. Havana, 1952, where art thief and smuggler Cantor Gold dodges gangland bullets and mobsters' schemes while she searches Havana's steamy red light district for her kidnapped love. (978-1-163555-153-2)

Isle of Broken Years by Jane Fletcher. Spanish noblewoman Catalina de Valasco is in peril, even before the pirates holding her for ransom sail into seas destined to become known as the Bermuda Triangle. (978-1-163555-175-4)

Love Like This by Melissa Brayden. Hadley Cooper and Spencer Adair set out to take the fashion world by storm. If only they knew their hearts were about to be taken. (978-1-163555-018-4)

Secrets On the Clock by Nicole Disney. Jenna and Danielle love their jobs helping endangered children, but that might not be enough to stop them from breaking the rules by falling in love. (978-1-163555-292-8)

Unexpected Partners by Michelle Larkin. Dr. Chloe Maddox tries desperately to deny her attraction for Detective Dana Blake as they flee from a serial killer who's hunting them both. (978-1-163555-203-4)

A Fighting Chance by T. L. Hayes. Will Lou be able to come to terms with her past to give love a fighting chance? (978-1-163555-257-7)

Chosen by Brey Willows. When the choice is adapt or die, can love save us all? (978-1-163555-110-5)

Gnarled Hollow by Charlotte Greene. After they are invited to study a secluded nineteenth-century estate, a former English professor and a group of historians discover that they will have to fight against the unknown if they have any hope of staying alive. (978-1-163555-235-5)

Jacob's Grace by C.P. Rowlands. Captain Tag Becket wants to keep her head down and her past behind her, but her feelings for AJ's second-in-command, Grace Fields, makes keeping secrets next to impossible. (978-1-163555-187-7)

On the Fly by PJ Trebelhorn. Hockey player Courtney Abbott is content with her solitary life until visiting concert violinist Lana Caruso makes her second-guess everything she always thought she wanted. (978-1-163555-255-3)

Passionate Rivals by Radclyffe. Professional rivalry and long-simmering passions create a combustible combination when Emmet McCabe and Sydney Stevens are forced to work together, especially when past attractions won't stay buried. (978-1-63555-231-7)

Proxima Five by Missouri Vaun. When geologist Leah Warren crash-lands on a preindustrial planet and is claimed by its tyrant, Tiago, will clan warrior Keegan's love for Leah give her the strength to defeat him? (978-1-163555-122-8)

Shadowboxer by Jessica L. Webb. Jordan McAddie is prepared to keep her street kids safe from a dangerous underground protest group, but she isn't prepared for her first love to walk back into her life. (978-1-163555-267-6)

Racing Hearts by Dena Blake. When you cross a hot-tempered race car mechanic with a reckless cop, the result can only be spontaneous combustion. (978-1-163555-251-5)

The Tattered Lands by Barbara Ann Wright. As Vandra and Lilani strive to make peace, they slowly fall in love. With mistrust and murder surrounding them, only their faith in each other can keep their plan to save the world from falling apart. (978-1-163555-108-2)

Captive by Donna K. Ford. To escape a human trafficking ring, Greyson Cooper and Olivia Danner become players in a game of deceit and violence. Will their love stand a chance? (978-1-63555-215-7)

Crossing the Line by CF Frizzell. The Mob discovers a nemesis within its ranks, and in the ultimate retaliation, draws Stick McLaughlin from anonymity by threatening everything she holds dear. (978-1-63555-161-7)

Love's Verdict by Carsen Taite. Attorneys Landon Holt and Carly Pachett want the exact same thing: the only open partnership spot at their prestigious criminal defense firm. But will they compromise their careers for love? (978-1-63555-042-9)

Precipice of Doubt by Mardi Alexander & Laurie Eichler. Can Cole Jameson resist her attraction to her boss, veterinarian Jodi Bowman, or will she risk a workplace romance and her heart? (978-1-63555-128-0)

Savage Horizons by CJ Birch. Captain Jordan Kellow's feelings for Lt. Ali Ash have her past and future colliding, setting in motion a series of events that strands her crew in an unknown galaxy thousands of light years from home. (978-1-63555-250-8)

Secrets of the Last Castle by A. Rose Mathieu. When Elizabeth Campbell represents a young man accused of murdering an elderly woman, her investigation leads to an abandoned plantation that reveals many dark Southern secrets. (978-1-63555-240-9)

Take Your Time by VK Powell. A neurotic parrot brings police officer Grace Booker and temporary veterinarian Dr. Dani Wingate together in the tiny town of Pine Cone, but their unexpected attraction keeps the sparks flying. (978-1-63555-130-3)

The Last Seduction by Ronica Black. When you allow true love to elude you once and you desperately regret it, are you brave enough to grab it when it comes around again? (978-1-63555-211-9)

The Shape of You by Georgia Beers. Rebecca McCall doesn't play it safe, but when sexy Spencer Thompson joins her workout class, their nonstop sparring forces her to face her ultimate challenge—a chance at love. (978-1-63555-217-1)

Force of Fire: Toujours a Vous by Ali Vali. Immortals Kendal and Piper welcome their new child and celebrate the defeat of an old enemy, but another ancient evil is about to awaken deep in the jungles of Costa Rica. (978-1-63555-047-4)